Robert Winder was literary editor of the *Independent* for five years and subsequently deputy editor of *Granta* magazine. He has written two other novels, as well as a groundbreaking non-fiction book, *Bloody Foreigners*.

'It's an audacious author who dares to emulate Shakespeare. But Robert Winder pulls it off with aplomb . . . A sophisticated romp . . . The book's languid humour and shrewd allusions to the *Collected Works* make this a hugely enjoyable read' Stephen Morris, *Financial Times*

'A joy to read. Here is a novel packed with arcane information and full of learning – but just as full of jokes . . . There is a magnificent, melodramatic dénouement. [The play] is a tour de force, sometimes knockabout farce but occasionally, seriously lovely poetry' *Tablet*

'An entertaining and skilfully constructed book' Charles Nicholl, *Guardian*

'Carefully crafted . . . Winder handles the blank verse of the fragment *Henry VII* with impressive masterly' René Weis, *Independent*

The Final Act of Mr Shakespeare

ROBERT WINDER

LITTLE, BROWN

First published in Great Britain in 2010 by Little, Brown
This paperback edition published in 2011 by Abacus

A CIP catalogue record for this book
is available from the British Library.

ISBN 978-0-349-12250-2

Typeset in Fournier by M Rules
Printed and bound in Great Britain by
Clays Ltd, St Ives plc

Abacus
An imprint of
Little, Brown Book Group
100 Victoria Embankment
London EC4Y 0DY

An Hachette UK Company
www.hachette.co.uk

www.littlebrown.co.uk

To Hermione, Luke and Kit

HISTORICAL NOTE

This is by no means a true story (so far as we know), but the historical background is, I hope, accurate. All the characters are authentic historical figures except for those without surnames – servants, innkeepers, spies, shopkeepers, carters and soldiers. William Shakespeare *did* return to London in 1613 when his plays were being staged to celebrate the wedding of the King's daughter; he *did* buy the gatehouse in Blackfriars; and he *did* (it is commonly thought) collaborate with John Fletcher in the writing of *Henry VIII*. Sir Walter Raleigh *was* imprisoned in the Tower; the court of King James I *was* louche; the atmosphere in the years after the Gunpowder Plot (a bona fide terrorist atrocity) *was* tense; Sir Edward Coke *did* prosecute Guy Fawkes; Richard Stanyhurst *did* write for Holinshed; and the Globe *did* burn down in June 1613.

In the interest of dramatic effect, however – and as a re-enactment of Shakespeare's own easygoing attitude to historical fact – I admit to taking a few notable liberties.

The scheming Margaret, launching plots against Henry VII from Flanders, is a composite figure based primarily on Margaret of Anjou, the wife of King Henry VI. In fact, Queen Margaret was exiled in France and died in Angers in 1482, several years before the action of the play in which she now appears. In this I was following the inspiring example of Shakespeare himself, who raised the same queen from the dead to shout curses at the King in his *Richard III*. In the pages that follow she is occasionally (and wrongly) disparaged by her enemies as a 'Yorkist', on the grounds that the Wars of the Roses were so chaotic that even Shakespeare's associates might sometimes have been confused!

In line with the fashion of the time, one or two men and women who are not related at times refer to one another as 'cousin'. I have also nudged several of the characters' ages into line. Stuart children such as Constance Donne and John Harvard entered adulthood early, and would have seemed very young (by modern standards) to play the roles assigned to them. I therefore added two or three years to the age they had actually attained in 1613. And there is not the remotest indication that Sir Edward Coke, one of the father figures of the English legal system, ever stooped quite so low as he does in these pages.

Nor is the book's vocabulary entirely Jacobean. Some words – tremendous (1625), blunderbuss (1645) and menagerie (1700) – are usually thought to have appeared in English rather later. Words such as steeple-chasing, torrential and fumarole are nineteenth-century inventions that Shakespeare would almost certainly not have known. But he was an inspired and relentless coiner of new words, so I hope it is not fanciful to imagine him ranging ahead of his lexicographers on such occasions. I am more than happy to suggest, even in the case of phrases or sentiments that seem modern to us, that Shakespeare put his fingerprints on them long, long ago.

As for the more sensational aspects of the tale, there is no evidence that they are true – but neither is there proof that they are false. Some are historical controversies that have intrigued or enraged scholars for years. Others (such as the notion that Shakespeare may have had a hand in the King James Bible) are complete fiction. When in doubt, I heeded Oscar Wilde's famous dictum that the only duty we owe to history is to rewrite it.

Throughout the novel, Shakespeare and his friends recall lines that they themselves wrote or performed. Sometimes their memories are accurate, sometimes not. They are certainly not 'quoting' from the plays as we might do today, because these plays did not yet exist in an authoritative form. The first folio would not be published for a decade, and the King's Men were too inventive to be word-perfect. Sometimes they even blend or merge disparate lines into one.

The character with whom I have made most free is William Shakespeare himself. His personal mannerisms are entirely imaginary, as is his dialogue (except where he quotes his own plays and poems).

It is nowhere suggested that he befriended Sir Walter Raleigh, and he is hardly ever named as a contributor to the King James Bible (especially not in 1613, when it would have been too late). Such are the gaps in our knowledge that I was obliged to spin his motives out of thin air. It is thought he *may* have worked on a new play at this stage in his life, but there is scant evidence for it.

I like to think that he would have written *The True and Tragicall Historie of King Henry VII* if he possibly could. The first Tudor monarch is a beguiling figure and an oddly neglected one. Most bookshops have a long shelf of biographical works concerning his son, Henry VIII, yet stock next to nothing about the father. This may be because we do not have the Shakespeare play to illuminate his life, character and times. This is a shame, because Henry VII is a good story: among his other achievements he turned a swamp of warring barons into the cradle of modern England, oversaw the first nautical steps into the Atlantic and played midwife to the birth of printing.

The novel offers a description of Shakespeare at work, so I should state here that I do not find the various attempts to find alternative authors for his plays persuasive or even interesting. The documentary record is sparse – though it supports Shakespeare's authorship more amply than any other claimant's. It is possible that the sketchy trail of evidence suggests nothing more than that a writer as prolific as Shakespeare led a quiet and orderly life. We like to imagine genius as having a rumbustious streak, and a bohemian appetite for the kind of incidents that make headlines, but the production of literature on this magnificent scale requires an abundance of peace, quiet, and clearheadedness. In any case, I have assumed a free hand here and attributed a significant measure of Shakespeare's creative power to his fellow actors. We do not know the truth, and probably never will, but drama is a team sport, and I suspect that if Shakespeare had to address an award ceremony, the list of people requiring thanks might be longer than we suppose.

Novels do not usually require a bibliography, but in this case there were some extremely informative guides, so I am grateful, among others, to: *Shakespeare's Life and Stage* by S.H. Burton (Chambers, 1989), *Shakespeare of London* by Marchette Chute (Souvenir, 1977),

John Donne by John Stubbs (Norton, 2006), *Will in the World* by Stephen Greenblatt (Norton, 2004), *The Age of Shakespeare* by Frank Kermode (Weidenfeld, 2004), *Elizabethan London* by Liza Picard (Phoenix, 2004), *Shakespeare* by Anthony Burgess (Penguin, 1972), *William Shakespeare: A Compact Documentary Life* by S. Schoenbaum (Clarendon, 1977), *Big Chief Elizabeth* by Giles Milton (Sceptre, 2001), *The Perfect Prince: The Mystery of Perkin Warbeck* by Ann Wroe (Random House, 2003), *The Power and the Glory* by Adam Nicolson (HarperCollins, 2003), *Oxford History of England: The Early Stuarts* by Godfrey Davies (Oxford, 1937), *Henry VII* by Jocelyn Hunt and Carolyn Towle (Longman, 1998) and *Richard III: The Great Debate* by Paul Kendall (Folio, 1965). I apologise for so wilfully choosing, every now and then, to ignore or contradict these most impressive works.

Finally, a great many thanks to Toby Eady, Jamie Coleman, Richard Beswick and Rowan Cope for their redoubtable, sharp and repeated reading of the work-in-progress. For whatever lapses, misjudgements and other failings that still linger in the text, they are of course partly to blame.

Time's glory is to calm contending kings
To unmask falsehood, and bring truth to light.

Shakespeare: *The Rape of Lucrece*

Chapter
1

*T*he measurement of human emotions is not an exact science; there are very few remedies for real sorrow. Misery may be biological, born of some inherited uproar in the blood, or it may be circumstantial – down to bad luck, heart-stopping loss, or the cruelty of others. Either way, the qualities we count on to keep us balanced – equanimity, ambition, optimism – can slip through the cracks between nature and nurture, leaving us alone, fearful and on shaky ground.

In all the confusing terms that have tried to describe unhappiness down the ages, however, there is one common thread, and it has little to do with moody physiologies or life's feverish ups and downs. It is a straightforward question of narrative. Put simply: true despair – the sense that life is meaningless and not worth living – is the emotion that invades us when the story we tell about ourselves turns out not to be true.

Each of us wants to be the protagonist, the central character in the chronicle that is our life. Some, the more egotistical, give barely a thought to the hopes and fears of others, but none can shrug off the unease that grips us when our own life story turns out to be imaginary or, worse, an illusion. The warrior who finds himself a coward; the Puritan unable to resist the lure of harlotry; the truth-teller revealed to be a liar . . . these are predicaments from which there is no escape.

That is why life stories, like all stories, have to be edited, revised, corrected.

This can be true on the largest scale, when entire nations discover to their shame that they have been fooling themselves with falsehoods. But though it is the work of a moment to exercise the editor's pencil, the side effects of altering a story may be harder to contain. Human beings have never found it easy to believe new versions of old tales, just as they rarely give up discredited gods without a fight. It takes labour to invent a new narrative; time and patience are required to make it credible. And some people, embarked on a life of disbelief, wind up finding it difficult to believe in anything – least of all themselves.

These were the notions that tumbled through the mind of William Shakespeare as he sat in the Whitehall Theatre, watching a gala performance of his own *Richard III*. He had, as everyone in the audience knew, a mind of rare agility, so he experienced them as sensations rather than ideas. But he dared not move a muscle. It was late February 1613, and he was sitting only a few feet from the mighty King James himself, the blustering glutton who these past ten years had nudged England and Scotland towards their present uneasy union. The crowded aisles were only half aware of the stage – they had eyes chiefly for the royal party and its celebrated guest. Not for the first time – he turned heads wherever he went, and could not scratch his ear without sparking a flutter of interest – Shakespeare was a prisoner of his own fame, pinned to his seat as securely as a thief in the stocks. But while etiquette insisted that he remain impassive, the weight of his heart told him that he had suffered a blow from which he might not soon recover.

The culprit was in his pocket: a leather-backed pamphlet that had the temerity to criticise the play. Its argument was blunt, not to say waspish: 'Shakspere' had taken a well-intentioned and legitimate monarch (Richard III) and depicted him as a murderous hell-hound. He was thus the willing collaborator in a calculated piece of political myth-making. In crowing over the toppling of a king, he had written a disgraceful apologia for treason that falsely presented the greedy, usurping Tudors as a troop of white knights rescuing England from tyranny.

The criticism pierced Shakespeare's heart like a bolt from a crossbow, because he knew, not all that deep down, that it was well aimed. He had based his play on the usual sources, Hall and Holinshed, but had also leaned on Sir Thomas More's life of Richard, an unreliable and sycophantically hostile portrait clearly intended to impress and protect the monarch's successor. He had not heard the fashionable sneer that history was merely the version of the past written by the winner, but Shakespeare felt the truth of this cliché in his arteries without needing to form it into a shapely thought.

In normal circumstances he might have been able to shrug off such barbs. He was celebrated, wealthy and content, and could afford to ignore the cavils of lesser men. But now, watching his superb, vile crookback, Richard of Gloucester, scheming for the crown like a malignant spider, humiliation came in a single white-hot flash. The thrilling heat of his own rhetorical zest made it even worse.

It was not the easiest time for him to bear an assault of this sort. Only two weeks ago, on the fourth of February, he had buried his younger brother Gilbert – just one day short of a year following the death of his older brother, Richard. February had become a bleak month to him: he felt edgy, transparent, insubstantial.

He glanced sideways and had to stifle a gasp. The King's pale, fleshy face was slumped forward over the pudgy jowls of his outsized chins: a single fat bubble snuffled and popped in the loose corner of his baggy mouth. His famous horse's tongue lolled over his bulging lip. He was fast asleep.

His well-born neighbours were taking care not to notice.

Shakespeare stared ahead for a moment, then nudged his companion's arm.

'Do you think anyone would mind if we left?'

A selection of pampered heads twitched at this heresy while, down on the stage, Richard III began to shout at ghosts. Shakespeare sank deeper into his seat.

Perhaps he should not have come. He had been invited down to London to be the honoured guest at more than a dozen performances of his own plays, however, and ought by rights to be enjoying himself. He had been welcomed back in the capital like a Roman emperor enjoying a Triumph. The plays were being staged as part of the pageant marking the Valentine's Day wedding of the King's daughter, Elizabeth, to the German Elector Palatine, so it would have been churlish as well as dangerous to stand aloof. It was never politic to say no to kings, and in the present atmosphere of suspicion and unease a refusal could easily be taken as a slight.

Besides, if he was honest, part of him had missed the riot and bustle of London life. And until this evening he had half enjoyed pretending to be embarrassed by all the acclaim. But now he found himself pecking at it with a tetchy conscience. In the high court of his own opinion he was finding himself guilty of a historic error.

Could he really have displayed the birth of the Tudor monarchy in an unmerited heroic light? Had he sold his own virtuosity too cheap?

These were uncomfortable questions, even for a man as successful as he. The applause of the audience, even as it revelled in the cartoon villainy of his depraved King Richard, juddered in his ears like the cackle of a witch. All that hard-won fame – the high eminence that allowed him to patronise this theatre as if he too were a duke: it sharpened the fear that he had prostituted his gift. Had he really been a publicity scribbler, a pen for hire? The thought made him pale.

He forced himself to concentrate on the stage. 'If you do sweat to put a tyrant down,' said the actor playing Henry Tudor, then still Richmond, 'You sleep in peace, the tyrant being slain.'

Thank God: it was nearly over.

He was a theatrical man, and when he had a clear thought he acted on it, so he met this seizure in his self-confidence with a powerful urge to set things straight. Yet what could he do? It was too late to unwrite or disclaim *Richard III* – he was finished with plays. In theory, he supposed, he could attempt some new assignment and create a more truthful version of England's history. Nevertheless, he could not suppress the weary feeling that overcame him at the thought of such a task. He was two years retired and lacked the optimistic fire needed for such work. When it came right down to it, he was no longer sure he had it in him.

He slept fitfully and woke early. He knew that what a man felt didn't matter – it was what a man *did* that counted – but he was not a free agent, and much as he would have liked to spend the day sauntering around the bookstalls or in Field's Printing House, he had engagements he could not neglect. His week was filled with visits and meetings – feasts, society events, church readings and so on – and it had long been arranged, by well-meaning friends, that this morning he would visit the Tower of London's most famous guest, Sir Walter Raleigh. The great Elizabethan had been locked up in prison for ten years, and Shakespeare conceded with shame that he thought of him only rarely. Some scruple had prevented him from going till now.

In truth, the two had never been close. They had met a few times in the old days at the Mermaid; indeed, Raleigh had often favoured him with compliments. Even so the man was a florid Protestant, and a few minutes in his company sometimes seemed a good while. More significantly, Raleigh had always been a rival at court to Essex, Shakespeare's friend. They moved in different circles, and that was that.

Still, it was a gross injustice that the man lay confined in the Tower. Pondering it anew, Shakespeare gasped at the iniquity in the idea of such an epic figure – the first Governor of Virginia, no less! – brought to such a pass. How long ago it seemed, that lofty tide of Elizabethan glory: those stirring deeds on ocean swells, the spirited sonnets and ballads, the golden fables from Hispaniola and the glorious, heavenly routing of the Armada. What did it say on the medal? *Flavit Jehovah, et dissipati sunt* – God blew, and they were scattered. Even the heavens were on their side back then.

It was almost painful to recall such times now. And this wasn't the only reason why Shakespeare had mixed feelings about today's outing. He felt awkward in these ceremonial roles; it embarrassed him to think that this was what his life amounted to – courtesy visits to condemned men, staged opportunities for a couple of elderly refugees, heroes of a bygone age, to get together for appearances' sake.

There was one bright streak in the sky, however. Shakespeare knew that Sir Walter was working on a *History*, and the grey cloud that now hovered over his own *Richard III* made this a fine time for a conversation on this matter. He knew very well that history wasn't the past –

merely what he had *instead* of the past; if anything, it was an obliging pool of magical tales, a well of inspiration. These days, though, he had a swelling sense of the way the past shifted and danced as it grew remote. There were worse people to debate this with than Sir Walter Raleigh.

He dropped in on a bookseller and paid sixpence for a copy of his own Sonnets, as a gift. The price made him wince – it should not have cost more than fourpence – but who was he to complain? Outside, he tiptoed through the evil-smelling mounds of mud and refuse before taking a carriage to the eastern end of Thames Street. At the great Lion Gate he stood for a moment, the broad river at his back, gazing at the looming bulk of the famous Tower that rose high and mighty behind its moat and rampart. He had not been here since the imprisonment of his friend Henry Wriothesley, Earl of Southampton – locked up behind these walls for his part in a ramshackle rebellion a dozen years ago. A shudder passed through him, like the ghost of a guilty conscience, to recall the fearful circular stairs that led to Southampton's room in the Bell Tower. He could hear a few barks and howls from the caged animals in the menagerie on the other side of this wall, and for a moment fancied he could hear, in the raucous scream of gulls on the battlements, the cries of all the other battered souls that had passed this way. Southampton and Essex, those innocent young Princes, Thomas More, Anne Boleyn, Guy Fawkes and the rest . . . They had suffered bitter agonies within these haughty walls. Most had lost their heads.

Shakespeare himself had seen Essex's terrified face skewered on a stake at London Bridge. It had been boiled, to prevent rotting, but still bore an astonished look, as if it had glimpsed some unspeakable horror. The once-noble visage of a brilliant courtier stared with lidless eyes across the river like the blank skull of some gaping, nut-brown devil. It was dreadful: Shakespeare could neither eat nor sleep for days.

There was a pause while a guard was sent for to lead the way to Raleigh's rooms. Then Shakespeare was escorted beneath the great battlements, along the line of the outer wall by the river, and across a wide expanse of grass. Spring flowers were beginning to burst out along the verges, and birds sang in the trees. It was quite possible to forget this was a home to desperate souls; it was more palace than dungeon.

6

'Here we are,' said the guard. 'The Bloody Tower. A pretty name.'

He knocked at the door, pushed it open and stood aside. Over by the window Shakespeare could see a tall man, still slim but grey-haired, with a neat beard and a fine white shirt. He was holding a leather-bound volume in one hand.

'Yes?' said Sir Walter Raleigh, only half turning.

'A visitor,' said the guard.

Raleigh laid down the book. 'So I see.'

He seemed indifferent to the prospect of company.

'I am sorry. Perhaps this is not a good time.'

'There is no such thing as a good time. Not in these walls, and not in this world neither.' Raleigh turned away and took up his book again.

Shakespeare smiled. It was a long time since he had gone unrecognised.

'It is me, Will Shakespeare. I am sorry. It has been years.'

'William Shakespeare!' Raleigh hurried across the stone flags. 'Cakes and crocodiles! Come in, come in! They said you were coming tomorrow.'

'If they told you yesterday, they spoke the truth.'

'Ah, the truth . . .' Raleigh lifted his hands in a shrug. 'A slippery fish, the truth.'

His creamy Devon accent made him sound sad.

The room was larger than Shakespeare had expected and more cheerful. The stone walls were caked in whitewash, and there were rugs, drapes, chairs, a heavy oak desk full of books and papers, and a huge fireplace. The windows, though not generous, admitted a fair amount of light. It was a cell, but a comfortable one.

'I am sorry it is early. I vaulted in on the spur of the morning.'

Vaulted? Where did *that* come from? He took a nervous breath.

'It is just as well. They still take an interest in my visitors. Perhaps this way they won't trouble you.'

'Trouble?' Shakespeare had not thought of this as a perilous mission. Raleigh had been imprisoned for so long – surely he was not regarded as a danger any more.

'But never mind that.' Raleigh's low voice washed over

Shakespeare like a rolling sea swell. 'Please. Have a seat. Have something to drink.'

Shakespeare shook his head.

'I insist.' Raleigh poured water out of an earthenware beaker. 'I can vouch for its freshness. And I value your opinion.'

Shakespeare shrugged, accepted the cup and took a sip.

Raleigh was looking at him in a way that suggested he was eager for a response. Shakespeare was confused – it was only water.

'Like silver dew. Very refreshing.'

'I am glad you like it. I made it.'

'Made it?'

Raleigh beamed. 'From salt water, using a process of my own devising. I have invented a means of removing the salt. If we have time I will show you. There is an old hen house across the lawn – the constable lets me use it for experiments.'

Shakespeare relaxed. It looked as if Raleigh was happy to do the talking.

'All we need now is to find a way to take my method to sea. As yet the apparatus is too large and clumsy, but one day all our ships may have fresh water.'

'And you will be the patron saint of our sailors.'

'It's a shame Bess isn't here. She's back in Devon, I'm afraid. Adores your work, though. I know she'd want to ask you about *Romeo and Juliet*.'

Wait for it, thought Shakespeare. Here it comes. Was the play based on his own life? Where had he got the idea? Who was the unlucky lady? He hated to disappoint people by admitting that he had plucked the unhappy couple from an old book.

He was surprised by Raleigh's quick, fidgety manner. He would have imagined that prison bred a morose or sullen disposition, but it seemed to have produced the opposite effect here. The explorer was very talkative.

'She won't forgive me if I don't ask,' he continued. 'See, she's always believed that *Romeo and Juliet* was based on us. Forbidden romance, and all that.'

He arched his eyebrows.

Shakespeare hesitated. The secret wedding of Sir Walter Raleigh and Bess Throckmorton was, it was true, a famous scandal, so the pair did fit the part of star-crossed lovers – indeed, they had been imprisoned for it. Shakespeare could not now recall which came first – their stormy passion or his heartbreaking play.

'Well,' he said carefully, 'I wouldn't say "based". It crossed my mind that there were echoes, but you two resisted self-slaughter, I am glad to say.'

'That's life,' said Raleigh with a breezy smile. 'So much duller than art. No matter. It is wonderful to see you. You will have to forgive my excitement, but a visitor is a red-letter occasion. I used to receive a good many guests, but recently . . . Oh, but listen to me. You must want something more to drink – they give me gallons of ale. Or eat. Or smoke! I have this marvellous tobacco, just off the boat. This year I am going to grow some out in the garden, but this –' he snatched a long pipe with a silver bowl from the shelf by the fireplace, and held up a pinch of chopped leaf – 'this is the real thing . . . from Virginia!'

Shakespeare almost purred with pleasure. To be offered tobacco by Sir Walter Raleigh himself! It was almost enough to make him wish he smoked.

'Is it true, that story about the Queen and your smoke?'

It was a very famous incident. The Queen had refused to believe Raleigh when he said that he could, for a reward, weigh the smoke from his pipe – so he proved it to her. First he weighed out the tobacco, then he smoked it, and then he weighed the ash. A simple subtraction was enough to produce the answer.

The Queen's reply was what had made the tale endure. She said that she had seen many men turn gold into smoke, but none who could turn smoke into gold.

'Not quite,' said Raleigh, lighting the pipe. 'There never was a reward. Here.'

Shakespeare lacked the heart to decline. He took a light puff, gave an acrid cough, and felt tears leap to his eyes. When he tried to speak, his voice was a croak.

'Delicious.' He fought for breath. 'Sweet, sweet poison.'

'My comfort in miserable times.' Raleigh took back the pipe and

9

drew in a mouthful. 'Naturally the King disapproves. Oh, but maps and monkeys!'

Cakes and crocodiles? Maps and monkeys? Shakespeare, his eyes still watering from the bitter fumes, wondered whether Raleigh had been infected with these vivid tropical flourishes by solitude alone.

'Anyway, you caught me red-fingered. Look what I was reading when you came in.' He held out the book to show the gilt lettering on the spine: *Hamlet*.

Shakespeare smiled. 'Alas, poor Hamlet.'

'Poor?' said Raleigh. 'It is a miracle. That volley of revenges at the end – you surpassed even yourself. But be honest – those remarks about the kingdom: Something is rotten in the state of Denmark. Please tell me I am right to see them as barbs aimed at our own beloved Queen. I cherish the fondest hope . . .'

Shakespeare scraped a fleck of tobacco leaf from his tongue. It was true. King James's wife, Anne of Denmark, was a byword for vulgar excess, and everyone knew it. Most people blamed it on the eye-wrenching trip south from flint-poor Scotland – when she and her husband, stunned by England's wealth, had gorged themselves like cows in clover. Some predicted that she would rein in her extravagance, but there was no sign of it yet. Her famous masques were the butt of many a ballad: the guests sunk in a Bacchanalian frenzy; the King swooning in jelly, cream and cake, grovelling among the remnants; while his wife and her Viking friends bathed in pools of wine and gnawed at meat like ravenous animals.

Raleigh was right: London was full of carousing Danes, refugees from their country's war with Sweden. Those with more money than martial spirit had boarded the royal caravan to London, but none would have enjoyed Hamlet's description of their homeland as an unweeded garden, as rank and gross as a prison.

'I wish I could say so,' said Shakespeare. 'Alas, we wrote *Hamlet* years before we had a Danish queen. But this may be why it is never staged in London.'

'We?'

'The King's Men. We work on these things together.'

'Oh, but to think! After all our labours, all our victories . . . that we should end up with this weak Scottish king and his gross Danish queen. And both of them greedy sots. It is not right. I hear that the King looses only at fattened stags, and is fonder of his caged wolves than his subjects – except for his damned favourites. Is it true that he kisses his boon companions in public? We are worse than Roman, with our spectacles and taste for blood. Before God, it shames us, what we have become.'

'I myself have been away, but people say that it is so.'

'I trust you are no friend to Robert Carr. There is no man I detest more. The thought of him in my house—'

'Your house?'

'Do you not know? The King confiscated Sherborne Castle and has given it to this fawning Scottish lackey. And to think we named the Virginia settlement – Jamestown – in his honour. Oh, my heart aches . . .'

'I have never met Robert Carr. Nor do I wish to.'

'Well, if you *do* meet him, you have my full permission to put his eyes out. And the King's, while you are about it.'

There were daggers in the silence that followed. This went beyond grumbling. It was downright sedition. Oftentimes, to win us to our harm, whispered the voice in Shakespeare's inner ear, the instruments of darkness tell us truths. The glance he flashed at Raleigh was sharpened by suspicion.

Raleigh seemed to notice. 'I go too far,' he said. 'I apologise. It is easy for me to voice my thoughts – I am already a prisoner. But I see I have offended you.'

'Not at all.' Shakespeare was wounded by the implication that he was too timid, that he trimmed his sails to safeguard his freedom. He too was horrified by the coarse, gluttonous state into which the kingdom had fallen – and he did not often care who knew it. Everything fine and valuable lay smashed, drowned, dissolved. The England that he loved – the land of heron and buttercup, conker and rook, catkin, acorn and hawthorn hedge – lay ransacked under the clumsy wheels of its new rulers. This was the chief cause of his own heavy-hearted retreat to Stratford.

'Back to *Hamlet*,' said Raleigh. 'I don't care if you wrote it before the Queen arrived – I still credit you with the insight. Like a master mariner, you sniffed the storm before it broke, saw before any of us that England was sliding into the pit.'

Shakespeare sighed. Was it possible that he had foreseen this decadent royal spree? No. He could not accept the suggestion that he was any kind of seer. If anything, the accession of King James had lifted his spirits; he had even permitted himself to believe that the Puritan cause would be thwarted. Those hopes lay in ruins now.

'Maybe you should have set it in Spain. "Something is rotten in the state of Spain" – no one could have taken offence at that.'

'Have you not heard? We are friends with Spain now.'

Raleigh thumped the table with the flat of his palm. 'Yes, God help us.'

Shakespeare had no wish to be drawn into a theological argument, and sought to ease the tension by changing the subject. There wasn't time.

'But listen to me,' said Raleigh. 'I am too raw and salty. Excitement has stolen my manners. Let us talk of happier times, you and I.'

Shakespeare rubbed his head. Raleigh had been sequestered in this cabin for ten years, so had to be forgiven a few sour remarks. Nonetheless Shakespeare disliked bile and was not looking for trouble. He began to wish he had not come.

'Well, I shall sit,' said Raleigh.

Shakespeare took a seat opposite him.

'Tell me, why did you leave London? More to the point, what prompted you to stop writing plays? Those of us with time on our hands – we are distraught.'

It was a compliment, and Raleigh smiled to make sure it was received as such.

Shakespeare's eyes closed for an instant, the reasons for his withdrawal fanning out like a peacock's tail in his mind. Disgust at the grisly taste of the modern audience, which valued severed heads above wit; despair over the King's decision to suspend Parliament and rule like a tyrant; weariness with the endless need to cringe and simper after royal favour and patronage; impatience with the foul stink of a city that had become noxious and overcrowded; frustration at the intrusive attentions inspired by his own fame: these were the promptings that led him to seek a calmer life in Stratford, where willows grew aslant brooks and rabbits did not flee footsteps. There were other reasons too, which he barely admitted even to himself: a loss of drive, a fear that his talent was draining away, a cooling of all desire.

He shrugged. 'I missed my family,' he said. 'I had been away too long.'

And at once he felt a stab of shame. How could he have said such a thing to a man separated from his family for good?

Once again Raleigh noticed his discomfort. This time he laughed.

'Have no worries on my account. Bess and the boys live right here with me. Not in these rooms – they rent a house outside the walls. But they are about me all the time. I am by no means deprived of their society.'

Shakespeare breathed out.

'Let us be serious. You are a man of rare substance, so I know that you must fear for our kingdom, as I do,' said Raleigh. 'These last months, since the deaths of Salisbury and Prince Henry, who is there left to stand against the King's folly? Will none stand up for England?'

Shakespeare felt reproached, but forced himself to agree.

'It is indeed a dangerous time.'

'Worse than dangerous. A viper's nest.'

Shakespeare had to smile. Only here, in the chief dungeon of England, could a man speak so freely without fear for his life.

'It is not safe to say so, yet if it succours you to know there are those who feel the same, then count on it. When the King broke with the people, he broke with me too.'

'I did not doubt this, but am glad to hear it,' said Raleigh. 'Let's walk outside.'

He led the way up to a raised pavement that connected this tower to its neighbour.

'They allow me to me wander at will up here. We cannot be overheard, and the view is good. Though it is painful to see water so close and not be on it.'

He looked out at the river, at the swarm of ships and boats that nosed and wheeled in the centre of the stream. Just out of sight, in

Rotherhithe, a sturdy freighter called the *Mayflower* was unloading wine and nuts from Aquitaine.

'I refuse to be melancholy. There is too much to do.'

Shakespeare felt a miniature drill of shame. He faced inland.

'Tower Green,' nodded Raleigh. 'Where your friend Essex was executed. A long time ago. Even I wasn't here then.'

'He was hot, and loved not wisely, but he was never a bad man.'

'I know. And for the sufferings he endured here, in this accursed place, I swear I feel closer to him than to many a living friend.'

It was easy to see what drew people to Raleigh, Shakespeare thought, and just as easy to see what vexed them. The man was a confusing mixture – by turns as sombre as an ox and as eager as a puppy.

'What do people say about their king?' said Raleigh. 'Tell me the truth.'

'People, or me?'

'Both.'

'The people say he is a fine and noble leader – every inch a king.'

'They are not fools. They would be scalped if they said otherwise.'

'True.' Shakespeare groaned. 'Ours is a garden of beastly delights. The King showers wealth on every pretty upstart, while his queen . . . They serve thirty dishes at table, with Chinese silk and Venetian glass. It is . . . wanton.'

'Just as I said – a sty, stewed in corruption.'

'It is not only that. There is terror abroad. Since the Plot was discovered, we live under a tyranny. Fear stalks the alleys and the courtyards. It taps at the doors and windows, haunts the streets and doorways, and drips from the trees and rooftops. Who knows where it will strike? It turns people from their beds and makes honest men start in the night. Children scream at ghosts. Even the dogs cower. I do not know how long this state of things can endure. Something violent, something monstrous, is ripening in the body politic. We have been peaceable a long while, but I do not know—'

'It will not last. The injustice of kings is always punished.'

A gust of cold wind snapped through Shakespeare's hair. Raleigh was already changing the subject and stretching his legs. They strolled along the rampart, speaking about the latest news from the court – was it true the King was giving away more in gifts each year than the old Queen had done in her entire reign? They also touched on the chestnut colour of the Orinoco River, the number of deer in Richmond, the sickliness of the young Prince Charles, the whereabouts of mutual friends, the high price of sugar (Raleigh insisting that in the New World it grew like a weed) and the latest cures for plague.

After a while Raleigh returned to the subject of Shakespeare's plays, which he knew and loved well. He was not, however, above chiding his guest for his unfriendly portrait of Joan of Arc.

'You made her a madwoman,' he said. 'Yet she was a warrior and a saint.'

Shakespeare almost blushed. He had been young when he wrote *Henry VI* and happy to go along with the popular depiction of Joan as a demented French witch. He cleared his throat to apologise, but it was too late.

'Never mind. Do you know who I like best in *Hamlet*?' Raleigh was saying. 'Fortinbras. Now there's a proper instrument of fate.'

Shakespeare was surprised. 'Fortinbras? He is a man, neither less nor more. Not even that, if I am truthful. We needed *someone* to come on at the end and sweep away the corpses. He was near at hand, that is all.'

'Oh, your imagination knew better than that. Fortinbras is a pure angel of revenge. Vengeance: your great subject, and mine too. Who killed Fortinbras's father? Why, Hamlet's father! So here comes the son, at the bitter end, to avenge his father's death. Do you not see the parallel? Here, in just such a way, comes our own King James, bent on revenge for the wild spirit of his mother Mary – Queen of Scots, friend of Spain, traitor to our cause and executed by Elizabeth. Round it all goes. And here he loafs, a cuckoo in our golden nest, devouring all our fledglings.'

Raleigh smiled and again Shakespeare felt a wary ripple, like a shadow passing.

'We should have been friends before this day,' said Raleigh. 'We think alike, and both have cause to hate our king, who sues for peace with Spain and falls asleep in your plays – oh yes, he is famous for it! Oh, think back to when the world was bright, when we crossed oceans and mapped stars, and had your work to enliven our souls! Now . . .'

They stood in silence.

'When I say that injustice is always punished, do not mistake me. Things do not always get better.' Raleigh shivered. 'I have studied the Ancients, and this I know: nations and empires fall. Worlds decline. Look below us. There are only six firm roadways in the kingdom now: the Strand, Cheapside and four great Roman arteries. A thousand years ago you could travel the land on hard roads. We have fallen far.'

Something swam into focus in Shakespeare's mind.

'I too have feared the abyss,' he said. 'Ever since the murder of France.'

They stared out over the city once again, both thinking on the same event. Henry IV of France had been assassinated by a Catholic diehard enraged by the tolerant edicts the King was passing in favour of his Huguenot Protestants. Raleigh himself had fought alongside Huguenots in the Netherlands. The conflict between Catholics and Protestants was becoming sharp and raw; it was as if mighty armies were slowly massing across all Europe. If one sword were raised, if one blade flashed in the bright air, who could say how many might fall?

Shakespeare gazed over the rooftops that dropped away to the west. London was conquering its surrounding hills in a fabulous tumble of steep eaves, Roman walls and broken stones. St Paul's and Westminster Abbey stood like marooned hulks above a tossing forest of smoke and spires. From this vantage point it was hard to imagine the maggoty hovels that littered the public byways, the army of vagrants and beggars that flocked from the countryside these days. Shakespeare could sense the restless yearning of a man like Raleigh, who had seen the far side of the oceans – all silver pools in luxuriant jungles, rare fruits and grand forests of maple and mahogany.

'Good view, isn't it?' said Raleigh. 'I came up here to watch that naval battle they mounted on the river, for the Princess's wedding. Did you see it? Ridiculous.'

Shakespeare shook his head.

'Thank God the battlements of Durham House are obscured. That would be too painful.'

Shakespeare had passed Raleigh's old mansion often; it was one of London's most obvious landmarks. In some ways it actually resembled the Tower – it was a bulky stone fortress that rose on the bank of the river between Westminster and Blackfriars – and Shakespeare blinked at the thought of how much Raleigh must miss it. He had made it a temple to Elizabethan learning, a tranquil harbour for scholars and scientists.

'It baffles me now to remember those days,' Raleigh said in a low voice. 'Young Thomas Hariot was there, of course, building his telescope up on the roof. Did you know about that? And did you hear about those Indian fellows we brought over?'

Shakespeare shook his head.

'Before your time, maybe. Well, I took them to Hampton Court to meet the Queen. She loved them, of course. And Hariot set himself to learn their language. I tell you, we discovered more about the New World from those two astonished Virginians than from all our conquests. And the King thinks them savages!'

Shakespeare scratched his arm.

'You must have known the old Queen quite well.'

'As well as any man in England! But I will tell you something that most people *don't* know. I never heard anyone, man or woman, who could swear like Gloriana. My God! Even the windows had to stop their ears!'

Shakespeare grinned.

'And is it true, the other famous story . . . about the cloak?'

'Of course. The funny thing, though, is that it was – still is – a common practice in Spain. People were astounded, but it was not so very outrageous.'

'I suppose, in muddy England, men could not afford to be so free with cloaks.'

'I suppose.'

There was a pause.

'Anyway, I am glad to find you so well, though it pains me to see you here.'

Raleigh smiled. 'Oh, I count myself a king of infinite space, though I am, as you would say, bounded in this grey nutshell.'

Shakespeare registered the tribute with a faint smile.

'What scrapes at my heart is not my own trouble, but the national anguish. We let hard-won glories slip away like sand, and they call *me* a warmonger!'

Shakespeare had heard Raleigh thus described many times, without ever thinking to object. He was a well-known firebrand, itching to attack Spanish fleets.

'Believe me, no man who has seen war can endure it. *Dulce bellum inexpertis* – war is sweet to those who know it not. But war is not the point. Can they not see? The future lies to the west, in the colonies. Spain understands this. She is seizing all she can while we stand idle. I tell you, I know what befell the French Huguenots in Florida, and it was unendurable. Yet we do nothing! Our future is being written thousands of miles away, while we paddle our fingers and lick the grease from our spoons. All I want is an English nation at Roanoke, but this King – he sees the New World as a sewer, a place to toss penniless vagrants. I would harvest wheat; he seeks to plant convicts. I swear, Will, that I do hate war most truly. But if we permit Spain to conquer the new territories, we shall be lost, quite lost.'

Shakespeare could not let him continue. He could tell that this was a speech, and an argument, that Raleigh had made before; but he himself was more interested in the past than the years ahead. He had long since renounced such juggling fiends.

'I sometimes think,' he murmured, 'that when it comes to the future, history is the only soothsayer. There isn't much that happens that has never happened before.'

'Exactly!' said Raleigh, still agitated. 'That's what I am saying! Study the past to know the future. Oh, if I were not trapped under this rock. Snakes and seahorses!'

Shakespeare smiled.

'I am repeating myself, I know,' continued Raleigh, 'but if history teaches us anything, it is that time is an avenger. You of all people must agree. After all, you have given it magnificent, vivid names – fortune's wheel, fortune's knave, the whirligig of time. These are perfect phrases. Civilisations rising and falling to the thoughtless dance of a child's toy. The earth spins and nothing goes unpunished. Even kings have to answer for the cruelties done on their behalf.'

Shakespeare bowed his head, humbled by Raleigh's praise. It was true that he had put this story on stage time after time. The cruelty of kings did echo down the years. It haunted a thousand dreams and gave birth to vengeful children. Yet something new stirred within him now — a spasm of resolve, a tremor of desire. If Sir Walter Raleigh, unjustly locked in this place, could summon up such righteous fury, then who was he, William Shakespeare, to curl up and hide?

He had abandoned English history since Queen Elizabeth's block on such work — the Queen herself had counselled him against pitching his tent on such delicate ground. The previous day's shadow over his *Richard III* returned, here in this black heart of English power, and spread fresh gloom over his spirit.

In the depths of the shade, however, he heard the high, sad sound of a distant bugle. Someone had to dramatise anew the abuse of royal authority, and who was better suited for such a task than he himself?

Raleigh was looking at him with a watchful gaze. 'It is very good of you to come. I think something troubles you.'

Shakespeare shook himself. It was impertinent to seek sympathy from a prisoner. 'I reproach myself for not coming sooner. Is there anything I can do?'

Raleigh was leading the way indoors. With an ostentatious gesture he stretched out an arm, inviting Shakespeare to take precedence. With just such a flourish, Shakespeare thought, did once you cast your cloak before a queen.

'Actually there *is* something,' said Raleigh. 'You could speak for me, as Prince Henry used to. Poor man — they say he died from a chill, playing tennis. Infernal stupidity! He was a dear friend to my cause. Do you know what he said one time? That only his father would cage a bird as rare as me! But now he is dead; his brother Charles is too young and is, they say, a very paltry youth. So no one speaks for me now but Bacon — and you can't trust that snake.'

Shakespeare nodded. 'I will do what I can,' he said. 'Though in truth I too lack a friendly ear at court. Much has changed. I am no longer who I was.'

'I have offered to make another voyage, to find gold for the King, to crown his glory with all the treasure of El Dorado. I long for one last chance.'

'To whom should I appeal? Not Bacon, you said.'

'Not Bacon. But not Coke either. He would have my head if he could.'

Whilst Shakespeare did not know Sir Edward Coke – one of the Chief Justices involved with Raleigh's so-called 'trial' – he knew that the trial had been staged; it was common knowledge. It had made a fine play! The famous verdict – that Raleigh possessed 'the heart of a Spaniard' – was greeted with howls of mirth in the waterside inns and dens where the colonist was revered as a nautical hero.

'Of course I shall do what I can,' said Shakespeare. 'For old times' sake.'

'Old times' sake,' repeated Raleigh. 'I like that.'

He looked younger when he smiled: his teeth were still fair, and it was possible to glimpse, in these rare moments when his well-bred features lifted and lightened, the handsome visage of a courtier who had once charmed monarchs.

Shakespeare felt abashed. What do I know? he thought. *What do I know?*

It was time to leave.

'Well,' said Raleigh.

'Well,' said Shakespeare.

'In all honesty I should not complain. In court it was announced that I should be dragged through the streets, and have my heart and bowels plucked out. I was reprieved. I lost my estates, my houses, my hopes – but not yet my life.'

'I thank you for your hospitality.'

'Come again.'

'I should like to.'

Raleigh tapped on the door. It opened at once.

'Farewell, then,' he said. 'You have brightened a grey day.'

'So have you.' Shakespeare shook his hand. 'So have you.'

The door clanged shut with a deep, low boom, like a bell or gong – as if making some great announcement. Shakespeare leaned against the nearest patch of clean wall and sighed. The interview had been an ordeal and his shoulders ached. Yet he also felt a familiar tingle of exhilaration and renewal. He rejected the charge, often levelled at London's playwrights, that he was a parasite, feeding on the vitality of others, but he could not deny that he always found stimulation in human contact. Was that so strange?

Raleigh was a remarkable man. He had explored the Indies, supervised colonies and launched new trades. He had searched for gold in far-off mountains and he had written poetry. He had made fortunes and lost them, befriended queens and crossed them. His reward? To fret away his twilight years in this benighted cell. Who could fail to be enchanted by a man who refused to bow to such ill use?

The more he brooded, the more the spectacle of Raleigh's zeal made Shakespeare darken with self-reproach. He could not say when his own creative urge had faded, for he made a substantial effort to avoid self-examination. It had been a slow, sleepy process – a flame dying in the grate. Every now and then, if wind stirred the fine ash, he could feel flickers of warmth in the embers, but it had been a long time since he had written anything: he felt empty and in an odd sense inexperienced. He was too old to start over again. On the other hand, what had Raleigh said about the future – how it was being *written* far away? An interesting notion.

The guard was giving him a strange look. Shakespeare collected himself, nodded and followed him out on to the grass. He looked up, half expecting to see Raleigh's head at the window, but the casement was empty.

They reached the gatehouse and came to a halt in front of a heavy curtain by the oak door. It was locked. The guard stepped aside.

Shakespeare still had a book in his hand – the Sonnets he had forgotten to hand over. It made him feel clumsy, and for a moment he wondered whether he should return, but it was easier to leave the book with a guard. He had no wish to go back; he had both heard and uttered more than enough treasonous words for one day.

In the corner of his vision he sensed a quiet, silky motion.

The drapery behind him bulged and swished, and two men stepped through. One took hold of his arms and pulled them behind his back, twisting them up so he had to bend forward. Then a hood was bundled over his head, and the world went dark.

He had no idea what was happening. His instinct to cry out was stifled by the rough palm of a hand, which forced dusty sackcloth into his open mouth. The book dropped to the floor and something heavy slammed into his back; a piece of sinew or muscle dislodged, pushing him to his knees. He pulled free his arms, as if for help, and someone stood on them. Cold, damp boots ground into his hands and fingers. He tried to speak, but could not find air. There was a tug on the hood, jerking his head up and back. He felt his neck wrench.

He did not know which was worse: the physical shock or the shiver of disbelief.

Arms squeezed his chest and he trembled, but they only lifted him to his feet and shoved him forward. He was pushed down some steps into what felt like a dungeon – the air grew chill and damp, and he could hear dripping water. A fold of coarse sackcloth pressed into his eyeball. Above his head a door closed, and footsteps approached. He was pushed against the wall, face first.

'Name?'

The voice was rough.

The four simple syllables, echoing in this unreal, dripping place, sounded ridiculous even to himself. He heard the men laugh. They did not believe him.

He could hardly blame them – even to himself it sounded a silly name, and obviously invented. He almost smiled. Stripped of his prestige, he too was a poor, naked wretch. And my poor fool is hanged, he thought.

'Sir Walter can explain.'

'Is he telling us our business?' said a voice. Someone slapped the back of his head and squashed his face into the stone. He felt blood on his chin.

In the silence he could hear whispers, a door creaking and more footsteps.

'This way,' said a new voice.

Someone held his arm and steered him back up the steps he had just come down, out into the fresh air. After a short walk he passed indoors again and up a flight of stairs. This time they were made of wood – Shakespeare heard them creak. They came to a carpeted room much warmer than the staircase, and he thought he could hear the crackle of a fire. The footsteps retreated.

He did not dare remove his hood. With his head tilted, he braced himself against whatever was supposed to happen next. His back hurt.

He was surprised to find that he was not afraid: on the contrary, he was cooled by a perverse calm that shaded, as the minutes passed, into curiosity. He did not feel in danger; indeed, there was something about the violence that felt superfluous, theatrical. He was in the Tower of London, hemmed about by walls, guards, locked doors and – he shivered – instruments of torture. There was no need for this ham-fisted exhibition of force; this whole performance had some other purpose.

The thought soothed him. He was not, it seemed, in imminent danger. Someone was trying to tell him something. All he had to do was listen, and think, and wait.

He was a patient man, and he sensed he would not have to wait long.

Chapter 2

There was a hasty rustle of silk and the soft drumming of shoes approaching fast. A phrase flew into Shakespeare's mind: 'Tis now the very witching time of night.

'Good Lord,' said a voice.

Shakespeare did nothing.

'What on earth is that thing on his head? Remove it. At once.'

It was a voice used to being obeyed. A hand plucked at the hood, and Shakespeare's hair was snagged in an ungentle fist. It was all he could do to suppress a yelp of pain.

'So it is true,' said the voice. 'Please accept my heartfelt apologies.'

The room seemed bright. Sunshine poured in through enormous vaulted windows. Shakespeare threw a hand up to cover his eyes.

There was nothing to say, so he said nothing.

'Permit me to explain,' said the man facing him. He was standing by the fire, a decanter of wine in his hand. He wore a black gown with a broad, white ruff, and had pale features, milky eyes and well-fed cheeks. A politician or a judge, Shakespeare thought, dressed as if for a portrait. Perhaps the Constable of the Tower himself.

'My name is Sir Edward Coke,' said the man.

Shakespeare fought to keep the start of surprise (studded with fear) out of his face.

On a table near the fire was a dish full of coloured glass balls: red, blue, green and yellow. They reflected the flames and glared at Shakespeare like witch's eyes.

This was the man, he said to himself, who had prosecuted Guy Fawkes. He could not expect kindness here.

Coke smiled. 'I see you have heard of me.'

'It would be strange if I had not. You are a great man.'

'As are you.' Coke picked out a mustard-yellow ball. 'William Shakespeare.'

Some patronising accent in his voice suggested a cat inspecting food. Shakespeare inclined his head while his thoughts whirled. Patience, he told himself.

'I must apologise for any rough usage you may have suffered at the hands of those men. I am afraid they are not students of the theatre. They did not recognise you. Naturally, when I heard of your situation, I put a stop to it.'

Was he really looking for gratitude?

'If this is how they treat men they do not know, I am distressed to learn of it.'

'It is harsh, to be sure, but I am sure you understand. We have a duty to question Raleigh's visitors. It is one we perform in sorrow more than in anger, but he is, after all, a criminal. It is a matter of routine to keep an eye on his . . . confederates.'

Shakespeare could almost hear blood drain from his face. The pain in his back and the grit under his fingernails began to throb. Even so some part of him detached itself and floated free. Sir Edward's icy politeness resembled the small motion of a highwayman lifting his cloak to reveal the hilt of a knife. Shakespeare felt like a traveller who had stepped into the middle of a careering highway.

'I see.'

'Good,' said Coke, holding up the decanter. 'Wine?'

Shakespeare shook his head.

'You are probably in no mood to thank me. But it is fortunate for you that I was here. I would not have left you any longer in the care of those brutes. We try to educate them, but . . . *Semper idem*. Always the same.'

Shakespeare saw no need to answer.

Coke poured himself a glass, took a small sip and tutted with appreciation.

'Next time, perhaps, you should send word in advance.'

Shakespeare shrugged. Who said there would be a next time?

'So,' said Coke, gesturing towards a chair for Shakespeare before sitting down himself. He did not seem surprised or abashed by his guest's silence. On the contrary, he had the genial air of a man sharing a convivial glass on a balmy summer evening. 'How do you find our prisoner? Do not be misled by the comfort we permit him – he is a prisoner, under sentence of death should the King choose to be unmerciful.'

His eyes glittered. This was the man, Shakespeare thought, who had referred to Raleigh as a Spanish viper. His heart sagged at the thought of the countless humiliations Sir Walter had suffered at these hands.

Only minutes earlier he had promised to speak up for Raleigh. He could not with honour abandon him so soon. And it seemed wise at least to act as though this were a conversation between equals, as if candour was permitted.

'Sir Walter does not belong here,' he said. 'He is a man of the seas and oceans, a denizen of far-off continents and brave discoveries. I do not know what he has done to deserve this fate, but I am sure he is no traitor. He loves England.'

'England is no more. We are Britons now.'

'He loves Britain then.'

'Ah, but does he? His is a martial vision.'

'He fears the consequences of Spanish supremacy in the New World,' said Shakespeare. 'He wants England – Britain – to rule the waves. If that is treason—'

'It is. Raleigh harbours violent designs on Spanish power, despite the King's express command that we challenge it not. Is this not treachery?'

Shakespeare felt his toes curl. His memory flicked up the time, a few years ago, when the Thames had frozen over. The city had revelled in its broad and pristine new thoroughfare: market stalls and sliding games sprang to life on the huge white expanse. But one night Shakespeare had walked alone across the river and had been given a healthy fright by the high zinging note of ice cracking all around him.

The surface beneath his feet, which moments earlier had seemed as solid as dry land, suddenly felt as thin and treacherous as chilled water.

He had tiptoed home that night.

Coke was changing the angle of his attack. 'Let us not argue. I am delighted to see you. I did not know that you were friends with our resident seafarer. I do not recall your having come before.'

'It is my first visit. And we are not friends. I am retired in Stratford now, but thought, on this visit to London, that I should pay my respects. I was bidden by the King himself, as you may know. I did not realise how you welcomed guests . . .'

Coke waved a hand. 'A simple mistake. Are you sure you won't try this Rhenish? It is excellent.'

Shakespeare shook his head again.

Coke hesitated for a moment, then rose to his feet and walked to the window.

'Let me cut to the bone. I am glad to hear you have time on your hands. We should like to encroach upon it a little.'

'We?'

'All of us.'

'Us?'

'Counsellors to and servants of the King.'

'The King? What would he with me?'

'Nothing you cannot spare. A portion of your day. A little of your talent.'

Shakespeare shrugged.

'A commission, then. For a play.'

'I am honoured, but I have no more plays in me.'

'The King thinks otherwise.'

'Pardon me, but the King may not know how things stand. I am finished.'

'A gentleman of leisure. We all should be so fortunate.'

Serpent's teeth! It had taken thirty years of hard work, night and day, to earn such leisure as he now enjoyed.

'I am sorry,' he repeated. 'I am done with plays, and they with me.'

Coke smiled. 'Do you question the far-sightedness of our King?'

This was a charade.

'Of course not.'

'Yet you contradict his conviction that you can write this play?'

'Which play? He has one in mind?'

'Have I pricked your interest?'

Shakespeare rubbed his neck.

'Very well,' said Coke. 'His Highness *does* have a subject in mind. It should appeal to you – otherwise we should not even ask. King Henry VIII.'

Shakespeare was too busy thinking to be startled. The idea that a friend might have betrayed him made him stiffen. But no: this visit was not in any way secret. The Tower knew he was coming and had taken pains to welcome him in this crude way.

'Perhaps I *will* take a glass of wine after all,' he said. 'A small one.'

He tried to steady his galloping pulse. Down, climbing sorrow! He had faith in his ability to chase thoughts, but only if he relaxed. If he stood back and did not block the view with anxiety, the mist that obscured the truth usually burned away fast. Thus it was now: after only a sip or two of wine he saw what must have happened.

Coke had been alerted to his arrival in plenty of time to devise this whole tableau. It was a ruse, first to alarm and then to impose upon him.

It was good to be able to dispose of his first fear. No one had betrayed him. But now a new conviction jostled for his attention: there was not even a ghost of a chance that he could write a play about Henry VIII fit to be presented at court.

He still resented the official depiction of Bluff King Hal as the father of modern England and the intrepid hero of the break with Rome: the statesman who had set the nation on the path to glory. The man was a greedy tyrant who had executed two wives, murdered countless opponents, and ripped up the spiritual roots of the country.

Shakespeare was no longer quite a Catholic, but he was certainly no Puritan, and neither – he liked pointing out to his patriotic friends – was Henry VIII. The break with Rome was complete: the monasteries had been looted, the abbeys pillaged. Yet religious conflict still stalked the land and would surely erupt in bloodshed before too many years had passed.

He did not think that this version of the story would play well at court.

'Is it not too . . . delicate a subject?' he said.

'In the right hands, we think not.'

'Such work used to be forbidden.'

'*Omnia mutantur*. Times change.'

Shakespeare revered Latin and knew a good deal of it, but rarely admired the legal-minded wagtails who were so fond of spouting it.

'I must respectfully decline,' he said. 'London has better men, more equal to the task, than me. I have not written a play for years.'

Coke seemed to have anticipated this. 'So much the better,' he said. 'All England will clamour to see fresh work from your famous hand.'

Shakespeare had been flattered often enough to despise such weasel praise. He took care to banish all vexation from his voice.

'It is through no softening of the will that I must say no. But this I cannot do. I lack the wherewithal.'

Coke frowned, straightened and stared at the fire. Flames licked the branches like thirsty dogs. The silence grew heavy.

'I regret to say,' he said eventually, 'that I am . . . disappointed. Others may also be . . . dismayed. I hoped I would not have to mention this, but the King is most desirous that you accept, and means to reward you royally. He is open-handed when the mood is with him. And *pecunia non olet*.'

Shakespeare sniffed. He did not agree. Money *did* have a smell, sometimes a powerful and unpleasant one.

'There is no shame in accepting it,' said Coke.

Sunlight glinted on his wine and threw a sharp golden dot on to his chin.

'I mean no offence. I wish with all my heart that I could oblige you and the King. But my powers are not what they were. I cannot do it.'

He rested his glass on the nearby table with a distinct tap, as if to perform the role of full stop and bring this conversation to an end.

Coke, however, was not willing to let go.

'I am sorry to say that the King may not agree. He admires your work and may well claim the right to command more of it.'

Shakespeare cloaked his consternation in a shrug. *Command!*

Coke took a breath, like someone about to deliver bad news.

'May I be honest? I have said the King is generous, yet that is only half the truth. With friends it is so, but with enemies, well, his hands close. I trust you not to repeat it, because I should not speak thus of our King, but he can be . . . vindictive.' He paused. 'It would sadden me greatly if he took against you.'

The words floated above the silence. The room grew tense.

'He has no cause.'

'I know that, of course.' Coke was inspecting a fingernail. 'If a reprieve were mine to grant, I should not hesitate. But a known associate of Sir Walter Raleigh, who declines such a commission . . . I fear he may have difficulty understanding that.'

At last: like a serpent out of its burrow – an open and vulgar threat. Coke seemed serene in his confidence that no one could object.

'I am sure you can explain it to him,' said Shakespeare, his voice flat.

'You overestimate my powers.'

'I think that would not be easy.'

'Thank you.'

Shakespeare had heard enough, in this conversation, to know that there was no advantage in pressing his luck. It would be politic to feign willing.

'Very well,' he said. 'I shall think about it.'

Coke's eyelids flickered.

'I should appreciate it if you thought about it now.'

Shakespeare stamped on the rebel part of himself that wanted to yell defiance.

'Very well,' he said. 'I will do my best to bring it off.'

He was an actor. His voice assumed a reluctant sincerity.

'I am glad to hear it. And the King will be delighted. Another glass?'

'I have taken too much of your time already.'

'As you wish. Permit me a word, though, before we part. Our King is a scholar. But do not forget that he is also, above all else, your king. I am sure you will treat the idea of kingship with the reverence it deserves.'

'Reverence?'

'The King believes that Henry, and by extension himself, was divinely appointed. You will know of his belief that a true-born monarch carries "sparkles of divinity". He would be most distressed by any suggestion to the contrary.'

Shakespeare could not believe his ears. First he was being *commanded* to produce a play, much as a scullion might be asked to fetch milk. Now he was being told what to write. He did not mind *being* worthless, but to be *thought* worthless was more than he could bear. He could not restrain himself.

'I wonder the King does not write the play himself, seeing how well he knows what it must include.'

Although Coke seemed to be smiling, his eyes were without expression.

'He would not presume,' he said. 'And neither should we.'

It was growing dark outside. Shakespeare stood up.

'We agree, then. If it lies within my power, I shall be honoured to oblige our King.'

'I am pleased to hear it,' said Coke. 'You must let my carriage take you home.'

'Thank you.'

'And for the roughness of those soldiers downstairs . . . What can I say? Oafs.'

When Shakespeare looked across the room his gaze fell on the hood that had been forced over his head. It lay like a dark, ugly gash on the Flemish rug in the middle of the room. Once again he felt unhooked and adrift. He was gripped by an urge to flee these four walls, this place where the normal civilities of life were overturned, where orders came disguised as invitations, and threats swathed in silken compliments.

Controlling his impatience, he marched downstairs, passed through the Lion Gate and climbed into the waiting carriage without a backward glance. Not until the wheels clattered on the cobbles of Thames Street, a safe distance from the Tower, did he feel his breathing return to normal.

Only then did his true temper begin to flare into life. Destruction fang mankind! Who were these people? How dared they? His face grew pale, and he trembled.

It was as though he had seen a spectre. Something swept back the curtain before which everyday life was staged and flashed him a glimpse of the brute machinery behind.

Raleigh's words danced in his mind: time was an avenger, and the cruelty of kings would always be punished. How could he be sure?

He felt an urge to lash out, to act, and without delay.

But then a phrase from *Hamlet* came to him: It is an honest ghost.

Perhaps the time truly was out of joint – maybe it *did* fall to him to set it right.

He felt feverish, but when he put a hand to his forehead he was surprised to find it cool. A strange tranquillity seemed to have fallen upon him.

The carriage stopped at a crossroads where a seagull pecked at a carcass. The bird turned its head to reveal a slash of scarlet blood on its curved yellow beak. It glared at him with a cold, pebble eye; then the shoulders hunched, the grey wings opened, and the gull lifted itself up and away. It dipped one wing, caught a draught, veered high over a tall gable and vanished.

London had never looked so black. Soot crept over the sills and pulled soft, dark blankets across eaves. Black puddles lay across the pitted road, and black veils seemed to have been drawn across the sky. Ash crept over tiles and walls, drifted on wheels and boots, and swished up steps and gutters. London was a cesspit; not by chance was it home to thoroughfares called Dunghill Lane and Pissing Alley.

Shakespeare heaved a bitter sigh. And then, just like that, he had an idea.

He had never been able to explain where ideas came from: they were so plentiful, and fell into place so fast that it was impossible to describe the paths they took. On this occasion something in the notion of a *gull* provided the inspiration.

He knew what he had to do. The way ahead was narrow, and steep, and full of pitfalls. Now, however, it was brilliantly lit by his own blazing resolve. If a play was what they wanted, then a play was what they would have. It might not be what they expected – it might lack the candied tongue – but it would be what they needed. He himself could be the agent of history's revenge! If the whirligig of time was creaking around in its dumb, relentless orbit, why should not Shakespeare himself put his shoulder to the wheel, and help it to bring home its revenges?

Another line of his own darted up to his mind: Thus may we gather honey from the weed.

As the carriage squelched and rolled down East Cheap towards the bridge, he was startled to realise that he felt years younger. It had not been an ordinary day. The bruise on his back and the blow to his pride would fade soon enough, but the jolt to his will, he hoped, might change both the future and, better still, the past.

Chapter 3

Shakespeare was staying in a large room at the Elephant, a Southwark inn he had honoured with a mention in *Twelfth Night* and where, as a result, he was always welcome. It was not the most convenient choice so far as the city was concerned, but it was exciting to be back in the heart of the theatre district, and pleasant to be just yards away from the open countryside to the south.

He had no further appointments today so retired to his rooms, asked that he not be disturbed and took to his bed.

He could not sleep, however. The disturbing events of the morning made his mind race as fast as his pulse; rest was impossible. His supple intelligence, as quick and rangy as a hunting dog, gripped on the idea that had waylaid him in the carriage and would not let go. It was hardly a novelty for him to have a brainwave, but the one shaken free by the seagull was powerful. It reminded him of the inspiration (ignited during a stroll by the Avon back in the plague summer of 1603) that revealed the fearful outline of *Othello*. Like lightning in the night, it etched shade on to the visible world. Shakespeare blinked. The shadows cast by the trees lay dark as coal on the shining green grass. A thrill coursed through his bones and jolted him into silence; yet inwardly he quivered like a cat after a thrush.

From outside his window there came a loud series of splintering crashes and people started screaming. Shakespeare pressed a square of damp linen to the sore spot in his cheek, lumbered to the window and looked out.

There were soldiers in the road and broken furniture. Chairs, tables and even a bed were being tossed from an upstairs room. A small crowd was assembling, but people knew better than to interfere. It was folly, and hopeless, to protest.

Shakespeare turned away. Evictions like this were no longer rare, and King James's soldiers needed little excuse. A religious transgression, a financial lapse, a broken obligation, a malicious word from an informant: it hardly mattered. It was a matter of policy, in this royal effort to fight terror with terror, to harass, beat and imprison anyone suspected of sedition, however fanciful the evidence. London had become a city where neighbours looked the other way.

He had always been good at blocking out distractions. Large parts of *Coriolanus* had been written in a cowshed; *As You Like It* owed a good part of its rustic charm to the fact that it was born in the scything middle of a hay-harvest.

He closed his eyes and allowed himself to revel in the prospect of a new play.

Shakespeare had long been aware of the gap in his cycle of English histories. He had come to a halt too soon. The sequence that began with Richard II continued all the way to Richard III and his bloody death at Bosworth Field in 1485, but then it stopped. He had never dared attempt the final chapter. It had not been possible, with Elizabeth on the throne, to present the life of her own grandfather, Henry VII. True, he featured (as the one-dimensional saviour of the nation in *Richard III*), but only in a play composed many years back, when Shakespeare had not felt the sting of the royal whip.

When Elizabeth died – a full decade ago! – it seemed that such a piece might be feasible, but it soon became clear (Raleigh was proof) that King James was even more ferocious in defence of royal virtue than his predecessor. His blind faith in the sanctity of kingship outlawed the mildest criticism. So Shakespeare had been obliged to dismiss the idea all over again, and besides, other resounding projects –

Macbeth, *Othello*, *Lear*, *The Tempest* – had captured his imagination and led him into other realms.

Now, thanks to Coke, he fizzed with a warming glint of rebellious principle. Although the King and his henchmen might treat him like a lackey, he was not suited for such a servile part. There was power in him still and he would exercise it in the service of one more grand adventure. He would forget about Henry VIII and conjure instead the man who had sweated to put a tyrant down that he might sleep in peace. It would be called *The True and Tragicall Historie of Henry VII*. It would be high and strong, and full of tears. It would remind the world about the callousness of kings.

He knew that he could not attempt this alone. He would need to summon his old friends, like spirits from a former time. The King's Men was a brotherhood of souls as well as a company of actors. Shakespeare was sure the fellowship would not ignore his call to ride out together on one last quest.

It didn't take more than a day or two to find the rooms for sale in Blackfriars – the old brick gatehouse used to greet visitors to the monastery in the days before the Dominican friary was dissolved. He knew the place well: it was part of the hall that had for several years been used as a theatre by the King's Men. Before that it was a notorious Catholic safe house, riddled with a bewildering maze of tunnels and escape chutes through old crypts and chapels. This too was ideal: he liked the idea that his home was a false, theatrical stage for various concealments. It was only a short (if evil-smelling) walk from London Bridge, while the colourful dens, baiting halls and stews of Southwark were just a brief wherry ride across the river. Even though house prices had been booming for years, as the population of Elizabeth's merry capital surged, this broken palace had lain empty, its monastic past a commercial disadvantage. Now, for the less than princely sum of one hundred and forty pounds, it was his.

His old comrade John Heminge – the de facto business manager of the King's Men – had helped with the transaction and the paperwork. Whilst it was not an office Heminge sought, someone had to perform it, and he was by far the most efficient and reliable member of the troupe. In his day he had been a fiery actor – his Falstaff was famous – but in recent years had concentrated on management. There was always lots to do – venues to organise, people to hire or release, monies to receive, disburse or pursue. The King's Men was a company in both senses of the word: a theatrical association with its own unique repertoire of plays (by Shakespeare), and also a financial enterprise, with costs, revenues and profit-hungry shareholders. Heminge himself was a sharer, along with Shakespeare and Burbage. They had been successful for a long while; none of them had to worry where the next crust was coming from.

As soon as he took possession of the keys, Shakespeare sent messages to his old comrades requesting their attendance at his new home on the morrow. He engaged a young boy (sworn to secrecy with a silver coin) to deliver the sealed invitations.

The men on his guest list did not know what had prompted the summons. Their leader lived in Stratford now, and they heard only occasional news of him. He was prospering, by all accounts. It was said he had bought a handsome house in the centre of the town as well as a farm in the outlying fields, and that he was quite the wool merchant these days. To their intense regret, it seemed that he really had renounced any ambition to add to the corpus of plays that had made him (and all of them) famous. So it was not every day that Shakespeare beckoned, and each actor obeyed the call without a second thought. On the morning of the day in question, they set out from their various quarters and hurried towards Blackfriars.

All five of them knew the way well. They had presented plays in the Blackfriars Theatre for half a dozen years – the soft candlelit space created a shadowy atmosphere perfect for other-worldly works like *Cymbeline* and *The Tempest*. Blackfriars was a smart area, with solid houses, firm streets and only traces of the raucous squalor that surrounded the stages south of the river. But these men were sufficiently familiar to draw a hail of admiring comments (and the odd crude jeer) from the citizens they passed on the way.

The first to arrive was Robert Armin, a comic master who had played Dogberry, Feste and various other Shakespearian fools and clowns. He tripped down the road they called West Cheap, past the birds in their cages, the carcasses bleeding on butcher's slabs, and the barrows loaded with roots, cheese and beer kegs. When he slipped into the dank maze of alleys around St Paul's, anyone following might have been able to hear the strain of a melancholy tune: Armin was also a musician – the songs he created for *Twelfth Night* had won him both fame and silver.

Next came Edward Alleyn, the actor and impresario who owned the Rose and Fortune Theatres, and was now devoting his energy to his new college out in the fields at Dulwich. He came by horseback to the south side of London Bridge, entrusted his mare to a Southwark groom and then stood tall, surveying the Thames like one of the kings he had played on stage, as a boatman rowed him across. Alleyn was an Admiral's rather than a King's man, but the rivalry between actors was not implacable; he was a long-standing friend of Shakespeare's, and it was only a minor surprise that he was part of this morning's exclusive assembly. He was a man of influence, and influence – given what Shakespeare was planning – might well be required.

The third member of the troupe, Joseph Taylor, was a prodigy in his youth who had played queens and princesses to great applause. Now, as if in flight from this youthful fame, he was a trencherman to rival Sir Toby Belch; his appetite was hearty enough that he had no need for the padded shirt – he could fill any role without help. Though not yet a paid-up King's Man, he was a friend of Armin's and harboured keen hopes to join the group on a solid basis. His journey this morning was brief, for he lived in grubby rooms near the Temple. He paused at a public privy, then picked up a basket of sweet comestibles – apple wine and blaunderelles, roast larks with bacon, orange pudding and a bowl of almond milk – as a gift for his new colleagues.

Of all the guests, John Lowin was the most surprised and best pleased to receive an invitation. He was too young to count himself a particular friend of the group and had not played any of the major parts. Indeed, his great success to date was as a scoundrel in John Webster's *The White Devil* and he still smiled at the thought of

Shakespeare's succinct verdict – 'a silly piece, but an exhilarating performance'. He saw this morning's event not as a reunion but as an opportunity. Perhaps Shakespeare was recruiting! He travelled with bated breath, as if to an audition.

These were the men who marched through the confused and brawling streets of England's boisterous capital; a magical map would have seen them converging like dots on the muddy northern bank of the great sewer that the Thames had become. London showed only occasional signs of planning: it had grown organically in an unruly and ill-disciplined riot of private arrangements. Nevertheless, no architect could have surpassed the achievement by which the city had placed itself on a tidal river that emptied itself twice a day. There were several engineers trying to devise more hygienic ways to dispose of the waste expelled by the capital's growing population – Queen Elizabeth herself owned a Harrington water closet. But this was an infant science, and a river that flushed was better than nothing.

None of their journeys was peaceful, because London was still buzzing with anxiety. Armin found himself following a man whose earlobes had been slashed – a common punishment for clipping coins – and Alleyn had to leap aside to avoid a cartful of wailing prisoners en route to some grisly fate. Soldiers stood in knots on every corner, and the actors were careful not to return their malevolent stares. Only one man was missing: John Heminge seemed to have vanished.

Nobody was safe these days. Citizens scurried about their chores with their backs bowed and their heads down. Although the intense panic generated by the Gunpowder Plot just eight years earlier had subsided, caution was still a universal reflex. Citizens could be stopped, interrogated, or led away in chains, and only a fool dared affect the Spanish style – a clear invitation to be arrested. Anyone could be accused of Catholic sympathies, and many were: hardly anything was as dangerous as missing attendance at church, and the fines for recusancy were steep and ruthlessly imposed. Thousands had perished on the bonfires of the King's revenge; London Bridge had for centuries been a barbaric forest of severed heads on tall stakes. Some, like Henry Garnet, were indisputable Catholic martyrs on a Jesuitical mission to save England for Rome, but hardly any of them were authentic traitors. Most were merely the hapless casualties of King James's continuing rage against the plotters who had sought his death. It made Shakespeare frown: could they not see that by pursuing their enemies with such rabid and indiscriminate zeal, they were fanning an even deeper grievance?

The last man to arrive was the most distinguished of all. Richard Burbage had played Hamlet, Othello and Lear, and his booming voice and charismatic stage presence had won him a reputation second only to Alleyn's as a titan of the London stage. His father had built the very first theatre in the city – named simply The Theatre, for it had no rivals – and he had moved it, plank by plank, to Southwark, where it became the now-famous Globe. He was a trusted confidant and business associate of Shakespeare: they were as celebrated as a royal couple and were held, by the so-called common people, in the warmest regard.

Burbage lived in Shoreditch, a rough suburb where it was prudent to wear a sword in weak light, but he was too striking a figure ever to walk on foot through such a noxious neighbourhood. A talented painter, his clothes were often paint-bespattered. This morning he came by carriage and announced his arrival – he was the last to enter the yard where the gatehouse stood – with a metallic clatter of hoof on cobble. He was welcomed by a footman who took his cape, pointed the way upstairs and closed the door. The servant was under strict instructions. Today's meeting was not a public occasion, and any visitor should be asked – with all due courtesy and regret – to call again at some more suitable time.

Shakespeare knew that Joseph Taylor was unlikely to turn up empty-handed, but he had not seen these old friends for two years and the least he could do was feed them. The King's Men liked to eat like barons, so he ordered food from the markets: salt beef with mustard; legs of spit-roast veal and pork; capons boiled with leeks; and a turkey cock pie. The water in London could no longer be trusted, but there were flagons of beer, and since it was still possible to walk to green fields and buy a pennyworth of milk, Shakespeare sent out for some. Whilst the loaves of bread were fresh, the meat was dyed red with sandalwood to make it appear bloody, a luxurious effect heightened by some white potatoes, the fashionable 'root of great vertue' commonly imagined to be something of an aphrodisiac; it was, as the Leadenhall merchants put it, 'favourable to population'.

He himself had no interest in the feast – indeed, he could not bear the thought of being weighed down by such rich food – yet he had been in the theatre long enough to know that appetising props were essential when the troupe assembled.

The stage was set; the actors would play the guests.

The party began with a burst of back-slapping gallantry, but Shakespeare did not have to wait long for this to subside. His friends could see that he was vibrant with nervous energy and were curious to learn what had prompted this reunion.

'I am very glad to see you,' said Shakespeare, in the first appropriate pause. 'And it may not surprise you to know that I have a proposal to make.'

An expectant murmur ran through the room.

Shakespeare did not plan to tell them about his encounter with Coke. He had powdered the graze on his cheek (and the blow to his pride); there were few visible signs of his clash with royal power. The time would come when he would tell his friends what had happened; the priority now was to engage their enthusiasm. Whether or not this whole enterprise turned out to be foolish, he needed to know before anything else whether it was feasible.

He was about to speak when there came from below a knock on the door. It boomed into the silence, sounded dramatic and profound. No one reacted for an instant and then it came again, like distant cannon.

Shakespeare had only one thought: Coke.

Then he had another: they needed to have someone watching the door.

'Whence is that knocking?' said Burbage. Everyone smiled.

'Fear it not, Richard,' said Shakespeare, though in truth the noise appalled him.

The pounding from below continued, followed by footsteps on the stairs. Finally, before any of them could speak, the door opened and two men stood in the doorway.

'I am sorry,' said Shakespeare's steward. 'The man was most insistent.'

'I was,' said a tall, slender man with a pronounced stoop. 'I confess it freely. I crave a private word with William Shakespeare.'

He stood quite still, his whole body a question mark. Had they been casting a prelate, or the ghost of a monk, this man would have been perfect.

'If it is private, you may keep it to yourself,' said Shakespeare, nettled by the intrusion. But he understood that he needed to tread with care. This stranger might matter. He adopted a courteous air.

'Speak. This is a private gathering. You are among friends. They have kindly arranged this small reunion to honour my too brief return to London. What would you?'

'Very well. I bring not news, but a plea.'

'I like pleas,' said Shakespeare. 'I have written a few myself.'

'Yes,' agreed Burbage. 'Thou art the noblest of all plea-wrights.'

'No, a plea,' said the man. 'A suit. In the name of King James himself.'

'No name is more sacred to us than that,' said Shakespeare, ignoring the flutter in his jaw. 'But I am sorry. We are – were – in a cheerful mood. Continue.'

'My name is Beckinsale. I represent the honourable society of translators that has worked night and day to put the Holy Bible into English.'

'I know one of them,' said Shakespeare. 'Peter of Cambridge. A learned man, to be sure.'

'You know Peter?'

'Everyone knows everyone. He put my sonnets into Latin, I believe.'

'Well then, you have my drift. This translation has been a heavy task, and a triumphant one. The first copies were made a year ago. You may have seen them. However, the book is far from finished, and we ache to improve it. Fifty scholars have created this – some have poetry in their heart, some do not. We seek, in short, your help.'

'First, your book is done. Second, I am retired. Third, I am not a translator.'

'The work is done, but not yet perfect. There are delicate aspects. Some of the scholars complain that the English prose misrepresents the word of God. They have been unpicking and reassembling it. We ask only that you peruse, polish . . .'

'You would have me as an editor, then. I am sorry. I am not seeking work.'

'The Bible in English,' said Burbage. 'A fine thing. The word of the Lord walking the earth like a plain man. Shall we not hear a verse, Will? I am sure you could raise it into poetry with your merest touch.'

'Proceed, then,' said Shakespeare. 'Have you a page? Read, and we shall see.'

'I have it here,' said Beckinsale. He took a sheet from his pocket, slipped off the ribbon and unrolled it. 'It is literal,' he said. 'That is the whole trouble, as I said. It wants dignity.'

'Then you have come to the right place,' said Burbage.

The man took a breath, crossed himself and began to deliver, not quite for the first time ever, God's word unto the people.

God's word turned out to be tangled. Shakespeare let his eyes shut while thick, stony lines toppled into the quiet studio. When it was over he drew a long, slow breath, frowning as if (but only as if) at the stench from the road.

'There is only one word for that. It is wretched. I cannot say how it stands as a translation of Hebrew, a language unknown to me, but heavens above, if we are to have the Bible in our own tongue, then let it sing. Why don't they copy out Tyndale, or the Geneva Bible? Neither of those has this dead stink.'

No one spoke. The King's Men recognised the look on Shakespeare's face and knew that his creative pride was engaged. A half-dozen pairs of friendly eyes watched the master walk across to the casement window and stare at the rooftops.

'Very well,' he said over his shoulder. 'Repeat. I'll see what I can do.'

Beckinsale made as if to express thanks, but Burbage waved him to press on. So he nodded and did as he was asked.

'The word of God came before every living thing, and when God did speak that first word, the word was replete with godly truth . . .'

'See what I mean?' said Shakespeare. 'Dreadful. This is supposed to be holy gospel. The least it requires is the simple force of a charm, or a chant. Let me see . . . How about: "In the beginning was the Word, and the Word was with God, and the Word was God."'

Beckinsale's gasp could be heard across the room.

Joseph Taylor nudged his friend Armin.

'Good grief,' he said. 'I see what you mean. Is he always like this?'

Armin raised a quick finger to his mouth. It was important not to break the spell.

'I am glad to see that time and ease have not dented your gift, Will,' said Burbage in a soft voice, as if soothing a child.

'What comes next?' said Shakespeare.

The man put his hand on the page and read.

'God created all the world, and all the world was made by God.'

Shakespeare pressed his hands to his cheeks. He had an intense horror of sentences as clumsy and inert as this. Words, he had always felt, had vivid lives – they were like colours. When they collided he felt the jarring as a physical thud.

'Oh, who came up with this? It is dim . . . stupid . . . pedestrian. The task here is not to translate the word of God, but to dramatise it. We must give it a white beard, some dignity, and a glittering mind. Perhaps . . . "The same was in the beginning with God. All things were made by him; and without him was not any thing made that was made." See? All you have to do is make it cryptic, oracular, gnomic, as if it holds some strange and divine truth. If it seems repetitive, so much the better. This is the Lord's heartbeat. It's a dramatic fact that God could never reveal himself in mundane sentences. For his own sake, we must give him grandeur.'

Beckinsale licked a pencil and bustled to write down the new line.

'Carry on, friend,' said Shakespeare. 'You have put me in the mood.'

His visitor rustled the paper with a shaking hand:

'God was the source of life, and he shone upon the world of men like the sun.'

'God shone like the sun? Zooks! Is this supposed to render us worshipful, stun us into reverent awe? It sounds like a report on the privies, not a fragment of divine poetry. It needs majesty, contrasts, a luminous sense of fiery truth . . . "In him was life; and the life was the light of men. And the light shineth in darkness; and the darkness comprehended it not." Isn't that better? It really isn't so hard. It needs a drumbeat, that's all.'

'Are you sure,' said Beckinsale, 'you can't be persuaded to take this task? What you have just done . . . verily, it is verbal alchemy. The King will be generous—'

'I'll do it for *you* before I do it for the King.' Shakespeare's voice was sharp. Then he relented. 'Well, maybe I could look it over. Now where did I put my . . . but read on, I beg you. It begins to interest me, this Bible.'

'The next part is about John the Baptist. And I must say, very dim and flat. Maybe you could see a way to, I don't know . . .'

'Give it a halo?'

'Exactly.'

'We'll see. Read.'

'And God sent a messenger among the people of the world, and his name was John. He moved among the people, spreading the word of God so they might believe in the one true Lord. He was not the Lord, the great sun whose light shineth on all the world; but he was the Lord's messenger on earth. And the earth did not see that he was a reflection of the one true God, all hail, and John lived alone and wretched and ignored by the people.'

'Stop! For God's sake!' Shakespeare was clutching his head. 'You are wise to know that this will not do. Maybe I *can* help. When your dull . . . *scholars* . . . have finished mangling the lines, I could gild it a little. Can you not see? It must be supple, rhythmic, urgent. John must walk as an angel. He needs wings. Listen.'

Shakespeare walked to the window again, his heels the only sound in the room. After a moment he turned, and his eyes glowed as he delivered the trim sequence of words that those in the room would lock in their memories, and hang from their hearts like gemstones, for ever.

'"There was a man sent from God whose name was John. The same came for a witness, to bear witness of the Light, that all men through him might believe. He was not that Light, but was sent to bear witness of that Light. That was the true Light, which lighteth every man that cometh into the world."

'Isn't that more like it?' said Shakespeare, eyes flashing. 'Light, light, light. God. Love. Light. The big words must hum along the pulse. And then, for the finale, we need a flash of brilliant thought, something from the clouds. Like— "He was in the world, and the world was made by

45

him, and the world knew him not. He came unto his own, and his own received him not."'

No one said anything. People don't, when they have witnessed something so far beyond the ordinary. Their busy glances confirmed that they had experienced a wonder.

'I feel,' said Burbage, 'that I should fall to my knees. That was magnificent, Will. You *have* to accept this task, Will. The Bible! The King James Bible! You can't let them print some grey riverwater version of what you could do.'

'We'll see,' said Shakespeare and turned away.

Some of those present would later swear that he seemed almost unnerved by what he had so lightly accomplished. He was no stranger to party tricks; he loved to entertain friends by inventing rhymes and was a haughty parodist (his bawdy pastiche of Spenser's *Faerie Queene* was a popular party piece). But this spontaneous invention of God's word, which caught the spirit of the book, shook them all. Of course, they had been listening to the English Bible in church for years, but they had never truly *heard* it until now.

'I don't know about you,' said Alleyn, 'but hearing these verses gives me the shivers. I can't help feeling that men will come to blows over words like those.'

'They have gone to war for less,' said Burbage.

The scene came to a quiet, chastened end.

'Sometimes,' Shakespeare whispered that evening as he sat with Burbage, ignoring the oversized hunks of venison and bread, 'I feel myself to be a vessel, a mere mouthpiece.' He paused, and wiped weak ale from his beard. 'I do not know where the words come from. They just flow through me. And today, God strike me down if I lie, it was as though the hand of the Lord lifted my heart. I barely knew what I was saying.'

He paused to lay down his knife.

'I didn't find the words. The words found me. And let me tell you, Richard: I have never felt quite so small, nor half so frightened, in all my given life.'

Chapter 4

*I*t took a while for the Bible to leave the room. Shakespeare's solemn phrases hung in the air like the afterglow of a shooting star. The King's Men helped themselves to Shakespeare's provisions, their voices lowered. It had been easy, in the years of his absence, to forget this other-worldly gift for poetry. It was a feat of magic, an illusion as inexplicable as it was exhilarating.

One of them, Lowin, had the temerity to wonder whether the master had not stage-managed the event in order to impress them; but he did not deem it wise to voice this heresy. The rest, celebrities though they were, and masters in their own fields, were awestruck. For the most part they thought of Shakespeare as an equal; sometimes even as a rival. Yet every now and then he put on a display of poetic skill that reduced them to a thoughtful silence. This was such a time.

Shakespeare allowed them a brief pause to assemble their composure, then gave a modest cough and suggested they resume their discussion.

'Before we were so divinely interrupted,' he said, 'I was about to explain why I asked you all here today.'

He had their attention. Even Taylor put down his food.

'The first news is: I – that is, we – have been asked to write *Henry VIII.*'

The company twinkled.

'Hurrah,' said Armin.

47

'Bravo,' said Alleyn.

'Excellent,' said Lowin.

'I knew it,' said Burbage.

'I am not interested,' said Shakespeare. 'He is not here today, but I intend to ask Fletcher to undertake this task . . .'

The pause that followed skidded rapidly from surprise to dismay.

'Surely not,' said Alleyn. 'The man's a parsnip.'

'Oh, he's not so bad,' said Taylor. Along with Beaumont, Fletcher had written several plays for the King's Men; as it happened, Taylor had been invited to perform in a new one, *The Coxcombe*, when it was finished. Since it was partly thanks to Fletcher that Taylor was here at all, it would have been remiss not to speak up.

Burbage, however, agreed with Alleyn. 'You can't give a chance like this to *Fletcher*, of all people. He's a mooncalf. Why, any of us could turn our hand—'

'Of course you could. But I need you for something finer. You are right: Fletcher's no swan, but he paddles hard, and that is what we need. Fear not. We can give *Henry VIII* a leg up when the time comes. Until then I have something else.'

Alleyn was lighting a clay pipe stuffed with herbs. He puffed out clouds of thick smoke, his teeth clacking on the stem, wreathing himself in seriousness.

'Here is the thing,' said Shakespeare. 'There is a play missing from our pageant. It concerns King Hal's father, Henry VII – the man who overturned Richard III. This is the story I want us to tell. This is the siren that calls us now.'

The King's Men were not slow to rally round.

'I still say hurrah,' said Armin.

'Bravo,' agreed Alleyn.

'Alleluia,' said Lowin.

'It's all the same to me,' said Burbage.

There was a minor vacuum in the conversation. Shakespeare knew better than to fill it. After a brief silence, Taylor spoke.

'May I ask . . . why?'

'First, it falls next in our sequence. He begins where *Richard III* ends.'

'At Bosworth?'

'The same.'

'You said first,' said Burbage. 'What is the second reason?'

'Accuracy,' said Shakespeare. 'As soon as I conceived this plan I was struck by the extent to which Henry VII is a faded picture. He is colourless, inconsequential, dim. That is because we have not given him a play. We must correct this. We can't have England remembering Richard III, and Henry V, and Henry VIII, God help us, without finding a place for Henry VII – the only one of them worth a fig, I am beginning to think.'

'It might be wise to put a cloth on your voice,' said Burbage.

'The third reason is more sensitive,' said Shakespeare. 'I am also beginning to think that our portraits of Richard and Henry have achieved too wide a currency.'

'They have been successful,' said Taylor. 'And we are all glad of it.'

'But who can enjoy success when it flows from deceit?' said Shakespeare. 'Is it not poisoned?'

'How so?' Burbage was gentle.

'We played Richard false, and all for the sake of Tudor pride. He may not have been the black-toed villain we made him. He was like any other king: he defended his throne with steel. As for the idea that he was a usurper, well, his claim was better by far than Richmond's; now *there's* a man who really did seize the throne by force, through a rebel invasion. We have helped England forget all this.'

'Who wants to remember it?' said Alleyn. 'What good would it do?'

'When first we wrote our plays, we were young men, glad for the chance. We wrote to please the crowd. But something has changed. We prevailed beyond our dreams, and our works endure. Only the other day I watched our Richard, and it made my skin tremble. We have been agents of the state, friends, and I like it not.'

'What would you do?' said Alleyn. 'Make Henry Tudor a villain? No one will accept that.'

'Maybe not,' said Shakespeare, with a small inner curl of discomfort. 'Not yet, anyway. But don't forget, they *have* invited us to write *Henry VIII*, and just think what mischief we could do with *that* monster, if we wished. The man beheaded two wives – he's a barbarous villain. Henry VII isn't anything like so coarse a subject.'

'He's not even a subject,' said Armin. 'He's the King.'

'Thou ever wert a clown,' said Alleyn.

'He is still the founder of the line,' continued Burbage. 'The father of modern England. I'm sorry, but there are people who won't like us meddling with that.'

'But that's exactly why it must be us,' said Shakespeare, animated again. 'No one else can. Even we could not do it while the Queen lived. But there's a new king now, and we are the new King's Men. I just think we should set the record straight.'

'I don't like the sound of that,' said Taylor.

'I still don't see,' said Burbage, 'how we can murder our own play.'

'I agree, it is awkward,' said Shakespeare, turning to his friend. 'You played Richard whenever it was, twenty years ago. And you were amazing – thrilling. The whole town was your plaything. But it wasn't right; it wasn't true. The real Richard wasn't the devil we painted him. The man didn't even have a hunchback, for pity's sake.'

'What do you mean, didn't have a hunchback? That was his best feature! Richard without the hump? It'd be like *Macbeth* without the witches.'

'Who have you been talking to, Will?' said Alleyn. He was serious now. 'You've read something, haven't you? Those damned pamphlets, they'll say anything.'

'A shrewd thrust,' said Shakespeare. 'I expect nothing less. Listen . . .'

He was not entirely forthright about the features of Henry's reign that interested him most, and had no wish to inspire alarm by mentioning the full extent of the revisions he had in mind. And since his friends were already familiar with Henry VII's war-torn path to power, he dwelled for the most part on the resolve with which Henry quelled England's civil strife – the stern way two claimants to the throne were beaten off in battle, and the icy pleasure with which Henry dealt with his enemies. He mentioned the King's fondness for treasure, and the burdens he imposed on his long-suffering citizens. He summarised the King's private life: the marriage to a Yorkist princess, and the heartbreaking wound opened by the death of his beloved son and heir, Arthur. He laid particular stress on the background, the excitement of the age – the voyages of exploration and the rapid advancement of art, science, printing, literature and sport; he spoke breezily about the nautical stirrings that would lead, eventually, to the Armada-vanquishing prowess of Elizabeth's navy.

'I want,' he said in conclusion, 'to make a play about what kingship can achieve, and what it costs. We see a man who sincerely desires to be good, but is poisoned by his office – *and knows it*. He *knows* the crown will ruin him, as it ruined those who came before, but he is resolute: he will do his duty, like a sentry in a hurricane, or a stag too wearied by the chase to escape the dogs. I do believe there is meat on this. What say you?'

The King's Men were slow to respond. There was a strained element in Shakespeare's manner that they could not quite interpret. It was clear that his mind was made up and his heart fixed. However, they could not see quite what drew him to a tale that seemed, on the face of it, so ordinary. Perhaps it was because of the fireworks with which the morning had begun: traces of the English Bible still clung to the walls. It was hard to see how a pallid royal chronicle could excite him more than that. They were senior figures and they felt, if they were honest, a touch belittled and patronised.

Burbage was the first to speak.

'Will,' he said, 'If you want to do this, we'll do it. You know that. Just say the word. I ask only this. Let us do it properly, in the old way, all together.'

Shakespeare nodded.

'Dear Richard,' he said. 'That is my own most fervent wish. Let me add one more thing. If our work with English history has a theme, it is this . . .'

He paused. His mind was gripped by the poignant image of a tall, slim man in a clean white shirt, reading a book by a window and hiding his sadness with a smile.

'The cruelty of kings is always punished. All I want to do is say it again.'

Alleyn cleared his throat. 'Please don't take this as a criticism, Will.

But I too am troubled. Most of your histories start with someone toppling a king, and end with the new monarch being overthrown in his turn. Fortune or fate raises them up and then tips them into the mire. I don't see that shape here. We can hardly present Henry as a usurper murdering his way to the crown – can we? And he died peacefully, so I believe, leaving his kingdom safe, rich and with a genuine heir. Is there drama in this?'

'It is in there somewhere,' said Shakespeare. 'I am convinced that once we look, we shall find the arching parabola you describe. Here is my suggestion. Let us inspect the histories and satires. Speak to the balladeers; see what we can find to make a play with. I think there is plenty of arresting material, but if there is not, then what have we lost? What say you?'

The King's Men did not need to look at each other. As one, they raised their cups and rose to their feet.

Except for Joseph Taylor. He did not stand.

'I do not wish to spoil our sport,' he said, 'but may I take this occasion to remind you all what happened with *Richard II*?'

The others glanced at Shakespeare. There was a long silence.

'What happened?' said Lowin.

'It was a few years ago now,' said Shakespeare. 'In 1600. A man called Gelly gave us – we were the Chamberlain's Men in those days – forty shillings to put on *Richard II*. I remember the sum, because it was even more than Judas earned. Of course we had no idea quite what we were getting into. We staged the play at the Globe without any suspicion that we had been involved in a royal plot. The very next day, the Earl of Essex – a friend of mine, or so I thought – embarked on a wild revolt against the Queen. To this day I know not what possessed him. Our play was a gambit: the conspirators hoped it would rouse a crowd to side with sedition.'

'If you don't know the play,' said Burbage, 'it is about the toppling of a feeble king. Very splendid it is too. Let us sit upon the grass awhile, and tell sad stories of the death of kings . . . Something like that, anyway. It created the most delightful stir, the idea of a king actually sitting on the ground, where the common people dwelled. But in other ways this production sounded the depths of folly. It still amazes me that we escaped with our skins. Will here was summoned to explain it all to the Queen herself – fortunately his silver tongue found the right words.'

'The Queen declared herself willing,' said Shakespeare, 'against *strong* advice – I remember her emphasising that – to concede that we were mere fools. She spared us. But it was a reminder that there were sharp rocks in the waters around her throne.'

'What happened next?' said Harvard.

'Poor Essex lost his head,' said Shakespeare. 'For us, the chief consequence was *Twelfth Night*. The Queen urged me to try something less . . . political. I can still hear her saying it. I was so relieved, I went off to a farm and wrote it in a fortnight.'

He bowed his head, lost in the past for a moment. It was the nearest they had come to serious trouble – until the other morning in the Tower. And here he was, embarked on a far more dangerous subject, with eyes wide open.

He glanced up. His men were primed. It was a time to nudge them forward.

'It is good to recall such things,' he said. 'They remind us that we should regard our work as confidential. Massinger is in prison right now for writing too close to the seat of power. And then there's Raleigh, who dreams only of finding new stores of gold for the King. It will gain us nothing to have the authorities in our footsteps. So far as they are concerned, we are working on *Henry VIII*, by royal command.'

'You dog,' said Taylor. 'So that's why you want old Fletcher on board.'

'May I make a suggestion?' said Burbage. 'I take your desire for discretion very seriously. In fact, I think it essential. We might even move in secret, from place to place, incognito as some might say, to alert none rash enough to accept the King's shilling for news of our progress.'

Alleyn agreed. 'He's right. Things have changed more than you might think, Will. Elizabeth's spies may have rolled up their ladders and abandoned their vigils. But King James has soldiers everywhere, and they are the opposite of subtle. It's not quite as dreadful as it was after the Plot, but still . . .'

Shakespeare shrugged. He knew better than anyone – he still trembled to recall his encounter with Coke – the lethal reach of the modern Crown.

'I agree. It cannot be wrong to be cautious,' he said. 'If we meet here, the general tongue will soon rage with news of our doings. But it is not only for security that I urge discretion. We have a precious literary advantage too: the element of surprise. Let us keep this thing close, the better to let our imaginations roam.'

'We could meet at the Rose,' said Alleyn.

'There is always room at the Greyhound,' said Armin.

'My father is a schoolmaster in Clerkenwell,' said Lowin. 'He has a hall.'

'There are lots of empty spaces in the Temple,' said Taylor.

'Nor am I without connections of my own,' said Shakespeare. 'There is a chamber on the bridge, and a house in Westminster is ours for the taking.'

'It's easy enough to have ideas,' said Burbage, 'but this will need organising. Want me to take charge, Will?'

'I thought you would never ask.'

Burbage was already planning. 'Right,' he said. 'I will go ahead and line up rooms in different parts of the city. It might even be a good idea if we didn't all arrive at once. We could create a hierarchy – by age or alphabet – and land at intervals. I will see what can be done. When shall we start? Tomorrow?'

'Ideal,' said Shakespeare.

'Actually, that would be difficult,' said Alleyn. 'I shall need to clear the decks a bit.'

'It wouldn't be bad to have some time to research things,' said Armin.

'Quite so,' said Shakespeare. 'Shall we say . . . ten days from now?'

They looked at one another. No one voiced any objection.

'Sounds convenient,' said Burbage. 'I will make the arrangements and let you know.'

'On the subject of research,' said Shakespeare, 'let us divide it up. Ned, Richard, why don't you look at affairs of state and the intrigues at court. Robert and Joseph, perhaps you could explore the underbelly of the reign – the life of the streets. John, would it interest you to investigate the artistic scene? There was no theatre, of course, but it would be nice to know the other textures. I will study the King.'

'What are the key books?' said Armin.

'Hall and Holinshed, obviously. Polydore Vergil. Otherwise, see what there is. There are plenty of lesser chronicles.'

He paused. Something had just struck him.

'As it happens, I myself am trying to make an appointment with someone rather useful. It is not fixed yet – but I have friends working on it. A man called Richard Stanyhurst, one of the authors who helped Holinshed write his chronicle. He wrote the parts on Ireland, I believe. He got into trouble for including some pointed revelations about Henry VIII. He is in London, apparently, and I may be able to meet him.'

'I know who you mean,' said Alleyn. 'Didn't he go off to Spain, or France?'

No one was sure. And since none of them had anything further to add, the meeting began to wind down.

'My conscience is clear,' declared Taylor, 'but my stomach feels neglected. God speed our enterprise, and God feed its protagonists.'

'One last thing,' said Shakespeare. 'Would anyone be willing to place themselves in charge of food? We shall need sustenance while we work.'

There was a brief, sharp silence – then everyone laughed at once.

'I don't know what's so funny,' said Taylor. 'But yes, I am happy to do it.'

'Don't worry, I'll pay.' Shakespeare clapped him on the shoulder. 'Come then,' he said, picking up a knife and beckoning, as if to carve. 'Enough speeches. Next time we gather, we shall play different parts. Till then, please feast further on all these good things.' He put the knife down, selected a few nuts and some dried fruit, and allowed his friends to swarm about the table.

When the party broke up, Burbage was the last to go. He was Shakespeare's oldest and closest accomplice, and their similarity was famed: they had the same domed forehead, soft eyes and trimmed beard. That was not all; it was widely remarked, given their antennae for picking up each other's thoughts, that they could have been twins.

'What troubles you, Richard?' said Shakespeare.

'Only this. Did you not wish to include Heminge, or Condell, in this adventure? It surprises me much that they are not here.'

'I alerted them both. I too am sorry not to see them.'

'And Alleyn? An Admiral's Man? Is that wise?'

'Success has many friends, Richard. Ned Alleyn is a great and useful man, and we have need of those. Joseph too has mettle. You cannot say he is not one of us.'

Burbage did not look convinced. 'As you wish. But Ned is a different fellow these days – he aches for a knighthood. Still, I am pleased that you asked Heminge. He does so much – I think the King's Men would dissolve without him.'

'I know. And I know too that it is your company now, more than mine. And, believe me, I have no wish to come between friends, so if there is anyone else, then ask them now, with an open heart. And thanks, good Richard, for your counsel.'

'We have enough.'

'Very well.'

Shakespeare sat down and let out a sigh that turned into a groan.

'And yet I think there is something you are not saying,' Burbage said.

'There is much that I am not saying,' said Shakespeare.

Burbage waited.

'Do you feel old, Richard?'

'Well, we are not young.'

'And do you reflect on what we have achieved? It has been a miracle.'

'We have been fortunate. I thank my stars I live at such a time.'

'Yes. In our youth there were no theatres. Now there are scores.'

'In chief part, thanks to you.'

'I know you are impatient. Fear not: I will tell you all. I ache a little. The journey to London felt long this time. I came on horseback, by the Banbury route.'

He sighed. In his younger days he would have walked, so a horse was a luxury, and it was unseemly to complain. He closed his eyes. Burbage detected something more than tiredness there. He glimpsed a heaviness of soul he had never seen before.

'We were handed a wondrous opportunity, were we not?' Shakespeare smiled. 'Invited to produce, for the stage, the first great account of English history. Just think: we have told the story whole, from John to Richard.'

'It has been a grand adventure. And now you wish to ride out one more time, like a hero knight of old.'

'I am the opposite of a hero. And I wish not to extend the story, but to rattle it.'

'You think it can be improved? Yet it lives! The plays are performed everywhere.'

'That is why we must shake them up.'

'Oh, I meant to tell you. Have you seen Heminge? The works we performed for the royal wedding – they have paid us ninety-three pounds! Well done.'

'That's good,' said Shakespeare. He flapped an arm, then lowered it again. 'But our plays should be more than passing entertainments for an ungrateful court.'

'I do not call ninety pounds ungrateful.'

'No, we are well rewarded. But London feels sick and fearful. Our King wants to rule by divine appointment, yet he also desires the rapturous consent of his subjects and lashes out when this is not forthcoming. I do not think he can have both these things. I confess I am not sanguine. Do you not feel the tempest brewing?'

Burbage nodded. 'Most certainly. Some people even say that the recent plagues were God's punishment for the King's corruption.'

'What did we do to deserve a man who actually believes in his own royalty? Have our plays taught us nothing? At least the Queen knew she was playing a role.'

'I agree. It is . . . alarming.'

'Quite. And now even nature abandons us – the swallows flee, and there are no wildflowers in Gray's Inn. The mud is too thick.'

'But the plays, Will. The plays endure. Are you not consoled by that?'

'No. Something has happened that we did not intend. Our plays are more than plays – they are national myths. I was slow to see what this means, but it is quiet in Stratford; the days seem longer, and a man can see further.'

Burbage nodded.

'I met a fellow not long ago who told me something. The future was being written far away, he said, across the oceans. He was speaking of the New World.'

'I see.'

'And it struck me that we – you and I, Richard, and the others – have been writing England's future too. The stories we have told will shape the times to come. We have a duty to tell the truth.'

'I agree. But—'

'When I close my eyes,' said Shakespeare, 'I see future generations, crowds of men and women we shall never know. I imagine them crossing a bridge across a flood swollen with strange craft. They walk with their heads down. These are our children's children, and their children too. We cannot know how their lives will be, but their past . . . their past is our concern. This is what I believe, Richard: the past they have will be the one we compose. Our version – our drama – this is what they will inherit, believe, even fight for. I would not have them struggle for a lie.'

Burbage frowned.

'Do you see?'

'I think I do.' Burbage was too grand, these days, to be ruffled by any man in England – save perhaps the King himself. 'You said it yourself: uneasy lies the head that wears a crown. You feel the weight of your own high work. It is natural.'

'It is most *un*natural,' said Shakespeare. 'It feels like conceit. We have a duty to let the future see the real Henry Tudor, no matter what grief it may bring.'

'What grief do you anticipate?'

'For you, good Richard, I trust not much. But for myself, who knows . . .'

Burbage filled two cups with beer and handed one to Shakespeare.

'London is hateful to me now,' said Shakespeare, 'if for no other reason than that a man must drink ale. In Warwickshire we have fresh water every dawn.'

'How is the life in Stratford? Are you happy?'

'I could be. I love the meadows and the thrushes, the larks and the beech woods. But these damned Puritans, Richard, they have seized the town's pulpits. It is hideous. There are no plays. I believe they would ban music if they could. It isn't enough for them to renounce joy themselves – they insist that all men renounce it too.'

'I have always supposed that the way of suffering and self-denial must be insupportable if you are surrounded by people who take a different path.'

'It is hard for us, Richard. We belong to another time. I find myself stranded on a vanishing bar – I am of the people's party and I scorn kings. Yet I reject the people's dogmas and cannot accept their hatred of drama, colour, pageantry.'

'Poor, homeless Will.'

'You are right. I bleat like a goat.'

'You were saying something about the play, and why we must do it.'

Shakespeare sniffed. 'I was avoiding saying something, probably. But here it is. All my life I have fancied myself a boundless seeker after new realms. Where others traversed the waves, I sailed far in dreams. I reached high and never saw myself the lackey of any man. And now I fear I may have been the merest puppet all along.'

'You'll pardon me if I disagree. What has triggered this self-reproach?'

'You know that I came to your *Richard III* last week, in Westminster. You heard, perhaps, the applause for me before you began. Did you see me smile? I sat there, hot with shame: I felt mocked. The play is false, Richard. Oh, you were thrilling, of course – the fault is all mine. The story we have engraved on the future is wrong. I am ashamed to be the author of such ill-begotten work. I fear I am little better than one of the King's cut-throats.'

'What has led you to this? And why has Henry VII waylaid you so?'

'He was a tyrant, Richard – a despot, like all the rest. Oh, not as bad as some – not as evil as his son. It was not even his fault. History put him on the path to the throne, and he behaved as all men would. He killed his rivals and taxed his subjects.'

He looked at Burbage, who said nothing.

'I see you think me cracked.'

'On the contrary. I think you are *back*, and it is a very fine sight! All I can do is remind you of something, Will: trust your friends. What shall we not do for you? The fame we enjoy together flows, we know, from you. Hide not the truth, especially from the friends gathered here today. You yourself speak of the truth as something sacred, so please, be true to them. It is most sure that none shall want away.'

Shakespeare accepted the reproach with a smile.

'You speak in verse already. We are not yet begun.'

'Then let us at it, Will. That magic you performed this morning with the Bible: I know not how it came about, nor care I, because with that alone you snared us all. *Henry VII* will get the best of us. But if you had wanted to make a play about the King's cur, the answer would be the same. We are not the King's Men, Will, though some call us that. We are yours. Dispose us as you please.'

'You words fall hard, and I am humbled,' said Shakespeare.

'That's more like it,' said Burbage, grinning and scooping up orange pudding with his fingers. 'The play's the thing, eh?'

'Wherein we'll tell the truth about the King. Maybe.'

'One more thing.' Burbage grew serious again. 'This play. Do you really think it can be performed? Today, in London, where good men can be hanged for looking the wrong way when they say their prayers? The truth, now.'

'Honestly?' said Shakespeare. 'I don't know. If the play comes out as I expect, then I have to say – probably not. If we fail, if we produce something truly dull, then it may be a great success. But I have something in mind that . . . No.'

He slumped, defeat written all over his face and in the sag of his shoulders.

Burbage slapped his thigh. 'I knew it.'

'Knew what?'

'What do you think? Want some wine?'

Shakespeare held his hands palm upwards in puzzlement.

'I am glad to hear you admit the truth. Now we can get on with it, stupid.'

No one had called Shakespeare stupid for quite a while. He blinked. 'But you have just pressed me to admit that the play will not work.'

'Which is well. You said it yourself – we shall have a much freer rein if we don't have to fret about the practicalities. We can really let go, reach for the sun.'

Shakespeare rocked back, hands clasped behind his head, smiling.

'What is so funny?'

'Nothing.'

'I am not joking. What?'

'Nothing. I am just happy. Thank you, Richard. As always, you find a way through the marshes and the shallows. It is not important that this play is performed – it matters only that it is written. Remember *Julius Caesar*? How many ages hence, shall this our lofty scene be acted o'er in states unborn, and accents yet unknown? We are writing for the future, Richard. What could be more inspiring than that?'

'It calls for another drink, at least,' said Burbage.

Left alone, Shakespeare lowered himself awkwardly to the floor and stretched out his back, knees raised, eyes staring at the timbers in the ceiling. Even without the blow he had taken at the Tower, he was fragile – but that wretched guard had mangled him out of shape. His spine was tender and stiff, and lying on his back like this, legs in the air like a foal, was the only comfortable pose he could find.

As it happened, it was one that seemed conducive to reflection and soon his mind was drifting through wisps of smoke on a battlefield near Leicester, past gay banners and bursts of powder and shot, amid the shouts and cries of humble men and the defiance of a doomed royal host, staunch against well-born rebels and beset by tall pikes and stakes. It occurred to him that secretly, in the darkest corners of his heart, he *did* hope the play could be performed, however bitter and extreme the consequences. Half of him actually *wanted* to spit fire in defiance, just once. In idle dreams he could even imagine wanting to die – a hero of the resistance, a beloved martyr!

But now more urgent fancies were invading his restless mind. He could see the swaying carcass of a king slung athwart a horse, paraded through towns as a ghoulish warning to his followers. He saw the shimmer of a queen glowing in a mist of bright stars. He could hear the deep thump as carpenters pounded at keels, and thought he could make out the clink of coins as they trickled across the kingdom and into the royal treasure chest. He fancied he could even hear the howl of a leopard.

As the old king, Henry Tudor, took shape in his superlatively focused mind's eye, he could feel his iambic muscles twitching. It was as if the dim form of the man marched towards him through the fields of Wales and Leicestershire, through the fog of war and time – a ghost on the move, distinct if not yet clear.

He allowed himself a smile. It had been a rich morning, and in the exhilaration of the moment he was able to forget Coke's threatening words. With his men at his side again he felt invincible. A new play by Shakespeare would be so celebrated that surely no one, not even the King, would dare tamper with it. He had written English history before. Now the time had come to rewrite it.

The task fell to him, and it was one to which he felt more than equal. Whether the world would thank him was quite another matter.

Chapter 5

The following morning Shakespeare woke with the sun and the earliest birds, and spent a good while gazing at the wooden ceiling. His back was so painful he could scarcely rise from his bed. The mornings were always hard. He kneeled over a stool and stretched out the obstinate knot. His body twanged, and he grimaced.

After a while he climbed to his feet and shuffled to the small anteroom above the stairs. One of the happiest aspects of his relative wealth was that he no longer had to rely on the public privies, the infamous houses of easement. He was in possession of a private chamber with its own lead pots and cess-pans, and, what's more, could afford housekeepers to keep them clean. The same servants provided him with tall jugs of fresh water from the conduits and fountains that gushed into the city each day. He had long since refused to splash Thames sludge on to his face and now took for granted the sensation of morning-cool water in his eyes and hair. Not that he had much hair, these days.

He kept a ready supply of musk and almond washing balls; he had seen too many plague victims in his time and fought to scrub the evil poison from his skin before it took root. He had become as fastidious as a cat. Until his twentieth year (until he met Anne, pretty much) he had not once cleaned his teeth, but now he had a device – a sprig of dried rosemary packed in a silk purse and scented with mint, which could be rubbed around the mouth, leaving a man's gums polished and almost fresh.

By the time he had cleansed himself and dressed, he felt light-limbed and insouciant. He closed the door, glanced at the clearing sky and rubbed his hands against the chill. Then he turned down the slope to the steps that looked over the water and stopped beside a short, broad-shouldered stump of a man who was setting up barrels full of fish and bread. In Stratford it was hard to recall or even imagine the scale of the scene in front of him. The Thames was a hundred times wider than the sweet Avon – it was a great brown ocean, not a stream. And it was alive with boats; they swarmed on the water like flies on meat. None was large – the bigger vessels stayed in the deep waters on the estuary side of the bridge – but they made up in numbers for what they lacked in size. There were wherries, rowboats, fishing smacks, lighters, eelers, barges, schooners, cocklers and freighters, all drifting and rolling at clumsy angles. Some were ferrying goods into town: fruit, meat, poultry, cotton, brick, salt, wine and everything else the city might desire.

'Want something?' said the man.

Shakespeare shrugged, groped in his pocket for a coin and bought a walnut loaf.

'Still warm,' he said, pressing it to his cheek.

Across the river he could see smoke blossoming from chimneys and, behind the first rooftops, the high pitched turrets of the Globe, the Swan and the Bear Garden. There were treetops there too – the only patches of green he could see. His love for this city was often bad-tempered; he never stopped missing the ferns and bracken of his childhood, the bullrushes and reeds of the Warwickshire countryside. But he had wrestled with this townscape for longer than he could remember, and the sights and sounds rising to meet the new day filled him, as always, with a sense of promise.

On the dock below a crowd of men and women in loose black capes and blunt-topped hats were stepping on to a barge. A small crowd was watching them go.

'Friends of yours?' said the baker.

'No. Who are they?'

'Protestants, God help them. Brethren or some such. Bound for Londonderry, where there's empty land, they say.'

There was determination in the travellers' gait and the set of their shoulders. They looked ready to lean into the wind and take what came in a God-fearing spirit.

With a sudden clamour of hooves, three horsemen plunged into the scene – two soldiers and a man in a long cape. Swords drawn, the soldiers clambered on the barge, seized a young woman by the arm and dragged her on to the dock.

Shakespeare could hear rough shouts and cries. One of the soldiers beat at a pleading man with the flat of his blade. An older man tried to intervene but was swatted into the water like an insect flicked from a lady's gown. Hands reached down at once to haul him up. By the time he stood on the barge, clothes dripping, the woman had been hoisted on to a horse that clattered away angrily across the cobbles. He yelled and shook his fist, as the wind snatched his cry and tossed it west towards the sea.

Shakespeare exchanged glances with the baker, but neither man said a word. He looked at the loaf, thought for a moment and with one quick movement tossed it down into the boat below. It landed with a soft thud on the deck. A few faces looked up in alarm. Then a hand picked it up and held it aloft with a wave of thanks.

Shakespeare turned, made his own way up the hill along a tight alley and did not stop until he saw, rising far above him, the massive flanks of St Paul's Cathedral.

It was a relief to reach the churchyard and its warren of bookstalls. Shakespeare was familiar with all of them. The House of God had been turned into a market – a riot of merchants, lawyers, kiosks, barrows, agents and gallants. On days as fine as this most of them set up outdoors in the spring air. It could not be called fresh – there was too much refuse in the gutters; but there were moments, early in the day and upwind of the worst smells, when the air was by no means foul.

Shakespeare browsed along beneath the signs of the Red Lion and the Eagle, flicking through quartos, folios, pamphlets, ballads and plays. Some were familiar: Foxe's *Book of Martyrs*, Chapman's Homer, More's *Utopia*, Pliny's *Secrets and Wonders of the World*. But there were new and surprising volumes appearing all the time now. Some of the most exciting came from Catholic presses in Spain, shipped over in barrels like so much spice or grain. Sometimes they travelled in wine casks. Shakespeare himself had a Nashe satire that still carried the whiff of stale claret.

The shops were often raided by authorities hungry for banned material. This morning, however, everything was calm. As usual there were soldiers posted on corners and lounging in doorways. They scowled or glared at the citizens passing by; no man or woman could doubt that they were, in the eyes of the law, the enemy. Every now and then they would stop a man, seemingly at random, and surround him, poking him in the chest and forcing him against a wall. Who knew what they were asking? Who cared? Most people took pains to avert their eyes.

Shakespeare shuddered and forced himself to ignore them. He began to leaf through books like a dog after game, hungry for a scent of his prey. His hand rested on the three-volume edition of Holinshed, but he already had a well-worn copy (he called it his 'book of plots and legends') and had no need of another. Still, he smiled at the famous subtitle: *From the Time That It Was First Inhabited, Untill the Time That It Was Last Conquered: Wherein the Sundrie Alterations of the State Under Forren People Is Declared; And Other Manifold Observations Remembred.*

He opened it, turned a few pages and there it was: a grainy wood-cut of Macbeth meeting the Weird Sisters. Shakespeare's mind darted back to the time he had first seen this picture. He could vividly recall thinking that the sisters were, if anything, not weird enough. They wore long dresses and sulky expressions, as if someone had stolen their gloves. No witch ever stood in greater need of a bubbling cauldron.

It would be interesting to meet this man Stanyhurst, if it turned out to be possible. Men like him were the true historians – he himself had merely spun their work into plays. He would be counting on Holinshed again, for the main events of Henry's reign and for various set pieces. The same went for Edward Hall's dependable sourcebook, *The Union of the Noble and Illustrious Houses of Lancaster and York*. Whilst these two had seen him through several centuries of England's stormy past, he was looking now for something a little more peppery. There was an attractive volume of Vergil's *History of England* over there, but this,

Shakespeare knew, had been written to please Henry VII; it could not be relied on.

Here was something. An almost-forgotten verse drama by Edward de Vere, the Earl of Oxford, titled *Pleasure for Treasure* – a humourless and ham-fisted attempt to muscle in on the Shakespearian theme. It had made its author something of a laughing stock; some even said that it had hastened the poor man's death. Shakespeare buried the book out of sight beneath a pile of more deserving volumes.

In the end he picked out three titles: an essay on Henry VII by Francis Bacon, an anonymous play about the murder of the Princes in the Tower, and a pamphlet by one William Cavendish titled *The King's Right Arm*. It seemed to be about the link between physical deformity and divine right, with particular reference to Richard III. It had to be worth a look.

Behind him, someone screamed. An old man was being grappled by soldiers.

'Help me, ho!' he cried. 'Oh my sainted children! For God's sake!'

The people closest to him looked down. All knew that if they tried to help the poor fellow they would themselves be slapped in chains. It was not unknown for people to be executed in this very corner of this churchyard. In fact there was a thin, grey body hanging from a gibbet, in chains, to be pecked by crows as a warning to others.

Shakespeare swallowed, thought briefly of Prometheus . . . and did nothing.

No one knew what happened to those who disappeared, though there were stories. Some said that human remains were sometimes to be seen in the Hounds Ditch, the rancid gutter where they threw the dead dogs.

Please, he whispered to himself, let him be spared. He is only a man.

What else could he do? He turned back to the books.

They were all here, the classics – Chaucer, Malory, Bocaccio, Petrarch – and the best modern writers too – Sidney, Spenser, Jonson, Dekker, Lyly, Marlowe, Montaigne and a dozen others. There was a good copy of Galileo, but although Shakespeare was perfectly adept in Latin, he was not inclined to torment himself trying to decipher the man's strange Italian variant of the ancient tongue. Ah, this was what he was looking for: the Croyland Chronicle, a collection of historical observations written by a monk, in the time when there were still monasteries, where men could cultivate both crops and civilisation with the same strong, agile hands.

He spent the rest of the day reading, pacing his rooms, walking the streets and writing notes. A story began to form in his mind, of a young Welsh prince forced to take refuge from the wars in France; of a king who after Bosworth struck down his enemies and his rivals, and who by marrying Elizabeth of York (the daughter of Edward IV) brought an end to the Wars of the Roses, merging red and white into a single Tudor rose. He read about an industrious man who disliked frivolity – a Puritan before his time. He read of a leader who avoided war, yet had to fight a succession of claimants to his hard-won throne; a man who hoarded money and fined his subjects to the bone. He read about a man who lost a child to the plague, and lost too his appetite for life, his ability to feel pleasure, his love of games and laughter. He read about a man who retreated into a lonely, bitter, miserly silence.

Shakespeare learned all this and imagined more. For long periods he lay on his back, performing scenes on his inner stage, tingling with creative energy. Like a sculptor circling a lump of marble, he ran his fingertips warily, wonderingly, over the surface, his neck cold as he imagined the shape of the body within.

He knew this feeling. It was a good sign. It meant that he was ready.

The next morning he was about to head out into the city when he heard a scrappy commotion at the door. His steward was trying, and failing, to ward off an insistent stranger – a youngster, by the look of him, and a foreigner. For an instant his scalp crawled in fright, but in truth the boy looked placid enough.

'What is all this?' he said.

'Will Shakespeare? If you are he, it is you I have come to collect.'

Shakespeare looked beyond him. A carriage was waiting in the yard.

'You wish me to accompany you?'

'I do, sir.'

'And where, might I ask, do you propose to take me?'

'My master the Duke desires that you come at once.'

'The Duke of what, exactly?'

'Navarre.'

Shakespeare froze. Navarre was the kingdom in which he had set *Love's Labour's Lost*. It was to all intents and purposes an imaginary realm, a playground for games of disguise and deception. Its duke wanted to set up a court devoted only to manly scholarship – women were entirely banned – and the play had fun showing how quickly this whim fell apart; love would have the better of learning, in the end.

It was evidently a coded message – and from a sympathiser, it would seem.

Who could be behind it? He could not resist finding out.

'Come,' he said, taking his coat and marching past his nonplussed steward. 'What are we waiting for?'

The young man kept the curtain drawn, but Shakespeare knew the roads well enough to be aware of the route they were taking. First they rode up the hill and turned left across the Fleet ditch. Then they turned left again and trotted past St Bride's church. Then they stopped. They had performed three sides of a square and were not far from where they had begun: Shakespeare could see his own roof only a skimming-stone's throw along the river to the east.

'Here we are,' said the boy.

'Bridewell Palace,' said Shakespeare. 'It would have been as quick to walk.'

'This way. The Duke asked me to bring you up at once.' He turned on his heel and marched away from Bridewell to a more compact villa that stood alongside. He pushed open a door. 'Welcome to Salisbury House. Up the stairs, first door on the right.'

Shakespeare obeyed him. He was apprehensive, but not fearful. If Coke had plans for him, that rigmarole with the carriage would have been quite superfluous. More than anything he was curious. It felt like an adventure, and he liked adventures.

'William Shakespeare?'

The man at the top of the stairs was tall, dark, well groomed and as sunburned as a peasant. He was wearing a plum-coloured velvet suit and holding a silk scarf. He had bright, mischievous eyes and a scrupulously trimmed beard. He looked for all the world like the kind of European dandy Shakespeare had mocked in his play. There was the trace of an accent in his voice.

'Yes,' said Shakespeare.

'I apologise for the mysterious summons. You are most welcome.'

'Thank you.'

'I hope the timing is not too ill judged. You may be pressed.'

'I do not have all day.'

'Of course not. A busy man like yourself.'

'So . . . tell me. The Duke of Navarre?'

'I thought you would like that.'

'You *knew* I would like it.'

'I suppose I did.'

That accent – was it Scottish? Welsh?

'Perhaps you should start,' Shakespeare said, pulling off his gloves, 'by telling the truth about your identity. If you are Navarre, I must be Berowne.'

'You have not guessed?'

There it was – *Irish*!

Shakespeare smiled. *Of course.* 'I am willing to speculate,' he said. 'It has just now come to me. I do believe you may be . . . Richard Stanyhurst.'

'You have me! I am the very man! Will you take some ale?'

'No, thank you.'

'Wine?'

'A small glass would be welcome.'

'I am so glad to meet you. You must forgive the stealth that brought you here.'

'I promise to forgive, if you promise to explain.'

'With pleasure! Have a seat. Now, where to begin?'

Shakespeare took a sip of wine and waited.

'What think you of my disguise?'

'Disguise?'

'Do I look like an Irish ne'er-do-well?'

'I confess I was expecting a different . . . effect. Your complexion—'

'Hah! I know. I have been long in Spain, where the sunlight falls like fire.'

'Of course.'

'Anyway, here is the nub of it. I am banished.'

'It does not look that way.'

'I know. Yet it is true – they think I am in Brussels.'

'Forgive me, but you are not well camouflaged.'

'That is what I mean. This is a disguise. I am travelling incognito, as the Romans say. I was exiled from these shores as a traitor, and have travelled far and wide in all the Habsburg lands. I have become a courtier: they love me well.'

'You will excuse me for saying that you are not well hidden.'

'You mean this, my bright plumage? That is the whole trick of it. If I stole through London like a thief, I should be discovered at once. It does make it hard to issue invitations – I could not ask you here under my own name. But dressed like this, no one suspects me of anything worse than an offence against the laws of costume. You of all people must appreciate that.'

He raised his glass in a convivial salute.

Shakespeare accepted the compliment with a brief smile. It was no secret that he himself was addicted to the idea of disguise. His plays were full of girls dressed as boys, warriors dressed as monks, princes dressed as beggars. It was one of the first principles of acting – and of kingship – that a man could borrow robes. Whether it was Viola hiding her love, Henry V concealing his regal self, or Edgar putting aside his rank, Shakespeare's characters were always happy to swap costumes.

'But this house?' he said. 'How do you come to be here?'

'It belongs to the Earl of Devon. Poor man, he does not know who I truly am – he believes me to be an envoy from Austria. The large house to which we are attached, Salisbury House, was built by Robert Cecil – you probably knew him. This one is let to what they call "people of substance". I am honoured to have passed muster.'

Shakespeare listened patiently as Stanyhurst summarised his recent adventures: his work as a scholar and tutor in the Spanish court; his warm relationship with the Archduke of Austria, who retained him as his chaplain; his lavish romantic feelings for ancient Ireland; his hatred for the level Dutch horizon; and his undying love for Shakespeare's plays.

'To be honest, in all my wanderings I miss nothing more than the theatre. *Your* theatre, in particular. I have always wanted to meet you, so on this trip I begged my friends to set up an encounter. I don't think I can stay much longer, so I am afraid I took matters into my own hands. Anyway, you are here now. I salute you!'

'I in turn must thank *you*. The work you did for Holinshed is most rare. I prize it above all other books. I dare say we could not have made our plays without it.'

'I am very pleased to have been of service.'

'How did it all come to pass? Who *was* Holinshed? I never knew him.'

'Raphael? He was a man on whom the gods smiled, if you want the truth. The great book wasn't even his idea—'

'What?'

'It was Reyner Wolf, a fellow of resounding inspiration. From the Low Countries. It was his intention to produce a full, rich, sweeping chronicle of English history. Holinshed was a mere assistant. But then Wolf died.'

'Oh.'

'The book simply fell at Holinshed's feet. Having said that, he did a fine job. He set half a dozen of us writing passages, and he chose wisely: we were a boisterous crew. When we dined, it was a potted reformation. Campion and myself, we were of the Roman mind; Harrison and Fleming were ardent Protestants. Holinshed – and for this he deserves eternal bliss – had the wit to embrace all of us under one roof.'

'I met Campion once. A great man.'

'One of the greatest. We studied together at Oxford.'

'Ah.'

'But when Holinshed died, oh, what a falling off was there.'

'What happened?'

'Surely you know. The second edition was utterly spoiled and false.'

Shakespeare's ears grew warm.

'Utterly?'

'Yes. Oh, I didn't mind that they wanted more on Boadicea, to create a precedent for warrior queens. But the way they ruined our History of Ireland – unforgivable.'

'Ruined?' Shakespeare realised that he was sounding like a mere echo.

'My chapters were based on Campion's work and I, like him, was sympathetic to Ireland's Catholic past. In the second edition, that all changed.'

'How come?'

'The second edition was produced by Abraham Fleming – a contributor, a printer, and a thoroughly bad penny. He so far lacked respect for Holinshed that he asked John Hooker, as thirsty a Protestant as ever you saw, to revise my scenes. Holy Ireland was strangled in its sleep. And the Censor disposed of the corpse.'

'The Censor?'

'Oh yes. You think history is not censored?'

Shakespeare sighed. 'I know very well that it is.'

'Well, that's what happened. When I objected, I was banished. Interesting, is it not, how little patience Protestants have with those who have the temerity to protest?'

Shakespeare had to fight to prevent his thoughts from drifting away, like leaves on a current. Stanyhurst too was fired with the thought of telling the truth about the past! How many times, in this brief return to London, would he be visited by signs that history was a blank canvas on which each age painted its own story?

He did not share this idea, however.

'I am very sorry. It was most unjust. I wish I had known.'

'They won't silence me that easily. The sun may have passed behind the clouds, yet it burns still. I will not renounce my calling. History may have abandoned me, but I have not abandoned history.'

He was growing agitated, and took a deep breath to calm himself.

'Anyway,' he said, 'what are you working on now? A new play?'

'As it happens, you may be able to help with something.'

Shakespeare hesitated. How much should he tell? He recalled

both his promise to Burbage and his own request for discretion.

'We have been asked to write a play about Henry VIII.'

'My God!'

If it were possible for a tanned man to turn pale, Stanyhurst would have done so.

'I know you do not like him.' Shakespeare smiled.

'Not *like* him? I detest the villain.'

'Well, he is *our* subject now. And I want – may I be plain? – to tell the truth.'

Stanyhurst drained his glass, filled it and drained it again.

'I do not think so. I do not think you want to tell the truth. Even you.'

'I know it may seem unlikely,' said Shakespeare, 'but it is so.' He paused and met Stanyhurst's feverish glance with a level gaze. And he chose his words carefully before adding: 'I do not wish the future to hold any illusions about this king.'

Stanyhurst's breath came out of him in a rush and his whole physique seemed to crumple. The façade, the composed European aristocrat, seemed to dissolve, leaving behind an edgy Irish poet, historian, alchemist, teacher and refugee. It was not cold – there was a bracing fire in the hearth – but he was shivering.

'One more drink,' he said, reaching for the flask. 'And then I will tell you all.'

Shakespeare was a good talker but an even better listener. Whilst he did not interrupt Stanyhurst, like a quick-limbed sheepdog he contrived to steer him down avenues, padding ahead to block a digression, darting in to examine a detail, prodding and nudging him this way and that until he had teased out the revelations he sought.

He had a memory like flypaper and he held it before him now, anxious to capture the smallest nuance. Every now and then, despite himself, he trembled.

Stanyhurst's grudge against Henry VIII was twofold: first, he had broken with Rome, and cracked the holy compact between heaven and earth. Second, he had called himself King of Ireland. It was for a caustic pamphlet protesting against this outrage that Stanyhurst had been exiled. However, these principled objections were dwarfed by a personal distaste. In Stanyhurst's view, Henry VIII was a lecherous murderer, a thief, a duplicitous friend, a glutton, a bully, a tyrant and a pervert.

'I have studied the deadly sins,' said Stanyhurst, 'and that godforsaken man broke every one of them, twice a day, all his life.'

Shakespeare let this go, leaned forward and quietly changed the subject.

'What about his father? How did he get on with his father?'

Stanyhurst threw him an odd look. 'I should have known,' he said.

'Known what?'

'That you would be too shrewd for me.'

'I don't know about that. I am just interested.'

'I said I would tell you all. I have told you nothing. Somehow you have sniffed out my secret.'

'Secret?'

'How did you know?'

'Know what?'

'About Henry's father.'

'I know very little about his father. That is why I am asking you.'

Stanyhurst had a wild gleam in his eye.

Shakespeare tried again. 'Is it possible, for instance, that he was . . . an imposter?'

'A what?'

'An imposter. The young Earl of Richmond was quite unknown and far removed from any court. The man who came to Pembrokeshire and ousted the King at Bosworth . . . Well, he could have been anyone.'

Stanyhurst tipped his head back and roared with laughter.

'I've heard most things,' he said, 'but I've not heard *that* before.'

Shakespeare did not have time to feel proud of himself, because Stanyhurst was smiling, the distinctive glint in his eye once more.

'I am working on something, a scandal, a secret. I cannot tell you what it is. Not yet. The time will come for such revelations as will astound your ears. You question me about Henry's relationship with his father. Why, this is the cause that brought me to London! But I must not speak of it yet. There are things I need to find, to check . . . But my work is almost done. When it is finished you, my dear Shakespeare, shall be the first to know. My God! What a play it would make!'

Even though Shakespeare had no idea what he was talking about, he knew better than to press. A scandal. A secret. He itched to know more. Perhaps, if he made to leave . . .

'Very well,' he said. 'Please do not hesitate . . .'

He stood up.

Stanyhurst stayed his arm. 'You have to go? So soon? Come, man, another glass!'

'Alas, I am required elsewhere,' said Shakespeare. 'But thank you for your hospitality and your stories. I must confess, I burn to hear your secret.'

'Soon,' cried Stanyhurst as he left. 'It won't be long now! Then shall England come to know the wickedness that has been done in her name.'

Wickedness? Shakespeare almost changed his mind about leaving. Yet he sensed that Stanyhurst would not be swayed by entreaties, and he did not want to betray his true interest by pressing too hard. He grimaced, however. He hated secrets.

When he came out into the courtyard there was no sign of any carriage. He strolled up to the bridge, looked at the towering façade of St Paul's and slipped back to his rooms. He had a vague sense that something in them had changed, but could not say what.

At home was a note from Burbage, saying that he had arranged rooms for the next meeting of the King's Men a few days hence, at a house opposite the Bethlehem hospital.

Bedlam, thought Shakespeare. That was all he needed.

The Black House in Spitalfields, hard by the hospital in the old dissolved priory at Bedlam, was not a gentle place – perhaps not the sort of neighbourhood that might expect to host the theatrical elite. That was why Burbage had chosen it. The Bethlehem hospital was a famous attraction; Londoners would walk out to inspect the lunatics, displayed in their cages like beasts at a menagerie. The inmates – naked men and women – were chained and whipped, sometimes to calm them, sometimes to put on a better show. It wasn't far different from the bear-baiting rings south of the river; the human captives were prodded and goaded all day long. Their hisses and curses seemed as comical, to the onlookers, as the screeches of trapped birds.

Shakespeare had his own theatrical associations with the locale. The treatment of prisoners in this horrendous House of Correction lay behind the torments imposed on Malvolio in *Twelfth Night* – trapped in a darkened room, taunted with accusations of madness. And it had inspired Edgar's performance as Poor Tom in *King Lear*, gorging on frogs, toads, tadpoles, newts and whatever muddy amphibious life he could trawl up from the roadside ditches.

Burbage was waiting for him when he arrived.

'Here,' he said. 'There's someone I want you to meet.'

He smiled at a mild, pale man in dark clothes sitting on a stool by the wall.

'This is Andrew,' he said.

Shakespeare was not sure how to react, but he put out his hand. Andrew smiled, showing his teeth, and nodded vigorously.

'He can't speak,' said Burbage. 'He's a mute.'

Shakespeare understood.

'Good idea,' he said.

'I've known him for years,' said Burbage. 'He is as faithful as a hound. He will watch the door for us. Three taps means someone is approaching.'

Shakespeare looked the man full in the face.

'Thank you, Andrew,' he said. 'We will be counting on you.'

The watchman gave a bashful grin and moved away.

'As always,' said Shakespeare, 'I am in your debt. You think of everything.'

'Someone has to. How are you?'

'Very well.'

'Did you get to meet that man Stanyhurst?'

'Yes I did. Why do you ask?'

'Oh, an odd coincidence. Someone came looking for him, at the

Sign of the Eagle. Asked around if anyone had seen the man.'

'I hope you didn't say anything.'

'What do you take me for?'

'Sorry. It's just . . . He's an interesting man – had quite a lot to say about Henry VIII – but I don't think he wants everyone to know that he is here in London.'

'Why not?'

'He has his reasons.'

'I am sure he has. Shall we?'

He shoved the door open and ushered Shakespeare into the warm interior.

The room itself was light and airy, at the back of the house, facing away from the hospital. The windows commanded a view of open fields, with a row of handsome oaks, where half a dozen distant archers practised their skills at the butts.

The King's Men arrived separately, as Burbage had advised, but followed a similar route up Broad Street, along London Wall to the Bishop's Gate, and past St Botolph's church. While they took few extravagant precautions, they glanced behind them at corners. Alleyn ordered his driver to circle Smithfield twice before he felt it safe to continue.

There were two new arrivals waiting for them – a very young boy and an almost-as-young girl. The boy was too well dressed to be a street urchin and not quite old enough to be an actor. He had sandy hair, sharp features and an anxious expression. The girl might have been his older sister, except for her colouring: she was neat, pretty and pale; a vivid yellow dress glowed beneath coal-black hair.

Shakespeare waited until everyone had arrived before he introduced them. 'I am delighted,' he said, 'to be able to welcome two new faces. I know you will all enjoy working with them. This young man,' he gestured with his hand, encouraging the boy to stand, 'is John Harvard, a son of Stratford whose father has a position at St Mary's church, in Southwark. I know his parents – in fact, I introduced them. John is a very clever lad; he has not yet completed his studies, but has consented to be our secretary. His handwriting is beautiful. It will be a pleasure to read our words.'

A buzz of approving murmurs rippled through the company. The King's Men often placed scribes in one corner at their rehearsals to record their improvisations. The only man to show surprise was John Lowin, but although unfamiliar with the habit, he knew better than to venture an opinion at this early stage.

'How old *are* you?' said Armin to young Harvard. 'You are the size of a vole.'

'I am ten, sir. Nearly eleven.'

'I don't believe it. Will, he's a child.'

'Wait till you see his hand,' said Burbage.

'I can see it now,' said Armin. 'It is no bigger than a cat's paw.'

'And this,' continued Shakespeare, 'is Constance Donne. Some of you may know her father – poet, adventurer and soon, I believe, a prelate. The wittiest man in all London, they say, and father to the wittiest daughter. I met him at the festivities for the recent marriage of King James's daughter Elizabeth – he wrote a poem, an Epithalamium, to mark the occasion. Constance is a young lady of high education. She will be of great help with our queens.'

Not long ago this would have been a controversial novelty, but the playwright had for years insisted that the process of composition required female support. I want real women, he would say, not manly parodies. Nevertheless, the King's Men looked at the girl with alarm. She too was of tender years. Could she be worldly enough to impersonate a princess? Or brazen enough to impersonate an innkeeper?

More significantly, could she be trusted? This project was perilous enough without involving such innocents. However fine their intentions, these youngsters were unlikely to be tight-lipped.

'Now,' said Shakespeare. 'Let's begin.'

'Hold on,' said Alleyn. 'What about us? Don't *we* merit an introduction?'

'I'm sorry,' said Shakespeare. He stood between the two newcomers. 'Constance, John, allow me to present . . . the King's Men.'

The actors shuffled into line.

'First, but by no means foremost, this is Richard Burbage. Handsome fellow. They say he looks a bit like me, but I can't see it.'

79

They shook hands. Burbage made a fright-face, and Harvard giggled.

'And this well-tailored figure of a man is Edward Alleyn.'

'I have heard of you,' said Constance.

'If you stand in need of financial help, John,' said Shakespeare, 'Ned is your man. He is practically made of gold.'

'A rich man,' said Alleyn with a bow, 'is only a poor man with money. But I am at your service, naturally.'

He made a courtly show of kissing Constance's hand.

'If it were Donne,' said Armin, 'when 'tis Donne, 'twere well it were Donne constantly.'

'I'm sorry?' said Constance.

'Do not mind him,' said Shakespeare. 'That is Robert Armin, our resident fool.'

Armin made a mock caper. 'Talk sense to a fool, and he'll think *you* a fool,' he said, banging an imaginary drum.

The portliest member of the group did not wait to be named.

'I am Joseph Taylor,' he said. 'And the pleasure is all mine.'

'Very true. Pleasure is what he lives for,' said Shakespeare. 'But he always keeps some spare to give to others.'

Taylor shook Harvard's hand for long enough to make the boy laugh.

'You are very young, little man,' he said.

'I know, sir. But my father says that it is only temporary and will pass.'

Taylor laughed and clapped him on the shoulder. 'He'll do,' he said.

'Finally . . . John Lowin,' said Shakespeare. 'I confess I know him only slightly. On what stands your fame, John?'

'Given the weight of the reputations in this room,' said Lowin, 'my outstanding feature is the opposite of your own: my very *lack* of fame.'

'Modesty is finer than fame,' said Shakespeare. 'It is the battles to come that count, not those in the past.'

He flashed a smile at Alleyn, in thanks for prompting these formalities. There was an amiable sense of goodwill in the air. The arrival of fresh blood seemed to have rejuvenated the whole room. It boded well.

'Shall we?' he said.

Low benches formed three sides of a square. Shakespeare moved to the centre. Harvard sat at the table with his pot of ink and took a quill from a leather bag. His face wore an expression that plucked at Shakespeare's heart. Nothing moved him more than the unfeigned zest of boys, and Harvard's face was bright with nerves and resolve. Shakespeare rubbed his hands over his scalp, took a breath and began.

'Let us start by sharing what we have discovered,' he said. 'What do we know about our king?'

'He had thin white hair, blue eyes and black teeth,' said Lowin.

'Goodness,' said Alleyn. 'A veritable scarecrow.'

'He loved marrowbone pudding,' said Armin, 'and once paid a pound for a nightingale. A month's wages! For a bird that sleeps all day!'

'Yet he suffered from avarice,' said Shakespeare, 'according to Vergil. Especially in his declining years.'

'He had a very small claim to the throne,' said Burbage. 'He was a distant cousin of Lancaster abandoned in Wales and a refugee in Brittany. A colourful beginning.'

'And he kept moving his court,' Alleyn added. 'From Westminster to Winchester, Sheen to Eltham, and from Greenwich to Richmond.'

'What about his private life?'

'He married the Yorkist princess,' said Taylor. 'And listen to this: the Queen gave birth to their first child just eight months after the wedding.'

'Ho, ho,' said Armin.

'Perhaps the child was premature,' said Alleyn.

'What,' said Taylor, 'has the child got to do with it?'

'Everything.' Alleyn smiled.

'He was a peacemaker,' said Burbage. 'And a profiteer. He promised Spain that he would invade France, then went to the French and asked them to pay him off.'

'A businessman, certainly,' said Alleyn. 'The first year of a bishop's revenue went to the Crown, so what did he do? He kept appointing new bishops. And justice, in his time, was most profitable.'

'He actually gave Greenwich its name,' said Armin. 'Before that it was called, would you believe, Placentia. And of course Richmond was named after him too.'

'The main thing,' said Shakespeare, 'is that his first act, on gaining the throne, was to move against his rivals. There is our beginning.'

It was the story, he went on to say, of a man who aspired to be good, but became mired in the same inevitable horrors that had besieged his predecessors. He was a warrior who hated war, a miser who sold his soul for his kingdom.

'As always,' he said, 'ambition will outreach itself. Like a ripple in water, it will spread across the lake until it weakens and dies. So it is with men who seek power over others – in the end they lose all power over themselves.'

The King's Men said nothing. They were ready.

'Constance,' said Shakespeare, 'I thought we might begin with a wedding. King Henry is marrying Richard's niece, Elizabeth of York. It may help if we imagine them as close, like sisters. She is furious; she had no choice in the matter; only in asides can she admit her loathing for her new husband – who may even, she thinks, have killed her own brothers. I'll be the King. I wonder, would you consent to be my bride? My friends may doubt you. I do not.'

She rose and joined him in the central space.

'Now entertain conjecture of a time,' said Shakespeare, and his friends smiled. They had spent the week wondering, sometimes aloud, whether their old friend still had the gift; now they would see. In the past it had been thrilling to watch him throwing out casual yards of rhetoric. There never was anyone like him.

'Transport yourselves to Westminster. See the proud roofs, palms together in prayer. And look! Here comes the royal train. Music. Robes. Flaming lights. Here is the King, here his reluctant Queen. They step out of a carriage and process through wild applause. The Queen is in a superb pink dress. It is pouring. They hurry in.'

The pair of them mimed ducking in through a door to escape the rain.

'The King,' said Shakespeare, 'is florid in his speech. He knows the importance of ceremony, but he is new – this is his first attempt to mimic the voice of kingship.' He cleared his throat. 'As follows,' he said.

The pause was thick with promise. The audience leaned in; Harvard's quill pen hovered above the empty page; and softly, without a sound, like a ship setting off on an epic voyage, a tiny crack appeared between the vessel and the dock, and *The True and Tragicall Historie of Henry VII* pointed its nose out into the world.

'Good people all, I shower golden thanks,' said Shakespeare, as if from a balcony. 'For gathering on this torrential day, to celebrate the marriage of the King, and this his true and most delightful Queen. Enjoy this happy deluge at our side, and celebrate with us the storm of bells, from spire to spire, and steeples everywhere, that hammer out with lazy peals the hour when we, the prideful flowers of this land – for so long sundered in a bitter war – have grafted in a single happy stem, a union of the white rose with the red . . .'

There was a burst of applause from Robert Armin. 'Excellent,' he cried.

'Long live the King,' said Burbage. 'But he will need to take a very deep breath, if all his sentences are as long as this.'

'I adore weddings,' said Armin. 'I love the storm of bells.'

Shakespeare bowed and gestured to Constance Donne that it fell to her to respond. Before she could react they were startled by three sharp knocks on an outer door.

They snapped out of their parts like bolts from a bow.

Burbage put a finger to his lips; the actors slid over to the table and transformed themselves into partygoers.

Knuckles rapped on the inner door. Alleyn opened it.

An elderly woman with a scarf tied over her grey hair stood in the entrance.

'Good morrow,' she called. 'I was just seeing you were all provided for. Would you like me to send out for ale? Or wine? Or water?'

Alleyn opened the door a little wider to show her the table, crammed with treats.

'Oh, you are well provisioned,' she said.

'Ours is not a long voyage,' said Shakespeare, 'and we shall not starve.'

'I'll not trouble you then.'

'Thank you,' said Burbage.

There was a collective release of breath as the door closed.

'Who knocked?' said Alleyn.

'Better safe than sorry,' said Shakespeare. 'Burbage has a man watching the street for us. It looks as though we can rely on him.'

'Oh,' said Alleyn. 'Good.'

'Meant to tell you,' said Burbage. 'Sorry.'

'Don't worry. It brings back bad memories, that is all, being in this place. My father was a warden at Bedlam. All my life I have listened to the screams of those poor madmen in my dreams. I hate it in these parts.'

'Forgive me, Ned. I did not know.'

'Shall we go on?' Constance was walking up and down with quick steps.

'Please,' said Shakespeare.

She paced on, wringing her hands, then turned aside and said: 'Did ever virgin bride so ache with grief, to walk the aisle in this too bitter dress? 'Tis not for love he smothers me in lace, kisses my hand and strokes my trembling cheek. Affairs of state do urge him to the deed, as they do bear my body to his bed.'

She turned to Shakespeare and, with a queenly tilt of the head, released a cloud-splintering smile, every inch the happy bride.

'Don't marry *him*,' called Taylor. 'Marry me!'

'Bravo,' echoed Alleyn. 'Better than splendid.'

Shakespeare ignored them both.

'But first, some thanks,' he said. 'To you, right noble Stanley, a prince among the barons gathered here. Whatever you demand of us is yours, excepting enmity – that you'll never have. Those words you shouted back at Bosworth Field, most bravely, in the frighted din of war. "I have another son!" – Such was the phrase you flung in Richard's foul and twisted face, when you did take my part on that grim day, furnishing debts we never can repay.'

He stepped aside, leaving the floor to Constance. She turned her face away and years of painful experience seemed to gather in her brow when she spoke.

'I hate him, verily.' she said. 'This demon killed my uncle – all unprepared, I trow. The truth will out some day, yet lie I must, and with the King, right soon, as his sweet Queen. Oh!'

'Fantastic,' said Taylor, laughing. 'No other word for it. This girl's tremendous.'

'See, there *is* another word for it,' said Armin.

'Hush,' said Alleyn.

'Stanley,' said Shakespeare. 'I name you Royal Chamberlain, our closest and most trusted counsellor. Morton, bright Ely, you shall be our lamp. Pray join us as our Chancellor elect. And Oxford, come with us. I here declare: let every inn that bore the White Boar's name henceforth take Oxford's colour, and be blue. Exeter, Lincoln, come. Let's haste to Hampton, where we'll have our feast.'

Shakespeare broke off. 'Actually, that is true,' he said. 'There really was a royal edict that all the white boars had to turn blue.'

'It is fortunate Oxford's colour wasn't purple,' said Taylor.

'And I've just remembered something,' said Shakespeare. Another line from *Julius Caesar* hovered before him. 'John, can you add a rapid couplet there, after the lines about Stanley. Something like: Lie not within the suburbs of our love, approach thee nearer to our inmost heart.'

'Got it,' said Harvard.

'We don't normally poach our own work,' said Burbage.

'Normally we just poach other people's,' said Alleyn.

'I know,' Shakespeare smiled. 'But an echo of Caesar's wife carries a whiff of danger, does it not? Stanley and the other nobles must watch their step.'

'I suppose. Was it Caesar's wife, though, or Brutus's?'

'I am not sure.'

Shakespeare glanced at Constance. 'I think we need one more strong aside from you. Declare war on the King. Say you have plans and strategies. Swear vengeance. The scene has started in a high, declaiming style. Now we must show that the King isn't going to have things his own way, that plots are already hatching.'

Constance gave a quick nod, paced up and down, then turned. A frosty quality of quiet fury sprang into her face. She looked cold, bleak, dangerous.

'Friends have I still, in Scotland and in France,' she hissed. 'Letters I'll send, and my deliverance shall be as bloody as it shall be swift. The battle may be lost, my honour drowned, but wars are long, and this one shall not end.'

'They move away,' Shakespeare said, taking up the narration and leading Constance by the hand. 'The feast is in full progress. Jugglers, flares, musicians, platters of food on shoulders, and . . . that's it.'

He made a small bow.

Constance did the same.

The others rose to their feet and clapped. When they stopped, the only sound was the scratching of a quill pen.

'John!' said Shakespeare. 'I am sorry. How did you manage? Can you keep up?'

'Very nearly, sir,' said Harvard, still writing. 'Did she say that wars are long, but this one shall not end?'

'I think so,' said Shakespeare. 'A very fair rhyme.'

'But end does not quite rhyme with drowned, sir.'

There was a burst of laughter from the men.

'You could try crowned, or frowned, or bound, or sound . . .'

'Or hound, or ground, or gowned,' said Armin.

'Confound,' said Taylor. 'Dumbfound.'

'You are a brave editor,' said Shakespeare. 'Constance, he finds you wanting.'

'I am sorry I do not please you, master,' said Constance, bobbing a curtsy.

'You please us more than well,' boomed Burbage. 'Impressive work, my girl.'

'Yes,' said Alleyn. 'Good. Very good indeed.'

They spent the next several hours discussing different ways of presenting the King and his courtiers. Wanting to catch a sense of the grave power these men held in their hands, they also knew from experience that if there were too many noblemen on stage at any one time, they would seem like mere servants. Alleyn and Burbage offered up some suggestive details about the origins of the King's private guard, the immediate confiscation of Yorkist lands and the roster of executions. Constance and Taylor made merry by imagining a pair of royal ladies at the feast, while Shakespeare's King tried, with some success, to soothe the furies in Constance's Queen.

Things seemed to fall into place with surprising ease. Harvard's pen filled sheet after sheet with his quick but uniform script. Armin, after a long silence, began to toss fool-proverbs into the mix. All their eyes were bright with work and hope.

At length the company began to disperse.

'Perhaps I had better keep the pages,' said Shakespeare, leaning over Harvard and lifting them up. 'I would like to look them over. Thank you.'

He followed Burbage across the room, took him by the arm and led him aside.

'So . . . what did we think?'

'It was fine work,' said Burbage.

'Fine?'

'Good.'

'Good?'

'Good. Are you going to repeat everything I say? I thought it went well, very well. Although—'

'Although?'

'Nothing.'

'You said *although*. Although what?'

Burbage frowned. He didn't recall having to humour Shakespeare like this – the idea was ridiculous. Yet the man seemed anxious, eager for praise.

'Will, what is the matter?' he said. 'It was good. Excellent, if you want. Whatever. And Constance, God, she is captivating. But since when did you need reassurance like this? I suppose, if you push, I'll admit that it felt a bit . . . routine. I mean, a good beginning, don't get me wrong. Absolutely fine. But where is it leading? This could be any king, and any queen. I don't feel the sting of a story, yet, that's all.'

'I knew you didn't like it.'

'It's not that I don't like it.'

'Never mind.'

'Will—'

It was too late. Shakespeare marched away, stiff and wounded.

Burbage hurried after him, but Shakespeare looked round with a smile.

'Don't worry, Richard,' he said. 'I can see that you are right. I made a mistake. I was lowering us into the heart of the work slowly. I'll waste no more time. In truth, it suits me better. There is much to show you. But first, are you hungry?'

He put an arm around Burbage's shoulder as they walked across the room. Burbage couldn't help noticing that he leaned on it more heavily than usual, as if for support.

Taylor had surpassed himself and provided a feast. There were clay pots of warm venison stew, mushroom pies and rook patties, bags of cheese, treacly loaves of heavy-grained bread and thick, rich custards.

Shakespeare had no appetite and wanted air. He carved off a piece of pie and took it out to Andrew, but the watchman – a good sign – was nowhere to be seen. He leaned against a door, and when he closed his eyes he could see the tanned, horror-stricken face of Stanyhurst frozen in consternation like a death-mask. My work is almost done . . . I must not speak of it yet. What on earth did the man mean?

He regretted now that he had left without wrenching out the truth. He disliked secrets and knew that this one would nag him day and night.

Inside, the actors shared a long table. Constance sat with Harvard, nibbling bread.

'I long for fruit,' she said. 'But there's none to be had yet.'

'It will soon be summer,' said a voice behind her. 'Then there'll be pears and cherries, currants and strawberries.'

Constance turned to see Edward Alleyn standing behind her.

'I am especially fond of apples,' she said.

'Then we shall find you some. I came to congratulate you, young madam. That was a fine performance. Very fine indeed. You have the gift.'

There was a shout of mirth from the table at the far end of the room. Burbage was laughing so hard he started coughing.

Alleyn seemed unsure what to say next. He had mislaid his lines.

'And well done to you, young Lackbeard,' he said. 'Your writing is most fair.'

'And fast,' said Constance.

'Thank you, sir.'

'How like you this method?'

'It is very quick,' said Constance. 'And Master Shakespeare – he says the most wonderful things.'

'Indeed,' said Alleyn. 'Though he does borrow lines from his own work, and not all of them are his. That thing about success having many friends, or the one about ambition being a ripple on water . . . I have heard those before.'

'How heavenly, to have such phrases at one's beck and call.'

'Oh, we all speak Shakespeare now. Every time you say that something is time-honoured, or has vanished into thin air, or is the be all and end all . . . every time you glimpse the seamy side or see a shooting star, or summon up the dogs of war: all these are Shakespeare, and countless others besides.'

'Shakespeare and Burbage,' said Constance, glancing. 'They are old friends?'

'The best,' said Alleyn, letting his gaze rest on a dark curl of girlish hair, which gleamed on her pale neck as if wet. 'But all of us go back a long way. Until recently there were only a few score actors in all London. Most of us have known each other for a very long while and have shared a stage together at some point. I myself am proud to boast that I was once Shakespeare's Bottom.'

'His what?'

'His Bottom.'

'I do not understand. What mean you? He sat on you?'

'No,' Alleyn smiled. 'Not his bottom. His Bottom. A character in one of his plays, *A Midsummer Night's Dream* – a very foolish fellow, too. Perhaps you are too young to have heard of it. But as I say: it was an honour to be thus immortalised.'

'I am not so dreadfully young,' said Constance. 'I shall soon be sixteen.'

'Do tell us when. We shall have cakes. Apples and cakes.'

'December,' said the girl. 'I am winter born. Most people give me gloves.'

'A well-thumbed idea,' said Alleyn.

'You were about to say,' said Constance.

'What?'

'About Shakespeare and Burbage.'

'Oh yes. Old friends they are. And rivals too, of course. You know the story?'

'What story?'

'There is a famous tale,' Alleyn began, 'but it is . . . private.'

'How can that be, if everyone knows it?'

'Very well, though you must not think me bawdy. This happened in the old days. They were playing *Richard III*, and Burbage was Richard, the star. He was splendid, everyone agreed. And there was a lady, a great, high-born lady, who came every night to see him. She wore silk. She gazed at Burbage through the long scenes and one night proposed an assignation: that he come to her rooms after the play.'

'She was forward, this lady.'

'Very. But so was the play. There is a scene when Richard seduces a royal widow. It is very strong. This lady would smile at Burbage all the while.'

'What happened?'

'Well, Burbage was as grateful as any man would be who has spent the evening being a king. After the performance he made his way to her apartments. And who should he meet on the stairs, making his way out, but Shakespeare himself!'

'Shakespeare?'

'Oh yes. He too lacked not for admirers, and since he had only a small part – in the play – he had time to beat Burbage to the post.'

'But the lady, didn't she notice?'

'They looked even more alike then than they do now. People have always joked that they could sit for each other's portrait. And the lady hadn't seen them without greasepaint. She thought her man was truly the King.'

'So what happened then? Don't tell me. A duel.'

'Of wit alone, and one-sided. Shakespeare was glad to see the astonishment on his friend's face, and said in a florid manner that it was all very proper, since, as history taught us, William the Conqueror always did come before Richard III.'

'Oh.'

'I am sorry. I have offended you.'

'Not at all. I am not a child. But I confess, I thought that Shakespeare, the great Shakespeare, might have been more noble.'

'He does not lack nobility. But he is only a man.'

'Yes.'

'And yet, something more as well.'

'How so?'

'He marches to a different tune. Oh, most of the time he is no better than anyone else, but every now and then something sets him apart. It is not easy to describe: it is partly his facility with words, but he also goes to bed later, and rises earlier, than the common make. His mind never sleeps. It has planes, facets . . . I know not how to put it. He is not quite like the rest of us. Of course, we have to be careful not to let him know this. He would be unbearable!'

'I know what you mean,' said Constance. 'It is a wonderful thing, his gift.'

'Indeed it is. And most of it flows from one great insight.'

'Only one?'

'One is enough, if it is sufficiently grand.'

He glanced across the room and lowered his voice. Constance had to bow her head to catch his words.

'Shakespeare's idea is simply this: that worms will gnaw on kings and knaves alike. It is so simple that it is easy to forget it. Shakespeare's strength is that he *never* forgets. He abides by this, and never deludes himself. Somehow he sees through and beyond death, and neither laughs nor weeps. It allows him to see life in the round. This is what gives him that far-sighted, other-worldly gaze.'

'There's a line from *Hamlet* my father often repeats. A man may fish with the worm that hath eat of a king, and eat of the fish that hath fed of that worm.'

'Quite so.'

Constance smiled. 'I think he may also be fortunate in his friends.'

Alleyn straightened, as if remembering himself. 'Well, yes, you are right. I have to remind him sometimes that it was I who discovered him.'

'Where? How?'

'As a theatrical force. We – the Admiral's Men – gave him his first chance, with *Henry VI*, oh, two score years ago now. All that water beneath the bridge, and our lives have advanced only as far as the next Henry in the line.'

Shakespeare appeared out of nowhere. 'What are you two smiling about?'

'Oh, I was just explaining how I taught you everything you know.'

Shakespeare smiled at Constance. 'That is true, actually. If it weren't for Ned I would still be stealing horses.'

'I doubt that,' said Constance.

'May I burden you with a task?' said Shakespeare.

'Of course.' Constance sprang to her feet.

'I think you have done enough for today. The best way you can help us now is to undertake some research. Look deeply at the Queen, and the royal children. The next scene is very masculine. There is a fellow downstairs to escort you home.'

'I am not tired. We have bare begun.'

'Nevertheless. Go, and with our thanks. You were magnificent. I salute you.'

Constance smiled at Alleyn, waved to the others and skipped down the stairs. Lowin rose to bid her farewell; the others stayed where they were. Heels tapped on the wooden boards, and then there came the uproar from the street. The door closed behind her and she was gone, leaving the room several degrees less vivid and bright.

'Well,' said Burbage. 'Quite a discovery.'

'Yes,' said Shakespeare.

'Exceptional,' said Alleyn.

'Fair Constance,' said Armin. 'Will, how are we supposed to concentrate?'

'You've said nothing, John,' said Burbage, turning to Lowin.

The man hesitated. 'What can I say? I am all undone by Constance Donne.'

There were several grunts of assent.

'Quite so,' said Taylor. 'I am in love too. Pray do not tell Mrs Taylor.'

'The first Mrs Taylor,' said Armin.

'Enough,' said Shakespeare. 'I am glad she pleases you. And I am sorry I sent her away. It is because I have something I did not wish her to see just yet.'

He let the smiles fade and the silence grow.

'The time has come to reveal more of what I have in mind,' he said. 'That scene was fair, but our play must not be meek. We want a dark deed, something to make the audience chew their lips and fear for their souls. I'll show you. Come.'

He led the way back to the performing space. John Harvard took up his seat at the table, a tense drop of ink hanging from his raised quill pen. Like greyhounds in the slips, Shakespeare thought.

'Let's go,' he said.

Chapter 6

Shakespeare began by asking them whether they remembered Tyrell.

They could not have forgotten. Tyrell was the hireling in *Richard III* who took the King's shilling to murder the Princes in the Tower. It was one of the very first collaborations between Shakespeare and Burbage, and it caused a mighty stir. Two boys smothered in a plaintive, agonising death scene, right up there on stage – all of London was rapt. Burbage had played the warped King with a malign glee that silenced the audience night after night. Shakespeare himself had played Tyrell and still smiled to recall the hectic boos and hisses.

It had taught him a valuable lesson: nothing played half so well as villainy.

Shakespeare took a breath. 'This is what niggles at me,' he said. 'What if Tyrell never performed this deed? What if they lived?'

No one spoke for a moment. Shakespeare let the thought sink in.

'Why not?' said Armin. 'We are gods. We can do as we please.'

'But can we raise the dead?' said Taylor. 'The story is so well known. Can we get away with changing it?'

'Oh, we can convince an audience of anything,' said Shakespeare. 'Don't worry about that. It may even be better this way. Everyone believes that the boys are dead, so it will be even more dramatic when we revive them. In a lightning flash.'

'People may rebel,' said Alleyn. 'They *saw* us kill those boys.'

'More to the point, these are dangerous waters,' said Alleyn. 'If Richard didn't kill the Princes, then who did? And do we really want to rescue that toad?'

'Patience,' said Shakespeare. 'I am still assuming that Richard *did* order the Princes' death – we absolve him of nothing; he remains as wicked as ever. Have no fear: I do not wish to launch another Yorkist plot! But how about this? Tyrell *ignores* the order. Conscience stays his hand. Look . . .'

He held up a copy of Sir Thomas More's *Life of Richard III*.

'We based the death of the Princes on this account. But More, I did not realise until lately, was himself in the employ of the Archbishop of York, who hated Richard and instructed his apprentice to sully the dead King's name. This whole portrait is a stark attempt to glorify Henry Tudor. Listen to what he says about King Richard at the critical time: "I have heard by credible report . . . that after this abominable deede were done, he never hadde quiet in his mind." Do you hear that? "I have heard . . ." He can only repeat what he has been told. A great man, More, but not a reliable witness.'

'Will, this is wild and dangerous talk,' said Alleyn.

'I trust you all.'

'And so you should. None here will betray you. But this is a play! A play, on a stage, with people watching. And you wish to divert them with a tale that will sully the repute of King Henry VII, the founding father of the Tudor house and the grandfather of Queen Elizabeth. I am sorry, Will, I do not know if this can be done.'

The King's Men glanced at each other in silent communication. Shakespeare knew that all of them were feeling the same lancing bolt of doubt. He could almost trace the outline of the phrase threading through their minds: *he has mislaid his wand!* He sensed too that he was running out of chances to persuade them that this idea was not the folly that suddenly, in the light of Alleyn's concerns, it seemed.

He smiled. 'I am sorry to say that it may be worse than you think,' he said. 'My idea is that it wasn't Richard who killed the Princes – it was Henry.'

The silence was almost perfect. Then a stool scraped.

Shakespeare raised a hand. 'Bear with me. Henry had the same motive as Richard – to secure the crown. His own claim was weak, so long as Edward's children lived, but here, right before him, was a great opportunity. Think of Macbeth. Henry had to act at once, and without hesitation. If he struck fast, and without warning, he could blame the blow on Richard. With a single hateful act he could remove his rivals, polish his prestige and give *us* our story: a man who kills for the kingdom, then struggles to conceal the truth. It is provocative, I know. I readily concede that we may not be able to perform it in this witch-hunt atmosphere of fear. But I beg you, at least, to help me write it. If not for us, then for future generations. It may, you see, be true.'

'Some truths are best left untold,' said Taylor.

'Oh, nothing is so dark as ignorance,' said Shakespeare.

'Even talking this way could be suicidal,' said Alleyn. 'Will, the quiet life has made you forgetful, or blind. If the King's people hear of this, they will—'

'Things have not changed, Will,' said Armin. 'If anything they are worse. We are the King's Men in name only. There are spies everywhere. Take that new house of yours – it is a well-known Catholic safe house; they have been watching it for years! That is why we are slinking about here in Spitalfields, is it not? My God: a play that sets out to blacken the name of Henry Tudor. I don't know, Will . . .'

Shakespeare shrugged. In truth, his meeting with Stanyhurst had left him feeling tipsy and light-headed. The Irishman had been even more outspoken than Raleigh, and Shakespeare found himself coveting the airy freedoms that these renegade scholars seemed happy to assume. It surprised him how intensely he envied them their glamorous, dissident roles.

All was not lost, however. He had spoken and the earth had not swallowed him up. He had tested the ground and it had supported his weight.

Only just. His friends were still shaking their heads.

'I can see that this could be great,' said Lowin. 'In theory. What I *can't* see is how we can possibly, in a thousand years, get away with it.'

It took courage for Lowin to speak up in this way. He was not part of the inner circle here. Heads turned in his direction, and he blushed.

'What *I* can see is that we stand to lose our heads,' said Alleyn.

'I think Will knows that.'

Burbage had held his tongue until now, which gave his words extra weight. He glared about him as he rose to his feet.

'I must say I feel,' he said, 'as if introductions may be in order. This man here, in case you have forgotten, is William Shakespeare. All of us know him. No one has ever called him foolish. So I do not think he can have failed to see that this is a grave and serious enterprise. To say, Edward, that we stand to lose our heads – do you honestly believe that this can be news to Will? Nor do I think that he would lightly invite any of us into such a lethal course. I sense, in fine, that he has not told us all. For my part I would, before I leap to judgement, hear the rest.'

Shakespeare could not have wished for a finer defence.

'Thank you, Richard,' he said, sitting down heavily on the nearest bench. 'I am touched by your confidence, and grateful. I have little more to say, save this. No man is a villain by necessity. Even kings have a choice. I wish merely to add Henry to our sequence and see how he measures up. I happen to believe that we could, if we find the right words, be the talk, and the toast, of England – for ever. Imagine: this could be more celebrated than *Julius Caesar*, could win us more acclaim than *Henry V*. I know as well as anyone – perhaps better – that it may prove impossible to mount this play. But only time, which devours all, can answer that with any certainty.'

'It does seem to me,' said Burbage, 'that posterity will not thank us if we let this opportunity pass.'

'Oh, posterity,' said Armin. 'Boo to posterity. Since when did we ever give a fig what future audiences think?'

'You are quite right,' said Shakespeare. 'It is a new sensation for me too. When we began, such thoughts did not enter our minds – and, if they had, we should have shown them the firm underside of a boot. What can I say? Things have changed. I cannot speak for you, dear friends, but it is my heart's desire to plant this seed in the crevices of time and memory, and let it sprout where it may.'

The room was very quiet.

'All I am saying is this: we do not have to make a decision about staging the play until we have finished making it.'

'It is a lot of work . . .' began Taylor.

'I was coming to that. We have a patron. You will not go unpaid.'

He reached under the table and picked up a small wooden casket.

'Our patron wishes to remain in the shadows. But he has been generous. Here are six bags of silver. One each. Mine I will share with John and Constance.'

'I like not this,' Burbage was shaking his head. 'A mysterious patron wants us to risk our necks with a play about Henry VII. This does not sit well.'

'Have no fear,' said Shakespeare. 'This is the money intended for *Henry VIII*. It is the Crown's money. It does not seek to lure us towards the flood.'

He rose to his feet.

'I would not bribe you. You are all great men; none among you weeps at night for want of a bag of silver. My only wish is to set our history straight. In *Richard III* we made Henry Tudor a hero, but it goes heavy with me that I should be the author of a falsehood that may outlive us all. Call it an old man's wish. If you desire no part of it, then leave, right freely, and with my fairest blessings. That is all.'

The actors looked at the empty platters and jugs. Nobody wanted to be the first to waver. If anyone had moved, it might have triggered a general exodus. But the bond between them – their long career together – held firm.

Almost. After a lengthy silence Alleyn cleared his throat.

'You will have to forgive me,' he said. 'But I must, after all, excuse myself.'

'Please,' said Burbage. 'Ned. Stay. We shall be careful. We need you.'

'I am sorry,' said Alleyn. 'Believe me, it is not danger that drives me away. I do not wish . . . I do not like . . . I would not want . . .'

'I understand,' said Shakespeare. 'There is no need to explain.'

Alleyn looked as though he wanted to say more, but the faces of the other men closed around him like flowers on a cold night. And since he was not sure that there was anything to add – his action in leaving being eloquence enough – he walked slowly round the group, shaking hands and saying his farewells.

'It goes without saying,' said Burbage, 'that we count on your discretion.'

'It did go without saying,' said Lowin. 'But you have said it now.'

Alleyn laid a hand on Shakespeare's shoulder.

'If I were ten years younger,' he said, 'I would not balk. But times have changed. My blood is not so easily roused by thoughts of unsettling a king. And I do not like patrons who stay in the shadows.'

'Neither do I,' said Shakespeare.

'I wish you had told him to keep his silver,' said Alleyn. 'I might have done the play for you, Will, but not for some murky lord.'

He turned to face the room.

'Forgive me,' he said. 'Good luck.'

And with one small step he vanished from their sight.

Shakespeare waited to see whether anyone else would move. No one did.

'Well, then,' he said. 'Shall we begin?'

'We may be better off without him,' said Lowin. 'He is not what he was.'

'Have a care, John,' said Burbage. 'He is a better man than I; perhaps than you too.'

Lowin knew he had overstepped. He blushed again.

'I only meant—'

'Why are we so glum?' said Armin. 'We seem to be forgetting what a *feast* this is going to be. Will, it sounds admirable, one of your very best. I admit I was taken aback at first, but now I love it. Who cares what the Chamberlain says? Does he think he can get away with persecuting William Shakespeare? Or Burbage? Come, where is our courage? We are not nobodies. Let 'em rot, I say. You can count on me. Armin, I'm in! And I shan't say no to the silver, neither.'

'Thank you, Robert,' said Shakespeare in a quiet monotone.

'I am staying, too,' said a high, clear voice.

Burbage laughed. 'Good for you, Harvard. You are a lion, a veritable lion.'

Good humour seemed to have returned to the room. Shakespeare let it bubble for a few more moments, then called the actors to order. It

99

was time to show them a little of what he had devised. It might, he knew, change their minds.

'I'll play the King,' he said. 'Joseph, can you be Tyrell? You are in hiding. You have saved the Princes and hidden them. I have tracked you down. You do not know whether you can trust me; you do not even know who I *am*.'

Taylor nodded.

'Ready, John?'

The boy nodded too.

'Enter players,' said Burbage.

Shakespeare pretended to hammer on a door.

'Knock, knock,' he said.

'Who's there?' said Taylor.

'A friend,' said Shakespeare.

'Unhood yourself,' said Taylor, 'and warm your face at my despondent fire.'

Shakespeare mimed an entrance beneath a low beam. 'Good evening, sir,' he said. 'I bring a token of fair friendship from the King.'

Taylor turned his face away and hissed, as if to the front row of an audience, 'What means he by this gift? What would he have that his commandment could not have more cheaply? I fear some stealth in this.'

He rose, offered the King his hand and spoke with all due courtesy.

'Who are you, sir?'

'I called myself a friend, and so I am. Yet I am no mere royal embassy. I am the King himself, and here I come, unarmed, in expectation of your help.'

Taylor kneeled before him: 'Your wishes will be father to my deeds,' he said.

There was laughter from the table.

'Sycophant!' said Armin. 'Dance a jig, why don't you! Lick a boot.'

'Perfect!' said Burbage. 'Good old Tyrell – still a damned buzzard!'

Taylor gave a deep, melodramatic bow.

Shakespeare raised a finger and continued. The two of them batted phrases back and forth for a few lines. The King sought news of the Princes; Tyrell made cagey replies. As the King pushed for information, something like a threatening manner began to enter his speech. Tyrell stuck to his story, however. He didn't know where the boys were – he thought they were dead.

'God's teeth, Tyrell,' said Armin. 'When you strangled them back in *Richard III*, didn't you actually *check*?'

'No, it's well enough,' said Shakespeare. 'That's what he *would* say. He's not about to admit he killed them. Continue. Where were we?'

Tyrell began to weaken. Henry produced a bag of gold. Tyrell, grateful for the opportunity to confess, admitted that conscience had prompted him to spare the boys. 'I would not call myself a good man, sir. Deeds have I done that poison sleep and dreams. But harm those Princes? That I never did. Richard commanded me to end their lives, yet these too disobedient hands rebelled against the thought . . .'

He paused to draw breath. Burbage clapped and nodded. Shakespeare described a circle with his hand, urging Taylor to go on.

'I took the boys,' continued Taylor slowly, as if thinking aloud, 'and lodged them in a wharf along the river. I kept the King's reward, meant for their slaughter. And now I hide, in terror of the wind.'

He kneeled before Shakespeare like a man at confession, or in search of a royal pardon. His manner suggested that he believed himself reprieved. Far from being a murderer, he had saved the royal Princes! Surely he would be a hero, a saviour.

Shakespeare, still frosty, urged him to reveal their whereabouts. Tyrell explained that they were not far from here, just across the water, by the windmill, 'where otters play at sunrise, and swans beguile the breeze that stirs their ruffled necks . . .'

'Not bad,' said Burbage.

It seemed happy, the scene Taylor was describing; the mood was warm. For an instant it seemed that the princely boys *were* the otters, playing innocently on the river bank. Then a cold look fell upon Shakespeare's face. He walked behind the kneeling Tyrell, reached around and, with a dramatic swipe of his arm, pretended to cut his throat.

Taylor was astonished, but his theatrical reflexes were strong. He writhed on the ground in some convincing death throes.

The quill pen scratched and scraped. Burbage and Lowin whistled.

'Great heavens,' said Lowin.

Shakespeare stretched out an arm, helped himself to the bag of gold he had just given Tyrell and made it clear that he had more to say.

'You'll have no need of this, I think, or this,' said Shakespeare, pulling away the purse. 'And none shall miss thee, neither. Traitor, die!' He shoved Taylor with his foot, knocking him to the floor. Then he straightened and looked about him, as if to make sure he was unseen.

'Bit of a soliloquy coming up,' he said. 'Like this. "So wherefore do I quake? How oft my blade has fallen on enemy heads. But that's in battle, not in this cold blood. Oh swans, what have I done?" Sorry, I don't know where swans came from. "Oh Gods, what have I done? Is this what kingship does? My brightest hopes for peace and justice sway, and fall and shatter in the smiling dust." That's not quite right, but the point is that, like every king of this accursed land, he's mired in plots and murthers of his own. In fact, let's work that in: "All mired in plots and murthers of my own. How better must I be than those before? I know not, and am weary, and I fear. There is no peace for kings in lands where men dread not to . . ." Something that rhymes with peace but means kill.'

There was a long silence. No one else moved.

'Decease,' said Armin. 'Cease. Crease. Geese. You're right. It's tricky.'

'It is brilliant,' said Burbage.

'Thank you,' said Shakespeare. 'It'll be better when *you* do it.'

'Oh, but it's good to hear Will on song again,' said Burbage. 'Pure alchemy.'

It was true. Shakespeare did not understand it himself, but some rhythmic uproar in his childhood had tuned his tongue to the tempo of the five-beat line, and it took a conscious effort, sometimes, for him to break it. Only the other day, in Stratford, he had caught himself asking a drover how many sheep a field could hold. 'I wonder, pray, if you might counsel me,' he had begun, before curbing himself.

He was enjoying himself again now, as the old metres rolled off his tongue. Even when he lampooned himself, the rhythms felt alive. And the cold violence in the scene had made his associates sit up. No one could say it lacked bite now.

'But it is impossible, surely,' said Lowin, cutting across the happy mood. 'Alleyn is right. We can't go round showing kings as common cut-throats.'

'Speaking as someone who has just had his throat cut,' said Taylor, 'I have to say he has a point. It is strong stuff, Will. Do you really think we can—?'

Shakespeare pinched a flea from his sleeve between thumb and finger, and held it up to the light for a moment. 'All kings are assassins. Name one monarch who never killed a man. Some – the good ones – have consciences. That is all one can say.'

He turned his head to listen to the roaring in his ears.

Quiet, hissed his inner voice. *You go too far.*

'Look, this is the way we've always worked. Doing the most adventurous, the best things we can think of. If we think any scene unfit for the play, so be it. Remember when we had Henry V running one of his soldiers through with a sword, to stop him fleeing the battle? We wanted to show him stiffening the sinews of his band of brothers; but it was too much, so we dropped it. Let us not clip our wings too soon.'

'I think we can be sure the King will not smile,' said Taylor.

'Impossible to say what will amuse this King,' said Burbage. 'I read his pamphlet against tobacco the other day. Insufferable priggery. And yet he is no Puritan. Did you hear what he said when his counsellors advised him to appear more in public?'

'No,' said Shakespeare. 'What?'

'He said: "I will put down my breeches and they also shall see my arse."'

'Charming.'

'Some would say that is his daintiest feature,' said Armin.

'Don't be fooled,' said Shakespeare to Harvard. 'Robert speaks lovely Latin.'

Lowin was staring at the floor. He looked unhappy. Finally he spoke.

'I am sorry,' he said. 'I wish I could stay to be part of this. But it is too close. My family fought for Henry, and for England. I wish you well, but in all conscience, I cannot make this play.'

No one tried to dissuade him; no one urged him to be discreet. They had no option but to trust him. In truth, no one knew him well enough to plead their cause. They let him go.

'And then there were four,' said Armin.

'I am sorry,' said Shakespeare. 'I should not have asked this of you.'

'And then there were five again,' said a voice at the door.

It was Alleyn.

'Edward!' said Shakespeare.

'You old dog,' said Burbage.

'I must be younger than I thought,' said Alleyn. 'But you are right about the dog. When I left, I felt like a cur that has been strapped. And like that cur, I crept back, tail down. I have been sitting on the stairs and could hear every word – even your more than generous praise, Richard; my thanks! Our late friend Mr Lowin is not wrong: this is the most damnable treachery. But my God, Will! What a conception! How could I think to absent myself from such scenes? I tell you, Richard, sitting on those stairs, it was like being in the gallery. The hairs rose on my neck. So here I am. If you will have me, I will join this endeavour.'

Burbage rested his hand on young John Harvard's shoulder.

'You must be wondering what you have agreed to,' he said.

'I confess,' said the boy, 'I am sometimes not sure which parts are the play. All these exits and entrances. I hardly know what is real.'

'Neither do we, boy,' said Taylor. 'Neither do we.'

'I was moved by you too, young Harvard, and by the girl,' said Alleyn. 'I didn't see how I could abandon ship when you were willing to face the storm.'

'I *said* you were an old dog,' said Burbage.

'By the way,' said Armin. 'No offence, but Will, should Henry really turn into Macbeth quite so soon, haggard with doubts and dreads?'

'It was only an experiment,' said Shakespeare. 'Yet in truth I think he should. It may be a redeeming virtue that he can reflect on his sins. He is our central character – we want him to be a man, not a monster.'

'By the by,' said Alleyn, 'I couldn't help noticing that you gave Tyrell the gold, then cut his throat. That's really why I returned. I feared the assassin's knife.'

'Quick!' said Shakespeare. 'Follow our hireling. Tell him to spare Ned. Tell him the assignment's cancelled.'

He grimaced and showed his teeth when he sat down.

'What's the matter?' said Burbage.

'Nothing,' said Shakespeare. 'This damned back. But you know what they say about pain: a man frets more over a minor scratch on his hand than he does over all the suffering in all the world. The wisest philosopher cannot mend an aching tooth.'

'Quite right too,' said Armin. 'Toothache hurts.'

They laughed, and drank, and laughed again.

Shakespeare took the pages from Harvard to scan them at his leisure, but no one seemed in a hurry to leave, and they munched on into the afternoon. On and on they talked, at peace both with themselves and with each other. Taylor fetched more beer and they shared it out as they discussed the work-in-progress. Although Shakespeare was looking forward to a rest, the enthusiasm of his friends buoyed him up. Armin promised to look into the life of the docks; Alleyn pledged to explore the intrigues at court. Shakespeare could not stop smiling. He loved this part; when the play glittered on the far horizon like a bewitching mirage; when nothing had yet turned out badly; when nothing had proved impossible or long-winded. He had put the King's Men to the test, and they were rising to the task like falcons. All he had to do now was let them go and watch them fly.

Before they parted, Burbage called the group together and issued his instructions. There was nothing more they could do this week. Alleyn had business in Westminster and Taylor was appearing before a magistrate in Holborn – something to do with chickens. Burbage had productions to supervise. They would not meet again until the following Monday.

'We will assemble at Will's house in Blackfriars.'

'How so?' said Armin. 'I thought we were going to lurk in the shadows, like trout sheltering beneath rocks.'

'Ned has arranged that the Chamberlain call on us. We do not want him to hear rumours that we are working behind his back. My information is that he will arrive in the middle of the morning. We must put on a plausible show for him.'

'In the meantime,' said Shakespeare, 'look to your books. I would like to pepper this stew of ours with some genuine spice. We have time. Let us use it.'

He looked at the men standing in a row before him. Their faces shone.

They were his to command.

He prayed, in the old-fashioned way, that he would not let them down.

Chapter 7

One of the things Shakespeare loved about the Globe was the way the scenery could shift in an instant. You only had to drop a curtain and Rome turned into Egypt.

This was one of the beauties of London, too. One moment you could see lordly stone towers brushing the clouds; the next there might be masts rocking on the estuary, or rats nosing in alleyways; now you might see a crowd fleeing a fight, but turn about and there would be a stately procession of clopping cavalry officers.

In the Warwick countryside the seasons crept along with soft, deliberate strides; but here they flickered to and fro like the backcloths in a theatre. In the evening the sky might clear, and soft red light would fall in rosy splashes on the warm wooden frames of the houses; the following morning could easily be cold, flat and grey, as if locked in ice. A man had to be light on his feet and quick with his wits.

He spent the rest of week reading and walking, musing and brooding. He toured the haunts of King Henry VII – in Westminster, Whitehall and Sheen – but as a tribute to his former life he also trudged through his own antique stamping grounds in Shoreditch, Cripplegate and the Clink. It was strange: his past seemed remote to him now – those first tentative steps in theatre at the Rose, the early struggles to make the Chamberlain's Men the best company in the land, the frantic efforts that went into proving himself with *Henry VI*, and the long drinking bouts with the other theatrical wits. It seemed another time, another life, another man. Was it possible that his whole career was nothing more than a preparation for this final drama? He did not know, but for some reason he felt that it might be.

In truth, it did not matter where he wandered, because most of the time he lost in thought. He often worked like this. One half of his preparation involved the discovery of useful knowledge; the other half required him to distil his stories down to their most resonant essentials. It had been on just such a ramble – in the chalk downland of Kent, he remembered – that *Henry IV* had reduced itself to a single theme: the balance of rule and misrule. And it was in the marshy byways out in the Thames estuary that he had glimpsed the conversation about money – the price of this, the value of that – which formed the heartbeat of *The Merchant of Venice*.

This is what he strove for now. He spent his evenings among books and papers, and in the daylight hours he sallied forth and tried to think, as it were, on his feet.

It was the bitter depths of March, almost New Year's Eve, and the clear blue sky was still alive with hints of snowflake and frost. When Sunday came, Shakespeare wrapped himself in his warmest coat before setting out. He had no particular object in mind. He thought he would wander to the church in his old parish of St Helen's and then follow the great easterly sweep of the river to Greenwich.

He was struck, as he passed through his sturdy front door into the yard, by the thrill it gave him to have his own house. All these years in London and he had never, until now, troubled to buy a property. It was partly because the city had become so vile, so scuttling with rats; but it was also connected to his inheritance. He was determined to leave his possessions to his daughters and shuddered to think that Anne might ever be able to pass them on to some new, bounty-seeking husband. But had he known how settled and permanent it felt to own a town house, he would have secured one sooner. In truth, he had never seen himself as more than a fleeting visitor in this city, lodging here and there as a guest or a tenant, never loyal to one particular roof, bed or church. As one century folded into the next, while squalid new buildings overflowed Roman walls, and a king replaced a queen, he continued to feel that his residence was temporary. To put down roots in London would have been to declare that he no longer belonged to Stratford – and this he had never been able to do.

In St Helen's he listened to the readings from the Bible and wondered what had become of that fellow – what was his name: Beckford? Beckingham? Strange that he had not heard from him since that day. Yet he did not dwell on it: there was enough on his plate without having to rise to another task. And maybe it was just because the Latin version was illicit, hunted, suppressed, but in truth there was something about biblical Latin – something to do with smoke, incense and magic – that he felt bound to find wanting in any English version, even his own.

At the bottom of the hill he turned left. The way ahead was crowded and filthy, but he knew that once he crossed the bridge his mind would be able to soar free of his feet. His supple inward personality was his most valued companion, and it spoke most vividly to him when he walked. Today he would liberate it from all other duties: it could fly untethered through time and space, dissolve the flimsy bonds of daily life and take him to those secret, sublime corners of the heavens that few but he could visit. On lucky days – and there had been many in the past – he had been privileged to glimpse, as if from an Olympian height, the boundless, luckless, ever-hopeful travails of this world, as if it truly were no more than a stage. It was in these silver pools of imaginary light that he had seen – almost whole, and in bright flashes of inspiration – *The Merchant of Venice*, *Romeo* and *The Tempest*.

It was sacrilege to wish for such luck today, but you never knew.

There was a cutting wind, he noticed. He pulled a scarf about his neck. He did not mind; if nothing else, it would freeze the stink of the Fleet ditch.

He pushed his way across the bridge and set course for Greenwich, along the southern bank. It would take only a couple of hours – nothing for a man who used to walk thirty miles in a single day. He was soon in open fields, where horses nuzzled reeds and sheep pulled their black hooves from the sticky wet clay. Every now and then a patch of blue sky would pick out the rising buds of crocus and early daffodil, shine on the wet grass and glisten on the birches that lined the track.

On the hill above Greenwich he turned and looked back at the great curve of water beneath his feet, the long panorama of London spread before him on the far shore. It was a spectacular sight: a pulsating arena of towers, turrets, gables and eaves, with boats and carts, horses, cattle, men, women, children and dogs all massing, moving, churning, gathering, spreading and ebbing like the mighty tide itself.

Magnificent as it was, it did not feel like home, and that, he sometimes thought, is what he had been seeking for so long. When he had first left Stratford and his infant family, with the furious cries of the townsfolk dinning in his disbelieving ears, he had thought, misled by the foolish optimism of youth, that he would soon be back – with wealth in his pocket and a tune on his lips. It had not turned out that way. He had fetched up in London like a castaway on a reef and stayed there, hiding among the rocks like a crab, dreaming his dreams and nursing hopes of a homecoming.

Though no one ever remarked on it, he himself was painfully aware that nothing inspired his work so keenly as the idea of shipwrecked souls. He felt helpless – doomed to perform the same scene again and again. In play after play after play, he had conjured storms at sea and thrown characters ashore to survive, as best they could, the violent accidents of fate. Viola and Sebastian beached on the coast of Illyria; Othello driven into a Cyprus harbour by a raging sea; Mark Antony adrift on the currents off Alexandria, ripped loose from his Roman roots; the grieving merchant of Venice marooned on a shrinking spit of debt by the deluge that had drowned his argosies; Lear flailing, like a man fallen overboard, on his thunderous heath; Timon ousted to his filthy Athenian cave; Pericles tossed on the Homeric tides like a cork; Perdita left to fend for herself on the non-existent shores of Bohemia; Prospero driven on to a remote island by his magical tempest. Even Rosalind, in the Forest of Arden, was thrust by banishment into her joyous new realm. And who were his kings if not capsized survivors, adrift and mewing like ships' cats on a sinking spar?

What did it mean, this unceasing taste for evacuees? Shakespeare shrugged. In part it was a mere narrative convenience – a shipwreck was as good a way as any (and quicker than most) of turning someone's life upside down. Yet there was also a more personal motif at work. He did not like to dwell on his own rough expulsion from Stratford; it was ancient history now, and there had been a golden compensation: however bitter, it was his own banishment that had spurred him to conquer the London theatre.

Still, as he strode back along the river, looking across at the tenements of Wapping and Shadwell, it was as if he had grit in his soul. Was it possible that he had done nothing, all these years, except write and rewrite his own sad life story, his own plot of heart-wrenching exile and patient, longed-for return?

Flotsam, he thought, as he picked through the crowds along the Bermondsey wharves. Flotsam. That is all we men are made of, in the end.

On the far shore of the giant waterway stood the high walls and grey ramparts of the Tower, curled around its mound like a reptile. Raleigh would be up in that stone fortress somewhere, shivering like a seaman on a broken ship, his head into the wind, dreaming of maps and monkeys, history and vengeance.

He crossed the bridge and was nearly home, rounding the final corner, when . . . what was that?

Two men in pale leather coats barged around the corner, almost knocking him to the ground. One of them glared at him; the other looked puzzled.

They knew who he was.

The door of his house was open, and there were footsteps on the stairs.

Shakespeare pressed himself flat into the nearest doorway and watched as a tall, bearded man stumbled into the yard.

'Richard!'

'Will?'

'What the devil is going on?'

'Did you see those men?'

'Yes. Who were they?'

'I have no idea.'

Burbage looked up the yard, but the pale coats had vanished. His face was white.

'We'd better go in,' he said.

'But who were they?'

'I told you. I have no idea.'

They walked upstairs. Shakespeare felt unable to breathe: his neat front room had been ransacked. The cabinets and shelves lay upended on the floorboards; books and papers were scattered all over the place. There were muddy boot prints on the linen and blankets, and a pitcher of water had been knocked over.

'I came to tell you about the arrangements for tomorrow,' said Burbage. 'And as soon as they heard my knock they rushed downstairs. I thought they were going to trample me to the ground, but they took pains not to touch me. Strange.'

Shakespeare had to stifle a gasp when he recognised the cause of this uproar. Blood ebbed from his face; there were suggestions of an ache in his ribs.

'Wait a minute,' he said. He hurried into the bedchamber, threw back the heavy lid of a large chest, flung aside some cushions and scarves, and reached in.

'Thank God,' he said. He held up a neat roll of papers.

'Is that what I think it is?' said Burbage.

Shakespeare nodded. He held it up so Burbage could see Harvard's handwriting.

'You really think that's what they were after?'

Shakespeare let out a breath. 'If so, then they didn't look very hard. It could scarcely have been in a more obvious spot. Anyway, it is safe.'

They returned to the front room. The only thing in its rightful place was the table in the centre of the room. Everything on its surface had been swept to the floor except for a single glass ball, which glinted yellow in the centre of the oak. Shakespeare walked over, kicking aside smashed plates, and picked it up.

As soon as he touched it he froze. The connections jolted into place and made him shake. He knew what it was and why it was there. He knew why the man had looked puzzled as he passed. He even knew why they had not touched Burbage.

It was simple. They thought Burbage was Shakespeare.

Shakespeare's mind whirred like a bee's wing. It meant they had orders not to harm him. It meant they had taken some pains to discover what he looked like. It meant that they were not desperadoes but part of an organisation, links in a chain of command. Those pale coats . . . they even wore a uniform.

He put out a hand to steady himself against the table.

'What is it?' said Burbage.

Shakespeare tapped the bead on the table top. It was as hard, cold and yellow as a death threat. Its cold glare put him in mind of lions and seagulls.

'Glass,' he said. 'It is a piece of glass.'

'Yours?'

Shakespeare shook his head.

'What in heaven's name does it mean?'

Shakespeare's face was blank, but his mind darted back to the room at the Tower, to a Flemish rug on a cruel stone floor, to a bowl of angry, glittering glass beads. This was a message, and he could read it well enough. The demon eyeball wanted him to know that he was being watched.

Coke, he thought.

'I could not say,' he said.

It took less than an hour to put the house back in order. The damage was minor, and Burbage was a man used to shunting scenery with one hand.

When it was done they shared a jug of ale, picked at some rye bread with cheese and discussed what had happened. Shakespeare's steward managed to come up with a dish of parsnips and some onions, so the old friends nibbled at those too.

Burbage was not able, and Shakespeare was not willing, to shed new light on the intrusion, so they did not have a great deal to say to one another. But Burbage insisted, and Shakespeare agreed, that it was an outrage.

'I say we raise the roof about this.'

'I agree. It would be odd if we did not.'

'I mean, who do they think they are?'

'They probably know who they are. We, alas, are the ones who do not.'

'Well, hang them, I say.'

Burbage was into his third glass, and his spirits were lifting like smoke from a fire.

'Oh,' he said. 'We have an appointment. The Chamberlain is coming to see us.'

Shakespeare frowned.

'Don't worry. It is Ned's idea, and he is quite right. The Chamberlain comes at *our* invitation, to hear news of your new play, *Henry VIII.*'

'Perhaps,' Shakespeare looked mournfully into the bottom of his cup, 'that really is the play we should be writing.' Ever since meeting Stanyhurst, he had been inclining to the view that Henry VII was a reasonable man; it was his son who offered melodrama.

'Never!'

Burbage's vehemence made Shakespeare sit up.

'Come, Will. Remember yourself! Are we really going to let a royal blunderbuss frighten us so easily? This bears out everything you said. It is high time someone brought these meddlesome monarchs to account. And since we lack expertise in the martial skills, this is a dragon we shall have to slay with mere words. Not just any words, fortunately – *your* words. Let us to it! What do you say, Will?'

Shakespeare looked at Burbage. He was ashamed of his own faint heart, and took no pleasure in his failure to be truthful with his oldest friend. Perhaps he should tell him everything. He was asking his dearest companions to sail into a hurricane; the least he could do was give them a map.

Soon, he told himself. Soon.

'Very well,' he said.

'And I have told everyone that since we are all gathered together, with nothing to hide, we might as well do a scene or two.'

'What should we say about . . . all this?'

Burbage looked surprised. 'What should we *not* say?'

'You are right, as always. I just thought . . . We don't want anyone to worry.'

'About what?'

Shakespeare put his head in his hands.

'I'll be honest, Richard. I don't know. I am shocked, I suppose. Forgive me.'

'Until tomorrow, then,' said Burbage.

His tread on the stairs was heavy and unbalanced. Once or twice he put a hand to the wall. He did not know where Will got his ale, but it was a stout brew.

The following day, Shakespeare encouraged Alleyn to explain once again why a visit from the Master of the Revels – the Chamberlain – was so necessary.

'It is a strange situation,' Alleyn said. 'This new Chamberlain is, to speak plainly, a simpleton, but do not be fooled: he is only a messenger. Sterner eyes than his will oversee our work. Nevertheless, we must have either his support or his enmity, and I know which I prefer.'

The actors nodded. It was straightforward politics to flatter the man.

'Just be sure to control yourself. I don't know when you last saw him, but his vowels skid more dangerously than ever. Whatever you do, don't laugh.'

'Have no fear,' said Burbage. 'We'll cut a proper garden path for him.'

Shakespeare tried to prevent his mind wandering, but the image of the men in pale coats could not easily be persuaded to fade. There was something so triumphant and careless in the half-smile of the second figure . . . Shakespeare had not slept well, and it had left him red-eyed and weak. He forced himself to pay attention.

'What is it you are waving there, Ned?' said Armin.

'A golf club,' said Alleyn.

'A what?'

'A club. It propels a ball towards a distant hole. There is a new field at Blackheath – I am a patron. It is great sport; the ball veritably whistles.'

'I believe I saw it once,' said Burbage. 'It is billiards, but out of doors.'

'It is a Scottish game,' said Alleyn, 'and well fitted for the King's Men.'

'It sounds hard,' said Armin. 'But I suppose someone must carry the coals.'

The thought of a shining ball made Shakespeare twitch like a deer at the crack of a branch. He could almost hear the clink of a wine goblet on Coke's jewelled finger.

There were three sharp knocks on the outer door.

'Andrew,' said Taylor. 'Whatever did we do without him?'

The Chamberlain swished into the house in a flurry of ermine and velvet. He seemed to feel the occasion called for full formal wear; he was only a trumpet short of his full regalia. Since his body was an almost perfect sphere, he resembled a scarlet bauble.

Outside, dark clouds hung over the cold, damp rooftops and gables. Snow fell like sieved flour, cooling the streets, hushing the hawkers and hucksters in the riverside alleys. Even the church bells were faint. London life felt stilled, almost suspended.

The house looked immaculate; no one would have suspected that clumsy boots had kicked it apart the previous day. And Taylor had provided a table piled high with the usual treats from the early-morning markets. It would soon be Lent, when the authorities would frown on meat, so there was plenty of beef and mutton.

The mound of flesh made Shakespeare feel queasy; he desired nothing more than fresh water and a handful of nuts. Even Burbage could not persuade him.

'Come on, Will. You are eating like a bird. Have some of this stew.'

Shakespeare smiled and shook his head. He had lost all enthusiasm for the groaning larder and this morning especially he was impatient to press on. He also wanted to get rid of the Chamberlain as soon as possible, though he allowed no trace of this wish to infect his voice.

'I am glad to have this opportunity,' he said, recalling his guest's weakness for orotund speech, 'to seek the advice of one who enjoys, I know, the King's perfect confidence. The work we propose may seem to court controversy, but I hope that we might, today, settle any anxieties you may harbour.'

Burbage smiled. Shakespeare was a magnificent chameleon. Chain him to a slave and he would talk like a vagrant; usher him in to see the Pope and he would bow like a baronet. He did it without thinking.

'I am,' said the Chamberlain, 'all ears.'

There was a shout and Robert Armin appeared at the door. 'Sorry,' he began. 'I was at St Paul's, and thought—' He broke off when he saw the Chamberlain. 'I apologise. I forgot you had visitors.'

'We are honoured,' said Shakespeare with a smile, 'to be entertaining the Lord Chamberlain. I was just telling him about our new play. Have a seat.'

'Oh, yes. Our play.' Armin sat down.

'It is a history, sire,' said Shakespeare, turning back to his guest. 'And the subject is a great one, as you know. We thank you for entrusting us with the times of King Henry VIII.'

He paused. The Chamberlain was not known for the speed of his thoughts, and he looked as if he might be trying to speak; his mouth was moving.

Shakespeare held up a hand.

'We understand all too well that this could be, in the wrong hands, a keen and treacherous tale. A king with so many queens. Allow us to set your mind at rest.'

'There is nothing yet written,' said Alleyn, 'but it will be a royal romance, and a patriotic one: we will put on stage a king who stands for England, and for love. He's a suitor and a warrior. He is fighting for the freedom to wed his beloved.'

'And bed her,' said Burbage.

'He needed no Pope's permission for that,' said Alleyn.

'We will end,' said Shakespeare, 'with the arrival of a new star in the firmament. The birth of Elizabeth, our future Queen.'

'A happy ending, then,' said the Chamberlain. 'I lake the sound of it. You say you have no lanes to show?'

'None, my lord, but we thought we would open with a simple Chorus, rather like the one in *Henry V*. Do you remember? It is a most useful device in these large new theatres: it gives people time to settle. Richard?'

Burbage assumed a heroic pose.

'I come no more to make you laugh,' he boomed. 'The time doth wear a grave and serious brow, sad, high and working, full of state and woe, while we with noble scenes must draw the eyes of these our rare and undishonoured guests . . .'

Even in a casual setting, Burbage was able to invest his voice with strong emotions. The Chamberlain clapped his hand on the arm of his chair.

'Oh, most worthy. A grieve and sarious brow. Most illoquent of praylogues. I lake it much.'

Shakespeare gave a small cough.

'If I may fill you in, my lord. We have two nobles, let us say Lincoln and Suffolk—'

'Those suns of glory,' said Burbage. 'Those two lights of men.'

'They mention Cardinal Wolsey . . .'

'I wonder,' said Burbage, suppressing a smile, 'that such a keech can with his very bulk take up the rays of the beneficial sun and keep it from the earth—'

'Keech?' said the Chamberlain.

'I expect he made it up,' said Shakespeare. 'But 'tis good, a bold word.'

'Indeed. Very bold. What does it mean?'

'These dukes are politic. They know it is dangerous to speak out.'

Burbage rose to the challenge. 'Heat not a furnace for your foes so hot that it do singe yourself. We may outrun, and lose by overrunning, that which with violent swiftness we run at.'

'Thou run'st too fast for me,' said the Chamberlain. 'But forsooth, it is well put!'

'You like it?' said Shakespeare.

'Lake it? Lake it? Of course I lake it.'

Shakespeare held out a plate of sugar sops – bread soaked in syrup – and offered one to the Chamberlain, who picked out two.

'This may interest you,' Alleyn said. 'Did you know that the hearing into King Henry's Great Matter was held just across the ditch there, at Bridewell Palace?'

A puzzled look washed over the Chamberlain's face.

'Of course he knew that,' said Shakespeare with a smile.

With Burbage's help he ran through the rest of the tale. Wolsey schemed with the Pope, Catherine wailed sad songs on a lute; and Henry married Bullen. Wolsey fell, Cranmer rose, England broke with Rome, and all roads led to Elizabeth.

When it was done, Shakespeare took one small bite out of a stewed fig to drown the bad taste. He did not like painting pretty pictures of such a disgraceful episode.

There was only one more matter to discuss.

'We have your blessing to proceed?'

The Chamberlain bit into another sop, his eyes wide in appreciation.

'My blessing? Of course. Proceed! But who shall play Bullen? Young Richard?'

He was referring to Richard Robinson, a fine-featured apprentice who had won many admirers for his fetching performance in Dekker's *The Converted Courtesan*.

'I fear,' said Shakespeare, 'that his pipe may be cracked. But there are plenty of other . . . gifted boys. We shall see.'

'Very well. I wish you God speed,' said the Chamberlain, climbing to his feet. 'I will leave you to the fire curse of tame.'

Half a dozen years of banquets had taken their toll; he had eaten too many swans for a man of his modest height. Alleyn drew back the chair for him.

'Before I go,' said the Chamberlain. 'I wonder if you'd take a look—'

He produced a package of papers from beneath his robe.

Shakespeare opened it and read the words on the front.

'*The Lion of Albion*. What is it – a play?'

'I hardly dare call it one. But should it please your eye, maybe . . .'

Something in Shakespeare clamped shut, but duty called.

'I'll have a look.'

He even produced a warm smile.

'You are too kind.'

The carriage door slammed, and with a metallic clatter the Chamberlain was gone.

Shakespeare's shoulders slumped.

'Farewell, Monsieur Chamberpot,' he said. 'Thank God that's over.'

Armin joined him at the door, grinning.

'Magnificent,' he said. 'What a woven tongue is there!'

'You *like* him?'

'We'll need a clown. And one who mangles words like that. I lake it not! Quayte!'

'Fair enough,' said Shakespeare. 'Now I did ask Fletcher today. As you know, we want *him* to write *Henry VIII*. One thing: I don't propose to tell him the truth.'

'He may not care,' said Burbage. 'Have you not heard his news?'

'The grapevine bears very dry fruit these days. I know nothing.'

'He is sad. Beaumont is to be married, and is quitting their rooms.'

'Married? But I thought the two of them shared food, cloaks, all.'

'They did, Will. That is why he is melancholy.'

'Well, this work shall keep him warm.'

'These are pretty good, these sops,' said Alleyn.

'Should be,' said Taylor. 'They cost a fortune. Sugar is twenty shillings a pound, the baker said, and going up fast. There's a shortage, apparently. Sorry, Will – hope you don't mind.'

'Toss one over,' said Armin, 'before they all go. Will?'

'Thank you, no.'

There was the sound of wheels below. Shakespeare looked out of the window and saw Constance being carried over the gutter towards the house by a tall, fair man wearing a short purple cloak. His heart snagged on an imaginary scent: apples, honey, spring grass and some sweet, rare spice – vanilla. He felt his chest constrict.

Soon everyone was helping themselves.

'Try these,' said Taylor. He held up dishes of smoked pork and herring, a plate of hot oatcakes, roasted nuts and the stewed figs Shakespeare had tasted. 'Oh look,' he said, holding up the jug. 'It is chipped. What happened?'

Shakespeare glanced at Burbage.

'Oh, a bit of an accident yesterday,' he said. 'Couple of chaps came looking for me, knocked it over.'

'Clumsy brutes. I know a potter in Wapping who can fix it, if you like.'

'That would be kind.'

Shakespeare turned to Harvard, who was eyeing the sugared rolls. 'Have as many as you like. Build yourself up. You'll need your strength in the days to come.'

Shakespeare had a clear idea concerning the overall shape of the play – he had discerned it in the clouds over Greenwich – but he knew better than to impose it now. He had learned long ago that things went better if everyone had their say.

'Now,' he said, when everyone was ready. 'What have we found? Richard?'

'Seems to me,' said Burbage, 'that Henry was a relatively good king, all in all. Single-minded, hard-working, a careful diplomat, a peace-maker – something of a bore, if anything. He made a lot of smart marriages for his children, all for the sake of the alliance. The main point seems to be that he left a well-endowed throne for Henry VIII.'

'True,' said Alleyn. 'A throne padded with gold.'

'It is a pleasing idea,' said Burbage. 'A king who sincerely *tries* to be good—'

'And fails,' said Shakespeare. 'Go on.'

Alleyn finished a mouthful. 'Henry VIII had this pair of wonder-fully sinister advisers, Empson and Dudley. They were tax collectors, and they were ruthless.'

'Why am I not surprised?'

'Empson was actually the son of a sievemaker. But he himself was a sieve through which nothing passed. The man was pitiless. Citizens could be fined for having too many windows, or too few; for using too much salt, or too little. If they cut hedges too short, or failed to cut them: any excuse would do.'

'That's all to the good,' said Shakespeare.

'And then there was Morton,' said Burbage.

Shakespeare grinned. 'With his famous fork.'

'While I remember,' said Alleyn, 'he made the Tudor rose – the red and white folded together. When he married the Yorkist Elizabeth, that became the royal emblem.'

'He understood the power of symbols,' said Shakespeare.

'When you are done with the King,' said Armin, 'I do have ideas on the low-life.'

Shakespeare held up a hand. 'In a minute. Joseph?'

'There's this description by a Venetian ambassador,' said Taylor. 'All very flattering. The King could speak Latin and French, even had a Latin scholar at court. Only thing against him is his miserly streak. Mad for money. Ended up sleeping with his coffers of gold and silver. We can have fun with that, I should say.'

'Indeed,' said Shakespeare, rummaging in a leather bag. 'Have you seen this? It is Polydore Vergil. Here . . . "His mind was brave and resolute and never, even at the moment of greatest danger, deserted him. But all his virtues were obscured latterly by avarice . . ." Now Vergil was loyal, so we can assume that this description actually flattered the King.'

'Did I see,' said Burbage, 'that he was the first king to put his head on a coin?'

'Yes,' said Shakespeare. 'As we have seen: strong on symbols.'

'And a great lover of animals, by all accounts – was always buying lions and leopards from the Portuguese. Built a menagerie for them in the Tower.'

'I like that,' said Shakespeare. Thoughts of the Tower merged with the memory of Bridewell and inspired a brief vision of Richard Stanyhurst waiting at the top of the stairs, dressed like a bruised plum, head tilted. His eyes swam. Raleigh, Coke, Stanyhurst, the men in pale coats, the Chamberlain, the King's Men, Constance . . . there were too many people trying to storm the ramparts of his mind. He felt unsteady.

'It might be good to set a scene at Bridewell too,' said Taylor.

Even in a haze of confusion, Shakespeare missed little.

'Not possible,' he said. 'Bridewell was built by Henry VIII. It didn't exist in his father's day.'

Armin giggled. 'We could put it in anyway. As a jest. See if anyone noticed.'

'I think I know what is coming,' said Shakespeare.

'Yes,' said Burbage. 'It could be another coast of Bohemia.'

The King's Men had been much mocked for imagining, in *The Winter's Tale*, that Bohemia had a coast on which the lost child, Perdita, had been cast ashore.

Shakespeare put an end to this by fetching himself a drink and draining it. When he turned he was himself again. 'So. Anything more about the King's love of money? It would be useful to have details. We know he made sure his son had plenty to waste.'

'Will!' said Alleyn.

'Sorry. I thought the Chamberlain had left.'

'Even so. Take care. It isn't safe to speak like that.'

'The chief thing about all this,' said Shakespeare, 'is that we can do something significant with the period here. Usually we neglect this—the plays are called Histories, but in truth care little for history. Our subject has always been the theatre of leadership – the way kings don robes like actors getting into costume, the way they play a part. This could be different. It was a remarkable time. Ships were heading off to the New World, and England was a modern state, not a playground for bickering barons. The wounds of the civil wars were still bleeding.'

'An ideal setting, I agree,' said Burbage.

'And some things never change,' said Alleyn.

'I'm liking this,' said Armin. 'A great big story, full of ceremony.'

'But moving,' said Taylor. 'With a plain man at the centre. The thing that strikes *me* most about Henry is his childhood. Hard, hard, hard. His family was scattered by war, and he fled to Brittany for fourteen years – half a lifetime! He was part Welsh, part French, and when he defeated the King at Bosworth and took the crown, well . . . he must have wondered what on earth he had got himself into.'

'Something else happened early in his reign,' said Harvard, eyes bright. 'But excuse me, it is not my place.'

'No, indeed it is,' said Shakespeare. 'What happened?'

'I've been reading about printing. And it was at this time that Caxton set up his press in London. He learned the craft in Cologne and brought it to Westminster. For the first time, people could read books and—'

'Wonderful!' said Burbage with a guffaw. 'Oyez! Oyez! Today we present, on stage – people reading books! By God, that will bring in the crowds.'

'Don't mock,' said Shakespeare. 'That is a good idea, John. Don't mind him. I agree: we could use Caxton and Vergil as commentators – rather like the Chorus that Richard produced for the Chamberlain. But

I think we need a scene at court first, to show the King going about his business, dispensing judgments and so on. Not a king at war, for once, but a king at peace.'

'A king at work,' said Armin. 'That is certainly something new!'

'Shall we?' said Shakespeare.

With Burbage's help he sketched out a scene in which the first Tudor appointed Polydore Vergil as official court historian and told him what to say about Richard III. It was simple but effective. At the end, however, Burbage just guffawed.

His laugh had a way of making a room shake. As Sir Toby Belch he had made the rafters shudder; now the cups and plates trembled at the resonance in his voice.

'Very good,' he said. 'People reading books! A king signing papers! People will faint, I tell you. They'll faint!'

His rollicking mirth drained the room of all subsidiary sounds.

In the quiet that followed, Shakespeare spoke. 'Would it help,' he said, 'if I ran through our story again?'

A murmur of agreement trickled around the gathering.

'I see it as *Henry VI* meets *Hamlet*.'

'Good Lord,' said Burbage.

'Sorry. But we want the contrast. The grand sweep of history, but with reflective turmoil as well. The outward show is easy: a new king consolidates power by marrying his enemies and eliminating his rivals. He puts down rebels, imposes laws and taxes . . . invents modern England, more or less. The second strand is more private. We will see an intelligent general become a jaded miser; we will see what kingship costs. We will give him soliloquies, to reveal the doubts behind the confident display.

'The third strand is everything else: the period; the explorers, printers, poets, ambassadors and moneylenders. The war between York and Lancaster was a family feud, but we can present Henry's England as more than a wrangle between dukes.

'That's roughly it. We can toss in everything: plots, battles, ghosts, love stories. I want this to be a compendium of everything we can do.'

'I think we can stand Andrew down, then,' said Burbage. 'I can't see anyone objecting to this.'

Shakespeare glanced at his old friend. It was obvious that something had nettled him. Did he sense that Shakespeare knew more than he had confided about the assault on his house the previous day? He would have to reassure him about that.

'One thing we need,' said Armin, 'is a way to weave those strands together. The life of the docks has to tie in with the royal world some- how.'

'Absolutely,' said Shakespeare.

'Are we still going with the idea that Henry himself kills the Princes?' said Taylor.

'Very much so.'

'Maybe that could be the link. If the Princes are hiding in the docks, Henry would have to descend from his throne—'

'A little touch of Harry in the night—'

'Exactly.'

Shakespeare paused to let a thought settle, like a bird in a tree.

'And also,' he said, 'we must take care that once the King has killed the Princes, he is haunted by the deed. Usually we have the spirits of murdered souls returning in dreams and visions. Maybe this time we should simply have the King meeting a couple of boys – he thinks them ghosts, though they be but plain lads.'

'Excellent,' said Armin.

Constance Donne raised her hand. Everyone looked at her.

'Yes?' Shakespeare said.

'It may not be my place to say it, but I don't see a great deal here that pertains to me. Are there to be no ladies in this story?'

'Whom would you like,' said Alleyn, 'apart from Elizabeth, the Queen?'

'In my reading,' said Constance, and she did not sound abashed to be addressing so senior a group, 'it struck me that something could be done with the figure of Margaret, the Lancastrian queen in exile who in *Richard III* vowed vengeance on the King. Why don't we have her launching pretenders at Henry's crown?'

Burbage laughed and rose to his feet.

'Mistress Donne,' said Taylor, 'you embarrass our greatest tragedian.'

'I am never embarrassed,' said Shakespeare, 'by good ideas – only by poor ones. Thank you, Constance. Margaret must play her part. She can be vivid – a banshee shrieking vengeance. But she also stands as an emblem of the old days, the feuding days, the days Henry wants to leave behind.'

'And best of all,' said Burbage, 'what a part for Ned!'

'You are laughing at me,' said Constance, not sounding especially hurt.

'Not at all,' said Burbage. 'Dear girl, I applaud you.'

'I can tell you one thing,' said Shakespeare. 'If this is the same Margaret that hurled curses against the King in *Richard III*, then we *do* have another Bohemian moment. This Margaret was the wife of Henry VI, his queen. She died three years before Bosworth, before Richard's reign even. We didn't worry about that when we made the drama, we plucked her from the grave to play her part. Can we really revive her once more for further scheming?'

'Why not?' said Armin.

'What think you, Edward?' said Shakespeare. 'How sits this plot with you?'

'I wish I did not like it,' said Alleyn, 'for I still consider this a barrel of powder that may yet blow off our heads. But how can I resist? I was an actor once, like you.'

'You're still an actor, Ned,' said Burbage. 'You have been playing a Distinguished Man of the Theatre for years now.'

'And I, an undistinguished one,' said Armin.

'Modesty,' said Burbage. 'The true insignia of the scoundrel.'

'One problem,' said Shakespeare, 'is that this Margaret had no reason to hate Henry Tudor. She was herself of the Lancastrian party. She was exiled in France, or Flanders, or somewhere, but she was no Yorkist plotter. She railed against Richard, remember.'

There was a silence. The actors looked at each other. Then they laughed.

Shakespeare looked perplexed.

'I'm sorry, Will,' said Burbage. 'It's just that – well, she's *dead*. It is somewhat idle to worry that she is ill-suited for the role in smaller ways.'

Shakespeare smiled.

'Very well,' he said. 'We will cast Margaret as the Yorkist menace, until such time as we can find a more honest enemy.'

'Speaking of which,' said Taylor, 'could we have some of that oatcake before it gets cold? And is there any wine? I'm sick of that thin beer.'

'Let us pause,' said Shakespeare. 'Thank you, everyone. Help yourselves to anything. Where the devil is Fletcher, by the way?'

While the company broke for more food, Shakespeare sat down beside Constance. For a reason he could not name, her shy smile made him sad.

'Tell me,' he said, 'how is your father? The last time I saw him he said he was still weak from the stomach colic he caught in Paris.'

'He is much improved, thank you,' said Constance. 'When last we spoke, I fear he was still of the view that the theatre was an unfit place for civilised men.'

'He is not a playgoer?'

'He is not. I, however, have enthusiasm enough for both of us.'

'I am very glad to hear it.'

'He is in Wales at present, visiting Sir Edward Herbert.'

'His patron?'

'His friend.'

'He travels a good deal, your father. It must pain you, losing him for so long.'

'As it must pain *your* family when you are in London.'

Shakespeare tried to smile, but could not. This was a delicate topic.

Constance hurried on, 'In truth, we manage quite well without him. Last year we went to the Isle of Wight and remained there for the whole long summer – the happiest, I dare say, of my life.'

'You liked the green countryside? You liked the sea?'

'Oh yes. In Mitcham we had little room, but on the Isle of Wight we had gardens to play in, and fields, and cliffs. I rode a mule and read poetry. It was not so good for Mother. She suffered a . . . gave birth to a . . . had a child who died.'

'I am sorry.'

'And now we are back in London. Almost together.'

'Your father is a great man, and a rare one. He married for love.'

'According to him, that is why he is so poor.'

'How are your lodgings? How is Drury Lane?'

'Very fine, thank you. My father is planning to enter the Church. But my mother is sick again, and abed. So I am very glad to be busy with this work. I cannot thank you enough for permitting me to join your troupe.'

'It is we who are fortunate to have you,' said Shakespeare. He felt a contraction in his heart. It was faint and muffled, an echo or memory of desire – he could hardly ignore the dark ringlet of hair on the girl's slender neck, or the silkiness of her cheek – fringed with something fonder, almost paternal.

It was a strange and new sensation. He had once enjoyed the idea that there were only two ways to evade Time's scythe: a man could re-create himself in children, or in eternal verse. His sonnets harped on this theme too much, perhaps, but in Constance he saw bright flashes of both these things. It made his head spin.

It had been a long while since he had felt such a tremor, and he permitted himself a smile. A long time ago he had, in a fit of angry self-knowledge, described lust as perjured, murderous, bloody, full of blame, savage, extreme, rude, cruel, not to trust. Now it felt, to his surprise, winsome and sad: like a warm kind of melancholy.

He shook his head to dispel the thought. 'And what think you of our play? We have made a beginning and soon shall have need of you. Your remarks about Margaret were perfect: I salute you. But I also have in mind a romance between a princess and a common man, maybe an explorer. Would that please you?'

Constance smiled. 'I think I should not mind, if he is handsome.'

'We do not yet know who he is. A navigator, maybe.'

'I can well imagine a princess delighting in intercourse with such a man. The court must resemble a prison, sometimes.'

'That is a common theme. Think on it. We'll try it whenever you are willing.'

'I shall be ready next time we meet. Tomorrow, if necessary. I have read most of the books you advised. I think I am getting a sense of the time.'

'Good,' said Shakespeare. 'Excellent.' He hesitated. 'Forgive me, but I must ask this. I have no wish to pry, but – the carriage that delivered you here—'

'Yes,' said Constance. 'It was most exciting. I felt like a proper lady.'

'But . . .' Shakespeare's tongue fumbled for the right word. 'The young man . . .'

It was Constance's turn to blush.

'Oh,' she said. 'He is not a *young man* in that way. That was Lord James Hay, a great favourite of the King's. He had some business with my mother, I know not what. He was delighted to offer me a place in his carriage.'

Shakespeare was startled. Lord Hay was one of the King's intimates. Another thought burst upon him. Could it be that the King himself wanted first-hand reports on Shakespeare's movements?

'Kind of him,' he said.

'Oh, my mother practically insisted. I don't think he dared refuse.'

Shakespeare was relieved. 'She sounds formidable, your mother.'

'It takes a brave man to deny her anything.'

Shakespeare hesitated.

'It is none of my affair,' he said, not sure he wanted to hear the answer to the question forming on his lips. 'It is just that . . . it is a matter of . . . confidence. We do not wish the world to know what engages us here. You understand?'

'Naturally,' said Constance. 'That is why I informed him that I was calling upon my brother's tutor. I don't believe it occurred to him to doubt me.'

'You are wise beyond your years,' said Shakespeare.

'I have years enough for some degree of wisdom to be expected, surely.'

'Of course,' said Shakespeare. 'Of course.'

He wished he had not broached the subject. He felt foolish, clumsy and old; and Constance seemed, in contrast, to have moved into some remote, mysterious realm of glowing smiles, pale skin and cool wit to which he had no access. He did not reproach himself for finding her so alluring: how could he? If I could write the beauty of your eyes. Feminine lustre was the most transient and fleeting light in this transient and fleeting world, measuring itself in months rather than years. Constance was as pure as honeysuckle on a dew-bright May morning, but she would all too soon be assaulted by the ugly poxes, fluxes, rashes and boils that squatted on life in this verminous city. In a year or two her bloom, a haunting marriage of peach and roses, would be overlaid by pitted skin, pondwater breath, blackened teeth and the weeping lesions of adulthood. Women like Constance truly did seem angels to men such as Shakespeare; the awe and rapturous yearnings they inspired was all the more intense for the certainty that it was rare and would not last.

He was amazed to find himself still capable of this sort of baffled tenderness. No man knew better than he that love was a blind fool, yet here he was, trembling like the fondest youth. What had Rosalind said: that men have died from time to time, and worms have eaten them, but not for love? This still struck him as an obvious truth, but he was aware equally that even truth could stutter and quail before beauty.

He smiled. The fact was, he did not know whether to treat Constance as a woman, a child, a colleague or a servant. All he could say was that she made his blood race.

Sometimes, he sighed, he knew nothing about human nature at all.

Chapter 8

$\mathcal{S}$hakespeare hadn't forgotten Armin's desire to have fun with the Chamberlain's tipsy intonation, so when they regrouped he said that their main task now was to improvise a scene at the docks, with common men grumbling about the state of the nation as well as their stomachs. If Armin could create a memorable clown – and it would be a shock if he could not – then the play would have a lively new dimension.

'I am thinking of Falstaff, and the chatter in the Boar's Head tavern.'

'I don't suppose Falstaff could be still alive,' said Alleyn. 'One of your greatest characters – still brings a tear to my fond eye. Sweet Jack Falstaff, kind Jack Falstaff, true Jack Falstaff, valiant Jack Falstaff . . . Banish plump Jack, and banish all the world.'

'His death was too memorable, alas,' said Taylor. 'Though *I* suppose, if we can bring those Princes back to life . . .'

'So long as I'm not a gravedigger,' said Armin. 'Once was enough.'

'You could always be a porter again. Many porters along these wharves.'

'No. Kempe's was definitive. Never again.'

'Strange, what happened with our Porter,' said Shakespeare. 'I don't think any of us liked that scene at first, did we? I mean, the man does nothing but open the door when Macduff arrives, and scratch his jewels a bit – but people just fell about.'

'That's right,' said Burbage. 'So we added that sycophantic stuff about equivocators – all quite superfluous. Yet still people loved the man.'

'Our old friend, the breathing space,' said Alleyn. 'A cushion for the nervous.'

Shakespeare smiled at the memory. 'Everyone enjoys a good grumble, but it taught us a valuable lesson. There are certain moments in plays that don't have to *be* funny; they just have to *sound* funny.'

'The main thing was that the King liked it,' said Burbage.

'So I should hope. Its only purpose was to tip scorn on Catholic plotters.'

Shakespeare frowned. Here was another thread to the whip with which he was lashing himself. An awful lot of *Macbeth* had been designed to flatter King James. The play had shown little respect for – even interest in – historical accuracy.

'I was thinking,' said Burbage, getting back to business, 'about the King and his menagerie. Perhaps we could use zookeepers. The animals were right there at the Tower. The keepers would be in a good position to see the King coming and going all the time, and they might make good, trenchant gossips.'

'I happen to know,' said Armin, 'that he especially favoured the flying squirrels from Virginia.'

Maps and monkeys, thought Shakespeare. Seize the world's most beautiful winged creatures and cage them in a cold, stinking castle.

He wondered whether Raleigh knew of this and could imagine his reaction to such news. 'What can you say about a fat-tongued King who thus despoils lands named for a great Virgin Queen?' Shakespeare found himself hoping that if they ever did establish a new province, someone would think of calling it Raleigh.

He smiled. 'I happen to know,' he said, 'that the King had no such beasts.'

'How so? I have it on good authority.'

'Then your good authority must also know that the New World had not yet been reached. Virginia did not exist – not for another hundred years. Unless those squirrels flew all the way across the ocean—'

Armin shook his head. 'I'll kill that damned tapster,' he said.

'I am sure he is a fine fellow,' said Shakespeare. 'But for now let's just call them citizens. What we want is a sense of unease, of ill winds blowing in uncertain times.'

Armin was not finished. 'This could be the time to mimic the Chamberlain.'

'There won't be a better one,' said Shakespeare. 'Have at him. But before we get to that, can we just spend one more moment on the King? I have been thinking . . .'

He paused, as the recent uproar in his own life welled up and flowed into the now-familiar figure of King Henry VII. It was wonderful to be able to lose himself again in an imaginary tale, even one peopled with an authentic past. Here, perhaps, was his true home. Yet it was not a comfortable one: never before had he cared for a character in this emotional way. The men and women in his plays were slaves, not friends; they did as he commanded. But now he throbbed with a stirring affinity for this king – so much so that his mouth felt feverish and dry. Like Henry VII, he himself felt beset by powerful enemies lumbering into position over the brow of a hill. Like the King, he began to sense pretenders, claimants and spies behind every arras. The fears that he felt in his own home – he wanted Henry to feel them too.

It mattered not that the King's motives were honest. Henry might well have hoped to rule wisely, not just fatten himself on the blood of his subjects. Good intentions led him down alleys every bit as dark as the ones haunted by his greedy ancestors.

There was no escaping it. Kingship gouged the soul of all who entered into it. And the loneliness! Shakespeare looked at the expectant faces of his friends, waiting – with expressions beginning to show concern – for him to beat the path ahead. There was much he had not told them, much that he had not shared, although that too was part of the burden. Writers wore no crowns, but if they did, they would be as hollow, as bloodstained and as heavy as a king's.

The thought made the muscles of his back twitch and pinch. 'How all occasions do inform against me,' he murmured, allowing his own quiet words to lift him like a sip of honey. Almost at once the welcome warmth of fresh resolution seeped through his veins. He would not be brooked. Coke could not be permitted to instal himself as the author of England's history: like any usurper, he had to be beaten off with clear eyes and, if necessary, valour. And since the only weapon of Shakespeare's revenge was this play, nothing could be allowed to check or hinder its advance. King Henry VII would have to obey his commands and beat back the rival claimants to his authority.

'I am sorry,' he said. 'On second thoughts, I think we should let the King be for a while. He is weary – let him woo his wife. We will to the docks once more.'

'As it happens,' said Alleyn, 'I had an idea about that.'

'Help,' said Taylor. 'There's something amiss with Edward!'

'No, really. I was thinking of this as I dined in Deptford the other day.'

'Deptford? What were you doing in Deptford?'

'Never mind. Raising a glass to Marlowe. And it reminded me that this was the time of the great ocean explorers. And I thought: why don't we include our own Columbus – Cabot?'

'Why didn't I think of that?' said Shakespeare, smiling at Constance.

'Giovanni Caboto. John Cabot. From Genoa or Venice, one or the other. He was seeking funds. Columbus was claiming Hispaniola for Spain, and Cabot offered to do the same for England. Actually he didn't care who claimed it – he just wanted someone to buy him a ship. He was a dashing navigator. A pretty situation, don't you think?'

'It sounds good,' said Burbage.

'So long as I don't have to do any actual sailing,' said Taylor. 'I hate boats.'

'I think he was from Venice,' said Alleyn.

'Weren't they all?' said Armin.

'How is it you know all this?' said Burbage. 'Have you been financing ships on the quiet? Own up: it was you who saw off the Armada, wasn't it?'

'Ned was too heartsick to set sail,' said Armin. 'Still furious about losing that game of bowls to El Draco.'

'I didn't lose,' said Alleyn. 'I let him win. There's a difference.'

'Very funny,' said Shakespeare. 'But time is short. Shall we?'

'It's called reading,' said Alleyn. 'A pattern of inkmarks on a page. Nothing to it.'

'Actually, this is good timing,' said Taylor. 'I heard the other day that a true English child has been born in Newfoundland, in Canada.'

'An omen,' said Shakespeare.

'Why don't I start?' said Burbage.

'Please.'

Burbage sat on a stool, legs spread like a quarryman, and waved a non-existent pot of ale in front of his face. In a single tremble of an eyelid they were in a tavern.

'There is a sickness so invades the air,' he declared, 'and so infects the kingdom, some believe a pestilential vapour has o'erthrown our strength. Thousands lie dead. The King has fled to Guildford, so they say, and I do sweat and shiver in the chill.'

Shakespeare knocked his knuckles on the bench and interrupted.

'I know,' he said. 'And I have heard of strange events in Kent, of hail-stones big as horseshoes that did plunge in the bat-benighted sky . . .'

There was a burst of laughter.

'Bat-benighted!' said Burbage. 'For crying out loud, Will.'

'You don't like it?'

'It's *awful.*'

'All right. How about . . . horseshoes . . . that did plunge in steeple-chasing sky . . .'

'Steeple-chasing?' said Taylor. 'Sounds wild. What does it mean?'

'I was thinking of the way clouds swarm around church spires on a stormy day.'

'Good. Like horses leaping.'

'Let's stop interrupting,' said Alleyn. 'Carry on.'

'Actually, I've got something,' said Taylor.

'Go,' said Shakespeare.

'And keen reports there are that comets lie abandoned in the heav-ens. When great men fall, the wheel that crushes them . . .'

'Not bad,' said Shakespeare. 'But why not try *wild* reports? And *extinguished* instead of abandoned. But . . . good. Not sure about for-tune's wheel, if I'm honest.'

'I think it still pulls its weight. And people expect it.'

'Fortune's ladder . . . Fortune's top . . . Fortune's dice . . . Fortune's lottery.'

'All good,' said Armin, 'but why reinvent the wheel?'

'Hah.'

There was a cough behind the table. Shakespeare turned to see Harvard drinking some water.

'Are you getting all this, John?'

'Most of it, sir.'

'Enjoying yourself?'

'Yes, sir.'

'No need to call me sir. Master will do well enough.'

'Yes, Master.'

'John, I was joking. Will will do.'

'Very good, Will, sir.'

'As in the saying,' said Burbage, 'where there's a will, Anne hath a way.'

Shakespeare glanced at Constance and felt a pang to see her smile.

'A very old saying,' he said. 'Too old, some say, to be repeated.'

In truth he was thrilled by the bantering rhythm the group had achieved. There were times, out on the river, when oarsmen swung in unison, and a boat could feel light and swift as a greyhound. So it was with the King's Men when they were dancing to the same tune. Nothing seemed impossible; phrase tripped after phrase like children skipping through a meadow. At times like this he felt that he could lean back, melt into the scenery and simply let them go.

Taylor wanted the citizens to reminisce about Bosworth and soon they were comparing tall stories. It took an hour or more – there were false starts, odd digressions and a few blatant dead ends – but slowly the scene took shape. Armin adopted the Plymouth accent of a sailor, sounding uncannily like Raleigh as he whispered that the *real* Richmond had been killed during the battle. Burbage disputed this, assuming the voice of a tinker to declare that he himself was on Ambien Hill when cruel Richard swooped from above.

'It would be a fine king who swooped from below,' said Shakespeare.

'That may be,' said Burbage. 'But I was there. I saw him, sword in hand.'

Alleyn became a foolish soothsayer, and Taylor impersonated a baker who said, behind his hand, that the new king ate like a horse, but by swallowing brimstone would void his stomach – all for the pleasure of filling it again.

'A king who gorges and ungorges. We are fortunate subjects,' said Shakespeare. It was time to move on. 'But let us away. Strange sunsets have there been, and heavy dew. All is not well, when monarchs play the fool.'

Constance Donne was the only person to clap, but her excited palms made a rapid crackle in the warm room.

'Do you always do it like this?' she said.

'It's the only way,' said Alleyn, placing his hand – Shakespeare flinched to see – on her slim shoulder. 'But don't be fooled. The real work happens later on, when Will here takes these ideas and writes them up. That's where the magic lies.'

Constance turned her gaze on Shakespeare with eyes, it seemed to him, as soft and mild as a foal's.

He almost stammered. 'He's too kind. I've got the best handwriting, that's all.'

'I wouldn't be too sure of that,' said Taylor. 'Look at this.'

He was peering at the lines scratched out by John Harvard. They were composed in a beautiful, roomy, cursive script.

'This is almost a fair copy,' he said. 'It looks perfect.'

'Then I am out of a job,' said Shakespeare, careful not to look at Constance, 'and will have to find another occupation.'

'I don't know about making it better,' said Constance. 'It sounded marvellous just as it was.'

'It won't really come alive,' said Alleyn with a gallant bow, 'until we encounter such queens and princesses as you can provide—'

'Tomorrow,' said Shakespeare.

'I am not sure I can seem a princess,' said Constance.

'If you do lack a virtue,' said Shakespeare, 'simply act as if you have it, and it may grow on you. It is one of the great secrets of theatre . . . Wear the costume of the role you seek and it shall be yours.'

'He means: dress for the part,' said Armin.

'More than that. Wear the right dress and *become* the part,' said Shakespeare.

'In that case I shall find a new gown.'

'Your gown is perfect. True costume comes from within.'

'Actually, you were talking earlier,' said Constance, changing the subject away from herself, 'about a scene where a lady of the court meets the explorer, Cabot.'

'Yes.' Shakespeare tugged at an earlobe.

'Well, Henry had no sisters, but the Queen did. One of them was called Catherine. Maybe she—'

Shakespeare groaned. 'I have always hated the name Catherine.'

'The patron saint of wheels,' said Burbage. 'Often considered unlucky.'

'We could call her something else,' said Alleyn. 'What is your mother's name?'

'Mine?' said Constance. 'Anne. In fact, that might even be the name of the Queen's other sister.'

'How about Anne, then?'

'I like Anne,' Shakespeare's head came up. 'Anne is good.'

'Capital,' said Alleyn. 'You be Anne. I can be Cabot. I *am* half Italian, you know.'

'And half Scottish, half English, half French and half Spanish,' said Burbage.

'Then he is twice the man I took him for,' said Constance.

'Touché,' said Taylor.

'But never half-hearted,' said Alleyn.

'Robert,' said Shakespeare, frowning, 'want to have a go at that clown now?'

'I was hoping you would ask,' said Armin. 'I am thinking of someone a bit like Dogberry, with perhaps a sprig of Chamberlain thrown in.'

'He'll need an accomplice,' said Taylor. 'A fishmonger or some such.'

'Why not a butcher,' said Burbage, 'since we want him to slaughter words.'

'We could call him Bacon,' said Taylor.

Shakespeare blinked at a memory: The earth spins, and nothing goes unpunished.

'Ouch,' said Alleyn. 'Sir Francis will be thrilled.'

'Perhaps not,' said Constance.

The whole room turned and looked at her.

'I'm sorry,' she said. 'I should not have spoken. But I know Sir Francis Bacon. Our patron, Sir Robert Drury, is married to his niece.'

'And what has your father done to earn his patronage?' said Taylor.

'He helps him with his papers,' said Constance. 'And letters. Courtiers have to write many letters, and poor Sir Robert can barely write a word.'

'And your father can?' said Alleyn.

'Oh yes,' said Constance. 'The most beautiful poems. You might know them. *Songs and Sonnets. An Anatomy of the World.*'

'Great heavens, Ned,' said Armin. 'She is John Donne's daughter! Did you not realise? I love the *Anatomy* dearly, though 'tis a sad story.'

'Is that the one about the girl who died?'

'That's the one. She whose rich eyes perfumed the East. She, she is dead; she's dead; when thou know'st this, Thou know'st how lame a cripple this world is. It is absolutely damned wonderful.'

'The girl who died,' said Constance in a quiet voice, 'was Elizabeth Drury, daughter of our patron. She was fifteen, and her death followed hard upon the death of her sister Dorothy. Some say she died of a broken heart. She loved a groom on the country estate, but he shot himself in an accident. The parents have been drunk with grief ever since. I sometimes think they keep us in their household just to have people in it. Sir Robert took my father with him to Italy last year.'

Someone cleared his throat.

'I am sorry, but where were we?' said Shakespeare.

'No, I'm sorry,' said Constance.

'No, *I'm* sorry,' said Alleyn – for what exactly, no one could guess.

'No need to apologise,' said Shakespeare. 'But we do have work before us.'

'We were auditioning buffoons,' said Burbage. 'And it reminds me that once, in Banbury, I met a town crier. And do you know, he could not read.'

There was a smatter of laughter.

'That is all very well,' said Armin, 'but it's one of those true stories that sounds quite *un*true on the stage.'

'Fair enough,' said Shakespeare. 'However, if this Bacon is as great a fool as I think you intend him to be, he would be easily gulled. The crier could feign ignorance of the words, to have the pleasure of hearing Bacon foul his lines.'

'That could work.'

'Well then,' said Shakespeare. 'Want to start?'

'You set the scene. I'll be Bacon.'

Shakespeare nodded.

Behind his back, Alleyn put a hand on Constance's shoulder. When she turned her head, her neck curved like a shy swan's.

'Watch,' he murmured. 'These two are pretty good at this.'

Harvard dipped his quill into the jar of ink and waited, hand poised.

'It is night,' said Shakespeare. 'There are torches. We are in a courtyard before a tavern. We can see water and sails behind. A town crier enters and prepares to read a paper. But here comes Bacon, a butcher.'

Armin adopted a superior air and began. As quick as fish flicking between rocks, they nipped at each other's lines. Eventually Shakespeare's crier admitted he could not read.

'Piglet's eyes!' said Armin. 'A crier that cannot read? 'Tis like a butcher without a knife. Give it to me. "The King, to all to whom, et cetera." What means this nonsense?'

Burbage stood up to interrupt. 'What have you got there, Robert?'

'A pamphlet,' said Armin. 'It is the actual proclamation honouring Cabot.'

'That is quite a find. Can we put in a chunk of it?'

'If you would just sit down . . .'

'Oh. Good.'

'Here goes.' He read the announcement in an urgent, high-speed rattle. '"Greetings! Be it known and made manifest that we have given and granted as by these presents we give and grant, for us and our heirs, to our well beloved John Cabot, citizen of Venice, and to Lewis, Sebastian and Sancio, sons of the said John, and to the heirs and deputies of them, and of any one of them . . ." By God we have a wordy king.'

'Indeed. But who is this citizen of Venice? A merchant?'

'I once saw a play of that name. A very dull piece.'

'As dull as the ear it played to.'

'List . . .'

On and on they went, carving through the past like silver ploughshares on a chalk down, lifting the soil and drawing wriggling life into the sunlight.

Eventually they began to wind down.

'Speak to me more of this Venetian!' said Shakespeare.

'Cabot? I lake him not.'

'You know him not.'

'I lake not what I know not.'

'And if ye . . . *laketh* . . . what ye knoweth, then . . . *laketh* you all parts of the pig?'

'A straunge quistion. The pig, sir, is of all creatures the most deciduous.'

And with that Armin turned on his heel and marched gravely away, like an archbishop engaged in a solemn mass.

Shakespeare held a hand out as if he really did carry a bell. With a final, slight swing of his wrist, like the leader of a musical troupe, he announced the end of the scene with a sweet closing passage – concluding, as he liked to do, with a moral about the way kings suck wealth from the furthest corners of their wide domain.

'And so the world stands upside down, when all its treasure trickles uphill.'

This time the applause was louder, and more sustained. Shakespeare put a finger to his lips, but inwardly he smiled: the play was coming to life.

'I never saw,' said Constance, 'a clown with so quick a tongue.'

'Best mend thy words, my lady, lest the fool deliver thee a licking.'

Constance flushed.

'I am sorry,' said Armin. 'But a man must be a scholar to play the fool.'

'Robert is no fool,' said Alleyn. 'He has written plays of his own, and they are not all awful. *The Two Maids of Moor-Clacke . . . A Nest of Ninnies.* I was nearly in one once, though good sense prevailed in the end.'

'A shame,' said Armin. 'You would have made a perfect Ninny.'

'John,' said Shakespeare, ignoring this exchange, 'while you have that pen in your hand, can you take this down? I think we should give that free-for-all a semblance of order, and boil it down to just three citizens, or zookeepers, or whoever they are . . . They should have clear personalities from the start. The first is a spreader of rumour, quick to pass news. The second is less easily swayed, more sensible. And the third is scurrilous, a mischief-maker.'

'A gossip, a bore and a wag,' said Burbage. 'A pretty group.'

'Poor Bacon,' said Armin. 'I fear they will fry him proper.'

'I must say, I feel sorry for him,' said Constance. 'The citizens are cruel, yet they are not so very much wiser than he.'

Shakespeare slapped his knee. 'That is exactly right. Let us not mock the poor man too roundly. So majestic a fool could not swim long in such company.'

'Perhaps all his wit went into butchery,' said Taylor.

'Or perhaps he was not always a butcher,' said Shakespeare. 'Maybe he has sunk in the world, like so many men we know . . . like Raleigh. I met a man at the theatre the other day, selling brandy. In Elizabeth's day he was a Master of Horse, owner of a fine holding in Kent, but under our gracious new King he has lost everything – house, lands and all his treasure.'

Burbage sighed. 'Poor fellow. How so, a recusant?'

'The only author of his downfall was error. His name, Catesbury, so resembled the name of one of the Westminster plotters that he was undone by a simple mistake. Ill luck is mischievous. It flies in unannounced and sometimes will not depart.'

Alleyn was nodding. 'Bacon as a fallen soul – I like it. It will echo with today's citizens, who know well that fortunes can sink more swiftly than stones.'

'And fortune toys with fools just as it plays with kings,' said Armin.

'Jeer at him all you like, for now,' said Shakespeare. 'But the time will come when we must take pity on poor Bacon. He was not always thus. Life has played him false, left him ill fitted to his place and scrambled his wits. And where he goes, there, but for the grace of God, go all of them.'

'Not to mention . . . all of us,' said Constance.

'Bravely said. What think you, John?'

'I like this Cabot,' said Harvard. 'I have never seen the sea.'

Shakespeare smiled.

'We shall show it you when we are done,' said Taylor.

'I should like that.'

'Maybe you too will sail off into the west,' said Alleyn.

'I don't know about that. I cannot swim.'

'No need,' said Armin. 'Take the boat.'

'Well then,' said Shakespeare. For an hour or more he had hardly been aware of the pain in his back. Now he gasped as it juddered up his spine. He gathered himself fast, however, so none but Burbage noticed the ashen shadow that crept over his face and tightened his smile.

'A word about the arrangements for next time,' said Burbage. 'Some of us have a busy week, but we shall meet on Friday, at the sign of the Greyhound, in Cheapside. There is an upstairs room at our disposal. Our host believes we are having a reunion and could not be restrained from providing vittles. So please bring your appetite.'

'What time?' said Taylor.

'Prudence insists that we take turns to arrive. The world does not need to see the group massing. Will and I will be there at eight. The rest should arrive separately, every ten minutes. Andrew will be there to keep an eye on things.'

'Does everyone have a dial?' said Alleyn.

'Mine never works,' said Armin.

'Then thy dial goes not true,' said Shakespeare, 'You mistake larks for buntings.'

'I'll manage somehow.'

'I would like,' added Shakespeare, 'to work up a scene at Henry's court. The King surrounded by his advisers. Affairs of state. Noises off.'

'And our princess?' said Alleyn.

'We shall need her too,' said Shakespeare. He was beginning to sound weary. 'So let us do a scene in which the King seeks to pacify his angry new Queen. And Ned, if you do want to do something with that brave sea captain of yours, then go to it.'

The King's Men clattered down the stairs. Shakespeare lowered himself into a chair and beckoned Burbage to sit beside him.

'What have you got there?' he said.

'It's for you.'

Burbage held up a strong leather pouch with a shoulder strap. 'For the pages.'

Shakespeare rubbed the leather with his hand and smelled it.

'Perfect,' he said. 'Still no sign of Fletcher, I suppose.'

'No.'

'I've been thinking about Lowin.'

'And?'

'I don't blame him for leaving. He's not like us. He's young. You and I, we have age and fame to keep us from harm.'

'Speak for yourself. I am a merry gallant of forty-four years.'

'And I shall soon be fifty,' said Shakespeare. 'It is the strangest feeling, Richard, to feel that your life is behind you. Even the stage is not what once it was.'

'How could it be? When we were young, it was young too. We were the first. Remember that night we moved The Theatre?'

'As if it was yesterday. The men's faces glowing in the torchlight. The guards shaking their heads. The scrape of saws and the pounding of mallets, the curses in the dark. It could hardly be done now.'

'There is no need. The Globe is ours.'

'Yea, the great Globe itself. A world upon a stage, and all for us.'

'I like what you did with Bacon,' said Burbage. 'Typical of you to find dignity in the life of a prating fool.'

'I cannot help it. Fortune plays with butchers just as it does with kings. And laughing at the misfortunes of others – that is a vicious sport, is it not?'

'Indeed.'

'We have been favoured by fate, have we not? We survived the turning of the world – we prospered! It troubles me that I might endanger that.'

'All of us know,' said Burbage, 'that if we have prospered it is largely because *your* plays sustained us in the warm light of the King's favour.'

'But I was politic in those days. I was a diplomat. Now . . .'

'You have earned the right to speak your mind.'

'I have earned the right to folly, then.'

'Something else struck me during that scene.'

'I am sorry to hear it.'

'It was when you and Robert were clowning. I thought of what you have said about posterity, and the future, and could not help imagining how it would be if someone, one day far into the future, wrote a play about *us*.'

'I think not.'

'You never know. The time might come when plays have no need for kings and queens, when the adventures of common men might do for an hour's amusement. And suppose that we put some players into our *Henry VII*, to perform a masque or something. It would be strange, would it not?'

'Ah,' said Shakespeare. 'A play within a play within a play.'

'A world of mirrors, up to nature held.'

'And all the men and women merely players.'

'Exactly.'

'And all the more lifelike for that. Each of us acts out a life. A king on his privy is a man like any other, though he must perform royally in other fields.'

There was a silence.

'What were you saying about Lowin?' said Burbage eventually.

'Oh yes,' said Shakespeare. 'Only this. Shall we offer him *Henry VIII*?'

'The play?'

'The part.'

'Oh. I see.'

'I know you think it should be yours,' said Shakespeare. 'But you can be Henry VII – a better man by far – if our play turns out to be possible. We need to keep John in our party, don't you think? He's not a bad fellow, but even good men talk.'

'How about this?' said Burbage. 'If *Henry VII* goes ahead, so be it. If not, he and I can share Henry VIII. I would not like to miss out on such a part altogether.'

'Dearest Richard, I should not want you to.'

'To show Lowin we bear him no ill will, we should do it right away.'

'We should.'

'I shall send word.'

'And if you see Fletcher, tell *him* that if he doesn't reply we'll ask Middleton.'

'That'll wake him up.'

'Poor Fletcher. But good for Beaumont. Who has he married?'

'No idea. It was all very rushed and secretive. She has money, I believe.'

'Much joy may it bring her.'

Burbage didn't answer. He poured ginger wine into a beaker and took the last of the sugar sops to dip into it.

'Can I ask you something, Will?' he said.

'Anything.'

'I still feel you are holding something back. I mean, today was wonderful. The play is alive – it has lungs. But there's more, isn't there?'

'What makes you think so?'

'I go along with everything you say about the history – setting the record right. But you are animated by more personal feelings, I can tell.'

'If a king had such a counsellor,' said Shakespeare, 'he would be well advised. What can I tell you?'

'The truth?'

'Ah, the truth,' said Shakespeare. 'The truth is that I feel the pulse of real tragedy in this story. And it lies in a fiery arena – the arena of faith. You and I are one on this, old friend. It moves me that Henry, with his fondness for astrologers, clung to the old faith. He left a grand kingdom for his son to squander, and when that fat cuckoo had spent all the money he raided the Church. And for what? Lust and vanity, vanity and lust.

'You are wise to worry, Richard. Our play *is* dangerous. Not for the barbs it aims at Henry VII, but for the scorn in which it holds his son. Henry the Ape. This is why we must work fast, and close. This can be the story of Eden before the Fall.'

Burbage looked at the floor. 'Will,' he said, 'are you sure about this?'

'I have no choice,' said Shakespeare.

'It is a risk.'

'Danger's a nettle that must sometimes be seized,' said Shakespeare. 'We pledged, did we not, to let our imaginations roam? This play will out, Richard. It is inside me, pressing to escape. I think of it as a message in a glass, tossed into the brawling ocean of time. Who knows on which rough coast, or in which fair city, it will land. But it must, at least, be written – I am most certain of this.'

'You sound like a man at the gaming table who imagines he wants to win, but knows that the likely outcome is irreparable loss. Losing is his dream.'

'That is deep, Richard. I know that the truth can be painful. I am no martyr.'

'So I should hope. When are you going to tell the others? They may not wish to join this – I know not what to call it – this counter-reformation.'

'Soon. I want them intrigued first.'

'They are.'

'I know.'

'Damn it, Will. It isn't just us. We are old men; we can look out for ourselves. What about Harvard? And Constance? They are young, Will, and will do whatever you ask. You are risking their necks with this.'

'I know.'

'Then—'

'Richard, I can't argue. There is nothing you can say that I do not think already. I have no wish to deceive anyone. But the truth, which is what you asked for, is this: if no one will help me, I will write the play alone. I have to.'

Shakespeare looked, Burbage thought, as pale and tired as he had ever seen him. A dark thought flew across his mind like the shadow of a bird. His old friend seemed to have abandoned the usual ambitions entirely. He was being driven by something more profound than a commission, a licence to divert, a purse. He was engaged on some more necessary level – almost as if he were writing an elegy for himself. He spoke as if this were the last throw of the dice; he seemed compelled to undertake this final act. Burbage actually found himself wondering whether the man was dying.

'How is your back?' he asked.

'It will bear up,' said Shakespeare. 'The odd twinge. Needs rest, that's all.'

'I shall see you at the Greyhound, if not before.'

'That's right. Eight o'clock.'

For an instant Shakespeare almost blurted out another truth – that his back had been injured during that scuffle in the Tower. But he hauled on the reins of his own candour. They had exchanged more than enough truths for one day.

'I wonder if we aren't overdoing the secrecy,' he said. 'It is a known fact that we are at work; it might make it worse if people think we have anything to hide.'

'True,' said Burbage. 'But we should avoid becoming a spectacle before we are ready. And we do want peace and quiet. Remember what it was like with *Timon*, out in the open like that? It was like working in a barracks.'

'Good point. I sometimes think that's why the play is so furious.'

Outside it was growing dark and the temperature was falling towards freezing. Burbage was surprised, on leaving Shakespeare's house, to find the streets alive with fires, flares and merriment. It was rare to see people out after dusk, but this was a carnival. Chestnuts roasted on braziers; a juggler threw wooden stakes in wild circles; songs echoed among the half-timbers, and people danced around flames. It was, he remembered, the great spring festival of New Year's Eve. For a moment he was tempted to rouse Shakespeare for a seasonal feast. But he decided to leave the man in peace.

What did they have to celebrate? They were embarked on a lonely voyage into *terra incognita*. Who could say when, or even if, they would return?

Chapter
9

*T*hat night, Shakespeare propped himself on silk cushions and read Holinshed by lantern-light until his eyes hurt – he no longer had to endure the sour and smoky tallow that lit his nights in earlier days; he could afford beeswax – then slept like a rock, unperturbed by any of his usual dreams. He had an imagination that rarely rested; his nights swarmed with hags, demons, witches, ghosts, dragons, spirits and other spectres. In recent times, feeling himself to be on the outer limits of his life expectancy, he had been more than usually troubled. The weird sisters who nagged at Macbeth cackled through his own reveries, and the ghoulish father who begged Hamlet for vengeance was as familiar to him as his own shadow.

Had there been ghosts in his sleep, they might have looked like Richard Stanyhurst and Edmund Campion, sorrowful Catholic veterans haunting a blinded world. However, this time nothing stirred the mirror-calm surface of his slumber. For a few brief hours he was entirely inert and when he woke it was with a bewildered jolt. He felt empty, placid and even-keeled – most unlike himself.

The week passed slowly: he was impatient for Friday. He had a number of duties to perform: there was paperwork and financial administration to be done on the house; there were meetings with printers and theatrical supplicants; there was even a midday feast in Whitehall – the Earl of Rutland was hosting a banquet. One day had to be spent with Fletcher, running over the outline of *Henry VIII*, urging him to examine the original Holinshed, not the corrupt, censored second edition. But Shakespeare could keep only half a mind – perhaps less – on this subject. Thoughts of the fat King's father kept drifting to the surface, like casks from a sinking ship.

When Friday came he hurried through his routine and was soon marching along Thames Street, past the high walls of Baynard's Castle and down to the noisy fruit wharf at Queenhithe. When he turned left up to Cheapside he quickened his stride. He hadn't visited the Greyhound for years. Would it still be the hot, merry tavern where he had spent so many long evenings in the old days?

Far downriver he caught a glimpse of the high turrets of the Tower and wondered whether Sir Walter Raleigh would have begun his day. Probably he had been up for hours, Shakespeare thought – experimenting with his water filter and tobacco plants, plotting courses on charts, writing ancient history, dreaming of gold and making ink drawings of the view from his pavement. What kind of world was it in which a man like that was penned away in a pitiless gaol, with only enemies for friends?

He would visit again. But not yet. Coke would surely see it as a provocation and he could not afford to draw undue attention to himself until the play was done.

He was approaching the crossroads at St Mary-le-Bow when he had to stop: the way ahead was choked by sheep. It would not have been hard to wade through the bleating animals, but Shakespeare treated himself to a pause. There was nothing strange about the sight of livestock on London's roads – the city's meat arrived at Smithfield on foot – and it was clear from the curses of the drovers and the laughter of the onlookers that these two flocks had collided at the junction of two alleys. Both had the same – or a similar – blue daub on the left haunch, and while the drovers needed no brand to tell their sheep apart, since they knew them all by sight, the animals were flowing together too smoothly and too fast for anyone else to keep track of them.

There were several incurious cows dawdling behind, trying to graze on the vegetable rubbish in the gutter. Shakespeare sensed a brief clamour in his imagination. Dumb beasts: they had no inkling what lay in wait for them at Smithfield, where butchers ground knives on stone wheels, and cats loitered to scavenge on warm offal. How far had they come? Just the other day he had heard talk of calves that had trudged all the way from Wales in order to provide fresh veal chops for a London dining vault. Not for the first time he felt like the author of their lives; at any rate, he knew their future. It was a familiar sensation: the characters he propelled through the action of his plays never guessed what lay ahead. They nuzzled forward as blind as moles, to meet fates already assigned by a power beyond their conception. Theatre, he thought, inspired a dangerous arrogance. He had juggled with the lives of kings for too long; how could he not feel them to be dim, minor figures who knew not what they did, as they stumbled towards their violent ends like bleating lambs?

One more time, he told himself. Once more into that famous breach.

He did not look away when he saw the ragged, pustular beggars hunched against the wall, too exhausted and ill fed to move. London was as full of poverty as it was of wealth, and Shakespeare had never been able to banish either one from his field of vision. He glanced at the hideous new houses on the smart side of the street: garish brown-and-white monsters, giant toys, at once grandiose and infantile.

As he approached, he heard whimpers of pain. One of the vagrants had been chained to a cart and he was kneeling, head down in the dirt, shaking with misery and pain. His back was a scarlet patchwork of whip strokes.

Shakespeare sighed. In recent times there had been some relaxation of the stinging laws against vagabondage, but in practice these unhappy wretches could be seized, beaten and branded with irons at will. It was not just. As he often said: both the rich and the poor believed that God was on their side – but only the rich had proof.

He reached down, slid a penny into the man's shoe and backed away.

The view of London made him feel bloated and almost glad it was time to renounce meat. There were laws against the eating of flesh in Lent, but exemptions were cheap and he often threw a few shillings into the poor box in exchange for a bishop's licence. This was primarily (he told himself) to provide for his carnivorous guests; for his own part, the prospect of austerity was quite pleasing. There was work to be done and a full belly, he knew, was the enemy of inventive thought.

When a path opened between the sheep, Shakespeare, along with a few others, took an optimistic stride forward. A couple of swollen ewes dashed into the gap, though, and soon the road was again a mélange of wailing wool and drumming hooves.

He decided to take another route. But as he turned something in the background scenery jarred. The thronging sheep had attracted a number of amused spectators and one of them was discordant, out of place. It wasn't easy to say why: he was too scruffy, or too neat; too dirty, or too clean. Either he held himself with more delicacy than his clothes required, or his costume was too suave for his physique. While he could not be sure, Shakespeare had done enough poaching in his youth, stealing through the Warwickshire forest at night, to detect the dissonance at once.

It made him shudder, but he had no need to examine his unease in detail. It was as clear and mysterious as the sudden flight of a bird, the quivering tail of a squirrel or the flared nostrils of a deer. It might have been nothing more than that the man's hat and beard seemed unmatched: it didn't matter. Whatever it was, it fell upon Shakespeare as clearly as the mute thump of a cracked bell.

His first instinct was to smile. People had been following him for years, nudging one another as he passed. The theatre had created a celebrated new class of elite people for whom there was not yet a word – celebrities, perhaps; they were commoners, but well enough known to attract curious, admiring or envious glances from the general public. Shakespeare was not as discomfited as most people would have been. He was used to it. Sometimes he could almost hear them whispering.

There goes Shakespeare!

Who?

The playwright! You know: 'If music be the food of love, play on.'

Oh, I thought that was Jonson.

Even Shakespeare was sometimes able to forget that not everyone shared his own devotion to the theatre. He could barely imagine a life not ruled by staged events. As a result, he was not too intimidated by this stranger. London was full of people who might recognise a famous playwright. It meant nothing.

His second thought was less confident. Memories of Sir Edward Coke and the men in pale coats clutched at his heart. He could not ignore this.

The leather bag, he thought – a succulent target for any cutpurse. He wrapped his elbow around it and squeezed.

The man was taking ostentatious care to look the other way – a clear mark against him. Shakespeare sensed a burly body in these fine clothes and noticed a flash of neat gingery beard above the dowdy scarf. And on the man's feet: strong, costly leather boots. There could be no doubt – these were the boots of a soldier.

Implications barged through Shakespeare's mind like housebreakers. He was being watched, and by a man with royal connections.

Be calm, he told himself. It is most likely a coincidence.

This was a rational response. Shakespeare was not an entirely rational man, however, and could not suppress the rumble of a more substantial alarm. Yes, he had been followed before – but not by a man of this sort. There was a negligent, loafing swagger in the fellow's bearing. He would be a difficult man to frighten.

Burbage was right: the King had eyes everywhere.

For a moment he was tempted to rise to the bait. He was confident he could lose himself in the warren of shops and stalls around the Royal Exchange. He knew the area well: had lived down there in Cripplegate with the Mountjoys. But it was a long time since he had attempted such evasions and he was too old for games. Nor could he risk acting in a suspicious manner; nothing would stiffen the hackles of a Crown agent more reliably than stealth. As matters stood, he was attending a meeting of old friends at a well-known inn. He would have to leave it at that.

As he walked on, anxiety still nibbled. Could Lowin have said something? Or Alleyn? Burbage had expressed doubts about both.

Had he been reckless? Lowin had actually admitted his royalist sympathies, and Alleyn, well, he did live a different sort of life now. He consorted with dukes and courtiers, and such men, as Shakespeare well knew, were capable of anything.

He began to relax when he strolled into Cheapside. It was his favourite street in all London: an immense thoroughfare, broad enough for jousting and lined with grand buildings on either side, but with a lively array of smaller enterprises jostling in the middle. The grocers and apothecaries gathered around the Great Conduit so that they could splash water from the fountain on their fruit and flowers. There, in the Mitre, were the smoky rooms where he used to meet Dekker, Jonson and the other wits. Further down were the foreign craftsmen, goldsmiths, silver-workers and jewellers who turned out counterfeit gems and sold them in a blizzard of Flemish and Italian accents. There were bookbinders from Holland and lacemakers from Normandy. There were blackamoors hauling barrels of ale through the mud, and away towards Finsbury Fields was the famous African pinmaker known to London's seamstresses as the Moor of Moorgate. There were fiddlers, vintners and balladeers. There were printers, bakers, costermongers and butchers. There were colourful signs – dragons, swans, roses and keys – over doorways, and clothes hung from lines stretched between the upper floors. And of course, as everywhere in London, there were inns.

The Greyhound was one of the oldest. It had crooked walls, crooked ceilings, crooked stairs and a crooked innkeeper who had salted away a modest fortune by overcharging customers, especially the foreigners who slept between his well-laundered sheets and knew no better. Few of the men who gorged themselves on his famous pies, or availed themselves of his useful latrines, knew that they were helping to pay for a large house on the river in Essex; and the innkeeper also collected rents from several farms out at Whitechapel. He did not dress like a rich man; on the contrary, to his guests he seemed almost to require a charitable expression of gratitude.

He had long been a good friend to the theatre, however, and Shakespeare knew that they would be well looked after. There would be oysters and capons, hot wine with sugar, spiced puddings and warm broths of every flavour. Taylor would likely bring more, so there would be far too much.

Most important of all, no one would disturb them.

On the way in Shakespeare turned his head to see whether his consort had kept pace. Yes, there he was, sauntering with brassy insouciance on the far side of the road, feigning to read an advertisement nailed to a post. Shakespeare smiled. He hoped the man had something to while away the hours, because he was in for a long wait.

The King's Men arrived at staggered intervals, and in an assortment of different ways: Armin on foot, Burbage on his horse, and Taylor burdened, as usual, with a basket of warm treats.

Shakespeare waited for them inside the door.

'Got them in Pudding Lane,' Taylor said cheerfully. 'What a place! All those bakers – furnaces everywhere. Piles of wood and butter, straw all over the shop, and the roofs almost touching. I tell you, that lot will go up in smoke one day.'

'If it does,' said Shakespeare, 'the whole city will go with it.'

'Morning, Will,' said Burbage, scraping cabbage leaves from his boots. 'All well?'

Shakespeare glanced outside. 'Not quite,' he said. 'There's a man over there. See him? He followed me all the way from Carter Lane.'

'He *what*?'

'Wasn't even careful about it.'

Burbage made a gruff noise, like a bark. 'That's all we need,' he said.

'Let's step outside,' said Shakespeare, 'to greet the others.'

'Are you mad?'

'Richard, he knows I am here. Now he knows *you* are here. The only thing now is to act as if we have nothing to hide. It's a reunion. Come on.'

They stood by some baskets of fish.

'I don't see Andrew anywhere,' said Shakespeare.

'I would be dismayed if you could. He is out there somewhere.'

'Can we find a way to ask him to keep an eye on our foe?'

'We can. But reporting back is not really his strength.'

They watched a carriage worming its way through the crowd of strolling citizens.

Burbage groaned. 'Is this Ned's idea of keeping his head down?'

'Good morning!' cried Alleyn. 'I took the liberty of arriving in style.'

'What is liberty for, if not travelling in style?' said Shakespeare.

'I thought our young princess, so green in years, wanted not the walk.'

Constance stepped down into the road. She was wearing a pale blue gown the colour of the sky in spring, and as she bowed her head out of the carriage Shakespeare was stirred by the sight of her slender body pressing on stiffened silk.

'Good morning,' he said. 'You look . . . splendid.'

Entrancing, he thought, smiling at his own soft heart.

Constance smiled. 'Then I am well dressed for making an entrance. Mr Alleyn has given me this gown. He said it would help me to look the part.'

'The part of what?' said Shakespeare, a hot flush on his face. For an instant she was abhorrent to him: a fledgling decked in garish feathers; lamb dressed as mutton. But then his flash of distaste fell instead upon Alleyn. What right did he have to dress this glorious young woman? The day, barely begun, was not going well.

'Let's in,' he said. 'Is John not with you?'

'His father will bring him presently,' said Alleyn. 'I called. They were at prayers.'

Shakespeare blinked at the gnat's buzz in his temples. There was, he knew, a wicked dart of jealousy lurking inside the more respectable sense of himself as Constance's patron and protector; and he was astonished to find himself still susceptible to such unsteady thoughts. It might have made him feel kindled and alive, but in truth it felt wretched. He murmured a favourite line: When in disgrace with Fortune and men's eyes, I all alone beweep my outcast state . . . The bleak comedy of the situation did not elude him. He did not pride himself on much, but he had always been aware that all men, even the mightiest, could be floored by the fluctuations of this uncertain life.

He looked at his old companion. It was undeniable that in recent years Alleyn had gone up in the world. His heavy yellow cape – Burbage said it cost a full twenty pounds – was laced with threads of gold, and he treated his carriage with the ease of a man used to such luxuries. Perhaps he really did belong to another milieu now. He had walked out on them once. Was it friendship, or policy, that had lured him back?

'Let's make a beginning,' he said. 'There is much to do.'

The actors were shown up to a room at the top of steep stairs, with a long table in the middle. The innkeeper had brought jugs of ale and wine. Taylor emptied his basket, and a servant brought platters of baked meats and warm pastries.

They sat down, helped themselves and waited for Shakespeare to begin.

'I recall saying that we should try out a court scene,' he said.

'True,' said Burbage.

'Right,' said Taylor.

'True *and* right,' said Armin with a grin.

'We might as well start at the beginning,' said Shakespeare. 'Let us imagine that Henry hears news of a plot against him . . .'

'How would it be,' said Burbage, 'if a messenger brings the news, but we can see that Henry already knows it?'

'That could work,' said Alleyn.

'Yes,' said Shakespeare. 'Imply that Henry is resourceful without him having to say a word. Excellent. It tells his nobles that their new king is a force to be feared.'

'And wise too,' said Alleyn. 'And confident enough to take up the reins of the kingdom in his own hands. He is nobody's puppet, this Welsh usurper.'

'Exactly,' said Shakespeare.

There was a scraping sound and a burst of noise as the door opened.

'Ah, John,' said Shakespeare. 'You are welcome.'

'I am sorry I am late,' said Harvard.

'You are not late,' said Constance, helping with his coat. 'We have not begun.'

'We are about to try another scene at court,' said Shakespeare. 'Get ready. We will be with you in a moment.'

'Maybe we should move this table to the side,' said Burbage.

'Good idea,' said Taylor.

'And a good idea,' said Alleyn, ' is a job half done. This looks pretty heavy.'

'There are plenty of us,' said Burbage. 'Come on.'

They half lifted, half shoved the table over to the wood-panelled wall, leaving clear space on the other side. This, for the next few hours, would be their stage. Shakespeare closed the door, glancing down the stairwell as he did so. Satisfied that no one would overhear, he turned to the players.

'We are ready,' he said. 'Richard, want to be King today?'

'I think it had better be you,' said Burbage. 'You have strong thoughts on the man. Set the tone. I will help later on.'

'Very well. We need nobles: Oxford and Stanley are the King's great allies; Suffolk and Lincoln are not to be trusted. So let's start. I was thinking I would begin with a small soliloquy, just a few lines, to give us a glimpse inside Henry.'

He put his fingers on his forehead and paced the scrubbed floor-boards. He stopped at the table, picked out a piece of sausage and chewed. Then he looked up.

'Good,' he said. 'John?'

'Ready, sir,' said Harvard, his quill blooming with ink.

'Right,' said Burbage. 'Peace, now.'

Shakespeare walked into the centre of the space, then turned. Although he made no attempt to adopt a regal air, some trick in his bearing suggested kingly poise.

'I am sorry,' he said. 'Forgive me, but can we push the table back?'

'Perfect,' said Armin, with a clownish groan.

'My apologies. But I think the King should circle this table. His noblemen are seated. He will be a ghost, a presiding spirit.'

The men stood up, pushed the table back into the middle and sat down again. Shakespeare began to pace behind a ring of hunched backs.

'They see me not,' he said, 'these noble men of England. They think that I, a Welshman born and bred, and exiled in the courts of Brittany, know little of this war-torn realm of theirs. Yet I have studied while I've been away. Much have I learned and this I surely know: a king must be a dragon, or a lion.'

He paused behind Constance and passed a gentle hand over her bent head, like a priest administering a blessing.

'My Queen I've softened; now I must impress these great men of the land. Look at them chatter, these grey-bearded geese. I will astound them yet. Good morrow, all!'

He spoke these last words with extra weight and geniality, and the room came to life in his presence. Alleyn was the first to react.

'Good morrow to your noble majesty. Your humble servants ever.'

Shakespeare raised a finger.

'I thank you, gentle sir, but let's be on. What's first? You, sir, what is it furrows your brow and weighs upon your honest-hearted soul?'

He was looking at Burbage, who had risen to his feet.

'Unhappy news, I fear, most royal liege. A young pretender has appeared abroad, in Dublin, so the messengers vouchsafe. Bishops and barons both do flock to him, raising once more the banner of revolt.'

Shakespeare took his place at the head of the table. 'I know this news and will away tonight. Tomorrow I will break this lizard's back.'

He tapped a spoon on the wooden goblet in front of him to signal a break.

'So now another messenger arrives,' he said, 'with news that soldiers are on their way. This is the magic of the Globe – we can wage and avert wars in the turning of a pause. The nobles are flustered. They suspect rebellion but the King is way ahead of them. Guards march in with a prisoner, a ten-year-old boy.' He paused, a smile on his bright face. 'Goodness, if only we had someone like that to play the part.'

'I am not so very much more than ten,' said John Harvard.

'We are an open book,' said Shakespeare. 'You are Warwick, pretender to the crown. This plot was none of your doing, but here you are, captive before a king.'

'I will play the part of the scribe,' said Constance, taking up the quill.

'Thank you, my dear,' said Alleyn, with too much zest for Shakespeare's liking.

There were three sharp knocks, low down on the door. Shakespeare raced to open it, peered out, but there was nobody there.

'Come and look at this.' Alleyn was over by the window.

There was no glass. The Greyhound could not afford such expensive novelties, and had instead thin cloths soaked in linseed oil, which admitted light without offering a view.

A well-appointed carriage was moving through the crowd. It had a polished black car, with black wheels and black drapes in its windows. A black-gloved hand drew back one of the shades, and a pale face looked out in their direction.

Shakespeare suppressed a gasp but could not prevent himself taking a step back. He was fairly sure – there was something in the curve of the jaw and the self-satisfied tilt of the man's brow – that the passenger was none other than Sir Edward Coke.

A coincidence? Shakespeare had made a fine living out of far more fanciful things than this. He could not persuade himself that it was an accident.

But what did it mean? That he was on a short leash?

He knew that already.

The others didn't seem to notice anything amiss.

'False alarm,' said Taylor.

'Where were we?' said Burbage.

'The soldiers were about to come before the King,' said Shakespeare. 'Here they come. Left, right, left and . . . what's this?'

'Guards! Guards!' said Taylor, waving a half-guzzled chicken leg in the air.

'Magnificently put,' said Armin. 'If a hind could be downed with rhetoric alone, then should none go hungry.'

'Be calm,' said Shakespeare. 'Soothe yourselves. We have already taken regal steps. See who they bring? Young Warwick, is it not? Excuse our haste; inform us if we err. An Irish army has proclaimed you king.'

There was a silence. Everyone looked at Harvard with indulgent smiles.

Harvard did not have to act to look nervous. He took a breath.

'I've never been to Ireland, good my lord, but if you wish it I will gladly go.'

'Bravo,' cried Taylor. 'Bravo.'

'I wish you no such thing,' said Shakespeare. 'Indeed, I must insist that you remain with us, our guest in this our proud and well-appointed Tower.'

He signalled with his hand. Burbage and Alleyn took Harvard's arm and steered him back to his desk.

Shakespeare waited till they were seated again, then approached Burbage.

'The King has shown himself to be decisive. Now he will show himself to be fierce. In a way — it is a nice touch, this — he can use the rebellion to stage an instructive little morality play for his own nobles.'

Burbage waved him on.

'How now, my lord?' said Shakespeare. 'This messenger of yours, arrayed in blue, with silver badges, emblems of your house. Have you not seen our order, lately read? No baron is to hold a private troop, and there can be no livery but the King's.'

Burbage produced a mock-fluster to signal consternation. Constance laughed.

'I have, my lord, and heartily concur. But servants of the house—'

'May soon turn soldiers,' Shakespeare said. He lifted his head and made it clear that he was addressing the whole room.

'I would I could evade this heavy duty,' he said, in a declamatory voice. 'You are my stout right hand. But twenty thousand sovereigns is the levy. For you, dear friend, and in the name of love, we'll clip it to a delicate fifteen.'

Burbage kneeled before him. 'Your noble wish is ever my command . . .'

Shakespeare prowled behind, letting silence fall like an invisible axe on his subject's neck.

' 'Tis with a heavy heart that I perform this role. This rising was a ruse to test our strength. Firm must I be; orders have I dispatched. Our noble cousins, whom we late thought friends, have all betrayed us quite. The scaffold waits; the whetstone grinds the axe. Their souls must fly to heaven, or to hell.'

He sat down, indicating with a hand that his men could leave. There was shuffle of feet. As they processed past, he tugged Burbage's sleeve and led him aside.

'Without ado, I here annul the fine. It was a stratagem, I do confess. I hoped that when the others heard your fate, knowing how close our friendship, they would quail, and look upon our throne with more respect. Come now, good Oxford! No one here can say, I have not made my presence felt today.'

There was a flurry of noise as the actors tapped the table with spoons.

'Terrific,' said Burbage. 'Quick, clear, bold. I fear this King, but like him too. Am I supposed to?'

'Of course,' said Shakespeare. 'He may soon be yours to play. But you may like him less as we proceed. Did you know that one of his first acts, on becoming king, was to change the date on his amnesty? Anyone who had opposed him at Bosworth was deemed a Yorkist and had to pay a heavy fine.'

Armin smiled. 'A king who changes dates. We can't have that.'

'We could always change it back again,' said Burbage. 'Or fight the Battle of Bosworth in a different year.'

'Yes, yes,' said Shakespeare. They never seemed to tire of poking fun at his easygoing attitude to names and dates. He had written one play in which Ulysses quoted Aristotle (hundreds of years before he was born); another in which the Athenian Timon had quoted Seneca, a much later figure. He had given Florence a port, and put gunpowder in King John's artillery. He had even, in *Julius Caesar*, let a clock strike the hour – long before the invention of the European timepiece.

None of the King's Men ever let him forget these lapses.

'Excuse me,' said Alleyn, 'but I wonder if a few of these nobles shouldn't talk among themselves, behind their hands, muttering about this first sight of their king. It could be ominous, letting us know there are clouds over the throne.'

'Very good idea. A play should not steer a path. We must bring *all* sides to life.'

'Want us to try it?'

'Absolutely.'

'You said something about Suffolk and Lincoln,' said Alleyn.

'Yes,' said Shakespeare. 'And Stanley too. Henry has a plan for Stanley. It would be good to put him in with the doubters at this point.'

'Very well. Richard, Joseph, Robert? Let us to our grumbling! I'll be Stanley. I imagine he'd be happy to gossip about his prince, this stepson, who can turn so swiftly on his friend. So here goes . . . What think you of this boy we have made king?'

'I think that he is young,' said Taylor.

'And Welsh,' said Armin.

'And wild,' said Burbage.

'All qualities I hold in high esteem,' said Alleyn. 'But how find you his manner? Was it regal? Blunt was he now with Oxford; rough, too rough. It must be said: he was not born to this. Unversed is he in statesmanship and war.'

Shakespeare tapped his foot in appreciation. 'Excellent. Very courtly.'

'Just so,' said Armin. 'And look you, sirs, at this unhappy coin, stamped with the King's own likeness. Look at his eyes, a-frown with heavy thoughts. I like it not.'

He walked over to address Harvard.

'And that's *like* rather than *lake*,' he said. 'We are not a buffoon.'

' 'Tis said he loves to play at games of chance,' said Burbage. 'Like Flux and Plunder, Pillage, Freeze and Plug – and other sports as dangerous as these. And gazed at stars through telescopes.'

Alleyn had something to add. 'His claim is small, and on his mother's side. When kings are weak 'tis best to be prepared. For when they fall, their consorts are not spared.'

It felt like the end. But Harvard was still scratching at the paper, so it was only Constance and Shakespeare who could play the part of Audience and applaud.

'Coward,' said Shakespeare, smiling at Alleyn.

'Villain,' Armin grinned.

'I thought it was excellent,' said Constance. 'Is that true, the games he played?'

'I believe so,' Burbage said. 'He favoured boisterous diversion in his early years.'

Alleyn was frowning. 'I am not sure about the telescope, though. I don't believe they had been invented at that time.'

Armin slapped his thigh. 'You're right! Master Galileo, in Italy, is even now perfecting his instrument, though many swear that Master Hariot has been peering through one for years.'

'No matter,' said Shakespeare. 'Cleopatra played billiards. No one noticed. We can give the man a telescope.'

'One other thing,' said Burbage. 'Does the King need a companion, a fool?'

'I think so,' said Shakespeare. 'A big part of this story concerns the solitude that haunts a throne – a king has officers, not friends. But audiences love a truth-teller. I once conceived of a fellow named Bergamot, who speaks in proverbs. "A farmer who plants onions never reaped carrots" . . . "Do not ask an eagle to catch a fly." Things like that.'

'I like the sound of him,' said Alleyn. 'Tell him to join us with all speed. He is most welcome.'

'Any man may be well come,' said Armin. 'And many are well done. But 'tis only a rare and drunken fellow who is well gone.'

'See what I mean?' said Alleyn.

'I am worried,' said Burbage, 'that the King begins the play with such ferocity, killing the Princes, that we will never again believe him capable of tenderness.'

Shakespeare smiled. Actors – and they did not come finer than Richard – always wanted their characters to be consistent.

'Oh, I think we can stretch him a bit. It is the tale that shapes the character, not the character that shapes the tale.'

'I know, I know.'

'Though it did strike me the other day that it might be amusing to move our characters from play to play, to see what happened. Put Othello in *Hamlet* and he would not hesitate – he would cut Claudius down. There would be no story.'

Constance grinned. 'And if you did it the other way round, then Hamlet would *never* fall for Iago's coarse scheming – he would expose him in a flash.'

'That isn't so far from what we did, actually,' said Shakespeare. 'The whole idea of Hamlet was that he was miscast – the wrong actor for the part he had to play. I remember us saying that if the Ghost had given the job to Coriolanus, or Hotspur, or even Prince Hal—'

'I confess I never appreciated this till now,' said Alleyn, 'but it's true.

If Lear strolled into *The Tempest*, he would divide the isle between Ariel, Caliban and Miranda, spark a wrestling match, and go raging alone among the waterfalls.'

Shakespeare smiled and undid the top button of his shirt; it was getting warm.

'The more important problem,' said Taylor, 'is that there is nothing yet for me.'

'Or me,' said Constance.

'We are saving the best till last,' said Shakespeare. 'But first, do have something to eat. Our host was anticipating a regiment of stomachs, so do not stint.'

Everything looked delicious: the fried mushrooms, the porridge with raisins and nuts, the roasted kidneys with Portugal eggs, the stewed trout and gammon pie.

'Look, marchpane,' said Taylor, dipping his finger in the sweet almond paste.

Shakespeare shrugged. 'Maybe later. I am not hungry. But help yourself.'

'I can't resist.'

The Greyhound boasted that its froize was the best in London, and it had a point. A soft pancake of eggs, cream and flour was wrapped round bacon and fried with a fistful of onions and cheese – delicious. When Shakespeare imagined Falstaff and Belch feasting with their friends, this is what he pictured them demolishing. Today, however, he watched Taylor scoop it up and knew that he himself could not face so much as a mouthful. He met Burbage's eye and nodded at the door.

On the way down he grabbed two tankards.

'Props,' he said. 'Follow me.'

He led the way outside, and sat on a sawn-off log.

'He's still there – over by the water trough?'

'He has the boots of a soldier, and looks Scottish. His beard is freshly trimmed.'

'I've half a mind to go and talk to him.'

'If he knows we've seen him, he'll be replaced by someone we won't notice.'

'What news of Lowin? Did you find him?'

'I sent word. He is honoured to play Henry VIII and says you won't regret it.'

'Good.'

'Were you worried that he . . . that someone—?'

'I confess to a mild alarm. But I don't think so. If the authorities knew what we are doing, no one would follow me – they would know already where I was going.'

'Shall we warn the others?'

'I don't want to make them anxious.'

'No. But why conceal it?'

Shakespeare's eyes clouded. 'You are right. We will tell them straight.'

'Shall we get back?'

'Lead the way.'

Shakespeare followed Burbage, slapping him on the back and laughing at an imaginary jest. From a distance they looked like a pair of friends who had stepped out for a breath of air. A golden sun flared out of a cold blue sky, and the street glittered in the spring light. A cart laden with caged birds nosed its way through the bustle. A group of soldiers lolled outside a tavern, and someone scraped a fiddle near a shop full of woven baskets. It seemed a normal day.

He paused for a word with the innkeeper. He wanted, he explained, a service that required discretion. The innkeeper did not need to have it spelled out. It took him less than a minute to fetch a dark and wiry boy, wearing loose trousers and a tipsy beret. He had a keen, intelligent face. If he had sworn that he had stoat in his ancestry, nobody would have argued the point.

There was no need for small talk.

'I need a service,' said Shakespeare. 'In a while, one of our number will leave in a carriage. I would like him followed. There is a fat purse for the man who can tell me what he does, who he sees, where he goes. Might you be such a man?'

The boy nodded.

'The gentleman I am interested in is grand and wears a yellow cape. I shall meet you here tomorrow morning, an hour after first light.'

He paused, and suddenly, like a jester teetering on high stilts, felt a cold rush of trepidation. Was he about to take an irrevocable step? He had not thought of *The Two Gentlemen of Verona* for years – he was not even proud of it – but now the play stirred in his remote memory. Two friends in love with the same woman: one gullible, one two-faced. What had he said? Who should be trusted, when one's right hand is perjur'd to the bosom? That was understating the case. If he were writing it today, he would press further into the dark chasms opened up by the treachery of a friend.

The abrupt glimpse of himself as a woolly-headed dreamer from one of his own comedies made him wince. It was easy to smile indulgently at the antics of fools in love; it was much harder to remain composed in the face of a real-life quandary.

He had no choice. However great his reluctance to believe the worst of Alleyn, he could not afford to believe the best. He took a light breath.

'He may suspect he is being watched. Be careful.'

'I will be as quiet as his own shadow,' said the boy. 'He never shall see me.'

Shakespeare gave him a coin, then turned to the innkeeper.

'Where do you find these people?' he said.

'They are not rare,' said the innkeeper.

'Tonight I shall forget my gloves. That will be my pretext for returning.'

'Does sir need a pretext?' said the innkeeper.

'Your cheese soup is sufficient, you think? You are probably right.'

Shakespeare reached inside his shirt and pulled out a purse.

'For your labours on our behalf,' he said. 'I thank and salute you. Joseph has fallen upon your marchpane, and the froize was perfect.'

'Was?'

'I doubt there is any remaining.'

'If you need the room again, let me know,' said the innkeeper. 'It'll be quiet all through Lent.'

'Thank you,' said Shakespeare.

'The young lady is pretty.'

'Very.'

Shakespeare did not wish to discuss it further. His legs felt sluggish as he climbed the stairs, so he rested at the top to avoid seeming breathless. The door was half open, and Shakespeare could see Alleyn with his hand on Constance's waist. The devil! He was teaching her a dance step. Something gave way in Shakespeare's breast, as if he stood on a crust too thin to take the weight of a boot.

He pushed open the door with a sharp thrust. Most of the actors looked up from their food, but Alleyn dropped his hand and took a step back. An awkward silence strangled the life out of the room as Shakespeare strode over to the table, his leather boots clacking on the bare boards. For a moment it looked as though Alleyn was going to speak, but Shakespeare held up a hand to prevent him.

'There is something I need to tell you all,' he said. 'I was worried, this morning, that I was being followed on my way from Blackfriars. It seems I was right.'

There was a rumble of consternation.

'Now anyone embarking on a play about Henry VIII can expect interest from the King's spies. We are fortunate: we have royal permission and the Chamberlain's blessing. But we should be careful not to reveal our real purpose, or draw attention. This may not be the best time to steal your neighbour's ass . . . or covet his wife.'

'What a pity,' said Armin.

'Or daughter,' said Taylor.

'Or son,' said Constance.

There was an abrupt sense of shock, then a shout of mirth.

Constance did not blush.

'I am no longer surprised,' said Armin. 'This woman is beyond compare. Where on earth did you find her, Will?'

'I didn't find her,' said Shakespeare, looking at her softly. 'She found us.'

Constance's reply was calm. 'My father says there is no sin a man can commit that a woman cannot do just as well.'

'I have never met your father,' said Armin. 'But I like him very much.'

'And he would like you, I am sure,' said Shakespeare. He let the silence hang in the air for a moment. 'But we have work ahead of us. What is next?'

'Actually,' said Alleyn, 'Constance and I were speaking of that scene you mentioned yesterday, between a princess of the court and the sailor, Cabot.'

'You have some thoughts?'

'I have been reading this book, *A Brief and True Report of the Newfoundland of Virginia*, by Thomas Hariot – a Devon man, I believe.'

Shakespeare had to suppress a pang of surprise. 'I don't know about that, but he was a good friend of Raleigh's, who pretty much lived in Durham House, performing his experiments with charts and instruments. He's mentioned in Hakluyt, isn't he?'

'Could be.'

'Either he is or he isn't.'

'I'm ashamed to say I have never read Hakluyt. Tried. Couldn't get through it.'

'Persist, it is full of fine stuff,' said Shakespeare. 'Anyway, let's see.'

He sat beside Harvard, bit into a mustard dumpling and settled down to watch.

Chapter 10

Shakespeare's heart was not cheered by the prospect of Alleyn making Italian eyes at Constance, but it was improper to object. While the actors readied themselves he glanced through a gap in the window shades. The man was digging the dirt from his fingernails with a knife. Shakespeare frowned.

Then his face brightened. A slim figure in a green cloak was hurrying towards the Greyhound, stepping over the piles of rotten vegetables and dung that lay in the gutter. He looked pale and fastidious; no one would have guessed that this man had created fat, merry Falstaff – the old Queen's favourite character.

'John!' he said and turned to face the room. 'It's Heminge. About time. Excuse me for a minute.'

He ran down to find Heminge stamping his feet on the brushed stone flags.

'Will!' he cried. 'I have only just discovered your message. I went to the house and they said I'd find you here. How are you?'

'Where have you been? We've been trying to find you for days.'

'Oxford. Just got back.'

'What on earth took you to Oxford?'

'The usual. Brushing away offers from printers to copy your work.'

'You didn't agree to anything, I hope.'

'Who do you think I am?'

They had spoken often enough about selling rights in their plays to a printer. In recent years the offers had grown more and more tempting. Heminge, Burbage and Shakespeare, as leading sharers, could have pocketed a fat purse, but each knew that this would spell the end of the King's Men as an active theatrical concern. Their plays were their chief asset: once published, they could (and would) be performed by anyone. A number of their works *had* been copied, printed and distributed, and Shakespeare was keen to keep a tight grip on those that remained.

'While I was there I saw Sir Thomas Bodley and had a look at his new library,' said Heminge. 'It is wonderful. Two thousand books. I could happily live there. He is so scared of thieves, the books are chained to the desks.'

'A prison for learning, then,' said Shakespeare. 'I am not ready for that.'

'He's not ready for you, either. Still won't give house room to plays.'

Heminge was grinning; he seemed relaxed and happy. He was always fretting that Shakespeare might want to sell his copyrights and sought constant assurances that he had no such plans.

'Portia, Hamlet, Macbeth, Romeo: these are our children,' Shakespeare would say. 'Stop worrying, and you may stone me if I sell a line.'

The innkeeper hailed Heminge and offered him a drink.

'We've plenty upstairs,' said Shakespeare, taking his friend by the arm and steering him to one side. 'But before we go up, I have news.'

It didn't take him long to tell Heminge all and he enjoyed watching his friend's surprise turn into interest. At the end Heminge hesitated.

'You do realise how dangerous this is,' he said.

Shakespeare nodded.

'I wonder.'

Shakespeare did not rise to the challenge. He was not ready to describe his brush with Coke. However, there was one thing he could share.

'There's a man over by the pump cleaning his fingernails,' he said. 'He was watching your arrival with interest. He followed me here this morning.'

'Are you serious?'

'Absolutely. But worried? No. The Chamberlain believes we are working on a play about Henry VIII. That is not a lie. So while I cannot say what this man wants, I feel sure he presents no imminent threat.'

'I hope you're right. Who else knows about this?'

'Apart from us?' said Shakespeare. 'Richard, Ned, Robert and Joseph. Oh, and Lowin, too. He has left us now. We've offered him the lead role – he's going to play King Henry VIII. I don't think he'll let us down.'

'That's a good many people,' said Heminge.

'There are two more,' said Shakespeare. 'We have a pair of young stowaways called Constance Donne and John Harvard. You'll like them, I'm sure. No one else.'

'I wish I had been here from the first,' said Heminge.

'It is better this way,' said Shakespeare. 'You might have persuaded us to desist. But do not rush to judgement – it is coming along well. Come.'

He led the way upstairs. The others turned as they arrived and smiles broke out as they all exchanged greetings. In Shakespeare's absence, Burbage may have been the theatrical leading light, but it was Heminge who kept the King's Men together, handling all the company's payments and business affairs. He was everyone's best friend; he was privy to their secrets and kept each of them close. He knew what they wanted before they knew it themselves. Nature had given him a refined sense of discretion, so he was a warm confidant to all. When he introduced himself to Harvard and Constance it was with the easy air of a man who seemed to have already spent many cheerful hours in their company.

'I am John Heminge,' he said. 'Some people put an S on the end, but good fellows like you two need not trouble yourselves with so saucy a consonant.'

'Be seated,' said Shakespeare. 'Ned and Constance have cooked up a scene for us. The renowned – though renown lay ahead of him at this stage – Italian explorer Giovanni Cabot has come to England, seeking funds for a voyage to the New World. He is about to meet the Princess Anne.'

'We imagine it this way,' said Alleyn, taking up the baton. 'Cabot needs a patron and hopes that the Princess will help him win the King's favour. She is only too eager to assist. The man is an explorer, and the princess has led a sheltered life.'

'We were thinking,' added Constance, 'that they could bump into each other at the royal wedding, right at the beginning. It would be an outrageous friendship. Everyone would be horrified.'

'That way we start with the politics,' said Armin. 'The union of York and Lancaster, followed by this glimpse of a gentler world.'

'And audiences will love it,' said Shakespeare. 'A princess and a humble mariner, with the clamour of gulls, the chafe of rigging.'

Harvard took his place at the table. Heminge sat beside him.

'The party is in full flow,' said Alleyn. 'The dignitaries are about their business; the ladies-in-waiting are giggling at the men. The radiant Princess Anne is bold enough to engage the sailor – me – in conversation. So: ladies and gentlemen, I give you the beauteous Princess . . .'

Constance spun on her heel and bowed her head. When she turned to face them she had pushed a glittering tiara high into her jet-black hair. The light sparkled in her eyes and made her even more luminous than usual.

She walked towards Alleyn with an amused half-smile.

'Good morrow, sir. Perhaps . . . Is't aid you seek?'

Shakespeare could not stop himself interrupting. 'I should have said,' he said. 'I don't think we need verse in this scene. Good stout prose will do.'

'I am sorry,' said Constance. 'That wasn't meant to be verse.'

'Like father, like daughter,' said Armin. 'She speaks fluent sonnet.'

'I'm looking for the King,' said Alleyn, with only a faint Italian accent.

'Why then, you seek unwisely,' said Constance with a giggle. 'I am not he, nor is he hiding among my skirts.'

Alleyn allowed a smile to lift a corner of his mouth. 'What say I look there for myself, my lady?'

'Sir!' said Constance. 'I would not speak to the King with such insolence.'

'I have no wish to explore *his* skirts. With him I have other business. In Venice, my home, we often—'

'You are from Venice!' Constance's eyes shone. 'Is it true what they say? Rivers instead of roads, boats instead of horses?'

The rapture in her voice seemed unfeigned.

'It is true,' said Alleyn, sounding more Mediterranean now. 'The lagoon laps the lintels of the houses. Visitors come by boat.'

'Such a voice!' Constance turned aside for a moment. 'Oh tell me all, good sir. My heart pines to see such marvels.'

'Mine longs for stranger sights. This is the favour that I ask the King.'

'How can anything be stranger than a city built on the sea?'

Alleyn flung an arm out to indicate the far horizon, as if he were atop a mast. 'The land across the oceans! That's what calls my heart. The paradise beyond the foaming billows, and the icy floes that guard the Arctic flood.'

Taylor laughed. 'Good for you, Signor Ned. Foaming billows!'

Constance ignored him.

'You speak good English, sir, too good for me. What do you mean?'

'There are new worlds waiting for us,' said Alleyn, reaching forward to take Constance's hand. 'In Spain and Portugal, new ships are rising on their keels, bigger than castles and as swift as eagles. Their ropes and spars snap in the wind. Like hawks, they strain at the leash. Let them slip, these dogs of peace, and they'll race to find unfathomed wonders – ambergris and alabaster, gold and pearls, and unknown peaks to climb. This is what I seek.'

'Don't hold back, Ned,' said Taylor.

'Sssh,' said Shakespeare.

'What has this to do with the King?' said Constance, as if rebuking the man for too much poetry.

'I need money,' said Alleyn. 'To equip a boat. I seek unconquered lands . . . But I am sorry. I wax warm in my own interest. What of you, fair lady, what seek you?'

There was a pause.

'Spin it out,' whispered Shakespeare. 'Squeeze it for every drop.'

'I'll have to ask my brother,' said Constance with a solemn face.

'A girl's reply,' said Alleyn, nodding.

'You mistake me, sir. I seek no favours that are not mine without the asking. The King, he is my brother.'

'A palpable hit,' said Taylor.

'Sweet,' said Armin, 'though not quite the truth.'

'Are we happy with this?' Taylor said. 'Anne is sister to the Queen, not the King.'

'It is close enough,' said Constance. 'We do not have to be exactly faithful, do we?'

'A woman after my own heart,' said Shakespeare.

'Let's carry on,' said Burbage.

'Oh?' said Alleyn, feigning dismay.

'Sir, I am too merry,' said Constance. Shakespeare took a breath as she reached out and patted Alleyn's arm. 'Come,' she said, tugging at him. 'He shall hear your suit. I'll take you to him, and he'll not refuse. But wait awhile, and tell me more of Venice, and the foaming billows, and all else . . .'

Constance and Alleyn looked at each other and smiled.

'You are, without a doubt,' said Alleyn, 'the fairest princess we have ever had. A pity you won't be able to play her on the stage.'

'Who says she can't?' said Shakespeare.

'Oh come now, Will. The Chamberlain won't allow it. The *audience* won't allow it.'

'More fool them,' said Burbage.

'Let us tame the horse before we hitch the cart,' said Shakespeare. 'We do not even know if this can be performed. It is too early to talk about the cast.'

'Nevertheless,' said Alleyn, 'did it content the ear? Needs work, obviously.'

'Ned, Ned,' said Shakespeare, amused in spite of himself by the man's appetite for praise. 'It was excellent. Did you get it all down, John?'

'I believe so, sir.'

'Let's see,' said Heminge. He took the book and held up the loose, unbound pages in a shaft of soft light. 'Good,' he said. 'Very good indeed. Scarcely a blot, and very clear. You could print from this.'

He inspected the front.

'No title?' he said.

'It'd be tempting fate,' said Burbage.

'Plus it's a secret,' said Armin.

'Be as well to call it something, though,' said Heminge.

'We could give it a coded title,' said Taylor. '*A Private Word. Seven Days.*'

'I like that,' said Alleyn. 'How about . . . *Giovanni the First?*'

'How about *Henry VIII?*' said Shakespeare.

'Could get confusing when we really *are* talking about Henry VIII,' said Armin. 'It needs to be something different, a title we'd never use.'

'At school, when we wrote things in code,' said Harvard, 'we took names at random out of books.'

'Very well, let's find a book,' said Alleyn.

'I have one,' said Constance. '*Don Quixote*, by the Spaniard, Miguel Cervantes. A most excellent work.'

'Perfect,' said Alleyn. 'May I . . . ?'

He took the tubby volume and flicked over the pages.

'Here we are,' he said. 'Sancho . . . Carrasco . . . Cardenio. That has a ring to it. Cardenio . . . What do you think?'

'I think Cardenio will do as well as another,' said Shakespeare.

Harvard took back the book, set it on the table and inked his quill.

'May I ask something?' he said.

'Of course.'

'Is this play a comedy, or a tragedy, or a history?'

Shakespeare patted his head. 'That is a very good question. Most of our plays are a mixture of all three. Comedies end with a wedding; tragedies end in a funeral; histories end with a coronation.'

'A touch simple,' said Burbage. 'But true in its essentials.'

Alleyn agreed. 'I always say that comedy is just tragedy with a happy ending.'

'And the whole point about the history plays,' said Burbage, 'is that they mix the two. They are sunshine and rain, at the same time. What seems tragic to a king can be comic to his grumbling subjects, while in the tavern the fall of a king is fine sport.'

Shakespeare stooped low, hands on knees, until he was Harvard's height.

'The best answer to your question is that we don't know . . . yet. A play is like Cabot's voyage: we do not know quite where the four winds will take us.'

Harvard held up his pen. 'I understand. There is acreage enough in our plot.'

'Not another one,' said Burbage. 'There are enough punsters in this company.'

'Do you mind,' said Shakespeare, 'if we break? I need to speak to John.'

There was a mutter of assent, followed by a move to disperse.

'No need to leave. We will have a drink downstairs and return in . . . half an hour?'

'Before you go,' said Taylor, 'can I bring to your attention that I have done almost exactly nothing so far today? I don't know what you have planned for later, but if you like I could push ahead with a docklands scene or two. Maybe Robert and I could rough out an episode.'

'Good idea,' said Shakespeare, as he ducked away towards the stairs. But his mind was already pressing into the waves, skipping on white crests, surging into troughs and tacking towards new realms.

The innkeeper placed a jug of ale and a basket of bread on a crooked table in a gloomy corner. The two friends sat in silence, each waiting for the other to speak.

'I've been thinking,' said Shakespeare, 'and you are right. That man who followed me here – the least we should do is track him, see whose colours he wears.'

'I'll organise it,' said Heminge. 'Our genial host probably knows lots of spies.'

'I wouldn't be surprised,' said Shakespeare.

'I agree it would be helpful to know who he is.'

'He had the appearance of a soldier.' Shakespeare heaved a sigh; his shoulders slumped. 'But no matter. It is good to have you here. Richard tells me that the King's Men would be lost without you. How do you like our idea? Honestly.'

'Honestly?'

'Well . . . *quite* honestly.'

'It is splendid.'

'Really?'

'Yes. It sounds like a classic history play – well, a classic *Shakespeare* history play. Henry VII wins the throne, beats off pretenders, rules well – no major wars, at least – and has the wit to survive long enough for his son to succeed. A dynasty is born. Hurrah. The only problem I can see is the ending. A bit damp, as it stands.'

'I have a few . . . changes in mind.'

'Changes?'

Shakespeare summarised his findings so far, and the shape of the play. He did not mention Raleigh, Stanyhurst or Coke – and it gave him a fright to see how much was left unsaid by his unwilling tongue. He did not like close-mouthed people and had never been one of them himself. But some burdens could not be shared.

'I want the play to sing,' he said. 'I want to paint rainbows on the sky, over London and all England. I also want to tell the truth.'

'Very wise.'

'There is much to tell you. To start with, we have Henry VII murdering the Princes in the Tower. With his own hands.'

'But I thought that Richard—'

'That's what we all believe, I know. But we may have mistold history. I am determined to rewrite it.'

'I see.'

'We have an opportunity – don't you agree? Who else could do this but us? We have a measure of freedom because of our fame, and must make wholesome use of it. We have no choice: it falls on us to perform this task.'

Heminge clasped Shakespeare's shoulder. 'Fear not for me, Will. It is tremendous to see you ablaze with work again. That is what counts. Still, it is as well to be careful.'

'Yet not hide. I keep saying this, but our disappearance would attract more suspicion than a noisy get-together.'

'How much have you done so far?'

'We have made more than a beginning. There is meat on it now. You can read it – young John Harvard has been recording both our good words and our bad.'

'I look forward to it.'

'We had better go back up,' said Shakespeare. He did not move, however.

'Something else?'

'It's just . . . well, you'll see. Ned is behaving very fondly with Constance Donne. It is like watching an old buzzard circling a fawn. It grates rather.'

Heminge smiled. 'Not on him, evidently,' he said. 'Come, then.'

'Yes,' said Shakespeare. 'Air would be good.'

They strolled out into Cheapside, where lines of washing snapped in the wind, and a man on a ladder put the finishing touches to a new inn sign: a black bull.

Some screams echoed across the open space – impossible to say where from.

'God save some poor soul,' said Heminge.

Opposite them, in a doorway, a young boy polished a bell in the shadow of a pair of pikemen who held thick staves in meaty hands. There were soldiers all along Cheapside, standing in doorways and leaning on barrows. It was as if London were enduring occupation by a foreign army. The troops looked estranged and hostile.

'Every time I withdraw,' said Heminge, 'I forget how busy it is.'

'I am the same,' said Shakespeare.

'Even compared with Oxford.'

'I know. I broke my own journey there, spent a night. The next morning I was out early. The city was as old and silent as a crypt. Even the trees felt ancient. I seemed to be the only man abroad. I stood by the river for a while, watching kingfishers in the sunlight. Standing here, I find it hard to believe such places exist.'

He pushed his toe into a pile of peelings. Two rats scuttled into the drain.

'Oxford is beautiful,' said Heminge. 'But it is no place for us. No theatres.'

'Just like Stratford.' Shakespeare could not hide the sorrowful expression on his face. All his life he been seeking something, only to find himself now, at the peak of his fame, an outcast in the only two places he could even imagine calling home.

179

A roar of laughter burst from the room upstairs as they went back in.

'What's so funny?' said Heminge.

'I must be the devil,' said Shakespeare.

'Don't worry, Will,' said Burbage. 'We weren't talking about you, for once. Constance was telling a joke.'

'Oh?'

'Not so much a joke,' said Constance. 'Just something my father used to tell me.'

'Am I allowed to hear it?'

'He advised that whatever I did, I should be sure to marry a historian, because the older I got, the more interested in me he would become.'

The fact that the others had already enjoyed this pleasantry obliged Shakespeare to smile alone.

'Very good,' he said. 'Though, sad to say, untrue.'

'Anyway,' said Armin, 'we've made a plan. Shall we give it a try?'

'Why not?'

'Well then. We thought that down at the docks Cabot would run into the citizens, and two of our worlds would collide. I am going to be Bacon again. Will, are you happy to be the Town Crier – Hear ye and so forth? Then we have three citizens. Joseph, you are the first: he's the rumour-monger.'

'At last.'

'Ned, will you take second citizen – the sensible one? Oh no, you're the Italian, aren't you? And who wants to be the rogue? Richard?'

'Oh, I'll sit this one out.'

'He only plays grandees,' said Taylor.

'I'll pitch in if I think of anything useful,' said Burbage.

'As you wish. John?'

'I think not. I don't know the play yet. I would simply slow you down.'

'That might be a good thing. Go on: there's no one else.'

'Excuse me,' said Constance.

Everyone looked at her.

'Of course,' said Armin. 'Sorry – forgot myself for a moment. Yes. You will be our third citizen, and a very charming one too. Be mischievous.'

'I'll set the scene,' said Burbage. 'Let's have some fun.'

They took up their positions as idlers on an imaginary dock.

'It is early morning,' said Burbage, in a mock-heroic whisper. 'Gulls are mewling overhead, and a cold wind is whipping through the trees. A crowd has gathered to watch ships arriving on the tide. Gaunt cats scrap over rotting fish-heads . . .'

'Blancmange, blancmange,' said Armin. 'Blah, blah.'

Burbage laughed. 'Fair enough . . . Enter citizens.'

Taylor stepped forward, walked around in circles, then put his hand over his eyes as if to shield them from a glaring sun.

Off they sailed. Armin and Taylor traded nonsense, which Alleyn decorated with platitudes. Eventually he told how he had crossed oceans, seen whales as big as ships, fought with bears and eagles, and raced the wolves that howl through snow and timber.

Shakespeare nodded in appreciation, rose to his feet and strode towards his friends, raising and lowering a hand.

'Hear ye, hear ye! Citizens and subjects! An execution is announced on Sunday next, the fifteenth day in March, of Arthur Petticlough, for the crime of murder—'

'Murder?' said Taylor, anxious to join in. 'Whom did he kill?'

'One of the King's falcons,' said Shakespeare. 'For which foul crime he shall be hanged by the neck at the tenth hour, the eleventh being almost too late.'

'Fowl crime . . . very good,' said Heminge.

' 'Tis foul indeed,' said Constance, 'to kill fowl – if falcon do be fowl. But this is small news. Have ye not heard? Cabot is returned, and he has found new land.'

'Bravo,' said Alleyn with a smile.

'Thank you,' whispered Constance.

Shakespeare clenched and unclenched his fingers.

They kept going, taunting Armin until it became unbearable. He marched away with foolish ceremony and the others fell in behind, imitating his gait in a grotesque parade of elbows and knees.

'Impressive,' said Heminge. 'You have been busy in my absence.'

'Time waits for no man,' said Armin. 'And neither do we.'

'I don't know how you think of so many ideas,' said Constance.

'It is not magic,' said Shakespeare. 'It is a just reward for hard work. Learn from Robert. He plays the buffoon, but does not laugh at him. This Bacon knows not how tasty he is. Heed it well: to mock your own character is to steal the audience's part. As for the others, we have supped well enough on this Bacon. It is time to pity him.'

'Where have you been, anyway?' said Burbage, turning to Heminge.

'Oxford,' said Heminge. 'Come, I'll tell you all about it.'

'And what news of Condell?'

'Did you not know? He is in York.'

'York?'

'Invited by the archbishop to organise a library. It will take months . . .'

'Oh, I had quite forgotten,' said Burbage. 'Sorry, Will. Want me to send word?'

'Too late,' said Shakespeare. 'Let him see to the archbishop's books in peace.'

'Excuse me,' said Alleyn. The others turned. He stood by the window, looking down. 'My carriage awaits. I apologise, but I have business to attend to.' He gathered his cloak. 'I shall be passing the Lady Constance's lodgings. If you have no further need of her, perhaps I might claim the privilege of seeing her home.'

'Thank you, sir,' said Constance. She turned to Shakespeare. 'Of course I will gladly stay if you need me.'

Shakespeare hesitated, seeking a reason to refuse. It struck him that in Constance's company, Alleyn might miss the stoat darting in the shadows behind him.

'No,' he said. 'Enjoy your escort and his wheels. I am weary myself. We shall do no more today. Thank you for your excellent work, all of you. Joseph, Robert, I cannot thank you enough. You are performing marvels.'

'It *is* sharp, isn't it?' said Armin. 'Even the comedy has roots in the time. We have never done this – I don't know anyone who has. People will gape.'

'I agree,' said Taylor. 'The intrigue at court is strong too. This play has two thoughts, and both run as true and clear as Kentish streams.'

'Now: arrangements,' said Burbage. 'Unfortunately we cannot meet until next Wednesday. That's the bad news.'

'It is my fault,' said Shakespeare. 'I have business in Stratford. I depart in the morning. I will haste back as soon as possible. I am sorry.'

'The good news,' Burbage continued, 'is that Will has arranged a big room for us at Essex House, away towards Westminster. Does everyone know where it is?'

They all nodded except Constance and John.

'I will collect you both,' said Shakespeare. 'Or maybe . . . John, could you get yourself across the river? I could meet you at Puddle Dock an hour after sun-up. Better still, let's meet at St Paul's.'

'Of course. Would you like me to help Joseph get the food?'

'Does the Pope say grace?'

'It was a muddle this morning,' said Burbage. 'But please let us try to arrive at intervals again. Travel alone, and keep one eye in the back of your head.'

Taylor was playing with a knife. 'What are we to suppose about all this, Will?'

'All of what?'

'Your being followed this morning. The rest of us requiring eyes in the back of our heads. This journeying from place to place. Should we truly be fearful?'

'All we think,' said Burbage, 'is that it is wise to have care. We know how things have been in recent years, since the Plot. This King trusts no one.'

'I wonder if the memory of that day will ever fade,' said Alleyn. 'The people seem to make more of a festival out of November the fifth every year.'

'The flames in Stratford were as tall as a house,' said Shakespeare.

'It is already one of those dates that every child knows. They even have a rhyme for it – "Send them to heaven on five of eleven." It is like Armada Day.'

'We should have more such days,' said Armin. 'All fire and chestnuts.'

Burbage sighed. 'The point is, the King's watchfulness never slackens. He wants our love, but earns only fear. In preparing the story of

Henry VII we are, at the very least, ignoring a royal request. It is a risk we accept, but it is not one we can take lightly.'

'Thank you, Richard.' Shakespeare suddenly looked old beyond his years. 'I pray I have not embroiled you in anything worse than folly. The risks are real. There are those who will not like our play. It would indeed be foolish not to remember that.'

'I prefer to think of those who will love it,' said Armin. 'Cheer up, Joe. Your first citizen has got to be worth a severed limb or two, surely.'

As always, humour was the best medicine. The actors began to stand.

Harvard approached Shakespeare, holding out the growing book of pages.

'Perhaps I could take that,' said Heminge. 'I'd very much like to read what you've done so far.'

'I've a good leather bag for it somewhere,' said Shakespeare.

He knew he would have to tell Heminge that his own quarters had been searched. This manuscript was now a precious document – irreplaceable, in fact. His memory was good, but not *that* good.

'Did you say Essex House?' Alleyn was frowning. 'Are you sure that's wise?'

'Is that the same Essex who made the rebellion?' said Harvard.

'The same,' said Alleyn. 'Ever since his execution, the family fell into disfavour. An unusual gathering at their house seems guaranteed to arouse suspicion.'

'They know we are rehearsing. And we have Andrew. If anyone visits, we shall switch to *Henry VIII*. Honestly, Ned – if you heard that the Admiral's Men were meeting at Essex House, would you suspect covert work?'

Alleyn shrugged. 'I suppose not.' He put out an arm for Constance, stooping beneath the beam as he followed her down.

'I'll see you off,' said Shakespeare.

At the bottom of the stairs he held the innkeeper's glance and gave a tiny nod. Then he stood in Cheapside for a moment, watching Alleyn help Constance over a puddle and into the carriage. He looked past them to where his own escort had whittled at his nails, but the man was gone. Perhaps he had run out of fingers.

Armin, Taylor and Harvard stepped into the road beside him.

'We'll leave you as well,' said Taylor. 'Robert is due at the Globe, so we can escort young John here back to Southwark, if that helps.'

'Thank you, sir,' said Harvard.

'Your manners are as fine as your work. Thank *you*.'

'A fellow of great wisdom, too,' said Armin. 'He was just explaining why, when you lose something, it always seems to be in the last place you look.'

'That is indeed true,' said Shakespeare.

Harvard grinned. 'It is *always* true, and for this one reason: when you find what is lost, you stop looking.'

'Very clever.'

'Thank you, sir.'

Shakespeare grimaced.

'Get used to it, Will,' said Armin. 'It is not so easy to unsir yourself.'

Upstairs, Heminge and Burbage had already poured themselves a drink. Burbage had hoisted his feet up on a stool and was peeling an onion.

'Is all well?' he said, without turning round.

'That man out there,' said Shakespeare.

Burbage stopped peeling.

'He's gone.'

'I can't say I blame him,' said Burbage. 'A tedious assignment.'

'But good to know that his vigil was half-hearted,' said Heminge. 'It suggests you were right: they were only going through the motions. You're sure he was gone?'

'Well, I couldn't see him.'

'Not *quite* the same thing. But it will do.'

'Oh,' Shakespeare said. 'One thing. Do be careful with the manuscript. Richard came to my house the other day and surprised a couple of intruders. They barged past him and fled. And they didn't take anything, so we don't know what they were about. It doesn't seem likely they were after these pages – at any rate they didn't take them – but it may be best not to run any risks.'

'Intruders?'

'As I say, we have no idea who they were.'

Heminge scowled. 'Strange they did not take anything.'

'In truth, there was little to take. Some milk, a jug of ale, a few books. It was by no means pleasant, but there is no cause to panic. I confess, though, I do remain a little worried about Ned.'

'Worried?' said Burbage.

'You said yourself he was not one of us.'

'And *you* said that we needed him.'

'He's good, I admit it. But I'm not so sure we need him any more.'

'Bit late now,' said Burbage.

'It isn't that,' said Heminge.

'Isn't what?'

'Will doesn't like the way Ned paws at that young girl.'

'Oh . . . that. Well, he has a point there.'

'I am glad you agree,' said Shakespeare. 'It is painful to watch.'

'Well, he is a bit overfond,' said Burbage. 'But I think the little lady can handle herself perfectly well. Besides, Ned is the most uxorious man we know. I do not believe he harbours any untoward designs on Constance.'

'I didn't mean anything so coarse.'

'Didn't you?'

'I did not.'

No one said anything.

'I didn't,' repeated Shakespeare.

Burbage poured Shakespeare a drink and passed it across.

'Anyway, that's the least of our worries. The main thing is . . . this play. I am afraid there is a speech coming, because, by God, we're on to something here. You should be all smiles – you still have the gift, Will! And Robert's on fine form, isn't he?'

'Indeed. Never been better.'

'And the girl.'

'A revelation, I agree.'

'It could not have come at a better time. The fact is, we've all been aching to get our teeth into something strong again. London is rotting, and most of us are sick at heart. You are returning us to the old days, Will, and it's great. We're back, and we're giving them something new. So have another drink and stop worrying about Constance. She has all the bravado of youth. She can see off old Ned with one eye closed.'

'I do not think of youth as fearless,' said Shakespeare. 'Nor do I know why people think it so. It is a fearful time, a fretful time. But you are right . . .'

He put his hand over his cup, declining another drink, and tried to shake off the image of Constance. It was hard, but not impossible, because his head was already swimming with ideas for future scenes. He could see rebel armies gathering in the West, urged on by bitter curses from foreign courts. In the distance he could make out English ships nosing among ice floes, where white bears slid into green depths, and he could see courtiers fluttering at the King's displeasure. He could hear the infant cries of two boys, the King's sons. He saw craftsmen and poets labouring over presses, and candlelight in a window of the Tower, late at night, where a sleepless king muttered over sums. He did not have to close his eyes to see these things; they barged their way to the front of his mind and hammered at the door.

It was often like this. He only had to drop threads into his private pool of visions and haul out crystalline scenes. All he needed now was pen, ink and plentiful fresh paper. The rest, he hoped, would be history.

Chapter
11

The following morning Shakespeare pushed open his front door and breathed in the cold river air only a few moments after first light. It smelled of fish and dung. He did not tarry, but marched with rapid steps past St Paul's and up to the Greyhound. The streets were clear. More than once he glanced behind in search of his soldierly escort, but while there were various figures in his wake, flitting between doorways bearing baskets or sacks, there was nothing to make his pulse race. A kite flopped into a line of washing and tore away a strip of linen for its nest; a pair of carpenters hacked at a pile of logs; a goat relieved itself on a pile of sacks. But that was all. Maybe the man, bored by his slumber in Cheapside, had given up; or perhaps it was just too early.

After a few taps, the landlord let him in and ushered him into the back room. The stoat-faced boy was swirling a crust of bread in a bowl of warm ale. When he saw Shakespeare, he wiped his mouth with the back of a grimy hand and stood up.

'Well?' Shakespeare said. 'What did you learn?'

'I followed the carriage, like you said. It stopped in Ludgate and that tall man run inside. He didn't stay long. Came out with a leather book. Then the carriage moved on to Drury Lane, where the young lady got out.'

Shakespeare nodded. Crisp and brief: the boy was an ideal messenger.

'The carriage went down to Westminster going a fair clip. I had to run to keep up. Venturely it stopped in front of a big house, very important looking.'

'Where, exactly?'

'Part of the palace. On the flank of the inner yard, facing away from the river. He went through a great door, above it there was an emblem – a rose, with a star.'

Shakespeare shivered. He knew the yard, the building, even the motif. In his worst moments he had not anticipated this. He fought to keep his voice calm.

'What else?'

'He stayed best part of an hour. It was starting to get dark. When he came out, the carriage took him only a little way along the water to another great house.'

Shakespeare was about to speak, but the boy put a hand up.

'Don't worry, I know a name. Arundel House. Very big people, your friend knows.'

'Thank you.' Shakespeare reached in his pocket. 'Here.'

The money disappeared into a fold of the boy's jacket.

'You haven't heard the best bit yet.'

'There's more?'

'I hung about in a doorway, hidden from the road. And a good job I did, because other people started arriving. A couple I didn't recognise, but handsomely dressed, very senior, you could tell. And then someone I *did* recognise.'

Shakespeare waited.

'Want to know who it was?'

Shakespeare nodded.

The boy waited.

Shakespeare found a fresh coin and laid it on the table. The boy covered it with a quick hand.

'One of the great men of the country,' he said. 'Sir Edward Coke.'

It was as if someone had walked on Shakespeare's grave. A chill fell on his heart.

'No.'

'It was the man himself. I swear it.'

'Coke?'

Shakespeare could not believe it. His mind was beginning to race. What a blind, naive, provincial goose he was. For a moment he felt his brains slide about behind his brow like loose beads on a string. Alleyn and Coke? Heaven defend them all.

With a sigh he contemplated his folly. He had assumed, with an easygoing conceit that now bit deep, that his friends revolved around *him* – that he was their sun, their moon, their all-sustaining rain. Who could tell how many other involvements and obligations Alleyn had developed over the years? It wasn't as if Shakespeare's play was his only or even his main interest; he was a man of the world, with connections and hopes that even Shakespeare could only marvel at. He probably dined at Arundel House all the time, with Coke, the Mayor and the rest.

It brought back the stabbing sense of inferiority that had accompanied his very first steps in the city, thirty years earlier. He had walked these streets as a homeless newcomer, gaping and dazzled by the ease with which Londoners commanded the air. It made him shudder that he had changed so little; a couple of years away had been enough to turn him back into a country oaf, dumbfounded by the pageant.

He did not move; he had the sensation that he was sheltering from a storm, besieged by hostile forces he could not even see. It was like being harried by silent flies that stung him now on the shoulder, now on the thigh, now in the heart – all he could do was flick them away with his ears like some slow, lumbering ox.

When sorrows come, he said to himself, they come not single spies, but in battalions. It was not a cheerful thought, but somehow the words helped him regain his balance. He did not like seeing himself depicted, by his own mind, as a dupe, a plaything. And why should he endure all these whips and scorns without fighting back? He was not, after all, without powers of his own. This play, if it could be brought off, was a weapon. He must be calm, and then make medicine of his great revenge.

The boy was still standing there.

'What is your name?' said Shakespeare.

'Kit,' said the boy.

'An apt title. You have the right equipment. I thank you for your pains.'

He handed over some more money, and slumped on a nearby bench. Dinner at Arundel House was one thing, and Shakespeare could not deny that the thought of Alleyn reaching for the wine there in the company of Coke bothered him a good deal. It was the earlier visit that really made his heart knock in its cage. Shakespeare was not eager to confront the fact squarely, even to himself, but there was no shirking it. The dark entrance into which Alleyn had disappeared the previous evening was the worst place he could possibly have visited, home to the King's most feared enforcers. A few of Shakespeare's friends had been summoned into that shadow; none had emerged unchanged.

With a surge of fellow feeling he thought of Raleigh in his dark, lonely tower, a lighthouse keeper wrapped up in his sea charts and nursing the flame of exploration in an ocean of clouds. England was not, he reminded himself, at peace. He still had vivid memories of the time – the twins were squalling, and he had just begun *Venus and Adonis* – when Spain's hulking galleons were chased up the Channel and into the brunt of those North Sea storms; it seemed only yesterday that Fawkes and his idiot cronies had tried to blow up the King. Peace was always promised, yet remained no more than a dream. The Crown was ever-vigilant and numberless good men had languished in its cells: Raleigh, Essex, Southampton, Neville and so many others. Hundreds had been lost or abandoned in the dark webs of government power and intrigue, in plots so murky that even Shakespeare could only guess at them.

He looked up and saw quick scavengers wheeling overhead, eyes bright for carrion. He lurched with the kind of panic he had once experienced in the toils of a river, when chance had carried him out of his depth; like Harvard, he could not swim.

He closed his eyes and told himself that it would pass.

He might have stayed there for a while longer had the bells of St Paul's not clanged in noisy unison and broken his reflective mood. London was a city of chimes; in certain locales they had a gentle, neighbourly quality, but here they were urgent, explosive. His first thought was to go home – to rest and think. But he also needed breakfast. He stopped the innkeeper and requested bread with herrings and eggs.

'That reminds me,' said the innkeeper, advancing with a wooden board of food. 'I have something for you.'

He had pockets like saddlebags. One contained a package, wrapped in cloth and tied with string.

'A gentleman left it here for you. Remarkable fellow, he was. Most unusual.'

'How so?'

'All clad in purple, head to toe. And the biggest hat I have ever seen.'

Stanyhurst?

'How did he know to reach me here?'

'He did not say.'

'Did he leave a name?'

'No. Only this.'

Shakespeare began to open the package, then thought better of it.

'Thank you,' he said. 'And for this breakfast, too.'

He looked at it and sighed. The fish was black, the eggs grey and weak.

'You look like you could use a bit of strengthening,' said the innkeeper. 'I promise you it tastes better than it looks.'

He wasn't lying. Shakespeare gulped it down and almost asked for more. Odd: he had been ignoring mountains of delicious food, only to be rendered ravenous by this thin stuff. But he was anxious to inspect his parcel, so he tucked Stanyhurst's gift in his coat and hurried home. He found several pretexts – a dropped glove, the flight of a bird, the purchase of paper – to stop and look about him, without seeing a single sign of anything amiss.

When he reached his house he pushed the door closed, sat on the bench in the hall and unwound the packet. It was a collection of loose papers roughly bound between two coarse slabs of leather. The pages were handwritten in a small, determined script in – he sighed – Latin.

Curious.

A piece of parchment fell to the floor, and this time the lettering was in a careful, shapely English. It was printed in the form of a dedication.

TO.THE.ONLY.BEGETTER.OF.
THESE.ENSUING.PAGES.
MR.W.S.OUR.COURT.SHALL.BE.
A.LITTLE.ACADEME.
BY.
OUR.EVER-SEEKING.POET.
WHO.WISHETH.FAME.THAT.ALL.
HUNT.AFTER.IN.THEIR.LIVES.
IN.THE.NAME.OF.THE.FATHER.
AND.THE.SON.

He shivered like a rabbit hypnotised by torches. The layout and even the words were a direct echo of the dedication he himself had attached to his Sonnets all those years ago. It was cryptic, but addressed to himself – who else could be W.S.?

What was Stanyhurst up to?

There was no doubt that it *was* the Duke of Navarre. The purple costume implied as much and this inscription confirmed it. The 'little academe' was a reference to the scholarly court the Duke wished to impose in *Love's Labour's Lost*. And the fame that all hunt after in their lives: that was the first line of the same play.

The suggestion of a prayer at the end expressed something fervent – a plea? – but it was also infused with the sense of an ending. It felt melancholy.

This was a request, Shakespeare decided.

But for what?

He turned the parchment over. There, in chalk, was a hasty scrawl. 'Forgive this rambling envoy. I would not bring trouble to your door. Farewell.'

He scratched his head. This time the meaning was not remotely opaque: Stanyhurst was merely explaining why he had not dropped this journal at Shakespeare's own house; he knew where he lived, after all.

It was the final word that made him blanch.

Farewell.

It was like a coin settling on the floor of a fountain. Suddenly it reflected the light and became visible. Shakespeare could see it all now.

Stanyhurst had been discovered and was fleeing for his life. He was passing these pages to Shakespeare, not just for safe keeping but for inspection, perhaps even for completion. What had he said at their meeting? 'The time will come for such revelations as will astound your ears.' Shakespeare had taken this to be the overheated claim of an excited mind, but what if it were genuine? He himself had told Stanyhurst that he aimed to tell truths about kings. What if this were one, and he had been too dull to listen?

He pressed his temples, trying to recall exactly what the two of them had been talking about in Salisbury House, when Stanyhurst had made this bold protestation.

It would not come. It was something to do with a scandal surrounding Henry VIII, but that was not controversial: scandals about Henry VIII were ten a penny.

Maybe the book itself would hold the answer. Shakespeare pored over the early paragraphs, but the Latin was written in a compact script, as if Stanyhurst himself did not wish it to be easily accessible. It was not easy to translate a single sentence.

This would have to wait. He had a play to write. *The True and Tragicall Historie of Henry VII* was far enough advanced for him to see it whole now, and it was important that he set it all down – before, like a ghost at first light, it dissolved.

He walked upstairs, put Stanyhurst's book to one side, took out the paper he had bought on the way home and began to write.

He could not accurately have told anyone how he passed the next several hours. He was lost in his own creative reverie. In a rapid hand that skated across the white paper like a bird landing on water, he mapped out his scenery. The play would begin in Westminster, with those wedding speeches; and then would come badinage between ladies of the court. Scenes of subtle diplomacy would dovetail with Armin's talkative citizenry and then he would cut to the marrow: the death of Tyrell.

Act One would close with a shudder and a sense of rising apprehension.

Act Two would start with a flurry of episodes showing the King's public face. He would put down a rebel army at Stoke and harass his nobles. Cabot and the citizens would mock the New World, and then the King would steal downriver, disguised as an assassin, and murder the boy Princes. Shakespeare smiled to imagine it.

It was time, before the throne was even truly his, to summon up fresh enemies. In Flanders, Margaret would launch another claimant. The King would feel dogged, hounded, hemmed in. He would enlist his own spies and turncoats, and permit himself a soliloquy or two. The crown would start to weigh heavy on his soul.

Now the descent would begin, the trajectory Burbage wanted. Just when the King was flying high, ever nearer the sun, fate would steal upon him and exact its price. It would peck at his safety and his life; it would seize his first-born son, his queen and his peace of mind. He would begin the long, slow fall to earth, like a spent royal firework.

Nothing made Shakespeare laugh more than the idea that playwrights put their own life stories on the stage. In his time he had written about English kings, French dukes, Venetian Jews, Danish gravediggers, Scots, Romans and Egyptians. He had little in common with any of them except their everyday humanity: their fondness, fear and hunger. However, he was never averse to plundering his own emotions for verse. There would be opportunities to embed his high regard for Constance in some other lover's tongue, or to elevate his own suspicions of Alleyn into a proper royal intrigue.

For the final act . . . Well, Shakespeare had never planned too far ahead and he was not about to begin now. One way or another, the King's enemies would surround him like a pack of wolves. They would tear at his legs and snap at his throat. Eventually, like all kings, he would succumb. The dogs would have their day.

When he was done, he blinked. It was never easy, returning from these imaginary voyages into the lives of others. The daylight seemed unnatural and bright. And since he did not want his own affairs to interfere with the resonant world he had just wandered through in his mind's eye, he kicked off his boots, lay on his bed and slept for the rest of the day.

This was an unusual departure for him, which he found himself driven to because he could not allow himself to brood on Stanyhurst, Alleyn, Coke, mysterious packages, unwelcome visitors, imprisoned sea captains, dignitaries of the realm and the treachery of friends. Neptune, he sensed, was shaking his trident. Ink-black clouds were piling up on distant waves, and the nervous wind was whistling the arrival of a storm. There was no snug harbour now: he would have to face the tempest head-on – but he needed rest before it struck.

Shakespeare had never found it hard to think; *not* thinking was the hard part. This time, however, he tipped into sleep like a man who had stepped by mischance into a well; it seemed that nothing could stop his fall as he plunged into the consoling shadows below. It was just as well; one way or another, there would be plenty to do in the days to come.

The trip back to Stratford could hardly have come at a worse time. It could not be avoided, however. Awkward clouds were gathering over his holdings on the margins of the town – strips of farmland held as rents. One of Warwick's already-wealthy squires wanted to enclose fresh pasture for his cows. It meant that the tenant farmers – of whom Shakespeare was one – would no longer be able to collect their tithes.

Stratford was in an uproar. Councillors and aldermen were insisting that land enclosure of this sort was a devilish betrayal of both their ancestral rights and their children's future. Hundreds of poor families, they swore, depended on these small plots for their living. And this was only the latest outbreak in a continuing protest; half a dozen years earlier there had been an angry riot – almost a crusade! – in which several thousand people ranged over the countryside, pulling up hedges and filling in ditches, attacking enclosures wherever they could be found.

In private, Shakespeare could be heard to declare that enclosure was no bad thing, so long as tithe holders (such as himself) were properly compensated for their loss. Much of the land in question, though in theory held by villagers, was ill kept and unprofitable. It might indeed be simpler to collect a fee from a larger-scale farmer. He sighed. He knew that the township of Stratford would take a different view.

He might have declined the request that he return had it not coincided with an even more troublesome matter concerning his daughter Susanna. She was steadily, if not happily, married to a worthy enough fellow, Doctor Hall, but apparently a rascal called John Lane had been making crude accusations of unfaithfulness involving Susanna and a haberdasher, one Rafe Smith. The Halls wanted to file suit against Lane, for slander. Shakespeare was hoping he could persuade them to desist. Even a victorious suit would blacken their name.

He decided to ride – he needed the exercise – and joined a convoy of perhaps a dozen travellers on the same road. They set out early and were working their way through the magical Chiltern woodland by about noon, rocking in their saddles as squirrels and doves scratched and hooted in the branches overhead. They spent the night at a roomy old inn near Oxford, rose early and followed the Cherwell River north.

When he passed Banbury, Shakespeare began to look forward to seeing the low rooves of Stratford once more. He squeezed his knees into the horse's flanks, quickening the pace. Spring was bursting in the trees on either side; he was riding through a wild green tree tunnel. By the time he sighted the silver slash of the Avon he was a changed man: no longer Will, the playwright, scourge of kings and the toast of the capital, but Mr Shakespeare, gentleman, husband and merchant.

He didn't mind. He was used to wearing more than one cap. It would please him to see Susanna and besides, there was a five-year-old granddaughter to play with.

He stayed only one night. The following morning he rose before dawn and raced back to London, returning in plenty of time for his date with the King's Men.

On Wednesday he was ready and waiting when his carriage arrived. He climbed in with barely a word, and clip-clopped up to the cathedral.

Harvard was loitering in the spacious courtyard at the front of the great church. All Shakespeare had to do was open the door.

'Jump in.'

Harvard looked back and waved. A small knot of people shook their caps and cheered. They were standing round a gaily painted barrow out of which young boys in blindfolds would later draw lottery balls.

'Master Shakespeare!'

'Quick!' Shakespeare pulled the curtain closed. 'Let's be off.'

'Shakespeare! It's Will Shakespeare! Hurry!'

'I didn't tell them,' said Harvard. 'But somehow they knew it was you.'

'Did they now?' The word was out: Shakespeare was back in harness. It would not be easy to behave as if nothing was unusual.

They soon reached Constance. Harvard was about to tap on her door when it opened; she must have heard the trotting hooves.

Shakespeare stepped down, wrinkling his nose against the reek. Drury Lane was no longer the pestilential gutter it had been when he first arrived in London, but it was still an acrid, muddy slum. At the end of the road stood the Cockpit, where tormented birds flew at each other in front of a cackling mob.

Constance leaped up the step without requiring a hand. Harvard hopped in behind and Shakespeare took his own seat facing the front. Leaning forward, he knocked on the board between their heads to indicate to the driver that they could leave.

At first he was too preoccupied to enjoy the ride; indeed, he wished he were alone. Constance filled the emptiness by playing a game of fist-and-palm with Harvard, laughing merrily when she lost. Shakespeare sighed – oh to be so young.

He tried to draw back, but it was too late. Like a traveller marching towards a swamp, he had strayed into the central, thudding sorrow of his life. He had been on guard for so many years now and was usually skilled at keeping such thoughts at arm's length; but sometimes they sneaked through his defences. Not many people knew that he usually tied a black ribbon tightly around his upper arm as a permanent reminder of his grief. Today he had been in too much haste to wind it on.

When he looked at Harvard's grateful, happy smile he saw the visage of his own son, Hamnet, dead these two decades but as vibrant in his mind as ever. He shook his head as if to rid himself of a wasp, but it would not be repelled. He could feel his heart foundering, and a band of sweat formed on his neck. It never eased.

As they approached Whitehall the road grew wider and firmer. Shakespeare urged himself to descend to more level terrain.

'What think you of our group?' he said.

'What think I?' said Constance. 'I think you are all very distinguished.'

'I trust you have felt no cold shoulders.'

'None.'

'Burbage has been kind?'

'Very.'

'Robert and Joseph are good men.'

'They have made me – both of us – very welcome.'

'And Alleyn . . . a fine fellow, is he not?'

'Oh, very fine indeed.'

'And yet somehow . . . clouded?'

'Clouded?'

'I rarely feel I am seeing the whole figure.'

'You are playing with me, sir.' Her voice was grave.

Shakespeare leaned back, stifling a sigh. 'Very wealthy, of course. He does not need this work. He could buy the rest of us with the faintest rub of his fingers.'

'He does seem to lack for nothing. His new house is certainly grand.'

'He told you about it?'

'Yesterday. In his carriage. We stopped at Ludgate to pick up some books and papers.'

'Papers?'

'Drawings of the house. He showed them to me. *Most* grand.'

Shakespeare slumped back on the hard bench. This was one mystery solved. He hadn't even begun to speculate about the suspicious 'papers' Alleyn had collected in Ludgate; and if he had, he would have been plagued by the fear that they were a guilty secret. This news reminded him how easy it was to leap to conclusions. He of all people should have known – his own Iago had taught him all about the trouble a simple handkerchief could inspire, in malignant hands! Everything looked two-faced when seen through a jealous squint.

'Yes, he has means now,' he said. 'Still a man of the theatre, I suppose – but it is not stagecraft that keeps him in ermine. He holds the licence for bear-baiting – did he speak of that? If you have been to the ring, his are the pockets you have lined.'

'Not with my coin,' said Constance. 'I should be ashamed to take pleasure in the death of noble creatures. I consider it the darkest and most vulgar cruelty.'

Shakespeare felt an unvirtuous thrill run through him; he had dented Alleyn in Constance's eyes. Her vehemence took him aback, though. He knew there were people opposed to such rough entertainments, but he had never met one. It astonished him that a girl so young could be so original.

'Have you ever been?'

'Never. And I never shall.'

'It *is* rough sport.'

'Do you go very often?'

'Not for years. I too find it a grisly spectacle.'

'Is it true the bear is chained to a post?'

'Oh yes. He cannot escape. And then they set the dogs upon him. The hounds have speed, numbers and snapping jaws. The bear has his pink-eyed fury and fabled strength. He can cuff the dogs aside, and if his claws reach their bellies . . .'

Constance grimaced.

'I am sorry. You are right. It is a bloody and terrible spectacle.'

'Do the dogs always win? Does the bear have a chance?'

'Oh yes. The curs suffer too. I once saw one hurled high into a balcony. Landed on a fine lady. She was quite badly scratched. Everyone thought it was wonderful.'

'What's the worst thing you ever saw – in a bear pit, I mean?'

'One time they chained a monkey to the back of the bear. The dogs were leaping, and the screaming of the ape tore into the sky and maddened the beast. It was awful. But the most dreadful part is when men with whips assail a blinded bear. They lash away while the bear flails at their rods. *That* is torture. *That* is cruelty.'

'Why do men go?'

'It is not just men. But mainly they go to wager.'

'There must be more to it than that. They could wager on snails.'

'You are right,' said Shakespeare. 'And even I, when I say I hate it . . . there is a part of me that loves it too. It might be that I love it *because* I hate it. If it left me indifferent, I should be cold as a crab, and *then* I would be ashamed.'

'That is subtle,' said Constance. 'I know not why the sight of blood makes men's hearts jump with pleasure. It is hateful, and truly common.'

It had been a while since Shakespeare felt so chastised. But he was not as frail as at times, these days, he seemed. He smiled.

'I know I am common,' said Shakespeare. 'Yet hunting is not only a primitive pleasure; it is modern civilisation too – sport and theatre mixed. It was vital when men lived wild; but we are no longer lions. Food can be found more safely by growing it. So men merely play at hunting; they *act* it. It is a game, a stage for their stories. It gives pepper to their boasts. We do not call them *plays* for nothing.'

'I confess I had not thought of that,' said Constance. 'But surely this makes my argument for me. Killing animals for sport . . . As you say, in the old days there was nothing else to do. Now we have the theatres, we have . . . *you*. We need not prod bears to be entertained – or enlightened.'

Shakespeare took a deep breath. 'Have you seen my tragedies? *Lear*? *Othello*?'

'Both,' said Constance. 'Many times. I consider them – and I don't say this to flatter, believe me – as great as anything that ever was put on a stage.'

The compliment was so wholehearted and unforced, it made Shakespeare lurch.

'Why, thank you,' he said. 'I *am* flattered, whatever you intend.'

Her hand in her lap lay golden in the morning light, fingers forming easy curves.

'Oh, you must hear such things all the time,' said Constance, blushing.

'You'd be surprised,' said Shakespeare. 'People rarely fail to deliver criticism, though congratulations often stick in the throat.'

'I am sorry to hear it,' said Constance, turning her face aside.

'Here is my point,' said Shakespeare. 'Do those plays remind you of anything? If not, well, I am sorry to *bear* bad news, but I swear – on my son's grave – that they were inspired by nothing less than the baiting of those noble beasts. Sad grandees, lashing out at enemies they cannot see, who swarm about them, too quick for their stiff old limbs. The drama is the same, you see. A great soul under assault from lesser creatures, toppling and howling at the stars . . .'

'I had not seen it that way,' repeated Constance.

She looked crestfallen. Shakespeare kept his voice gentle.

'And consider the design of our theatres; look at the Globe. It is based on the bear-baiting pens; theirs is the architecture in which we work. Close by your lodgings stands the Cockpit – a dreadful arena, you say, foul and . . . common. What is it but a theatre, a forum where even Caesar could fall to the pack and die?'

Constance frowned, then brightened.

'But this too agrees with what I said. Because I really *do* prize your *Lear* and *Othello* above the baiting of bears. Far above. You have stolen all their thunder. Now that we have *your* plays, we can dispense with the clumsy murder of those poor dumb creatures . . .'

'I can't deny that it's cruel. But it's a *theatre* of cruelty.'

'A theatre of *mere* cruelty, you should say. Raised into true theatre, with great souls and mighty verse, as you do, we have tragedy.'

'How old did you say you were?'

'Sixteen,' said Constance. 'Nearly.'

'Your father has taught you much,' said Shakespeare.

'My mother too,' said Constance.

'Of course,' said Shakespeare.

The carriage was slowing. They were about to arrive.

'I surrender,' said Shakespeare with a smile. 'But please do not tell Edward that I am the man who has made his bear-pits obsolete. He may not thank me.'

'I will play the mute,' said Constance, smiling. 'I will be a second Andrew, and bite my feathered tongue.'

Shakespeare smiled. 'Be sure you die not in music.'

'If I do, sir, then you must bear the blame. You are famous for minting words.'

'You catch me incarnadine,' said Shakespeare. 'And I shall tell you a secret. It is only because I am always in such haste. If I had more time, I would correct half of them. Anyway, the truth is that I don't make up nearly so many as people think. A good number are things I hear at the market, or in the stables, or from the watermen.'

'I do not see how your plays could be improved,' said Constance.

'Thank you,' said Shakespeare. 'And by the way, please don't call me sir.'

It was warm in the carriage, and Constance's scent – apples and honey – was sweet. A drowsy feeling stole across Shakespeare like a mild, delicious breeze; he longed to give himself over, to surrender. At that moment the driver opened the door with a slap and a here-we-are, and cold air whipped their faces.

'I am so sorry,' Shakespeare said to Harvard. 'You have been so quiet; we have ignored you terribly.'

'I was happy listening,' said Harvard.

'I fear I was being very dull, all that talk of the theatre.'

'Not at all, sir. Though I, like Constance, cheer for the bear.'

A hat came through the opening.

'Morning, Will,' said Heminge. 'Morning, you two.'

'I am glad to see you, John,' said Shakespeare.

'I have news,' said Heminge. 'We need to talk.'

They clambered into the road and looked about. They were in a narrow street that led down to the river, but through a gap in the houses to their right they could see the immense summits of Westminster Abbey rising up into the sky.

Shakespeare peered up with an experienced gaze.

'Here we are,' he said. 'Essex House. I hope you feel honoured: this is where the Prince Palatine stayed when he came to woo the King's daughter.'

'Then we are going up in the world,' said Constance.

'I am afraid I must ask a favour,' said Shakespeare. 'Constance, I wonder if you would mind walking with John for an interval. I have commerce with Heminge a while.'

Shakespeare watched them go, then turned.

'How do you like our play?'

'It is perfect, but that is not what occupies me.'

'What news?'

'I tremble to deliver it,' said Heminge. 'It is as we feared. Worse.'

'Say it with all speed, then. Put it behind you.'

'Look at this.' He held out a torn sheet of paper. 'I pulled it from a wall at Aldwych. It is about that man you met – Stanyhurst.'

Shakespeare held the paper close and read. It was a crudely printed declaration of war, a paper bill depicting several 'prisoners-at-large' and 'ingrates'. It offered a reward of five pounds for news leading to their capture.

Shakespeare fought to ignore a roaring in his ears.

'What does it mean?' said Heminge.

'He should not have been here in London,' said Shakespeare. 'He is a Catholic apologist, and has been banished. His disguise must have slipped. He has been discovered.'

'Should we worry?'

'I told him nothing. I was hoping to discover what he knew about Henry VII, but he was more interested in Henry VIII. I did not tell him of our plan.'

'Thank God!'

Shakespeare stared at a pattern of deep boot marks in the mud. There was more to this than he could tell Heminge. Whilst he did not fear that Stanyhurst would incriminate the King's Men, he could not quell the sensation that he himself might have betrayed Stanyhurst. Could his own visit have been the spark that had lit this fire?

'That's not all,' said Heminge.

A cog slipped in Shakespeare's mental machinery; a wheel spun. *The book!*

Shakespeare closed his eyes so he could see the words in the inscription more clearly. 'I would not bring trouble to your door.' Stanyhurst was running for his life, and one of his final impulses was to hand over his secret papers. If Shakespeare, whom he barely knew, was his most trusted confederate, he could not have had many friends.

He clenched his teeth. Despite itching to inspect the book more closely, he did not want to cancel this day's work, or set tongues a-wagging. It would have to wait until this afternoon.

A shadow moved on his foot.

'I am sorry,' he said, looking up. 'You were saying.'

'The other news is no better,' said Heminge. 'You know that man we recruited to follow your escort? He trailed him all the way to this very neighbourhood, right by the Hall of Westminster itself, on the water.'

Shakespeare groaned. He thought he knew where this was leading.

'Would you like me to guess,' he said, 'which doorway he entered?'

'How could you possibly know?'

'In the East Yard, perchance? A long house with a rose and a star over the lintel?'

'What is this, Will?' said Heminge. 'It is not funny.'

'I heard the selfsame news myself only a short while ago.'

He waited for Heminge's reaction. None came.

'I might as well tell you, then,' he continued. '*I* had a man follow Ned—'

'Ned? Why? Will, what in pity's name is going on?'

'Never mind for now. I had . . . reasons.'

'And?'

'Ned went through that very same door.'

'I don't believe it. Are you sure?'

'Yes.'

They fell silent. The room behind the door into which Alleyn and the soldier had passed was one of the most famous in England, as well as one of the most feared. For a hundred years it had been a byword for the imposition of order and in recent times it had taken on an even more sinister association – as the ante-room of tyranny. Thanks to the celestial emblems on the dark ceiling it was known as Star Chamber. It gave Shakespeare only a brief flicker of pleasure to register the poetic justice by which this awesome institution had been founded by none other than their own great subject, the father of the Tudor line, King Henry VII himself.

'Let's walk,' said Shakespeare.

They wandered towards Whitehall. Both knew that on this cool April morning their lives had taken a treacherous turn. And while it wasn't easy to see an exact pattern in their discoveries, the connection between one of their intimates and the powers of the realm felt too close for comfort. The threat to Stanyhurst also seemed personal. Shakespeare himself had sharper reasons to be afraid – he had been

205

brushed by the flailing paw of political force – and he realised that he could not protect his secret for much longer. It was not fair on Heminge, Burbage, or any of them. He had led them into choppy waters; he could not in all conscience hide the chart.

He kept his head down as he walked, wondering how he could best raise this delicate theme, when he was rocked by a sudden commotion beside him. A young man in dusty, ragged clothes barged into Heminge and threw him to the ground.

Shakespeare could not tell whether he was slow to react, or whether time itself dawdled. Either way, the scene swam before him: he saw the assailant pawing at the strap over Heminge's shoulder – Cry heaven! He was clawing at the leather bag!

A thief. In broad daylight.

The observations marched past in an agonisingly slow parade.

Fortunately, someone else reacted instantly. A passing carter set down his barrow of vegetables, dashed into the fray and grabbed the man's hair. The thief rose up, yelled, lashed out with wild fists, broke free and ran off.

Heminge sat up. He was dirty and bruised, but otherwise unhurt.

Shakespeare was neither alarmed nor reprieved. Instead he felt marooned, bowed down by an overwhelming sadness. It was as though he were not present here, not standing in this road, not even a witness to this uproar.

'Will?' He heard a voice from far away. 'Will? Are you safe?'

He forced his head to turn. The carter was helping Heminge to his feet.

'Thank you,' said Heminge. 'How can I thank you? If you hadn't . . . Will?'

The blur passed. Shakespeare was again able to connect sights with sounds.

'I am sorry,' he said, a hand to his head. 'John . . . what happened?'

'Nothing. Thanks to this fine fellow.'

The carter beamed. He had obviously enjoyed it.

'Your friend seemed flustered. Skinny runt. After your bag, I'd say.'

'Then he would have gone empty handed,' said Heminge. 'There's nothing in it but paper.' He stopped. Something seemed to strike him.

He took the bag from his shoulder and inspected a deep gash in the strap.

'Thank God for the Italian who made this bag,' he said. 'That scoundrel was trying to cut it free. Nearly did it, too.'

Shakespeare swept dirt and stones from Heminge's back. 'You should have let him take it. He had a knife. He might have maimed you.'

'No matter,' said Heminge. 'I could not yield the bag.'

'Your courage steals much honour from the thief,' said Shakespeare. He sighed. 'But this man knew what he was after, we can hardly doubt that.'

Heminge nodded. Shakespeare frowned.

He trembled to think of what they had so nearly lost. He had read that in faraway lands, in China and the Orient, the earth shook violently enough to fell trees, fling buildings to the ground and crack open hillsides. Such catastrophes must resemble the way he felt now. Westminster, Whitehall, the whole city of London seemed to tilt and slide towards the river. He had a keen sense of ebbing, as if swept out to sea.

He groped for safety in the rigging of everyday manners.

'I wish we had something to give you for your trouble,' he said to the carter.

'You could buy some cabbages. Or potatoes. Look at these beauties. Fresh off the boat from the colonies. Hand-raised by the guv'nor, old Walter Raleigh himself.'

Shakespeare snorted. It was not always true that news travelled fast. Here was one man over whom the rumour mill had not yet ground.

'In that case,' he said, 'give us a bushel. Here.'

'All's well that ends well,' sighed the carter, scooping potatoes into a sack.

Shakespeare sniffed one. The soil smelled like the fields of Essex, sour and marshy, but it was more enjoyable to believe that these strange new roots had ridden the great swells of the Atlantic.

When the carter left they picked over the bones of what had happened.

'We can't be sure,' said Heminge. 'It could have been chance.'

Shakespeare didn't think so. Although he could not pick out the exact shape, there seemed to be a looming menace on all sides. There had been a battle once – he could not recall which – where an army was exposed on a frozen lake. It was too far from land to see the horsemen plashing through the woods, the warriors shifting in the wings, yet with every hour that passed the army's position became more and more exposed.

That was how it felt now: he was in the heart of a trap, its jaws closing about him.

'Fish do not see the net,' he said. 'Even so, they sense a disturbance in the tide.'

It seemed certain to both of them that they had put themselves in harm's way, and equally clear that someone was keeping a close eye on their progress. It did not take witchcraft to divine that Alleyn was betraying them all.

'It has to be him,' said Heminge. 'This is too rough a coincidence.'

'I wish it were not so,' said Shakespeare, in the flat tone of an almost-beaten man.

'What about that time you told me about, when he walked out and then returned? And it was Alleyn who organised the visit by the Chamberlain.'

'And Alleyn who protested that our plot was treacherous. Damn.'

'You must not blame yourself. These are precarious times.'

'And yet . . .' said Shakespeare, still unwilling to concede. 'I of all people should know that nothing is so deceptive as appearances. Oh, one may smile and smile and be a villain – but one can also frown and be a friend. I'll not hang him yet.'

'But Will, the *camera stellata*! We can't ignore that. It is serious.'

'You may be right.'' Shakespeare was animated. 'Yet if Ned is talking to the Star Chamber, why should they clip a spy to my heels? If he is telling them what we are doing, they have no need for the cloak and dagger. There are still mysteries here.'

Heminge frowned. 'If this be not so bad as it appears, neither can it be good.'

'I agree, John, but listen: the best response to adversity is to embrace it. Fight, and the whirlpool will drag us into its maw. Let us not doubt ourselves – doubts are traitors, whispering us to fail. I'll not assume the worst. I'll talk to Ned.'

'And say what?'

Shakespeare was surprised at his friend's bluntness. He stared at him.

'I'm sorry, Will. There are lives bound to this stake; we must tread with care. If Ned is consorting with the King's councillors, we cannot confide in him.'

'But if we push him away, we may only increase his desire to harm us.'

'You believe he harbours such a desire?'

'I know not. I hope not. It is possible.'

'What advantage is there,' said Heminge, 'in saying that we doubt him?'

'It would give him a chance to explain . . .'

'How would you feel if someone admitted they were having you followed?'

Shakespeare sighed. 'You are right. It would be a bitter insult.'

'Well, then. I beg you, say nothing.'

Again Shakespeare nodded, though he was puzzled by Heminge's firmness.

'Actors should be renegades,' said Heminge. 'We must keep our heads low. Alleyn has too many licences, too many friends, too many favours to repay.'

'So it would seem,' said Shakespeare.

Although a part of him still wanted to put a benign interpretation on the morning's events, it was hard to overlook the plain fact that Alleyn was consorting with one, or some – perhaps all – the men in that dreadful court of councillors learned in the law. In the Star Chamber, the prosecutors were also judges; they commanded dire powers of punishment and persuasion. They could (and often did) convict enemies on nothing more than a flimsy murmur. The fines they imposed were famous and feared, but in truth they were bribes. Great men paid small fortunes to keep the Star Chamber away from their door and themselves out of gaol. It was a savage expression of the royal whim, and it could never be trifled with.

Shakespeare hunched inside his cape. It was no longer cold, yet he felt a chill.

Constance and Harvard came racing round the corner carrying cakes.

'Honey and almond,' said Constance. 'Would you like a piece? We have lemon too.'

'No thank you,' said Heminge.

'Perhaps later,' said Shakespeare.

'Are the others here?' said Constance.

'Not yet,' said Shakespeare.

A memory stirred.

'I tell you what, though,' he said, turning and looking up at a high window on the opposite side of the road. 'Follow me.'

He led them into a tall stone gatehouse and knocked three times. An elderly woman opened a hatch and a pair of bright grey eyes peered out.

'Mistress Duncan,' said Shakespeare. 'Is that you?'

'Master Shakespeare! What on earth brings *you* here?'

The door opened to reveal a cool stone courtyard.

'I am about my business,' said Shakespeare, 'with these two young associates. I wanted to show them the family trophy. Is it still there?'

The old lady put a finger to her lips.

'Shh,' she said. 'We never talk of it, especially now. Bad luck. But come . . .' She beckoned them in and closed the door behind them. 'I'll show you up.'

'No need. I know the way,' said Shakespeare.

'Would you like some cake?' said Constance.

'Why thank you,' said the woman. 'What a kind young lady.'

Shakespeare led them up three steep flights of stairs and walked to the end of the corridor, to a recessed window that overlooked the street.

'A good view of Essex House from up here,' he said. 'A few years ago you would have seen all sorts of comings and goings.'

There was a cabinet in the niche, which Shakespeare lifted away from the panelled wall, then pulled into the light. He angled it so they could see the back.

'There,' he said. 'Look.'

They craned their necks together. Shakespeare looked at the perfect whorl of Constance's ear and the rich loops of raven-dark hair that fell lazily down to her shoulder. She had rubbed oil into her hair to make it gleam.

'See anything?' he said.

'Letters,' said Harvard.

'Can you read them?'

'I . . .' he read. 'And then C, followed by U and S . . . X . . . E . . . R . . .'

'Very good.' Shakespeare let the cabinet leg down to the floor again. 'What do you suppose they mean, those letters?'

'No idea,' said Constance. 'I can't even remember what they were.'

'I bet *you* can, can't you, John?' said Shakespeare with a kind smile.

'I think so, sir.'

'Then write them again, here, on this tablet.'

There was a small board and a piece of chalk on a shelf. Shakespeare passed it to Harvard and helped him write out the letters.

'I still have no idea,' said Constance.

'Try saying it aloud.'

'I . . . C . . . U,' she began.

'I get it!' said Harvard. '*I see you* . . .'

'So S . . . X means *Essex*,' said Constance.

'And ER?'

'Of course! The Queen!'

'What Queen?' said Harvard.

'It's a famous story,' said Constance. 'About Elizabeth and Essex. My father actually sailed with Essex to Cadiz, a long time ago, in the last century.'

'That's right,' said Shakespeare. 'Someone saw the two of them together, down there in the garden, and scratched out this testament.'

'What are you talking about?' Harvard frowned in puzzlement. 'Who saw whom?'

'That place opposite, where we are going to meet the others,' said Shakespeare, 'is Essex House. I know it well – I was once friendly with the family.'

'Essex was the late Queen's lover,' said Constance. 'But they quarrelled and she sent him to Ireland. When he tried to depose her, she had him executed. There used to be a joke about it. Why was the Queen of

England an ironing table? Because the Earl of Essex was always pressing his suit upon her.'

'A witty summary,' agreed Shakespeare. 'Of course it was a tremendous secret – that is why everyone knows all about it. What is this?'

He was looking down at the black roof of a horse-drawn carriage. A tall man with a distinctive yellow cloak stepped out with an unhurried air. The rapid intake of Shakespeare's breath was sharp enough to turn Constance's head.

'We'd better go down,' he said. 'But before we do, can you see that house down there, behind the tree, on the corner?'

He pointed.

'The small one, with the chimney?'

'That's the one. Any idea whose it is?'

Neither of them knew.

'That,' said Shakespeare to Harvard, 'is for you. It is the place where the great William Caxton had his first press.'

He was pleased to detect reverence in the gaze of his young consorts.

'That's where it all started?' said Harvard. His eyes were wide.

'That's right,' said Shakespeare. 'In the beginning was the word. And the word was God. I thought we might do something with Caxton. I worked on it a bit last evening. He could have a nice long speech, like a Chorus, telling the audience all the amazing things that are happening under the new King.'

He ushered them towards the stairs.

'We are covering a fair span of time in this play,' he said. 'When Caxton talks, we will feel the years passing. This is one of theatre's best tricks – it can make time fly. Seasons can revolve in the space of a single line; crops can grow and be harvested in a single sentence; kingdoms rise and fall in the span of a single speech.'

'You make it sound so easy,' said Constance.

'Don't tell anyone,' said Shakespeare, 'but it is not as hard as people think.'

'Not for you, perhaps,' said Constance.

When they reached the bottom he stopped to bid farewell to the lady who had let them in. She held his hands longer than necessary, and urged him to return.

There were tears in her eyes. 'We have so few visitors. Not like the old times.'

When they crossed the road to Essex House they could see that Alleyn's carriage had left a calling card: a mound of damp horse droppings steamed on the sand.

Shakespeare sent the two young ones on ahead like harriers and took a moment to compose himself. The more he tried to relax, however, the more he fidgeted. Bright images, blurred phrases, half-imagined conversations and wild surmises converged in him like tributaries pouring water into a river. He overflowed with trepidation. There was no alternative, he realised: he would have to call a halt to this reckless plan. Too many things had happened. It was not safe to continue and it was down to him to sound the retreat.

It was his absolute duty; he could not shirk it.

And yet . . .

It was no light matter to abandon a play. Every scruple chafed at the idea. And the sense that there were forces massing, armies marching through the night, actually sharpened his determination to press on, because this was not just a play: it was an enterprise of great pith and moment, and he should not steal the wind from its canvas simply because he was a-feared. Was the hope drunk, he wondered, wherein he dressed himself? Would act and valour fall so very far short of desire?

A chip of ice formed in his heart. He had not come so far to let one ambitious impresario, with inflated hopes and friends in high places, ruin the whole game. He would obey the letter of his promise to Heminge: he would not confront Alleyn. But he was no saint either, and would be damned if he turned the other cheek.

Even an ageing horse, he thought, had a kick in him.

As he stood there, an idea came to him. As always, it took theatrical shape and came wreathed in magic – a jewel dropped by a bird, a shooting star. Not for the first time, he smiled, the play would be the thing. It was high time they worked up a scene in which King Henry dealt with his fractious subjects and showed himself to be mettlesome. In a single startling flash on the blank page of his mind, he could see it all: the court assembled, the trap set, the traitor exposed.

He pursed his lips. Today might not be so bad, after all.

Then he sighed. He could not unmake the morning's events, nor pretend that they meant nothing. His time with Constance and Harvard had been a delicious distraction, but the dangers they faced were immediate, pressing and inescapable. And though he had immense faith in the power of men to write their own stories and wish them into life, he knew that he was not the author now. He was only a player; perhaps not even an important one. He would have to do as he was told.

He had to join the others, before the prompter reminded him.

With a silent groan he bowed his head and went inside. When he passed Andrew, he had recovered his poise sufficiently to hand him a coin and force a smile.

Chapter 12

*E*veryone stood up when Shakespeare marched into the ballroom on the first floor. Although not nearly so grand as the name suggested, it had a polished wooden floor and the King's Men made a drum-roll with their feet as they rose.

'Come, come,' said Shakespeare. 'Friendship needs no ceremony.'

He attempted nothing further in the way of small talk.

Everyone was present except Taylor, who sent word with Armin that he would join them as soon as he could. All of them could feel the urgent heat sparking from their leader. After a cursory round of blunt greetings Shakespeare rapped his knuckles.

'You all know I hate long speeches,' he began.

The others smiled.

'Tell that to Henry V,' said Burbage.

'Not to mention Hamlet's father,' said Armin. 'He was damned talkative for a dead man.'

'Point taken,' said Shakespeare. 'Can I begin today by running through the story so far and summarising what is to come?'

It was a rhetorical question: he wasn't proposing a vote.

'Our King has won the throne and married Elizabeth. Our Margaret is launching new claimants at the throne from her exiled court in Flanders. In the port of London, John Cabot is wooing the Queen's sister. While the citizens grumble, the King beats down his enemies and deals death blows to the Princes.'

'Well, *someone* has to keep up the old traditions,' said Burbage.

'Quite,' said Shakespeare. 'But from this point onwards, the action will accelerate. The King has climbed to the summit. By marrying his children to foreign powers, he secures peace and harvests gold for the royal coffers. Now the gods come knocking. They are hungry for their pound of flesh. The King must pay the price . . .'

'Can I say something about the marriages of his children?' said Constance.

Shakespeare gave her the stage.

'It's just that it always seems short-sighted to me. Kings think they are forming alliances, while in reality they are storing up problems for the future.'

'Problems?' said Alleyn.

'This is a perfect example. Henry marries his daughter Margaret to the King of Scotland, and *her* daughter begets Mary Queen of Scots, an enemy of the state, yet one with a claim to England through her great-grandfather. The result is that her son James becomes *our* king.'

The silence was tangible.

'Very true,' said Heminge. 'Most wars are family quarrels, in the end.'

Constance was still.

'By that argument,' said Armin slowly, 'can we expect, following the wedding of the Princess to the Elector Palatine, to have a German prince one day?'

'I would think it inevitable,' said Constance.

'Oh, I can't see it coming to that,' said Alleyn.

'What, you think our scrawny dwarf of an heir, that feeble princelet Charles, will be a match for the Rhineland?' said Burbage.

Alleyn smiled. 'Truly he will be a pattern of kingship, a model for all monarchs.'

Shakespeare ignored them. 'The King's conscience gnaws at him. The death moans of those fair Princes cloud his waking hours. And then something unexpected happens that shakes his soul.'

'What?' said Constance.

Shakespeare took a deep breath.

'His son dies,' he said.

He tried to keep the emotion out of his voice, but failed.

'The King's first-born, Arthur,' he said, his voice sounding strangled. 'He is carried off by plague when he is barely older than Harvard here. The King, cracked with grief and guilt, retreats into an endless winter of the soul.'

'That's strong,' said Richard with a serious look. 'And I see the grief. But guilt?'

'When King Henry died, he left instructions that ten thousand masses be said for his soul. No one could require clearer proof of an uneasy conscience.'

'In truth,' said Alleyn, 'this was also the King's avarice, even in death. It cost sixpence to say mass – a day's wage for a carpenter. So the King's death was excellent business. It enriched the Church no end.'

'The main point is that the King's soul was burning. God had turned on him.'

Constance's cough sounded forced, so the others turned to look.

'Excuse me,' she said, 'but when a king loses a son, then so does a queen. She is grief-stricken too. It would be odd for us to overlook a mother's sorrow.'

'Quite,' said Alleyn.

'So, should I work up something for our Queen to say?'

'In fact,' said Shakespeare, 'I was imagining her so torn with sorrow that her heart gives out. In truth she did die soon afterwards, leaving the King quite alone.'

He was alert enough to see the shadow fall across Constance's bright face.

'It would be wonderful, however, if you could do something with the vengeful Margaret, in Flanders, spitting venom, engendering rebellion, that sort of thing.'

'As you wish.'

'The good thing about Arthur dying, rest his soul,' said Burbage, 'is that it clears the way for the emergence of the King's younger son, the new heir: Henry.'

'Exactly,' said Shakespeare. 'And here is where we will find the end of our play. I cannot say quite what form it will take, though it is safe to assume that the ageing King and the greedy Prince will argue. The King's grief is consuming him quite.'

Alleyn began to pace up and down during this speech. Now he erupted.

'Good God in Heaven!' he said. 'I have given myself permission to present Henry VII as a cold executioner. Now you are suggesting that we make Henry VIII – the late Queen's own father – a monster too!'

'Well, he *was* one,' said Shakespeare. 'Nothing controversial about that.'

'There's plenty controversial about *saying* it, Will,' said Burbage. 'Come. You know as well as anyone—'

'It is true,' said Taylor. 'And while King James might not feel loyal to the Tudors, he *does* believe in the divinity of kings. And he is the most superstitious man in all Christendom – he believes in witchcraft and curses. That's why we put those hags into *Macbeth*, remember?'

'Actually,' said Constance, 'he may also feel a kinship with Henry VII. He is a direct descendant, after all.'

'I am sorry. Excuse me.' Shakespeare pulled up a stool, sat down and almost put his head in his hands. He felt dizzy. None of this was news to him, but he was always amazed by the intimate and violent family history that lay behind the endless saga of the English throne. It baffled him to think he had once applauded Seneca's famous Stoic faith in a benign providence. Who now could believe that suffering was a minor tribulation – an occasional sling and arrow – on an otherwise sensible journey? He could only laugh, these days, at such complacent philosophies. The vagaries of royal life fell on the innocent people of England like the hawkish whims of gods. It was the greedy squabbles of brothers and cousins that had left all those thousands of ploughmen, shepherds, cattlemen and children lying dead and bleeding in the crimson fields of Towton and Bosworth.

And then there were the divine punishments – plague and fever, fire and famine. Who could remain balanced in the face of such horrors as these?

His face was pale. The others flitted about him like gulls on a new-turned field.

'Do not worry,' he said. 'It is just . . . I must confess, I wonder if

Ned is not right. I pray I have not led you down a path too steep and slippery to permit a safe return.'

'We all have sure feet,' said Armin.

'But this present King of ours: he is wild and vengeful. He was reared in poverty and scholarship – he learned to speak Latin before Scottish – and it has deranged him. I am no Puritan, but the vulgarity of his speech, the way he strokes his manly consorts . . . it is too much. I hear that at hunting he likes to stand inside the body of the deer, with all the blood and bowels on his boots. He *never* washes his hands. He hates the good people of England and means to drive them into ruin. Is *this* a little god? I do not think so.'

Only Heminge knew the true source of Shakespeare's gloom, and it was impossible to share this knowledge with his friends – especially while Alleyn was present.

'Perhaps some broth,' said Shakespeare. 'I am not hungry myself, but feel free. Richard and Joseph have excelled themselves.'

The sideboard was loaded with bull's cheeks, spiced eggs and black bread, but no one wanted to eat. Shakespeare's outburst had made them uneasy.

'What is it, Will?' said Alleyn. 'What is behind this?'

'It is nothing,' said Shakespeare. He felt as if he were on a cart that was running too fast; the wheels juddered on the ruts. 'My sleep was troubled . . .'

He looked at the faces before him.

'Very well. You wish me to give treasonous voice to my fears again. I am in woe for our kingdom. The Queen had her faults, but this King multiplies them beyond imagination. Can you not feel it? Our England is sinking towards a new catastrophe as surely as a ship sails into the night. A shade has crossed the sun, and I fear we shall all be eclipsed.'

He forced himself to bite his tongue. In seeking not to speak, in seeking to hide his recent escapades, he had said a deal too much.

It was Burbage who came to the rescue. 'I think the best thing to do,' he said, 'is press on. Your fears may be baseless, Will, or they may be well founded. But they are only fears – horrible imaginings, no more. I say we do not smother ourselves in surmise, but trim and pilot our craft as best we can. You have not misled us, Will. Whatever may come, it will not be of your doing.'

Shakespeare wanted to rise to his feet, but his legs were weakened by this naked display of friendship, which he knew to be both generous and undeserved.

'Richard . . .' He reached out a hand. 'Oh, Richard.'

No other words came to him. There were tears in his eyes.

The men in the room would remember this moment and talk about it for the rest of their lives. They had seen Shakespeare speechless: a rare and moving sight.

It took Shakespeare less than ten minutes to collect himself. The transformation was amazing. It was as if he had dipped himself into some fabled spring of restorative holy water. Colour returned to his cheeks; liveliness crept back into his heels.

Burbage was not surprised. He knew Shakespeare well enough to understand the recuperative powers of creative work.

'I think we should begin by showing Henry in command,' Shakespeare said, 'full of pride and power. What say you? Let's see how our King handles battle. News has reached London of Simnel's uprising, and the King leads an army to face down the rebels near Stoke. No need to waste time on actual fighting, so you can put up your bright swords. I think we can show Henry triumphing merely by raising his voice. I will be the King. Richard, Robert, can you be Oxford and Morton, trusted advisers? Oh, there is one missing. Ned – can you be Stanley, hero of Bosworth?'

Alleyn nodded.

Constance was looking at the floor in dismay.

'And you, my dear, can be everyone else who comes up. Will that serve?'

Constance gave a weak smile.

'Good,' said Shakespeare. 'I am ready.'

Harvard sniffed. Alleyn cleared his throat. Shakespeare began.

'They think me brave,' he said, 'a dragon warrior, who breathes Welsh fire across the battlefield. But I would win this fight *without* a fight, and have within the enemy installed my acolytes to spread the royal word. Those troops are weak. They fight for coin, not life. When battle comes, we'll see whose army thrives.'

Shakespeare walked in a tight circle, explaining the *mise en scène*.

'Outside the nobles are gathering. Cockerels. The King swoops on the dawn, an eagle, and says: "Good morrow, friends. I know that on the eve of Bosworth Field the black usurper passed a dreadful night, all haunted by the shades of those he'd killed. Such evils plagued me not."'

He levelled a fierce glance at Alleyn.

'Nor me,' said Alleyn, surprised.

'Nor me,' said Burbage. 'Though I confess I suffered some disquiet, that tugged me from my bed before the cock. Your grace, we are out-numberèd . . .'

'Weep not. Be calm. Your King has set in train commotions that may help us win this war. Give me your shield, I must a sign convey to those men opposite who fear this day.'

Shakespeare marched forward, then turned.

'Will no one raise a hand to bar my path? Will all my nobles watch their King court death?'

Was this Shakespeare speaking, or the King? Burbage was the first to react.

'My lord! I do beseech you,' he said, taking a stride forward.

'Wait!' said Armin.

'Hold fast!' said Alleyn.

Shakespeare waved them away.

'At this point,' he said, 'I go forward and make a colourful speech. This will be a big moment. The King will seem both fearless and to be feared. John, set down your pen. We need someone to play young Lambert Simnel. You're the right age. Come!'

'Here,' said Constance. 'Give it to me. I can't write like you, but—'

'Good,' said Shakespeare. 'Now, remember Henry V before Harfleur, when he brought down a city with rhetoric alone – oratory his only battering ram? Our Henry will do the same: he will win this battle with words, not cannons.'

'Excellent,' said Burbage.

'If any of you brave and eager troops possess the stomach to betray your King, unloose your arrows now, for here I stand. If any of you brave and eager men have heart enough to unseat England's King, I here salute you all and wish you well.'

He stopped. He seemed possessed of a regal fire. The gloom that had weighed him down only moments ago now provided fuel for a righteous flame.

'I'll really pour oil on this part, warn them of the pride and frenzy of our steel and so forth. Perhaps throw curses on their sacred souls. Then, as I return, the opposing ranks will grow ragged. Men will lay down their arms. The army will dissolve.'

'And their leader will turn out to be a mere stripling,' said Alleyn.

'Exactly,' said Shakespeare. 'So, John, you have been placed at the head of this rebellion. You barely know what it means, but you have been abandoned by the troops hired to win you the throne. All is lost. What might you say?'

Harvard looked as pale and nervous as any failed rebel, but there was only a slight quaver in his unbroken voice.

'We crave your mercy, sir. We meant no harm.'

'Perfect,' said Shakespeare.

'Well done, John,' called Constance.

'So good,' said Shakespeare, 'that it allows us to jump ahead. Young Simnel is so innocuous, so disarming, that Henry can make a goodly show of magnanimity.'

He walked to Harvard, put a hand – friendly, but with a hint of menace – on his neck and led him across the floor like a farmer hauling a calf to market.

'No harm?' said the King. 'An army raised to overcome the King that means no harm? I like your cheek, you fox. Fear not, young man, your head is safe with us. The royal kitchen is the place for you. Return with us to London: stir our stew.'

Shakespeare had not finished. He stood still, as if composing himself before some fearful plunge. A frost fell on his features and his face, when he turned, was glacial.

Alleyn seemed not to notice. He had played only a small part so far and took the opportunity to keep the scene moving forward.

'Most gently do you deal with traitors, sire, and greatly it becomes you. Yet do I doubt that kingdoms can be safe while such men live. I know he's yet a boy, but he will grow, as acorns do to oaks.'

In most circumstances this would have been useful, a mild dissenting voice. In the present angry atmosphere, however, it fell flat. Shakespeare, in an exact impersonation of a man who had been struck a thunderous blow, walked calmly back to Alleyn until their faces were only inches apart. He half-turned to one side, as if to give orders to an officer. His voice shook with a dreadful calm, like simmering water.

'My true and noble friend, you speak the truth. Guards, take this man, and long before this night, remove the head from these broad shoulders here.'

He brought a hand up to his own cheek and pointed at Alleyn's eye. The tip of his finger was stiff with anger. It resembled an icicle – or a wand. Everyone's gaze was drawn to it: tense, accusing, implacable. Shakespeare's voice remained measured and companionable – and more malign than ever.

'See how he seeks to flatter and to soothe,' he said. 'To foes who show their face I can be kind. To friends who veil their thoughts I am of stone. Take him. Leave us. Away. Let's on to London.'

He spoke as mildly as if he were ordering a beaker of milk, but his voice abruptly broke the silence as if he had screamed. Everyone knew that a line had been crossed. This was more than acting. Something cold and furious swayed between the two old friends.

Shakespeare wore a mirthless smile. There was anguish written on his face.

'So,' he said, 'what do we think? A fearsome King, have we not?'

The others said nothing.

Alleyn seemed pinned to the spot by disbelief. Eventually he unhooked himself and walked stiffly over to the bench.

'Is anything wrong?' said Shakespeare.

'I do not know,' said Alleyn, taking up his cloak and pulling on gloves.

'You are not leaving us?'

'I do not think you want me to stay.'

'Ned, I was acting. *Acting*.'

Alleyn shook his head. 'I have seen you act. Forgive me, you are not that good.'

'What are you suggesting?'

'The question is what *you* are suggesting. I have no idea. But I am very certain that I shall not remain where I am so unwelcome. Farewell.'

'Oh Ned . . .' Burbage took his arm. 'I'm sure there's a . . . Will?'

Shakespeare said nothing.

'I see,' said Alleyn. 'Then I wish you all well. Constance . . .'

He made as if to bow.

'If you are going to leave, then leave,' said Shakespeare.

Alleyn turned, a hurt and hunted expression on his face.

'Ned, don't go,' said Burbage. 'Will, what *is* this? Come now . . .'

Too late. Alleyn was marching down the stairs, fury loud in every stride.

Heminge approached Shakespeare, seemed about to say something, then thought better of it and followed Alleyn. The others could hear him running down and raised voices echoed up from below. When Heminge returned no one had moved. They stood quite still, like statues in a mist.

'That may not have been our finest hour,' said Burbage.

'What's done is done,' said Shakespeare.

' 'Twere much better it had *not* been done.'

'I do not understand,' said Armin. 'What just happened?'

Heminge paused, restrained by the curiosity of Constance and Harvard.

'Will,' he said, taking Shakespeare's shoulder. 'A word.'

Burbage accompanied them; the others did not move. There was a hierarchy in the company, and no one was surprised that these three should seek private conference.

'If this is about Constance,' Burbage said, 'then I really must—'

'It isn't,' said Heminge. In a few swift sentences he told Burbage of the morning's discoveries and their suspicions concerning Alleyn.

'Even so,' said Burbage, 'you should have spoken to me first. You're a damned hothead, Will. Haven't you learned by now to quell that boisterous temper of yours? If what you say is true – which I doubt,

224

by the way – then upsetting Ned is the worst thing we could do. Will, I don't believe it. What possessed you?'

Shakespeare looked pale. 'Lilies that fester smell far worse than weeds. I had no choice. I am sorry.'

'Go after him. Apologise. Say your back is killing you.'

'It has nothing to do with my back – which is better, since you ask.'

'Well, we can make our peace with Ned,' said Burbage, 'if we crawl and scrape with sufficient humility. But that was stupid. Ned has friends in high places.'

'Precisely. That is the whole problem.'

'I can't believe you had him followed. And how was it I knew nothing of this? Are you having *me* followed too?'

He touched a nerve. For the first time Shakespeare wondered whether his assault on Alleyn wasn't the production of his own tangled nerves, his own private dread of that dripping dungeon at the Tower. That piece of yellow glass on the table in his house: had it jolted his own compass so thoroughly that he no longer knew who his friends were?

What had he done? King Lear had felt few pangs when he banished Cordelia and Kent – only the reverberations of his wrath. Shakespeare had no such immunity from self-doubt. Had he forsaken a friend for nothing?

'I thought I had no choice,' he said.

Nothing is but thinking makes it so, whispered the voice in his ear.

'I must say, I too think our fears may be justified,' said Heminge.

Burbage turned to him. 'You really believe Ned would betray us?'

'It is not a question of betrayal. It is a question of where his interest lies. I fear it may lie elsewhere. He does want to be a knight.'

'I won't believe it. We've known him for more years than I can count.'

'There is more, Richard. A lot more.' Shakespeare told Burbage the news about Stanyhurst and recounted the tussle over the bag in the street.

'I'll still not credit it. Not for all the wool in Bristol.'

'Remember that time he arrived at the Greyhound in a rich carriage, when the rest of us were trying to slip unnoticed through the crowd?

What was he thinking? And he did go to the Star Chamber,' said Heminge.

'You said yourself that those are the circles he moves in now. He probably goes there all the time. Maybe they are squeezing *him* for money. He's rich, the kind of man they like to tease with hot irons while they drain his pocket.'

'I really don't—' said Heminge.

'The point is, surely we should give him a chance. What if there's an explanation?'

Shakespeare groaned.

'And Will, no offence, but there is another suspect in this case.'

'Another?'

'You mentioned a patron, one who wished to remain in the shadows. No one has complained, but we are all nervous about this mysterious sponsor of yours.'

The air hissed out of Shakespeare's lungs. He wished he could call back the hour, bid time return and conceal his harsh judgement of Alleyn. Right or wrong, it had been a mistake to confront the man.

'Oh, Richard, there is no such patron. I made him up! I had no wish to embarrass anyone, but *I* am the man in the shadows; I am the hero with the purse. Your secretive benefactor is . . . me.'

'Oh,' said Burbage. 'Why in Heaven's name didn't you say?'

'I thought it would seem improper.'

'But did you notice the point at which Ned first left?' said Heminge, returning to the theme. 'I heard it was just when Will was laying out his plan to paint King Henry VIII in a wicked light.'

'Meaning?'

'That he wanted no part in such a work.'

'John, John. No one has ever called you a fool, but if he were truly offended by such talk, and had the least intention of betraying us, then that is exactly the kind of speech that would have obliged him to stay.'

Heminge's mouth moved, but no words came out.

'Anyway, what if he did not wish to vilify Henry VIII? That is no capital crime. I too am not convinced that insulting kings is the wisest route to a long life.'

Before Shakespeare could reply, fresh footsteps thudded up the stairs.

He found himself hoping that it was Alleyn.

'Am I late?' said Taylor, stepping into the quiet room. 'Here, I've brought some salted kidneys.'

'Joseph!' said Heminge. 'Exceptional timing.'

'Really? Have I missed anything?'

'Oh, nothing much,' said Shakespeare.

Out of the corner of his eye he could see Burbage smiling.

'I am glad,' he said, 'that you find this funny.'

'Oh pish, Will,' said Burbage. 'It *is* comical . . . can't you see?'

'I'm not sure I can. I feel I may have offended everyone. Ned, you—'

'Be calm. It is just . . . Look: you are acting like all the kings we have ever played. All of them see the world through eyes snake-green with fear and suspicion. Now you too have allowed yourself to become enmired in imaginary plots and conspiracies. Honestly, Will, I do believe that you have pictured Henry VII warding off plots in such rich detail that you now suspect them here. You feel that all occasions inform against you, and perceive enmity in the shaking of a leaf. It is poetic.'

'If only that were true,' said Shakespeare, but he knew that Burbage had a point. For an instant he was Othello, hounded beyond endurance by enemies he could not detect. Trifles light as air are to the jealous confirmations strong as proofs of holy writ.

'It is. I am sure of it.'

'It has been said that life will mimic art.'

'And also that appearance conceals the truth.'

Shakespeare sighed. He stretched out his arms, baring his teeth, then slumped on to the bench. 'You are a fine man, Richard,' he said.

Something tottered at an odd angle in his heart. Out of the vaults of his imagination came a vision, riding on pale and glorious wings. A succession of children's faces described lazy circles against an azure sky: two princes murdered by a king, Macduff's pretty chickens, a pair of royal heirs (Arthur and Henry) a hundred years apart, his own son, Hamnet . . . So many tender youths, all with spring dancing on their cheeks, all cut down by cruel fate. In his mind they merged with Constance and Harvard, making his chest ache. He knew more than he wished to know about the death of children, and though there was no conscious progression of thought, his heart drummed him into a firm decision.

His fingers sought the tight black ribbon on his arm. It was not there, but he pressed his flesh anyway. He would not be involved in the further betrayal of young lives.

He blinked. He seemed to have travelled far, though in truth barely a second had passed. He ushered his friends together and addressed them as a group, in a voice that had suddenly become flat, desolate, drained of all life.

'I have sorrowful news,' he said, 'which may require your forgiveness. For a long while you have suspected me of withholding something. You had every right. I have not been quite level with you. The time has come for me to reveal all.'

Burbage, Heminge, Armin and Taylor stood in a crescent, loyal soldiers awaiting orders from a general.

'Where's Constance?'

'Here,' she said, joining the men.

There was a pause.

'Would anybody mind,' said Taylor, 'telling me what is going on?'

Burbage made a wary face. Taylor held up his palms and retreated.

'Patience, Joseph,' said Shakespeare. 'Time will answer all. John?'

'Sir?' Harvard was ready with his quill.

'No need for that now,' said Shakespeare. 'We have no further need of you today. This scene requires no clerk.'

Even in the heat of his distraction he knew he had been unkind. His shoulders sagged.

'Heaven knows I mean you no hurt. I am sorry to speak roughly. You are our excellent and most trusted secretary. It is just that I have tedious business to discuss with the others. We make no more scenes now. Really, you may go home.'

A cloud passed across Harvard's face, but he did not protest. With an uncertain gait, as if he had made a blunder, he backed out of the room.

Shakespeare waited a moment longer, as pensive as his friends had ever seen him.

'I have come to a decision,' he said. 'And I won't sauce the meat with words. To quote myself: we shall proceed no further in this business.'

'What?' said Burbage.

'No!' said Armin.

'What are you saying?' Constance put a hand to her mouth.

'Please,' said Shakespeare. 'There is something I have not told you. It grieves me more than I can say, because I do not want this to end, but listen and you shall see.'

The murmurs subsided and Shakespeare continued.

'Several weeks ago, some days before we met, I went to visit Sir Walter Raleigh in the Tower. An exceptional man, who has been in prison these ten years, for no greater offence than disagreeing with the Crown. On the way out, something happened. I was seized, hooded, beaten, and interviewed – by a very powerful man, a courtier.'

'Beaten?' Constance's eyes were wide.

'By whom?' said Burbage.

'It doesn't matter,' said Shakespeare. 'The rub is that he asked me to write *Henry VIII* – a patriotic version, to show the King in a radiant light – with all his famous sparkles of divinity in place. I hid my distaste for the task, but not well enough. My interrogator let me know that it would cost him little sleep if I were to find myself at the mercy of his guards again. I was angry, vengeful.' He paused. 'So there it is. Our little play – *Henry VII* – is in part the fruit of that wrath.'

'God stand up for wrath,' said Armin, 'if it bears such plums as this.'

'I do not jest,' said Shakespeare. ' 'Tis said that barking dogs rarely bite, but this was no barking dog. My prosecutor spoke with all due modesty and restraint, the better that I should understand how gravely he was in earnest.'

'So?' said Burbage, beginning to see where this was leading.

'So this is where it ends. Recent events confirm that my experience at the Tower was no accident. I was wrong to think we enjoyed any sort of immunity: our play is too dangerous, and there is an end of it. I cannot delude you – or myself – any longer. The perils we face are not playful or imaginary: they are harsh . . . and close. For myself I care little, but I cannot put you in the way of such terrors. It is thanks to providence and our own care that we escaped the royal scythe till now. It was no accident that we managed to turn the Queen's Men into the King's Men – we steered a sage course far from the rocks – and I have no right to change the course of our craft. So while it has been an honour to work with you once more, our revel now must end. I thank you, I salute you, and I bid you adieu. The rest, I am sorry to say, is silence.'

His conclusion was so abrupt that no one knew what to say. Shakespeare rose to his feet, walked across the room and folded his cloak over his arm.

'I will leave you now,' he said. 'Let us meet again soon, for companionship. I am truly sorry to have trespassed on your safety. If anyone should ask – and I pray no one does – please say I sought your help and you declined. That will be my story.'

He looked at them. They looked at him. No one breathed.

'Goodbye.'

He stooped at the doorway and passed out of the room.

It was a long walk home, and the sky was grey, but Shakespeare wanted to be alone and was happy to drag himself back to Blackfriars on foot. He ignored the cries from the boatmen – 'Eastward ho!' – as he turned away from Whitehall and curved towards the City. He felt half lightheaded, half awash with gloom.

If he had wanted peace and quiet, he was in the wrong place. London was bigger and rowdier than ever, like a river that had burst its banks. Even in his own short life he had seen changes that his own poor father would not have believed. The great migration from the countryside was ballooning the population with hectic speed; even plague could not arrest the multiplying numbers in this seething hive. But though it was hard to be alone in London – the clamour and rush were too insistent – in some ways it was easier to be solitary. Stratford was peaceful, but there was no such thing as a secret; a man was never unobserved. In London it was possible to hide, to drift, to disappear. That is what Shakespeare wanted to do now.

When he left behind the wealthy villas of Westminster, with their spacious gardens and steps, the streets narrowed and filled with straw, dung, dogs, cats, chimney sweeps, puppeteers, physicians, thieves, herbalists, musicians, peacocks, monkeys and parrots. Cottage industries churned in the squalid alleys, where busy-fingered men and women worked up textiles, hats, shoes, needles and pipes. London teemed with vagrants and confidence tricksters; there was hardly a gallant who had not been cheated of a purse, a ring, a chain or a jewel. And everywhere lay signs of the general unease. In the Strand, Shakespeare saw a group of prisoners, chained by the neck, being dragged along the centre of the road by two men on horseback. Their ears were scorched red and raw where they had been scalded and branded – a standard punishment for cutpurses. The people alongside leered and laughed as they passed. A couple of children ran after them like terriers after game.

There were guards everywhere. They loitered in groups on corners, leaned against walls and sat in huddles on steps, their long swords and pikes resting on their shoulders. Dark birds wheeled overhead; this city was their refuse tray, and they were thriving. Gulls cackled and shrieked over crusts of bread in the filthy riverside ditches.

Shakespeare wandered until it was almost dark. The rain grew heavy and sluiced down his hat. Water slapped his face and dripped through his beard. A brief image flashed in his mind, of a mariner braced against an Atlantic gale, swaying lantern-light on his face, salt water sheeting down on his shoulders, masts creaking against tarred rope, and a shout that could not be heard above the storm.

Genuine explorers did not turn back when the weather worsened. Cabot, Raleigh, Stanyhurst, even Burbage: they held fast, gripped tight and pressed on.

He sighed. It was not cold, so he did not bother to wrap himself against the breeze. There was nothing so cleansing as a spring shower, and London stood sharply in need of a purgative downpour. He watched the bellmen emerge, lanterns on sticks, and prepare to patrol the streets, shouting their shrill warnings against robbery and fire: 'Curfew! Curfew!' He could still remember when they used to shout the original French – 'Couvre feu! Couvre feu!' – ordering all citizens to douse their lamps.

It was an apt phrase for his own predicament. He too was putting out the light.

He felt strangely detached, as if he might wander the streets all night. But he was too old for such dramatics. It was something to sigh at when even the King seemed young. He himself felt like an elderly grandee, superfluous, a botched story.

At Ludgate the grocers were packing away their pudding pies, oyster rolls and turnip cakes, and wheeling their barrows into the dusk. There were a few late cries from the river as the gates of the city prepared to swing shut for the night.

The only thing that made his pulse quicken was the memory of Stanyhurst's book. With his own work cancelled, he had time to look into it. Yet he could not summon more than a pallid spark of curiosity even for this. It was not as if he really knew the man.

He was surprised, when he reached his house, to see lights burning. And as soon as he pushed at the door he knew that he had visitors. He could hear voices and then a hush of anticipation as his own feet sounded on the stairs. A tremor of apprehension passed through him and made him shiver.

Was this it? Had Coke's men come for him at last? If so, should he retreat while he still had the chance, or should he, like a bear bound to the post, stay the course?

He had no choice, he thought. Even villains had to stand the hazard of the die.

He took a deep breath and opened the door.

They were standing by the fire, warming their hands in silence. Heads turned when Shakespeare arrived, and all wore the same expression: nervous, yet firm and elated. The room had the sour scent of damp wool.

'Very well,' said Shakespeare. 'Who wants to tell me what is going on?'

Burbage looked at Armin, who stepped forward. 'To cut a long scene short, after you left we spoke among ourselves, and it turned out we all agreed.'

'Agreed with what?'

'We are of one mind,' said Armin. 'Don't even try to talk us out of it.'

Shakespeare didn't want to play this guessing game.

'Talk you out of what?' he said in a quiet voice.

'The play, of course,' said Burbage. 'Surely you can divine our purpose?'

Shakespeare dared not believe it.

Burbage was smiling. 'That's right,' he said. 'We've decided that even after taking into account everything you said, we are going to continue.'

Shakespeare felt the room shake. The street noise seemed to melt away; one of the walls seemed to tilt, and a chill leaped to the back of his neck.

'No,' he said. 'You are good people, and I expected nothing less. But no.'

'We are not good,' said Armin. 'We are simply men of the theatre, as you are. We cannot turn aside – nor shall we.'

'You may do it without my help, for I'll none of it,' said Shakespeare.

'See?' said Burbage. 'We know you well enough. I *said* you'd say that.'

'I am happy that you find me so . . . predictable,' said Shakespeare.

'Only a little,' said Burbage, stepping forward and grasping his old friend's arms. 'Will. We mean what we say. Understand this: we decline to stop. All of us knew it was risky, from the beginning. Our eyes were open. I know you are worried about Ned, but your fears may yet prove groundless, and I for one will not believe him false without proof. I propose we restore him to our cause and finish this work.'

'Hear, hear.' Taylor stamped his feet.

'And so say I,' echoed Heminge.

'Don't forget me,' said Armin.

Constance did not need to speak: her eyes flashed and her smile was soft.

Shakespeare looked at them, and they looked back at him.

'You have no choice,' said Burbage. 'We are adamant.'

The pause that followed resembled the tense interval that precedes the felling of a tree. The axes had done their work, and the silence that followed their blows was whetstone-sharp. The King's Men, like foresters, stood back to watch. For a moment the tree was motionless, but soon there was a faint rustle high in the twigs and branches, and then the whole proud trunk began to fall.

So it was with Shakespeare. He stood quite still, aware that he had no defences left – only pride kept him upright. And then, with a slow crash, he toppled.

'You shame me,' he said. 'I swear I never knew what friends were until this day. Good fellows . . . Constance . . .'

Words did not often fail Shakespeare, but they did so now. His spirits bobbed on a warm tide of comradeship until they were held aloft like heroes on the shoulders of a crowd. His dark feelings faded; all of a sudden there seemed little to fear. He bowed his head like a child that has been beaten, nodding his gratitude to the floor.

'I am sure you are wrong about Ned,' whispered Burbage. 'Do nothing further. I will go and talk to him. Perhaps there is an explanation. We shall see.'

'You are a dear soul,' said Shakespeare. He clung to the hand of his old friend, leaning into his care like a deer sheltering beneath an oak.

'I'll after him right away.'

'Tell him what happened to me at the Tower.'

'Don't worry,' Burbage grinned. 'I shall blame it all on you.'

Shakespeare followed him to the top of the stairs.

'I hope you're right, Richard,' he said. 'I do hope you are right.'

When Burbage had gone he picked up a goblet and filled it with wine. He swilled it around, watching the luxurious ruby liquid slosh up the sides of the heavy green glass. It looked like blood.

'But what if you're not?' he muttered to himself. 'What if you're not?'

The others were tucking in. If nothing else, Shakespeare thought, they were not starving. Someone had brought in bowls of fresh onion broth. It was filling the room with a rich, warm smell that made Shakespeare's stomach beg for a spoonful.

'May I say something?' said Constance.

'Of course,' said Shakespeare.

'I just want you to know that it will not trouble me if we paint Henry VIII as a villain. I say this in case you think we all feel as Mr Alleyn did.'

'Brave girl,' said Shakespeare. 'You are your father's daughter.'

'I hope so,' said Constance, making a face that drew a giggle from Armin. 'But in truth, a king who executes wives: how could I admire such a beast?'

'I wish,' said Shakespeare, 'that the rest of England were as clear-thinking as you. I fear that many flinch to cast aspersions on a monarch, however grotesque.'

'No one minded your rendering of Richard III. All London applauded.'

'True. But Henry is a different animal.'

'I doubt the late Queen would have taken too much offence. He did imprison and kill her mother. She must, as a girl, have lived in daily fear for her life.'

'It was not a happy childhood,' said Shakespeare, impressed. 'I suppose that is why she never married, when she had the choice of any man in Europe.'

'My mother says that the Queen's refusal to marry was perfectly logical. It is only men who feel she lost or sacrificed anything. What advantage could wedlock bring? Women marry for security or advancement, and she had need of neither. She was free. If all women had her freedom, why, there might none be married at all.'

'Bravo,' said Armin, applauding. 'Truly, you are a marvel.'

'Yet the man *you* marry will require strong nerves,' said Heminge, smiling.

'Who says I'll marry?' said Constance.

'You hope to be a queen, then?' said Shakespeare. 'A modest ambition.'

'You should marry young Harvard,' said Taylor. 'He can write down all you say and make it into a great book, and we shall all be the wiser for it.'

'You mock, sir.'

'He teases,' said Shakespeare. 'But that's because no woman will marry *him*. He's asked hundreds.'

'Then they are all fools!' said Constance with a theatrical curtsy.

Armin picked her up by the waist, held her high and set her gently down again.

'Why, you're light as a mosquito,' he said. 'I wish we'd had you when we did *Lear*. If ever a man needed a queen, it was him.'

He stopped, struck by an idea.

'Will?' he said.

'Robert?'

'Do you think that if we cut Constance's hair she might pass for a boy?'

Shakespeare glanced at Constance. The suggestion that she might, disguised as a man, actually join them in a stage performance: this was a rare compliment, one that went against every stage tradition Armin knew. He smiled – partly at Constance, twinkling with unfeigned, girlish pleasure – and partly at his own tumbled response. The idea of seeing her doubly costumed at the Globe – girl dressed as boy dressed as girl – made him shake his head. Words from one of his sonnets crowded upon him. Would not all nature fall a-doting at so beautiful a merger, so passionate a master-mistress?

'I think she might,' he said. 'Whether we *should* is another matter. It would be like crushing a snowdrop.'

The silence that followed was tinged with embarrassment. He had gone too far. But for once he did not notice; instead his mind raced ahead, and gave him a flash of excitement at the prospect of an amicable reunion with Alleyn. The friendship with his fellow actor was too long-standing to be lightly tossed aside, and he had enough confidence in Burbage to feel that all was not yet lost.

Best of all was the sense that his play was once more alive – vibrating inside, close to the surface, pressing from under his skin. It wanted to burst out into the air. All he had to do was stand back and let it find a graceful shape.

'Perhaps,' said Heminge, as the silence grew painful, 'since we are here, we might worry away at a scene. There was talk of doing something about Caxton.'

'So I did,' said Shakespeare, glad of the interruption. 'So I did.'

'That is settled, then.' Heminge was calm. 'Since Richard has gone, I will take care of the arrangements. It is late now, but let us begin first thing tomorrow.'

'Where?' said Armin.

'Good point. I shall need a day to organise something.'

'I would like that,' said Shakespeare. There was nothing in particular to do, but he was aware of an acute need for a space in which to regain his balance.

'Good. I will talk to Richard, and let you know where and when. What else should we be working on?'

Shakespeare rubbed his eyes. 'We do need a bit more from the citizens. We must speed up the manoeuvres at court, let the King feel the fates turning against him. And Margaret – it is time we heard from her.'

'Should we get out of the city, somewhere quiet?' Armin suggested.

'In good faith,' said Shakespeare, 'it might work better if we stay hereabouts. The day after tomorrow is my birthday. We can disguise ourselves as revellers. My friends are giving a small party. What could be more natural than that?'

'Excellent,' said Heminge. 'Leave it to me.'

'Many happy returns,' said Armin.

'I'll bring a syrup pudding,' said Taylor.

'Please don't,' said Shakespeare.

The fading sound of feet on cobbles was still audible when Shakespeare picked up the book Stanyhurst had left for him. He stared at the dedication and was touched anew by a needling sense that there was a hidden meaning – some instruction or plea – in the careful, ceremonial phrases. Those references to *Love's Labour's Lost*: what did they signify? Shakespeare wished he had a copy to hand, because in truth he did not remember the play very well. A handful of lords in disguise climbed trees, wrote sonnets and courted the wrong princesses. There was a good deal of lovesickness and verbal jousting. It didn't seem to have any bearing on the present predicament at all.

He bent over the tiny Latin, but it would have been hard to read even if it had been written in English, so cramped was the calligraphy. The title contained an unambiguous reference to *Henricus VIII*, but otherwise, though a good number of recognisable words shimmered in the crowded lines, it was incomprehensible.

As he peered closely, however, two words began to glow and lift away from the page: *rex . . . princip, rex . . . princip*. There was a rhythm to them, like a chant: *rex princip, rex princip* – and suddenly Shakespeare gasped. It was no accident that these words stood out, because they really were illuminated. Each had a tiny yellow dot in the centre. Stanyhurst had deliberately highlighted them.

A king and a prince. And not just any king and prince.

A shadow passed over Shakespeare's memory. He remembered now the point at which Stanyhurst had become agitated. It was when he had pondered the tension between Henry VIII and his father. That was when his face had gone as purple as his gown, and he had talked excitedly of his great, scandalous secret.

Now that his eye was attuned to the yellow dots, he picked them up elsewhere. They lay like footprints across the page. All he had to do was follow the trail.

The dots led to numbers. There seemed to be three of them, repeated at various points, and they were almost but not quite identical.

II – II – IV – I – V – IX
II – IV – VI – I – V – IX
II – VIII – VI – I – V – IX

The numbers were not hard to read – the first was 224159, the second 246159 and the third 286159 – but Shakespeare could not imagine what they meant.

He scratched his head. He was no good at this sort of thing. He had heard of boxes with elaborate dials built into the locks, which could be opened only by arranging a correct sequence of numbers. Or could these numerals be measurements, numbers of yards north or south of certain landmarks? They could be days of the week, months of the year or pages in a book. None of these ideas seemed helpful here.

What else? Could it be a numerical code, with each number a letter?

That would mean that he was looking for three six-letter words.

Using the most obvious key – in which the Roman numeral I represented the letter A – he calculated that the first number came out as BBDAEI – obvious nonsense.

How many words could begin with a double letter? Not many: it could only be an E or an O. And if II stood for E, then the word came out as EEGDHL. And if the second letter was O . . . No, that didn't work, either.

He knew that the number two was sacred in ecclesiastical symbolism, standing for the dual nature of God and man in Christ. He knew also that the Roman numerals were based on the shape of a man's hand – the four digits and the V of an open palm. What he did not know was whether such knowledge was of the slightest use here.

He looked harder at the final lines of the epigraph and swallowed.

IN . THE . NAME . OF . THE . FATHER .
AND . THE . SON.

On a first reading, this had sounded like a prayer, a purely formal expression, but now he could see that it was more literal. The hairs on his scalp stirred when he saw its meaning: Stanyhurst was advising him that what followed was a revelation about the father and the son. He probably suspected that Shakespeare's Latin – or his eyesight – might not be up to the task of reading his book. This dedication was an oblique but pointed attempt to alert him to the nature of the book's contents.

Shakespeare almost shouted when the last piece of the puzzle slipped into place. The reason for those allusions to *Love's Labour's Lost*, he now saw, was to announce that there was an element of disguise in what followed. Stanyhurst was urging him to look behind the surface of the words themselves.

The man had thought of everything. But why? Why so much subterfuge?

Shakespeare stood up and ran his hands through his hair. His face felt hot. The story was coming together in full view: he could see it clearly now.

Stanyhurst was running for his life and his final act had been to hand this book to a man he had met only once. It was a desperate throw, but also an ambitious one: he clearly wanted to pass on his findings (or theory – or whatever it was) to someone who might complete or at least publicise his work. There had been enough in their talk that day to persuade him that Shakespeare was an ally.

And there could be no doubt: Stanyhurst's secret, grave enough to force a man to flee, concerned the balance of feelings between Henry VII and his own son and heir.

Shakespeare looked at the manuscript again, but it was hopeless. He was all at sea with respect to those mysterious numbers and would never be able to decipher the text without help – expert help.

Then, for the first time since his friends had left, he smiled.

He knew just the man.

Chapter

13

*T*here was no time to arrange an appointment, but Shakespeare was content to travel hopefully. On another day he would have walked – the path to Fulham was about the same distance as the one he had taken the other day, to Greenwich – but he was impatient, and damp grey clouds were scudding low over the city. There was rain in the air and he was not in the mood for a soaking.

Neither did he fancy one of the long ferries that ran a regular service between Richmond and Gravesend (with a change of boats at the bridge). Some of the passengers on these foul craft had horns and hooves, and nothing spoiled a journey faster, Shakespeare liked to joke, than having to sit next to a boar.

Fortunately there was space on a tilt boat. Shakespeare paid his pennies and stepped on board. The awning over the benches flapped in a wind that was chilled by the river, but it would keep out the worst of the rain. He was lucky: the tide was turning and the boatmen were impatient to leave. No one wanted to row against the current of grey water on its relentless return to the sea.

It had been a long time since he had taken this river voyage. The first great building on his right was Bridewell Palace, and there, set back from the waterfront, was Salisbury House, where Stanyhurst had received him only a few weeks ago. Soon, however, he was able to set that troubling memory to one side, and surrender to the changing scene.

There were hundreds of boats on the river, all going in different directions. The growth of the entertainments on the south bank had created a surge in the demand for rapid crossings and the watermen had multiplied. Yet while near misses were common, collisions were rare. It did not occur to Shakespeare to be nervous.

He smiled when he saw the Middle Temple Hall behind its hedge. It was warm with memories: that was where they had first staged *Twelfth Night*, and Shakespeare had a vivid recollection of the afternoon when the Queen herself had come to see it.

Here stood the palatial houses of the kingdom's richest landowners: not just Essex and Arundel, but Suffolk, York, Northampton and Lancaster. Most of them had formal gardens laid out in terraces, with steps leading down to private jetties, and they were far enough from the city's bustle to enjoy air, trees and a river view. Shakespeare raised one finger in a discreet salute as they passed Durham House, the mansion Queen Elizabeth had given Walter Raleigh in the years when he was in favour.

How things had changed.

The contrast on his left was striking. The theatres and bear-pits poked up above cheap tenements and crowded hostels. Once the Paris Garden landing stage fell behind there were damp, marshy fields crisscrossed with ditches until, in the distance, the palace at Lambeth shone red against a screen of pine and elm.

At Westminster, Shakespeare could not quell a shudder as they lurched past the entrance to the Star Chamber and the steps used by the Gunpowder Plotters. There, too, lay the royal apartments of Whitehall. This stretch of water was better dressed. Silk pennants streamed in the wind above gold-and-scarlet bargemen standing on the prows of their elaborate, carved cutters. Even the blades of their oars, as upright as soldiers on parade, flashed blue and silver in the cold spring air.

After they had crossed the route of the horse ferry, the city fell away and the riverside became green. Ducks, geese and other waterfowl bobbed among the drowned branches. Thomas More's beloved village of Chelsea – his handsome house was right on the river, with the parish church and a clutch of more humble dwellings nestling alongside –

emerged and slid past. It was very quiet this morning, though a small group of labourers were felling trees in the woods behind the church. The rhythm of their axes blended with the whoosh of oars in a strange, mesmerising dance.

As they approached Fulham, Shakespeare stood up and stretched. He was hungry.

One of the boatmen looked up. 'Is this where you stop?'

Shakespeare nodded.

'Fulham. *Foul* ham, more like.'

It was commonly supposed that the place was named after the malodorous burial ground and cesspit in the fields just north of the village, near the hurling ground.

'I always thought it was named for the birds,' he said. '*Fowle* ham.'

'You can believe that if you want to,' said the boatman. 'But you might want to hold your nose just in case.'

The boatman leaned on his oar and swung the boat neatly alongside the landing stage.

'Thank you,' said Shakespeare.

Platforms such as this always made him feel as though he was performing, so he made a brief bow before moving off towards Fulham Palace.

It was a hard place to love. The building was delightful, a tall, proud house surrounded by grassy meadows and impressive trees, yet it was here that a number of Protestant heretics had been butchered on the orders of Queen Mary. Whilst Shakespeare sympathised with her religious beliefs, he was not fond of executions. This was also where his old friend John Florio lived, however, and he could think of no one better able to solve a problem such as the one he gripped in his cold right hand.

Florio was the translator of one of Shakespeare's favourite books – the essays of Montaigne – but he had also been tutor to the young Prince Henry. That was why he had an apartment here in the palace of the Bishop of London.

The boatman was wrong: the air smelled sweet. Some previous bishop had ordered the planting of a forest of rare trees – there were cedar and maple, walnut and lime, cork, pine and cypress. A stone path led beneath the trees to the front entrance of the palace; Florio lodged at the back, facing away from the water.

A row of enormous stumps lined the path. Shakespeare recalled hearing that Queen Elizabeth had complained, on her visit, that the tall elms blocked the view. Here were their remains. They had not given up; all were putting out new shoots and reaching for the sky once more.

A footman answered Shakespeare's knock with the news that Florio was absent. He had gone to Richmond on a royal errand and would not be back before sundown, if that. He was dining in Parson's Green.

What were his plans for the coming days? The footman did not know. He retired for a few moments and returned with an assurance that the master was due back on the morrow.

That was good enough for Shakespeare. He wrote a hasty message that he would return the day after that, adding that he had urgent business with his friend.

The footman was visibly impressed when he learned Shakespeare's name. There was little chance that he would mislay or forget the message.

Shakespeare retraced his steps through the arboretum and sat on a rock beside the riverbank. A vole nosed along the muddy margin; a swan preened itself in an eddy of still water; an otter arched its back and wriggled in the stream. And here came a boat curving towards him. He was relieved: the breeze was blowing in rain.

By the time he got back to Puddle Dock he was wet through. He marched up to the Mermaid, bought a small piece of ginger loaf and ate it while looking over the water to the Globe.

Ah well, he thought. He rubbed his smooth scalp, then went to bed early and slept like a young boy. It had been worthwhile for the fresh air, if nothing else.

He was delighted when word arrived from Burbage that the meeting would be at Windsor House in Cripplegate. It was a place he knew well, hard by his old rooms in Silver Street. The large walled garden would be ideal if the weather was kind.

'It has been empty for a while,' said Burbage when they met, 'and for a small consideration – a florin, to be exact – the sheriff made it ours for the day. The man even promised to warm the rooms, and I see he has done us proud.'

Flames danced in the grate and the room smelled of cherrywood.

'Any word from Ned?'

'He is in Dulwich. I have sent him a letter begging him to forgive us. Of course I could not write in detail, but I expressed the hope that we could meet as soon as possible. I doubt he will nurse a grievance for long, though we – you in particular – owe him an apology.'

'I hope you are right.'

'I will call on him as soon as I can. Anyway, how are you? I trust you passed the time well. When I dropped by, they said you had been out since first light.'

'I went to visit an acquaintance in Fulham. John Florio – I don't think you know him, but he's a deep scholar, a faithful tutor and a dear friend. I took the boat.'

'Any reason in particular?'

Shakespeare hesitated. Should he relate what he had discovered? How could he when he himself did not know? It would have been delightful to confide, but it would precipitate a lengthy conversation. The others would be here soon and there was so much to do. He bit his tongue.

'I am only rarely in London these days. If I fail to visit old friends when I can, I will never see them again. And I felt, I confess, a desperate thirst for fresh air. But it did not matter in the end, because he wasn't at home.'

He tugged an earlobe.

'We will get through this,' said Burbage. 'We have been in tighter spots.'

'You are too kind, as ever,' said Shakespeare. 'Thank you, Richard.'

The day began with a bewitching feast of warm walnut biscuits, cinnamon pudding, buttered raisins, honey rolls and other sweet delicacies. Taylor had surpassed himself. None of it appealed to Shakespeare, but he did not wish to seem churlish, so he toyed with some jelly and forced himself to nibble a chestnut.

'All the way here,' said Taylor, 'I swear, I heard nothing but French.'

'I know. I used to live in these parts myself. Remember the Mountjoys?'

'Of course.'

'They introduced me to a lot of French people in the area. Good souls, I found, who worked hard and hid their sorrow well. I took them to Field's Printing House for tidings from home. I felt for them, I must say – humble refugees, battered by their King's dragoons. And though they were devout, they were not like our Puritans. They drank wine like sailors. I went with them once to Tilbury, to meet a ship. It was a fearful sight, piteous beyond imagining. Scores of hollowed pilgrims, babes at their backs and without a shred of luggage, struggling in search of salvation.'

'Poor, naked wretches,' said Constance.

'Exactly.'

Burbage had his own news. 'Sorry to interrupt, but have you heard? Overbury's in the Tower.'

'What?' Shakespeare was horrified. Another one! Overbury was a friend of the present Lord Essex, whose marriage had been the talk of Whitehall for months. His wife, Frances Howard, was pressing for a divorce as she wanted to marry the King's new favourite, Robert Carr. Overbury had been agitating on his friend's behalf to prevent it. His sudden arrest could only mean that the King had swung against Essex (and the laws of matrimony) for good.

'From what I hear it's all political,' said Burbage. 'Those damned Howards want to bind themselves closer to the royal household. I don't know why: they say that Carr is more anxious to catch the King's eye than that of any lady.'

'And if he does catch the King's eye,' said Armin, 'he will torment it.'

An uneasy feeling stole over the group as they realised that one of the places they had chosen for their work was the home of the King's newest enemy.

'It is as well we didn't go there again,' said Taylor.

'Yes,' said Burbage. 'We are much safer here, so long as we sing drunken birthday songs from time to time.'

Shakespeare's blood ran cold at the thought of Overbury in the Tower. Where was he now? Stumbling down those cold stairs, somewhere far below Raleigh's light, restless feet, with water dripping down the walls and a dark hood over his eyes? He recalled the eruption of fear when he himself had been seized. It had happened with no warning; the talons clawed into your neck before you could blink. There could be men approaching the house even now, their boots drumming in the dirt.

He shook his head. He had to push fear aside. It was time to play the King.

Everyone else was settled. He gulped in air and began.

'The important point about Caxton is that he is a well-known emblem of the reign, so his commentary has authority. He is one of the fountainheads of our times: he printed Malory and Chaucer; people will hang on his words. The way I see it, Act Four should open with him describing the turning of the world. There's a good deal to narrate: an end to the quarrels of York and Lancaster; the landfalls out in the New World; the paintings of the Florentines; the peace falling like quiet dew on England's green pastures. One thing we must mention is the marriage between Prince Arthur and Catherine of Aragon, because that's where all the trouble begins. So shall we go round, taking it in turns? Keep it simple. I'll start.'

Burbage smiled: the man was a marvel. In circumstances where others would have balked, Shakespeare could dig in his spurs and throw himself at imaginary hosts. The news about Overbury must have rocked him and the situation with Alleyn remained tense. Not many men could carry burdens as lightly as Will.

'Ready?' Shakespeare said. 'Here goes.'

'May I suggest something?' said Harvard.

'Of course.'

'When Caxton tells us how the world turns, why doesn't he actually turn the world – by spinning a globe?'

'John, that is so clever.'

Harvard blushed. 'I like maps and things,' he said.

'I mean it,' said Shakespeare.

He picked up a ball of twine and held it up like the globe they were imagining.

'The world we know is changing every hour,' he began, spinning the sphere. 'Look how this toy, our planet, doth revolve, passing from darkness into radiant light, from this most lustrous day to blackest night . . .'

Burbage leaned down and whispered in Constance's ear.

'The truth is that we could slip away and he would barely notice. He would just carry on panelling the walls with verse.'

'. . . With mountains, rivers, cities, deserts, seas, clung fast to this old orb we once thought flat . . .'

There was a pause. No one else chipped in, so Shakespeare continued.

'Since Henry plucked the crown at Bosworth Field, a dozen years have run their fertile course. Now England lies, well fed and satisfied, in warm and dewlapped pastures of sweet peace . . .'

It was time. Armin took a step forward and offered some lines about schooners and rough seas, and hungry sharks that leaped to feed on seals, and tigers that padded through the spice-filled East.

'Superb,' said Shakespeare.

Constance had a line about Leonardo and Raphael, and then it was Taylor's turn.

'The Queen spills sons and daughters like ripe fruit,' he said, 'in some bewitched and melon-fabled orchard, while Henry makes alliances and deals . . .'

'Not sure about melon-fabled, but keep going,' said Shakespeare.

It was Burbage who took up the baton, however, with a neat story about the pretenders pining in the Tower.

'I like it,' said Shakespeare, stepping forward. 'That is ample – we can put more beef on this later. Are you keeping up, John?'

'I believe so, sir.'

'Good. Now, the next thing we need—'

He was all business, as quick and accurate as a snake pouncing on a mouse.

'Caxton needs to wind down with a soft cadence. Any minute now, Henry's world is going to collapse. A messenger will bring news – awful news. Joseph?'

'Will?'

'When I stop, you arrive with dreadful tidings. My bright son Arthur, the blinding light of all my hopes, is dead. Can you do that?'

Constance fought to ignore a stab of apprehension. There was a brittle note to Shakespeare's voice that made her nervous. No sooner was she aware of this than it changed. With a flick like a lizard's tail, the shrill edge melted and Shakespeare became calm. Once again he was Caxton – bumbling, short-sighted, an elderly craftsman pottering among his papers in search of a comb.

He described a land in which kingfishers slept safe, flashing on rivers in the shade of oaks, their mates furled in gauzy nests. A land whose future was assured by Prince Arthur's sacred marriage to bright Catherine, who sailed from Aragon bedecked in gold, with swan-drawn carriages of pearl.

'But soft . . .' He looked up. 'What news?'

Taylor caught the sombre mood and kept the volume low. 'Most solemn tidings, noble Caxton. News that will stop your heart.'

'How about press,' said Shakespeare. 'Let the news stop his press.'

'I mean *stop* in the musical sense. The news plays on his heart as on a pipe.'

'I missed that. Very good. Carry on.'

'News that will stop your heart. Eyes, prepare to weep, for I have tidings fit to drown a fleet.'

'That is good except for the rhyme. Weep . . . fleet. How about . . . *flow*.'

'Will.' Burbage smiled. 'Let the man speak. You cannot drown a flow, anyway.'

Armin offered a short, grave speech charging Caxton to print, in the King's name, a thousand copies of the news. Arthur, the King's son and heir, was dead.

'The beacon of our happiness is dimmed. Tomorrow shall we drape ourselves in black, and ring out bells, and make such lamentation as we may.'

There was a long silence. Shakespeare's Caxton was as motionless as marble.

'Ill met indeed,' he said at last. 'I will to work tonight. How died he? From the pestilence, you say? And what of his poor widow, how grieves she? But time enough for that another day. For now we can do naught but print, and pray.'

He glanced heavenwards for an instant. Then, like a magician hidden in a secret compartment, he stepped out of character and back into the present day.

The hush lay on the company like a blanket. No one wanted to bruise the tranquil atmosphere with speech. Shakespeare remained in a daze.

Eventually Burbage felt he had to say something.

'That was awfully good, Will. You excel yourself.'

'Thank you,' said Shakespeare. 'At some point we will see how the King receives this blow. But not now.'

Burbage glanced at Taylor, who hurried off for a flask of ale.

'This calls for a drink,' he said.

Shakespeare's smile was only a little forced.

'Was it that bad?'

'You know it wasn't,' said Armin.

'You are very kind. I think I might take a piece of that cake now, if we still have some.'

'About time,' said Constance, fetching a slice. 'It's good.'

'But this isn't a break,' said Shakespeare. 'We must keep going.'

They spent the next few hours discussing the stratagems by which Henry secured his strength. Armin did an impressive turn as the Scottish poet Dunbar, who travelled south to London with a marriage proposal that fell on favourable ears: Henry's daughter Margaret – a child – was promised to King James IV of Scotland in a marriage of political convenience that would open the English throne to the Stuarts. Shakespeare inserted a smiling suggestion that the King did not enjoy poetry.

'The King will like this part,' said Heminge. 'It will remind him of his daughter's nuptials. Perhaps we should make a longer scene of it.'

'If we have time,' said Shakespeare.

'I have always felt,' said Constance, 'that if *I* were ever to write a play, it would be about just this, the roots of the rivalry between Elizabeth of England and Mary of the Scots. When their joint ancestor Henry VII sent his daughter north to marry the Scottish King

James, he hoped to unite the kingdoms; yet all it did was divide them. Years later, Mary clung to the old faith and wasted her life in plots to supplant her English cousin. Poor Henry. The best-laid plans . . .'

'I wouldn't put it past you,' said Armin.

'We owe much to Queen Elizabeth,' said Shakespeare. 'The greatest actor I ever saw, present company excepted. She played the regal part better than anyone – trod the court as if it were a stage. That speech at Tilbury, when she roused her men to face the Armada – "I know I have the body of a weak and feeble woman, but I have the heart and stomach of a king" – it was the model for all the speeches of all our kings.'

'I never knew that,' said Constance.

'There is often less to these things than meets the eye,' said Shakespeare. 'And luck plays a surprising part, too. Remember when *Othello* caught fire? The script, I mean. Someone's pipe fell on it.'

'By God, I'd forgotten,' said Burbage.

'Or maybe it was a candle, or a hot coal. Anyway, we lost a long scene where Iago admits that he is enamoured of Desdemona. We were panic-stricken, because we felt it was important – it explained Iago's vindictive malice, and suggested that *he* was the truly jealous man in the play.'

'Yes. And there was no time to write anything new, so Will came up with a flash of such adroit wit . . . How did it go? I hate the Moor, and it is thought abroad, that 'twixt my sheets he has done my office: I know not if 't be true, but it will serve. That was all, but that line made the whole play sing. Instead of being a spiteful love-rival, Iago was a force of nature, pure evil. People loved him. They still do.'

Shakespeare smiled. 'As I say, it was just luck really.'

'I think we should move on,' said Heminge.

'I've been thinking,' said Burbage. 'I don't know if it's because of our own situation, but I wonder if we need more on what a fearful and uncertain time this was – spies, emissaries, soldiers.'

Everyone agreed this was a good idea, and Burbage mentioned a noble called Clifford, who had been engaged by Henry to infiltrate the rebel court overseas. Armin and Taylor outlined some boisterous new material for Bacon and the Crier. Heminge made several suggestions regarding the King's financial position and was especially cutting in a clever scene showing the King's devious way with taxes.

'One last thing,' said Shakespeare. 'With the death of Prince Arthur we are approaching a climax and a turning point. The King needs a long speech. I have prepared a few thoughts, although I welcome any suggestions.'

Constance coughed. 'It may seem improper, but I read that there was much consternation, following his death, about Princess Catherine of Aragon. If she had been pregnant, then the young Prince Henry would not have been the heir.'

Taylor almost shouted. 'That is *tremendous*! What a story.'

'Apparently,' said Armin, 'there was quite convincing evidence that she might have been with child. On the day after his wedding night, the Prince was heard to boast that he had spent a hot night in Spain.'

'What elegant tongues they have, these royal husbands,' said Burbage. 'May I ask how old Prince Arthur was?'

'Fifteen,' said Shakespeare. 'Old enough for those rumours to be true. But I must admit I was thinking of making him fourteen, perhaps even younger.'

'Good idea. Audiences weep more freely for boys than for men. A beard is a great suppressor of woe.'

'It might just give Henry's heartbreak a more plaintive note.'

'That's decided, then,' said Heminge.

Shakespeare nodded. 'Now,' he said, 'I have changed my mind about something else too. People love swords, so I think we *do* need a bit of action, with soldiers rushing about. I was thinking of a scene with Warbeck's rebels, a blur of one-line speeches to give the impression of an army on the hoof, events moving fast. Like this . . .'

With a nimbleness that surprised those who had not seen him do this before, he leaped over the bench and said:

'The men are ready. All our stores are horsed.'

He jumped back:

'And men do daily flock to swell our ranks.'

Again he spun about:

'Suffolk awaits at Exeter with supplies.'

And one more time:

'And spring sends sun to speed our hopeful feet.'

The effort left him panting. 'That's the kind of thing,' he said. 'I could carry on, but it wouldn't be good for my back.'

They were starting to enjoy themselves again.

'Come on, Will,' said Burbage. 'Try some of this potted meat. Pigeon, I think it is. Very good on these oatcakes.'

Shakespeare declined, then stretched and wondered aloud if it was time to break.

'Is it too early to go for that walk, John?'

'Any time is good,' said Heminge.

'While the sun's out, then. Shall we?'

Shakespeare looked out of the window at the street opposite. He saw no sign of anyone in the shadows, but it was impossible to draw any conclusions from that.

'Would you mind if we went back to Westminster? It is such a fine day, and there is something I would very much like to show the young ones.'

'Westminster?' Taylor looked shocked. 'That's miles.'

'Come. It is less than an hour away. And it is beautiful weather.'

'Is it prudent to march around together like this?'

'We don't have to stay in one large group. But since you ask: yes, it *is* a good idea. Today is my birthday. We are having a party. Let's go.'

When he looked out of the window again, it struck him that he no longer believed in Alleyn's duplicity – it didn't feel right. Spies did not storm off in self-righteous dudgeon; they pulled themselves deep into their camouflage and hid.

Unless . . . Alleyn knew more than enough already to have them arrested. Maybe *that* was why he had stormed out. His two-faced performance as a King's Man was done.

Was it true that time would answer all? What if it did no more than devour all? There had to be mysteries – *stranger things* – that would never be solved.

The others were pulling on their cloaks. Burbage made a point of bringing up the rear. On the way out he took Constance's arm and held her back for a second.

'If you permit,' he said, letting the others go ahead, 'I must enlighten you about something.'

'Am I so dark?'

'In this, perhaps you are.'

Constance was curious.

'Shakespeare had a son once,' said Burbage in an abrupt voice. 'Hamnet. He died quite suddenly when he was . . . oh, no more than twelve years old. There was no warning. Shakespeare . . . well, he took it hard. I dare say he has never been the same since. Something broke in him. He had been away so much, you see, here in London, so he did not know the boy as well as he wished. I think this above all is what haunts him. One day, Hamnet was gone. As a candle gutters and is extinguished, from light to dark in an instant. A message arrived. I mention it only . . .'

'I understand,' said Constance, frowning. 'This scene we are to play, the King and Queen mourning the death of the Prince – it may go hard with him.'

'Your years belie your wisdom,' said Burbage. 'To Will, Hamnet was a son; but he was also, as it happens, an heir. Interesting, is it not, the way art follows life? Now we play with kings and their concern for their inheritance.'

'Their heirs and graces.'

'Very good. Anyway, Will too is anxious that no man will marry his daughters for their – his – money.'

'What would you have me do?'

'Oh, nothing,' said Burbage. 'I mention it only so you are not deceived. When the moment comes he may be a man on hot coals. Perhaps you can indulge him.'

'I shall. Thank you,' said Constance.

They hurried down, caught up with the others and walked down to Cheapside. They turned right down the hill to the Strand, then pushed past the mansions Shakespeare had seen from the river. For once, nothing unusual erupted in their path. A one-legged sailor tried to beg coin for a journey to Plymouth, where he could (he said) find a new ship, but Burbage shoved him away with an exasperated yell. Eventually they rounded the curve at Whitehall, passed under the stone arches and saw, rearing above them, the resounding crowns of Westminster Abbey.

'Magnificent,' said Constance.

'It's not a church,' said Harvard. 'It's a mountain.'

'Have you ever seen a mountain?' said Shakespeare.

'No,' said Harvard.

'There are none in England. We have only hills. But go to Switzerland and your head will never sit square on your neck again, from all the looking up. The peaks blaze white in the sun, and thundering rivers of ice carve their way down their flanks. I should not say thundering, for they are as silent as clouds. It is heaven.'

'Apparently they planned to crown the abbey with towers as well,' Heminge was saying. 'But they never finished them. One day, maybe.'

'Better not call it an abbey, John,' said Shakespeare. 'That is heresy, these days.'

'You know that phrase about robbing Peter to pay Paul,' said Taylor. 'It's one of Fletcher's – he uses it all the time. I always wondered where it came from, and the other day I found myself reading about it.'

'Something to do with the Church?' said Burbage.

'Not just any church,' said Taylor. 'This church. It was called St Peter's before the dissolution and was one of the richest religious houses in all the land. It survived – Henry VIII made it a cathedral – but all its treasure was handed to St Paul's. So Peter was robbed to pay Paul. Interesting, eh?'

'Fascinating,' said Armin. 'Where are we going?'

'This way,' said Heminge.

They were surprised to meet a crowd of people streaming west towards the green acres on the far side of the square.

'Where are they all going?' said Harvard.

Shakespeare hesitated.

'An execution,' said Taylor. 'Tyburn is up that way. Want to see a hanging?'

'Joseph!' Constance put an arm round Harvard's shoulder.

'Amazing, isn't it?' said Shakespeare. 'All the work we do, all our thought and wit, and the only thing you need to entice a crowd is a man's neck in a noose.'

'This way,' said Heminge again.

They slipped in through the northern gate.

'Wait,' said Burbage to Harvard. 'Speaking of hangings – just round there in the old yard, that's where the poor devil Fawkes was done to death.'

'This way,' said Heminge. 'For the third time. I sound like Peter himself.'

'Where are we going?' said Constance.

'You'll see.'

Heminge led the way into a high, quiet chapel lit by a vast stained-glass window. Above them, far above, hung the lacy fans that vaulted the ceiling.

'Hard to believe they are stone,' said Burbage.

'They look like curtains,' said Harvard.

It was cool and still; the thick walls forced the outside world to retreat for a while. Splashes of coloured light – red, blue and yellow – fell on pale French stone.

'We cannot stay long,' said Heminge. 'But Will wanted us to see this.'

He pointed at a stone plinth with two golden figures supine on top.

'Henry VII and Elizabeth,' said Shakespeare. 'This is the Lady Chapel, built by Henry when his Queen – that's you, Constance – died.'

'How died she?'

'In childbirth, it is said. But we shall make her die of a broken heart.'

'She looks so peaceful.'

'Yes.'

Heminge leaned in and expanded the lesson.

'It's the work of an Italian sculptor, can't remember his name. He once broke Michelangelo's nose in a fist fight, so they say. Anyway, it's gilded bronze. The King's face is the more lifelike because it was taken from a death mask.'

Shakespeare looked at the effigies in silence, breathing an imaginary life into the glowing couple who lay on the slab, palms closed in prayer, elbows touching, a faint smile on the Queen's plump face.

'There we are,' Heminge said. 'These are our subjects. Look on them, think on them. But tarry not long. We should not be observed here.'

'I would like to stay a while longer,' said Shakespeare. 'I shall catch you up.'

'Can I stay with you?' said Constance.

'Of course.' Shakespeare was delighted.

'We'll walk,' said Burbage. 'You two take your time and follow on by carriage. It makes sense to split up. Someone here might notice us.'

'Very good,' said Shakespeare.

As the others wandered off, they sat down on a stone pew.

'Are you happy with the play?' said Constance.

Shakespeare shrugged. 'It needs lifting, of course – half the work happens later, when I paper over the cracks, stitch episodes together or swap scenes round.'

'Will it change very greatly?'

'It won't so much change as . . . cook. Ripen. That's the idea, anyway.'

'I never realised that plays grew like this. I always imagined you writing them alone somewhere, in a top-floor room with the window open to the starlight.'

'I do that sometimes,' said Shakespeare, 'but it is more sleight of hand. Just as with dates, I often shuffle lines around – take them from one man and give them to another. Or to a woman. It creates surprises.'

'I was so sorry to hear about your son,' said Constance. She blushed when she realised how abrupt she'd been.

The silence whined like a gnat. Shakespeare's voice was low.

'Ah. I suppose Richard told you about that.'

Constance nodded.

'That was good of him. He's a good man, Richard.'

'Yes.'

'So are they all. All good men.'

Constance did not know what he was suggesting.

'Mine was a country boyhood,' said Shakespeare. 'I grew up in woods and fields: gathered acorns for swine, cared for horses, made bread from rye, minded cattle to make sure their feet didn't rot from the boggy ground – even stole a deer once.'

'A thief! I knew it.'

'It wasn't thieving – it was hunting. You must remember, these were the days after the wrecking of the monasteries. Without the monks to tend the fields, England's crops were ruined. There was little to eat. The pastures were infested with weeds—'

'Fie, 'tis an unweeded garden.'

Raleigh's sad face rose up in Shakespeare's mind. 'Exactly,' he said.

'Sorry. I interrupted. Then what happened?'

'Let's walk.'

They strolled along the flagged stone aisles of the great cathedral, footsteps echoing in the soaring space.

'I admit, Constance, that this is one of my motives in making this play. After his ruthless ascent to power, Henry VII soon found himself, like all kings, in a swamp of corpses. His enemies, of course, but also friends, allies, family . . . even his children. I know not what draws such men to thrones, for thrones are steeped in blood. And so it is with me.'

A glance at Constance showed him that he was alarming her.

'But you are young,' he said. 'You should not have to listen to such talk. I am too morbid – I am sorry. My parents had eight children – the same as Henry. Two of my brothers have perished this last twelve-month. Only two remain: myself and a sister.'

'You have other children, though . . .'

'Two daughters. One is married to an apothecary. He makes health-giving beer from plant juice. It is vile, but we all have to swear by it.'

'And then . . . Hamnet,' Constance said. She felt compelled to repeat his name.

'Yes.' Shakespeare clenched his fingers and squeezed his arm. 'Hamnet. It was in the summer of 1596. As long as I live I shall not forget the day I heard the news.'

'Seventeen years ago,' said Constance. 'Before I was born.'

'Six thousand and sixty-seven days, to be precise.' Shakespeare wore a grave smile. 'I count them every morning.'

Constance gulped.

'The thing that tears at my heart is that I was not there. I was trav-elling with the players, in Kent. When I heard, he had already been gone more than a week.'

He paused. His voice was as a limp flag on a windless day, and he seemed to be addressing no one in particular.

'It was often said that my plays were coloured by his death, that I became preoccupied by souls in torment – Othello, Macbeth, Lear. But look at the other characters I created – Falstaff, Belch, Benedick. Bright and talkative spirits. Writers are like actors – we are not slaves to our tempers.'

Constance's head ached. She wished she had not brought this up.

'I don't know whether you have seen *King John*,' said Shakespeare.

'I don't believe I have,' said Constance.

'It is not one of our best,' said Shakespeare. 'But it is precious . . . to me. There's a scene where the heir to the throne dies – murdered by King John, more or less – and his mother has to lament his passing . . .'

He looked away, lowered his voice and recited his own words.

'Grief fills the room up of my absent child, lies in his bed, walks up and down with me, puts on his pretty looks, repeats his words . . . O Lord! my boy, my Arthur, my fair son, my life, my joy, my food, my all the world . . .'

Shakespeare's voice was shaking. Constance said nothing.

'A mother's words,' said Shakespeare. 'But a father's feelings too. Strange that the Prince should be called Arthur. I wonder if you know the mother's name?'

Constance shook her head.

'She was called Constance,' said Shakespeare. 'She is you.'

Constance looked at her hands. This was embarrassing. She felt as if she had strayed out of her depth.

'Tell me about Stratford,' she said. 'I have never been. Is it a fair town?'

There was an aching hesitation before Shakespeare answered.

'Oh yes,' he said at last. 'It is a ruby. There's a low stone bridge over the clear, swan-lapped Avon – markets, fairs, inns, stables. It is the town of a thousand elms.'

'What turned you from such delights into the theatre?'

'My father made gloves – and when I was young I helped him. He became an alderman and was given front seats when the travelling players came to town. He would put on his thumb-ring and his black, fur-lined gown, and I would sit beside him, watching Warwick's Men or Lord Strange's Men. I loved it from the first, though I did not fully appreciate it till I was deprived.'

'Deprived how?'

'My father fell into financial hardship. He outreached himself, branching into timber and textiles. He should have stayed with what he knew. But he flew too high and lost . . . everything, even his position.'

'You take my house when you do take the prop that holds my house; and so you take my life, when you do take the means whereby I live. Shylock.'

'Goodness. You really do know the plays,' Shakespeare said.

Constance gave a meek nod.

'I tried to help him recover, but his heart was crushed. In his anger and shame he would not let me see the players, and it was this that fanned the flames of my enthusiasm. As I say, deprivation sharpened my appetite. Absence made me yearn for the rhythms, colour, even the smell of the stage. I would sneak off, climb a tree and watch the actors at rehearsal in the woods. It was a dazzling sight, and I ached to join in. One morning they called me down from my tree – they knew all along that I was hiding up there – and asked me to help with a scene. I had found where I belonged.'

'And the rest was history.'

'Not exactly. My father was furious. He would not countenance my becoming a player – he thought it too low. He said that if I followed this vulgar trade I would not be welcome in Stratford. We argued. And then, well, I married when I was eighteen, and children came – Susanna first, then the twins. You can imagine.'

He fell silent. Constance knew he was thinking of Hamnet.

'Is that when you came to London?'

'Not at once. I joined those players and travelled. They needed young men, you see, to play the female parts. And I knew I could never prosper in Stratford. We journeyed far and wide, as far as France and Italy, Germany and Holland.'

'That is where you saw the Alpine mountains, all crowned with snow.'

'Yes. And the fairest city in all the wide world: Zurich.'

'My father too has ventured far. I should love to travel.'

'Then you must. In Zurich, ancient towers hug the mouth of a river, by a lake, beneath a ring of glistening white peaks. In the distance you see gleams of snow. It is delightful. But do not go today, I beg you. We have not finished with you yet.'

Shakespeare's eager smile made her look away. He noticed.

'Well, that is my life story, poor as it is,' he said.

'What about your father? Did he not come round to your art? Surely he knew in time that you were born for the stage.'

Shakespeare hesitated. He was rarely as confidential as this, but Constance's youth and guileless beauty lifted away the fetters in which he normally bound himself.

'I will tell you something very few people know,' he said. 'The truth is that my father never knew I wrote plays. I dared not tell him, and then it was too late.'

'I don't believe it. Someone must have told him, surely.'

'It is not probable.' Shakespeare looked up at the vaults and let out a sigh he seemed to have been holding in for years. 'You see, in Stratford no one supposes that I am a man of the theatre, even today. They think me a wool merchant, and I do nothing to undeceive them. The fact is, I shunned my home until I had the means to pose as a man of affairs. The theatre is not well loved there, even now. My family would have suffered much ignominy were it known that I was a humble player.'

Constance had no idea what to say to this, so Shakespeare rose to his feet.

'Perhaps we had better look for the others,' he said.

When she stood up he put a hand on her arm.

'Forgive me if I confide . . . too much,' he said.

Constance frowned and Shakespeare gave an inward groan. She seemed even more beautiful when serious. 'This afternoon we shall see a king bereft of a son,' she said. 'I am glad – honoured – that you told me.'

Shakespeare scuffed the dust with his toe. 'It is not as if I am the only one.'

'The only one?'

'Ben Jonson lost a son, a seven-year-old lad, to the sweating sickness. I never met the boy. And Robert Armin – he had three children, and right fair they were too. All of them died young. He does not act the broken heart, but scratch the surface of his comedy and you will find a sad soul. Feste? Touchstone? Much of that is him.'

'I had no idea,' said Constance. 'I have been blind. I know those lines of Jonson's: "Farewell, thou child of my right hand, and joy; My sin was too much hope of thee . . ." But I did not realise he was writing about himself.'

'He does not seek sympathy,' said Shakespeare. 'Not like me, eh?'

She swallowed. What could she say?

'There they are!' said Shakespeare. He could see Harvard standing in the light of a sunbeam that slanted down through the east window. A golden ring of dust swirled in the luminous air above his head, like a halo. Shakespeare's chest swelled with melancholy gratitude to see such a shining emblem of youth – so fine, so eager and so untrammelled by disappointment.

'He looks like an angel,' said Constance.

'All children are angels,' said Shakespeare. 'But so he does. So he does.'

As agreed, they took a carriage back to Windsor House, and the first thing they discussed on their arrival was the plan for the morrow.

'We are nearly there,' said Shakespeare. 'One long day might do it. I am sorry to say that I am not free tomorrow. Does the day after suit everyone?'

'Absolutely,' said Armin. 'Where?'

'Blackfriars is out of the question,' said Shakespeare. 'I wonder if the Globe . . . Richard?'

'Good idea. It will be like hiding a leaf in a glade. All of us are familiar there, so no one will think of wondering what we are up to. As it happens, I know that tomorrow is impossible – there's a performance. But I think the next day is free. Maybe it is as well to break for a day in any case.'

Shakespeare nodded. 'Good. We shall gather breath, complete our research and prepare for one last assault. I am still open-minded about the ending, so we can all brood on that. Where is the story leading? We have a promising situation – a king twisted by grief and putting England on the rack in revenge. But we need a climax. We also need more between the King and his advisers about money. And Robert, you might wind up the tale of Cabot and the citizens. After that, we'll see.'

Something occurred to Burbage. 'Will Prince Henry make an appearance?'

'Possibly,' said Shakespeare, frowning. 'Possibly.'

'I'll look in at the Globe tonight, make sure it's all clear.'

'What time?' said Taylor. 'I do have something I must do, the day after tomorrow.'

'As early as possible.'

'Oh, no matter,' said Taylor. 'I'll be there.'

'Is all well for everyone else?'

Shakespeare saw Harvard's face cloud for a moment, an instant as swift as one flap of a bird's wing.

'What is it?'

'Nothing. Only—'

'What?'

'At Westminster I saw a notice that said that the day after tomorrow, at St Paul's, there was to be a demonstration of calligraphy.'

'And you wanted to go.'

Harvard shook his head. 'It's of no importance.'

Shakespeare smiled. 'I shall be proud to take you. Come to my house at first light and we shall go together. Joseph can do whatever it is he needs to do, and we can all meet for a late breakfast at the Globe.'

'Thank you, sir.'

Harvard's smile gladdened Shakespeare's heart.

'If anyone wishes to join us, you are all welcome.'

No one rushed to volunteer.

'That is settled, then,' said Heminge, catching Shakespeare's eye. 'What next? I believe that the next scene is you being the King, um, lamenting the loss of his son the Prince Arthur. Yes?'

'Agreed.' Shakespeare pulled a scroll from his leather bag. 'In truth, I went to the trouble of writing it already, so we can skip this part.'

'Oh, just a few lines, Will,' said Burbage. 'If Constance is to be your Queen, she needs to know in what wise to approach her part.'

'If you insist,' said Shakespeare.

He let the room grow quiet. Then, in a movement whose swiftness startled his friends, he dropped to his knees and bowed his head. When he looked up, all the life had drained from his face: he looked as though he had seen a ghost.

'The doctors say that Arthur is no more. I do not, cannot, will not think it so. Death might have sought some weaker prey to stalk. Not fourteen springs have passed since his first breath, and he has yet – must I say had? – to bloom . . .'

He shed the mask for a moment to explain.

'It goes on like that for a few more lines: quiet, wounded. The King blames himself – he sees this as divine vengeance on him for the murder of the Princes. But as the speech proceeds, his guilt swells into rage. He calls God a trickster, who conjures with our hearts and, laughing, breaks them. And so he comes to his pledge. This should be an icy moment. He vows to rule in God's name, observant of all His virtues, indifferent to the cruelty it will impose . . .'

Once more he took up the King's position. He clutched his arm as if struck by an arrow and his voice was hoarse.

'I'll henceforth none of you. I'll use my power to stand athwart your purposes on earth. I said I would do good, and so I shall. Virtue shall so possess this barren isle, that she shall cry for mercy to the heavens. So come, you thought-obliterating fires, stoke my revenge and scald my black intent, to do such good as will affright the world . . . And Lord, I do beseech thee, hear our prayer: Our Father, who art not in heaven, harrowed be thy name. Give us this day our daily dread. Et cetera. Amen.'

He stopped, and time itself seemed to stop too.

There was a sharp inhalation of breath, but no one was willing to puncture the intensity of the moment with speech.

Nor could any of them resolve their warring feelings. They were horrified by the violence in Shakespeare's words, but at the same time awestruck by his audacity. It reminded Burbage of the day when Shakespeare, in a rehearsal of *King Lear*, had urged their Edmund, seemingly on a whim, to rip out Gloucester's eyes. The actor had quailed, but Shakespeare, eyes flashing with theatrical fury, had stepped forward with what seemed a genuinely wild glint to spit out the now-famous line: Out, vile jelly! Where is thy lustre now?

This time they were shaken, not by the physical surprise but by the brazenness of the blasphemy. All of them knew that the Church sent people to the gallows for less.

A quiet voice broke the spell.

'Enter the Queen,' said Constance, her voice drained of everything except a trace of lilting sweetness. 'My lord, I have been seeking thee betimes.'

Shakespeare complimented her with a pale smile. 'Thou'dst better seek our son, who is no more. My soul is stabbed, and night is come again.'

'There is no sense, my lord,' said Constance, 'nor should there be. 'Tis God's decree. Our part is to endure.'

Shakespeare took her hand and pressed it to his cheek.

'I am a king, yet would a different role, for kings have hollow hearts. 'Tis for those hapless Princes he is ta'en. They are no more, and so our son is dead.'

'Oh do not blame yourself . . .'

'How can I not? 'Twas I that them dispatched.'

Constance sat beside the kneeling Shakespeare, reproaching himself in solemn soliloquy, and laid her arm on his shoulder. By some alchemy of impersonation she seemed older than he, and stronger.

'Oh soft, my lord,' she said. 'It was a dreadful deed. And I have seen how heavily it weighs upon your royal conscience all the while. Sometimes, to save the herd, we cull a hind. A king must needs be cruel to be kind.'

'Good,' said Burbage.

'Better than good,' said Shakespeare. 'Inspired.'

'I think not,' said Constance. 'It is too trim, too tidy. I have a better notion. Why doesn't the Queen misunderstand what the King has confessed? I don't like the idea that she just forgives him for killing those

Princes – that is too easy. It is much more likely she would simply miss his meaning. Would she not assume that he was talking about the *other* boys he executed, the claimants?'

'Now we have something,' said Armin.

'Good idea,' said Shakespeare, all business. 'John, what was my last line?'

'My hand was forced, but I am mired in blood,' said Harvard.

Shakespeare repeated it and invited Constance to continue.

'Sit here, my lord,' she said. 'Lay down these savage barbs. The Princes rose – you acted like a king. Do not, I beg you, make this crime your own. Our son was killed by pestilence, not God, and it is not for us to try His grace.'

Shakespeare beamed.

'Yes, that really works. I confess to double murder, and you mistake my drift. And so our King stands reprieved!'

'Congratulations,' agreed Burbage.

'See how the world imagines not my crime,' said Shakespeare, allowing the King to recover his devious streak. He turned to Constance. 'Thou art too fine and noble, good my Queen. What swan bequeathed you so serene a smile, when heav'n throws down such heavy bolts as this?'

He climbed to his feet, happy to end it there. But Constance remained seated on the floor. In a very quiet voice, she continued.

' 'Tis inward, all my bitterness, my lord, like as the fumarole, awash with fire, seems from afar as calm and cool as snow. So 'tis with me. My outward chill is but for public show. My soul doth shake, as water when it boils.'

'Again, very good,' said Burbage.

'I am wiping away tears,' said Armin.

'Be serious,' said Shakespeare.

He sat beside Constance.

'Do you want to go on?' he said.

'Not really,' she said.

'Because it would be perfect, I fear, if we killed you now, right at the peak of your splendour. The Queen could just swoon away and be carried off to her deathbed. What do you think? It would make this a horrendous double blow for the King, to lose a son and a wife in one fateful stroke.'

'The Queen did not actually die at this time,' said Constance. 'She died a year or so later, I believe.'

'Hah,' said Armin. 'We are boating in Bohemia again.'

Shakespeare did not smile. He was concentrating too hard.

They tried several different ways and settled on the quickest. Constance said a few more words about her grief ('Arthur is gone; he'll never smile no more, nor lay his head on his poor mother's arm') and then collapsed. The King raved and shouted; attendants rushed in – 'Convey her to her bed, and, pray you, let your feet ignite the stones!' – and the Queen murmured a lingering farewell, urging the King ('Adieu, my dearest lord') to cherish their remaining children. And then, shattered by despair ('Oh why is it so dark?') she too was carried off.

'Someone should set this to music,' said Burbage. 'Such drama, I love it.'

Burbage offered to take Constance home, but Shakespeare insisted that there was room in his carriage and that her lodgings were on his route.

They didn't talk much; both of them were tired. When Shakespeare closed his eyes he felt Constance's warm, brown gaze on his face and opened them again.

She was smiling.

'I amuse you?' he said.

'Not in the least,' she said. 'I am just marvelling at the workings of fortune, that I should have played Queen for an afternoon, to Shakespeare's King.'

'You did not merely play,' Shakespeare said. 'Truly, you have the gift. Even I did not imagine you would be so . . . inventive.'

'Women must invent a good deal, since there appears to be so little we can actually do.'

Shakespeare shook his head in wonderment. Every day, all over the world, men strived after wealth, power, land and other toys; yet nothing, since time began, could match the beauty of a tender young woman – or man, come to that. And so a day that had started in confusion was ending in garlands, with rejuvenated hopes. Acting out the death of Arthur had been like fording a weir or crossing a bridge over a chasm. He felt flooded with the relief that flows from dangers safely passed.

He had admitted many motives with respect to *Henry VII*: that he wanted to set history straight, and to shed light on Tudor myths; he had even told Burbage he wanted to denounce the break with Rome. Yet only this afternoon had he revealed his most intimate purpose. The kinship he felt with Henry VII had become a real presence in his life – both had lost sons; both had stared into the abyss of an all-encompassing sorrow. Everything he had said about wanting to set the historical story straight was true, but he also wanted to show how a mighty king could be brought to his knees by loss. Shakespeare had the right to tell this tale; it was his story too. And it wasn't just a morality play in which the gods take their revenge on a murderous king, as usual; it was something much more rich and fraught and dramatic. Henry VII was both a villain *and* a man on the rack; he was both virtuous *and* malign.

This was the picture he wanted to paint – for every light, a shadow. The initial sketch was almost done. No amount of royal threats could stop him now.

Constance cleared her throat.

'I don't want to presume,' she said, 'but may I give voice to a thought?'

'You may,' said Shakespeare, feeling courtly.

'Please don't think I seek only to expand my own role. But I wonder if we should not give a little more weight to Margaret, in Flanders or wherever she is, sending her claimants against the King. At the moment they spring up from nowhere.'

Shakespeare nodded. 'You are quite right, though I hope I would not have failed to notice this omission. At present the antagonists are dispersed. Much better to concentrate them in one sinister opponent – audiences love having someone to hiss at.'

Constance seemed to be about to say more.

'So yes,' said Shakespeare. 'See what you can contrive. Let us see her plot. It will be a pleasure to hear what you conceive. If you wish, help yourself to my books.'

'Thank you,' said Constance.

Shakespeare sat back and let the quietness lap around him.

There was much still to confront. He had not totally vanquished his suspicion of Alleyn. The man had behaved strangely, and Shakespeare owed it not just to himself but to the whole company to be cautious. He could see, however, that his anger might have been magnified by Ned's unpleasing interest in Constance, and had to admit that Burbage was right: it had been a juvenile misjudgement to make his fears public.

This would have to wait, however: in the meantime he was keen to see what Florio could make of Stanyhurst's book; and he ought to see too how Fletcher was getting on with *Henry VIII*. Perhaps they should send Sir Edward Coke an act or two, to keep him happy – or at least quiet. He could ask Heminge to take care of it.

It made him sag to think that till this moment he had avoided fretting about such matters for a while, at least. But he pushed self-reproach away. For now he was happy – enchanted – to recall the silky touch of Constance's fingers on his cheek. He himself could hardly recall a sexual encounter that was not a hurried grapple, so the vision of sweet, unhurried, languorous love was an alluring one. He closed his eyes, indulged himself for an instant in a hazy dream of unrequitable bliss, then sighed. Constance was too pure and spirited to be false – she knew not what she did – but she was still a swallowed bait on purpose laid to make the taker mad. Fortunately, he knew that love could unseat the most placid of tempers, and that he himself was not above the silliest and most blatant folly. As a result, he was able to summon a weak smile at the vanity that led him to think, as the carriage swayed along the Strand, that maybe he was not, in the great scheme of things, so very old after all.

Chapter
14

The journey to Fulham seemed to take longer this time, perhaps because it was no longer an experiment. With tight lips Shakespeare watched the London waterfront slide past, willing the oarsmen to pull harder.

When they left Chiswick behind he leaned forward. It would be good to see Florio again. He had known and admired the man for years, not least because he was – like Shakespeare – the child of shipwreck. His father, Michelangelo, was a Protestant convert forced to flee Italy for his faith. Both he and his son John were almost excessively cultivated. They knew every language and had read every book. They seemed to have absorbed the wisdom of the ages, yet they wore their learning like a silk scarf, as light as if it were nothing, and they were not averse to pleasure; hardly anything pleased them more than a roast supper and good wine.

Florio was waiting at the jetty when the boat splashed in.

'It is good to see you,' he said. 'I hope there is nothing amiss.'

'I do not know yet.' Shakespeare linked arms with his friend as they walked up to the house. 'That is why I have such need of you.'

Inside, he wasted no time in declaring the purpose of his visit.

'This book,' he said, 'was left for me in rather mysterious circumstance, by a man who seems to have fled the country, pursued by our own loyal officers.'

If Florio was surprised he did not show it.

'A man you knew?'

'I met him only once. His name was Richard Stanyhurst. An Irish scholar, and one of the contributors to Holinshed. Quite an eccentric man.'

'I have never met him. I thought he was abroad.'

'He came to England for a brief visit. I think he wanted to finish this book, and when he had to leave in haste he passed it on to me.'

'It does not sound like an act of kindness,' said Florio. 'What manner of book?'

'That is the point. It is a life of Henry VIII, I suspect not favourable to the King. I am interested in it because . . . well, because we are writing a play about Henry VIII.'

'A play! Why, that's wonderful. I knew you had not finished with plays.'

'Anyway, it is in a pinched Latin. I can barely read it.'

'And you thought that I—'

'I *knew* that you—'

'Then let's see.'

Shakespeare passed him the book and Florio bent over it.

'My eyes are traitors,' he said. 'But on this occasion they may be allies.'

He walked over to a desk, opened a drawer and took out a disc of curved glass.

'It is called a lens,' he said. 'I had it sent from Italy. If you have not seen one before, you might be impressed.'

Holding the disc over the page, he indicated that Shakespeare should come close and take a look.

Shakespeare was stunned. The words leaped out at him large and clear.

'Remarkable.'

'Yes.'

'Truly astounding.'

'Indeed.'

'I would still appreciate help with the Latin. Could you bear to read it awhile, and advise me, even in a general way, what it contains?'

Florio smiled, nodded and rang a bell. A footman appeared.

'I think we would like some wine, Philip, and also some fresh water.'
He bent over the book again.

'Entertain yourself for an hour,' he said, 'and I will see what I can do.'

Never had sixty minutes passed more slowly. Shakespeare was too unsettled to read, so he took turns round the garden, sat on benches, kicked at dead leaves, even skimmed stones from the water's edge. He had not made any progress, himself, with the bizarre mysteries in Stanyhurst's manuscript. He knew it had things to say about relations between Henry VII and his son, but its meaning escaped him, and those inscrutable numerals remained as blank as an abandoned oracle.

Eventually the hour passed and he was able to return. His heart was thumping.

Florio looked grey, almost frightened. He jumped to his feet when Shakespeare entered, took him by the arm and led him over to the desk.

'I am going to tell you what this work amounts to,' he said, tapping the book softly with the tips of his fingers, as if it might explode, 'because you are a curious man, and I know you will not rest until you have learned all. But then I must urge you to do something decisive. You must destroy these pages. Burn them, drown them, scatter them to the four winds. They will bring you nothing but harm.'

Shakespeare thought it best to say nothing. He looked at Florio with patient eyes and waited to see what he had found.

Florio began to turn the pages and spoke in a low voice, almost a whisper.

'There are two tales here. The one that is in the lines, and the one that lies between. It is the latter that should make us nervous.'

He picked out passages from Machiavelli and extracts from Spanish diplomatic papers, referring to the story's protagonists: Henry VII and his son; Henry VIII and his father. In his account, the two seemed locked in some kind of dance. Florio's soft murmur stole into Shakespeare's mind like subtle poison, or like a wind through trees. Soon he was trembling at its quiet, insistent strength.

Slowly the evidence formed itself into a recognisable narrative. By the time Florio stopped, his face drawn and sad, Shakespeare could hardly breathe.

He had expected – even hoped for – a surprise, but nothing had prepared him for anything like this. Stanyhurst was claiming to have uncovered a secret that might topple nations. True or false, it had propelled him into hiding.

'Are you sure?'

Florio inclined his head. 'The more important question is whether *he* is sure? This book . . . it is such an extraordinary story, such an unbelievable idea. I do not know if it has any basis in fact, but I *do* know that it is deadly.'

'Is it true, do you think?'

Florio shrugged. 'I have seen too much to say that because something is unlikely it is not so.'

'No one will believe it.'

'Who can say?' Florio heaved a weary sigh. 'People love stories. You of all people know that.'

'Yes.'

'And power – it is like communion wine. Some men gulp it down.'

Shakespeare stood up. He did not know why, only that there was nothing more to be said. He was aware of several contrasting emotions, all of which collided like brooks under a bridge. He was one part shocked, one part thrilled and one part awash with guilt for putting his old friend in such dangerous straits.

'One more thing,' he said. 'What did you make of these numbers?' He laid his fingers on the Roman numerals illuminated by their yellow dots.

'It is plain that the author wants them to be noticed,' said Florio. 'Beyond that, I do not know. Page references? Distances? Sums of money? I cannot say.'

'I am glad there is *something* you do not know.'

Florio forced a weak smile.

'A wise sailor runs before a gale,' he said. 'I know that much.'

'How can I thank you?'

'By destroying this book.'

'I shall.'

'At once.'

'Soon.'

'Do not delay.'

'I will be careful.'

'And next time, please bring happier news.' Florio rose and seemed to totter a little, as if faint. 'Do come soon. For myself . . . I will not speak of this again.'

'I thank you for your learning and your counsel,' said Shakespeare. 'I do not know if I can destroy a treasury of such daring news, but I will hide it well.'

'Sink it in the bottom of the ocean,' said Florio. 'Bury it in the deepest shaft of the tallest peak. Nothing good can come of it. It will imperil all who touch it.'

He grasped Shakespeare's hand as if he was bidding him more than farewell.

'I will come back,' said Shakespeare. 'We will laugh and eat cake.'

'Or chew beef,' said Florio. 'Like true-born English men.'

He held up a single pale hand as Shakespeare wandered out into the drizzle, pulled his cape up over his head and ran at a crouch down to the landing stage. The ferry back to London was rounding the bend at Putney. When it saw the stooped, soggy figure on the bank, it took pity on the poor soul and veered in to pick him up.

The boat was crowded, and Shakespeare found himself squeezed between two talkative fellows on their way, of all things, to the theatre. He hunched low and tried to ignore them, but it was impossible. The man on his left, a stout figure with lank hair, began to hand out pastries. They smelled of onions and cheese.

'Help yourself,' he said to his neighbours. 'It is my birthday.'

'Thank you,' said Shakespeare. For some reason he was ravenous. 'It was my own birthday yesterday.'

'Well then.'

He felt as though he had been slapped. His words hung in the air like daggers. *Of course!* How had he missed it?

He excused himself, bent over to prevent the wind from whipping the pages from his hasty hands and unwrapped Stanyhurst's book.

There were the numbers: 224159 – 246159 – 286159.

A gust of rain struck him in the cheek, but he did not care. All along he had been puzzling over the first three numbers, but the answer lay in the trio at the end.

159.

It wasn't a number. It was a date.

1509.

In a flurry, the other numbers fell into place. They were all dates: 22 April 1509; 24 June 1509; and 28 June, in the exact same year. Water was slashing across his neck, but Shakespeare forced himself to concentrate. Like wild beasts prowling the darkness around a fire, the dates skulked in the shadows, half visible in the gloom. They seemed somehow familiar . . .

And then he saw it.

Cold raindrops hammered on the canvas roof and coursed down his face, but he did not care. In truth, he did not even notice.

This was what Stanyhurst was trying to tell him, and the man was right – it was a sensational secret. No wonder he had moved through London in that brazen disguise, like a ghost doomed to walk in the fires of purgatory until he was avenged.

Shakespeare hurried home, slammed the door and pored over Stanyhurst's book once more. Slowly, as night fell, a pattern began to emerge. It was like the way a cloud sculpts itself in the sky. Most like a whale, my lord. It was a wild story, and he knew that any sudden commotion might frighten it away, so he did not move. He had never felt so frightened and alone.

It took half the night, but slowly his fears settled. And though he knew that nocturnal resolutions were not trustworthy, the idea that took shape in his imagination began to set like clay in the heat of his resolve. He had been given a dangerous gift, and it would be cowardice to throw it away. He decided to cling on hard.

He had been looking for a way to end his play, for a final, heart-wrenching act. Here, perhaps, delivered into his safe keeping like a gift from the gods, was the answer.

The next morning, John Harvard was kicking his heels in front of St Paul's by the time Shakespeare reached the sign of the Golden Pen. An early fog scudded down the streets, but the air was mild so it would soon burn off. Word of the calligraphy contest had spread and a good-sized congregation had gathered, hoping for an amusing display of skill.

'Sorry to be late,' said Shakespeare. 'I trust you were taking care. There are pickpockets everywhere in these parts.'

Harvard looked pale. He said nothing.

'Are you sick, John?'

'Not really.'

'Should I get you home?'

'It isn't that. I have a confession to make.'

'We are in the right place,' Shakespeare glanced at the cathedral. 'But not the right country.'

Harvard did not smile and Shakespeare could see he was genuinely troubled.

'What is it? Can you say?'

'I am afraid I have done something terrible.'

Shakespeare felt a pinprick of anxiety.

'Go on.'

'It is about the play. I had some pages about me, spoiled scraps which I did not give you. I took them home. And last night . . .'

Shakespeare's heart skittered like a stone on a lake.

'My father had a guest for dinner. He found the pages and read them.'

Shakespeare's eyelids trembled. 'Who was he, this guest?'

'That is the whole trouble. He is a warden at St Saviour's, and an alderman, and also, I believe, a magistrate. He was quite agitated when he saw what we had done.'

'What did he see exactly?'

'Some parts bearing on the citizens. A speech by the King. And a bit of Caxton.'

Shakespeare winced. The first two passages might easily be mistaken for a work about Henry VIII, but there was no reason for Caxton to appear in such a piece.

'Who was this man? Has he a name?'

'Yes. I remember it well. It is the same as mine.'

'He is called Harvard too?'

'No. His name is John.'

'Oh.'

Shakespeare did not think it necessary to mention that there might be more than one John in London, yet in all honesty it did not matter. It was enough to know that the stranger was an alderman and a magistrate. He would almost certainly gossip, at the very least, and soon the whole world would know what the King's Men were working on. It was damnable luck.

'How did he react?' His voice was quiet.

'He made quite a retort. He asked who had written them. I wasn't going to tell, but my father said proudly that I was working with you. He went quiet then.'

It was tempting to make light of it, to insist that nothing would come of this, but that was wishful thinking of the cheapest sort. The most likely thing was that this man would pass on his news. It would not take long for it to reach the ears of Sir Edward Coke. And then . . . well, events might move quite fast.

Shakespeare looked at Harvard's white, frightened face. His shoulders slumped.

'Do not worry, John,' he said. 'It is good of you to be anxious, but I am sure things will turn out well. And I know you meant no harm.'

'I really didn't.'

'I know.'

Somewhere in the depths of his soul, a voice was screaming: *Why did I let him take those pages home? How could I have been so foolish?* However, Shakespeare had a plentiful store of benevolence, and he called on it now.

'I am just glad you told me.' He patted Harvard's arm. 'But we'll be careful in future, won't we?'

The news was still sinking in. It seemed to Shakespeare that he had two choices – to give up, or push on with all haste. Every fibre at his command, and most of those over which he no control, insisted that he take the latter course. He had passed so many rapids already, it was hard to imagine stopping. And his head was still vibrating with Stanyhurst's unbelievable allegations. He could not, in all conscience, give up.

In truth, Stanyhurst's book made Harvard's mistake seem minor. And another thought was winking at him. If he sounded the alarm now, it would expose poor Harvard to the dismay of the group. He owed it to the boy to spare him that.

He looked across the square at the people scurrying about their day. In the great fog of time, he thought, none of this would count for anything. It was time for him to stand, as others had stood, against the forces of greed and vanity. How often had he depicted characters refusing to compromise honour for the sake of safety. *The purest treasure mortal times afford, is spotless reputation. Take honour from me, and my life is done.* Who had said that? Richard II? Cassio? Banquo? It shamed him that he could have forgotten, but he had, he told himself, written a goodly number of plays. History would have to forgive him if he could not remember all of them.

If he did not want to lean on his own words, there was always Florio's great hero, Montaigne. 'Lying is a terrible vice, for it testifies that one despises God, but fears men.' Shakespeare had never minded small lies – he preferred to call them adjustments. It did not bother him to portray a dead Lancastrian queen as a foul Yorkist plotter, but this was something larger. If he destroyed Stanyhurst's book, as Florio had begged him to do, he would stand accused of Montaigne's worst sin.

He could not do it.

'Come,' he said. 'Let us see what the scribes have to say, and then to work.'

He led the way across the cobbles, and through the crowd, to the exhibition.

Harvard seemed relieved. 'What *is* the Golden Pen?' he asked. 'Is it real?'

'It used to be,' said Shakespeare. 'It was won by Peter Bales in a handwriting contest. He was a master of miniature script: he put the Lord's Prayer, the Creed and other Latin prayers within the compass of a single penny. He once squeezed the entire Bible into a book no bigger than a plum. Or so they say.'

'Is he still alive?'

'I've no idea.'

Someone was demonstrating the differing styles of writing –

Roman; French; French and English Secretary, full of ornate swirls. He compared different inks and parchments, and bizarre potions rendered visible only by heat.

'Bales was in Walsingham's household,' whispered Shakespeare. 'The grand inquisitor himself. That's where he learned his love of secrecy.'

They were about to leave when a man asked whether anyone knew how much vellum was required by the first vernacular Bibles. Shakespeare swallowed. The day he had been asked to improve the holy book seemed to belong to an earlier, more carefree age. Who said that time dragged its feet as a man aged?

There were some wild guesses, but the answer was chastening. It took the skins of three hundred sheep – an entire hillside.

'No wonder they talk about the faithful as a flock,' said Shakespeare.

He was pleased to see Harvard smile. He had thought the boy almost too serious for his age; now he saw that he himself had made little effort to amuse him.

It was time to go. The others would be almost at the Globe by now.

The carriage was waiting. Shakespeare smiled to see Harvard staring open-mouthed at the driver's ebony-black skin. He was a blackamoor, one of hundreds, if not thousands, of Africans who had been shipped into London in recent years.

'A slave,' said Shakespeare. 'Seized from a Spanish galleon, I shouldn't wonder.'

'Why doesn't he go home?' said Harvard.

'His occupation's gone,' said Shakespeare with a smile. 'Have you not heard? A foul commerce is springing up on the African coast – a miserable traffic in human lives. Men and women hounded and herded like cattle. At the docks you see them in chains, slaving in the King's galleys. It is a cruel trade – though a necessary one, they say. It is bound to die out soon enough. This man here is lucky: he is free, though an exile far from the green hills of his home.'

He pointed south. The man bared yellow teeth in a grin of recognition, shook the reins, and Shakespeare and Harvard were flung back in their seats as the horses took off, hooves skidding on the damp stones.

There was a surprise for Shakespeare when they arrived. The man he least expected to see – Edward Alleyn – was waiting at the entrance, one leg propped up on a water trough. He wore a red cape, which flashed when he moved his shoulders and gave him the look of a foreign count. In one hand he carried a riding crop and in the other a bundle of papers. He drummed on his thigh with the crop in a rapid motion that was either musical or nervous – Shakespeare couldn't say which.

He was also wearing something strange over his eyes.

'Will,' Alleyn called when he saw the carriage come to a halt.

Shakespeare just had time to compose himself. 'Morning, Ned.'

He would have preferred some warning of this conversation. He had not decided how much to say about Stanyhurst and did not know whether to pass on Harvard's unpleasant news. Now he had Alleyn to contend with, and although he had been moved by Burbage's faith, he could not bring himself to trust the man. He supposed that after Harvard's revelation – John of Southwark might be sipping Coke's wine even now – it did not truly matter what the old blackguard had been up to. It still pained him to look at Alleyn, though; he was affronted even by the idea of such treachery.

He wondered how much time he had. Days? Weeks? He did not need long.

Alleyn was holding the door open for him. Harvard had already made himself scarce.

'What *are* those things on your face?' Shakespeare said.

'Spectacles,' said Alleyn. 'Eyeglasses. Amazing things, I never realised how little I could see. Got them from a foreigner in Spitalfields – a Frenchman called Holland.'

'It is good to see you. I owe you an apology.'

'Richard called. He told me what happened.'

'He did?'

'Yes. How you were having that *other* man followed, and your spy saw *me* going into the Palace of Westminster. Incredible. I can see why you were alarmed.'

'Well, it did seem . . . unusual.'

'I can explain. There is much to tell you.'

'Let's walk,' said Shakespeare.

'Or we could go in there . . .' Alleyn gestured towards a tobacco house, one of hundreds that had sprung up on the highways of London these days.

'Very well,' said Shakespeare. He smiled to recall the painful effort he had made with Raleigh's pipe. The man had made so strong an impression that few hours passed when he did not think of him, yet he could not easily forgive him this evil-smelling craze.

'Will you take an ounce of sotweed yourself?' Alleyn beckoned for a jug of ale.

'No, thank you,' said Shakespeare.

They faced each other across a small table. Alleyn smiled, with an ease in his manner that made Shakespeare believe, despite himself, that all might yet be well.

'What a scrape, Will. What a scrape.'

'Yes.'

'I can see it must have looked bad.'

'We did not know *what* to think. I confess I remain . . . confused.'

'Not a word, Will, not a word. I was hurt, but only because I did not understand. You had every reason to be angry. In your place I would have been furious.'

Shakespeare braced himself for an explanation, but Alleyn was hesitant.

'Here it is, then,' he said at last. 'I am going to tell you something I am not proud of, but it may lift the clouds a little. Look at these papers . . .'

He unrolled some drawings, the ones, presumably, he had shown Constance.

'This is to give you an idea. You know, I think, that I lately contracted to buy the Manor of Dulwich from Sir Francis Calton. It was not cheap. I won't beat the carpet: it was thirty-five thousand pounds, a great deal of money. And that doesn't include the sum I need for the restoration. Here, this is what we have planned. It will be magnificent—'

'I am sure it will. But I do not see—'

'I am coming to that. Henslowe and I – we have done handsomely out of the bear-baiting. So I am fortunate enough to have a generous portion of the money to hand. The other part I am borrowing from the Lombards. The interest is severe, so I have been seeking to obtain . . . another source of income.'

'Oh?'

'I don't know whether you know, but I trade in sugar a little, on the side.'

'I did not know.' Was there anything Alleyn did *not* dabble in?

'And a number of us – fellow merchants, all reputable men – have been trying . . . how can I put this? . . . to increase our profits by buying up the store of sugar.'

'In some quantity, I assume.'

'As much as we can lay our hands on.'

Shakespeare could not prevent his eyes widening in surprise.

'Engrossing!'

Alleyn spread his hands.

This was a serious crime. There had been several well-publicised episodes in recent years where wealthy individuals had tried to corner the trade in a commodity. The laws against it were strict.

'I hope it is making you rich,' said Shakespeare, 'because I tell you this: it will not make you popular.'

The social taboo against engrossing was one of the sharpest in the land. No one liked to see prices forced up by greedy speculators and citizens were quick to inform on anyone suspected of such manipulation. The art of monopoly – the commandeering of an illicit advantage – was hated.

'It began as a small thing.'

'It always does.'

'But then I was invited to join a group of merchant adventurers and it seemed an honourable gamble. A careful inspection of the shipping timetable indicated that the demand for sugar would soon outstrip supply. We hoped to buy in size, restrict the amount delivered to the market and reap a high price later in the summer.'

'Why are you telling me this? I could have you arrested.'

'I know. I place myself in your power.'

Shakespeare was not sure that this was something he wanted.

'That is why I went to Westminster the other day,' said Alleyn. 'Some of my colleagues in this venture are members of the court, and occasionally we need to meet. The complicated part is that our opponents sit on the court too. And this is the point: the person being followed is *me*. I have been aware of it for some days – Sir Edward Coke's men are keeping an eye on me. Coke is a stickler and has the King's ear too. I wish I had never entered this thing, but we are embarked now.'

Shakespeare started at Coke's name, but hid his consternation. He shook his head. 'Well, well,' he said. 'I understand. Thank you for telling me.'

'I haven't finished. There is more. Remember the Case of the Monopolies?'

Shakespeare nodded. It was famous.

'Remember anything about the people involved?'

'No.'

'Well, the plaintiff was Darcy – a nasty piece of dirt who held the monopoly, you recall, for imported playing cards. Somehow he managed to convince the Queen that gaming was dangerous and needed to be managed by one man: himself. He then brought a case against a respectable defendant, a small shopkeeper. Does this ring any bells?'

Shakespeare shook his head again.

'The defendant was a simple man. All he wanted was to make a few playing cards of his own. Not too much to ask, you would think. But this fellow Darcy sued to the court and the case went to the King's Bench. Luckily the judges took the part of the shopkeeper. The monopoly was unlawful – an unnatural restriction of trade.'

'I sense that the name of this card maker is going to surprise me.'

'Maybe not. His name was Alleyn. A cousin of mine. So believe me, I of all people am ashamed to be thus involved. But there was no time to think. Although the trade is small, it will swell; soon it will be impossible to calculate. Every day new sugar fields are planted, new ships launched. And I need only one windfall – just one. Otherwise I shall be adrift for years on a sea of debt to the Italians.'

Shakespeare took a gulp of ale and ignored the drops that trickled into his beard. He looked at Alleyn. There was something else.

'That time you walked out, and then came back,' he said. 'What was that?'

'I weakened. When I saw that you too were playing with fire, I was nervous. I thought I was in enough trouble as it was. There is only *so* much danger a man can court. Call me a coward if you please, but I have important friends on whom I depend for licences, permits and the like. I took fright. I am a poltroon. Run me through.'

'I see.'

'But then I came back. And look, I am so glad you asked me to help. More than glad: proud. I think it is going to be marvellous, even that ugly scene you threw at me the other day. I have no idea whether it will ever be possible to put it on a London stage without first drawing its fangs, but that hardly matters: it is great work. Yet you are no fool: you must know that all of us have our reasons for wanting to be part of it. Mine, I am embarrassed to confess, is that it suited me at this time to be obviously engaged on a theatrical endeavour.'

'My play was your alibi.'

'I wouldn't put it like that, but . . . to some extent.'

'Did it not occur to you, knowing that *you* were being followed, that *we* would be followed too?'

'It did occur to me, although in truth I did not think you had much to fear. As you have said, they knew you were working on a play. They simply did not know *which* play.'

'Still, you *knew* we were trying to be discreet? You were there when we agreed that the fewer tongues there were to wag about our plan, the better.'

'Oh, Will, really . . . Even the knife-grinders know what you are up to. Do you not realise that London is all a-twitter about your return to the stage?'

Shakespeare felt like a scolded child.

'My purpose is not to chide,' said Alleyn, 'but to confess. I was not candid. I abused your trust. I am sorry. I should like to take my place at your side and finish this play. You know everything now. I place myself at your service.'

Shakespeare needed a moment to think. This was the second significant confession he was being invited to hear this morning.

'I haven't seen anyone follow me since the other day,' he said.

'That's because they've been following *me*. I expect they chased *you* that day because they lost track of me. I do have to . . . lose them every now and then. Not for long – just every now and then.'

'One more thing, a small thing. The man who followed you, he mentioned a big meeting, a dinner at Arundel House. He mentioned . . . Sir Edward Coke.'

Alleyn smiled. 'He did not miss much, your man,' he said. 'I didn't see the need to tell you about that, but yes, I went to dinner, and yes, Coke was there.'

Shakespeare waited for an explanation.

'I see you do not like him,' said Alleyn. 'Neither do I. The man is a prick-eared cur if ever there was one. But even dogs have their uses. Shall we just say that some very distinguished citizens were my partners in this venture?'

'I see.'

'Funnily enough, I mentioned you to Coke and he said he had never had the pleasure. What do you have against the man?'

Shakespeare had the sensation that someone was treading on his tomb. If he had a hundred inner voices, all but one of them was shrieking at him, begging him to confess, urging him to tell Alleyn what had happened at the Tower that day. There had been too many secrets, too many evasions and too many misplaced fears already.

The last remaining voice refused to bow to the majority. It clung to its private knowledge like a limpet to a rock and Shakespeare could not claw it off.

'I met him once,' said Shakespeare. 'What can I say? I took against him.'

'That is an understatement. But I would sooner have him with me than against me.'

Shakespeare felt old and foolish, a blind mole tunnelling in the dark. But at the same time it was as if a burden had been lifted. Not long ago he had wished that he could lay down his daily chores and care for nothing but his work, and now it seemed that his wish had been granted. He was just yards from the entrance to the Globe, the homely arena he had helped make famous, and he was surrounded by friends. Together they had nearly created an astonishing new story.

Nothing could ever match the old days – to start with, he never had spasms in his back in the old days – but this was as good as he could hope for. The world would shortly see that Shakespeare was a long way from being a spent force.

It occurred to him that this must have been how the plotters felt as they stacked their powder and iron bars beneath the palace of Westminster. He too was preparing to launch bold, unforgettable fireworks into the English sky.

He rose to his feet.

'What can I say? With all humility I here beseech you of your pardon, for too much doubting you.'

'Please. It is I who should beg your forgiveness.'

'I have done you a most grave wrong.'

'If so, then you have just commanded the grave to open, and released me.'

Shakespeare sighed. Relief washed over him like warm water. They clasped hands and did not speak for a moment.

'Shall we?' said Shakespeare. 'The others will be wondering where we are.'

'After you.'

Each man ushered the other to go first, hesitated, then gave way. In the end they dipped their heads under the lintel of the door at the same time and almost collided.

'Great minds think alike,' said Alleyn.

'Fools seldom differ,' replied Shakespeare.

The King's Men fell silent when the two men entered, unsure how things stood. Shakespeare ended the suspense right away by announcing the glad tidings of Alleyn's return to the fold and apologising for his part in the breach.

'I feel like the monk who boasted that he never made mistakes. The closest he came was when he *thought* he had made a mistake – and was wrong! But it is behind us now. Ned and I both had hold of the wrong end of the stick, if that is possible.'

'Happy is the stick that has two wrong ends,' said Alleyn.

The King's Men (and the sole King's Woman) beamed, happy that whatever had come between the pair seemed to have evaporated.

'It was a misunderstanding,' said Alleyn. 'No one's fault, really.'

Shakespeare was itching to resume work on the play, but he was also judicious enough to sense that this reunion had kindled a fertile atmosphere. A glitter had returned to every eye, a spring to every step. He himself felt thoroughly rejuvenated: he loved scenes of reconciliation and forgiveness above all others.

'I think we can finish this now,' said Shakespeare. 'Let me run through what remains. Arthur is dead, as is the Queen, and the King has cursed the kingdom. His daughter has gone north to marry Scotland, leaving him lonely and bitter. Now we will see him raining taxes on his people, strangling the joy from their lives. And then . . . well, the ending will be a surprise, I hope. I need to brood on it a little more.'

'We will see the citizens complaining, I hope,' said Armin.

'I am counting on you for that,' said Shakespeare.

It was a busy free-for-all. Alleyn and Burbage joined Shakespeare in constructing speeches for Henry, and Constance offered words for the King – good ones, too. Shakespeare's manner as the bereft, demented monarch was so cold and unfeeling that the air seemed to freeze around him. 'Put all their heads on stakes,' he said at one point, with the casual demeanour of a man asking someone to pass the salt. It was Constance, though, who suggested that any poet who so much as mentioned a white rose should have his bloody Yorkist fingers hacked off with a blade.

Just when he seemed as black a devil as ever faced an audience, Shakespeare gave the King a soliloquy painful enough to rake the blood. 'O cursèd crown,' it ended, 'I would I had the strength to set it down.' A roomful of people who had just learned to hate the King found their hearts unexpectedly melting.

After a pause for a bowl of pottage they started to show the King losing his wits, lashing out at enemies and bickering with friends. Will and Richard bantered lines for Henry as he drooled over his beloved treasure ('How now, my priceless stones, come out and play') and bellowed contradictory orders to hapless servants.

It went fast. Alleyn's return seemed to have inspired a rare concentration and sense of affinity: lines and speeches tumbled forth fully formed. Harvard's fingers flew across the paper, filling page after page with freshly minted drama.

When the King grew tired, Armin and Taylor stepped in and cooked up scenes for the citizens. In one they welcomed Cabot back and cheered his discovery of a new-found land; in another they lamented the blows and omens under which the kingdom staggered: 'I heard they found stones in the eyes of the hyena.' They spoke of spies and executions, vengeance, bloodshed and crime ('Here comes fresh meat from the slaughterhouse'). Someone informed Bacon that the oyster beds had run dry, and he was superbly downcast. 'Then truly,' he replied (Armin drawing himself up to his full height), 'is night come at daybreak.'

No one's concentration faltered; they did not break or pause. Scene followed scene, and line replied to line. The sun rose high above the Globe, arced down towards the New World and threw long shadows across the room.

Shakespeare clapped his hands. Even during this rehearsal his mind had been untangling the knots in his thoughts about Henry VIII and now at last he was resolved. He helped himself to a large goblet of wine and drained it in one heady draught. What he was about to propose was so brazen, so unthinkable . . . yet he had no choice. All that had happened in the last months, from that first moment of despair in the theatre to the astonishing episode in the Tower, from the raiding of Blackfriars to his suspicions of Alleyn, from the disappearance of Stanyhurst to that clumsy piece of daylight robbery in the Strand, the glacial distress of Florio: all of it compressed itself into a single flame. He blazed with indignant determination.

There was only one possible ending. Although his friends might never speak to him again, he had reached the mid-ocean point of no return, where retreat was impossible. It occurred to him that he should spare John Harvard this final revelation: the tale he was about to narrate was a dangerous thing even to hear. So he walked over, laid a hand on Harvard's small shoulder and swallowed hard.

'I think that is enough for today, young John. You have done splendidly, as always, but the things we have to speak of now have no need for your quill.'

'I don't mind. I am not tired.'

Shakespeare glanced at Burbage.

'Have no fear,' he said, not quite truthfully. 'You shall not miss a thing. I promise we will send for you if anything interesting happens.'

Harvard shuffled his papers into a pile and held them out.

Shakespeare's gaze fell on the neat, even script.

'Immaculate. Truly, you have the gift.'

Harvard's light feet made hardly any noise as he left, the others clapping him on the shoulder as he passed. Everyone knew that something serious was afoot and that Harvard had been dispatched for reasons of confidentiality and safety.

'We are almost there,' said Shakespeare as soon as it was quiet. 'And I know it's late, but one more hour and I believe we can complete this thing.'

'You promised us a last surprise,' said Taylor.

'I did. Here it comes.'

'Good. I love surprises,' said Alleyn.

'Don't tell me – you're pregnant,' said Armin.

Shakespeare actually chuckled, an expression of levity no one had seen for a long while. Then he grew serious. 'You may not like this,' he said, 'but I was thinking that we should end with a scene featuring Prince Henry – the man destined to inherit the throne. This is the controversial part: he will be an absolute monster of conceit. The King will loathe him, and his son will revel in this loathing like a pig in mud. They will become sworn enemies, the Prince and the King, the father and the son.'

'My God, Will.' Alleyn was staring at him, shaking his head.

'I am not making this up,' said Shakespeare. 'You know that fellow I met, the one who disappeared – Stanyhurst? Well, he sent me a book he was working on, and it is full of remarkable discoveries. Much of it comes from the Spanish envoy.'

'You want to rewrite our history on the word of a Spaniard? I don't believe it.'

Shakespeare looked at the uncertain faces of his friends. 'Bear with me. There is much to tell. But first, the story. Prince Henry's eye will fall on the Lady Catherine of Aragon, Arthur's widow. The King will bitterly oppose the match. He wants his son to make a different alliance, with the Habsburg Princess Eleanor. He will beg his son not to marry Catherine, and warn of the schism that must surely flow from such a union – but Prince Henry won't care.'

'What are you saying?' Burbage said. 'All these marriages. Is this a comedy?'

'No. A thousand times, no.'

There was a gleam in Shakespeare's eyes; he strode among them with the speed and grace of a dancer. It was as if he had drunk brandy: he seemed intoxicated.

'Prince Henry knows that his father compares him unfavourably with Arthur. He no longer minds; all he wants is to get his hands on his father's treasure. He is a born absolutist, as impatient for kingship as he is unready – which puts us back where we began. One king is waning; another is on the rise. Come: we know how to do this.'

Armin had an idea: they could first meet the Prince on his return from a hunting expedition. He would have sprayed the forest with arrows, killed an unfeasible number of deer and still be insufferable to his companions.

They tried it this way and that way and, with Taylor excelling himself as the amorous Prince ('Why should I lose a wife so richly left, who glances chestnut Spanish eyes at me?'), turned it into a more than useful scene.

'And now,' said Shakespeare, 'for the *coup de grâce*.'

The sense of expectation was acute. Every pulse was pumping.

Shakespeare paused. He had always admired the way magicians distracted their victims with merry chatter, but he also knew that he was the bearer of news whose consequence he could not predict; he could not allow himself to be distracted. It had been an unusual, twisting journey, and the end lay before them now – as welcome as a lake glimpsed from a desert, or a port from a stormy sea.

For the last time, he took a deep breath and told them the play's new ending.

There was a long, stony pause. The King's Men looked at one

another for some assurance that they had not misheard, but all wore the same sad, clouded look.

'You are joking, I hope,' Alleyn said.

'I am not.'

'I thought this was a history play.'

'How do you know it isn't?'

'This Spaniard of yours . . .' Burbage began. 'Will, this is madness. You'll hang.'

'I do not plan to. Listen, I understand that we could not present this at the Globe. Today's audience will need a simpler ending. I have one in mind: the King will see the error of his ways, repent him of his crimes and turn into a virtuous angel – and at just that moment he will be mauled by cruel fate. Thank you. Applause. Dinner.'

'That sounds much better,' said Alleyn.

'But let us seize this opportunity to make something new. Do you not see? The story I have outlined may be true, in which case it must be remembered. If it is not the literal truth, it is still a magnificent metaphor. It *enacts* the way Henry VIII betrayed his father's legacy, his country's birthright.'

Alleyn was not convinced. 'I don't care about *enacting*. The audience will see it as treason and so will the King. This goes too far.'

'The important thing,' said Shakespeare, 'is that it sing to Heaven.'

'It is well and fine for you,' said Alleyn. 'You plan to retire to Stratford. The rest of us desire to stay here in London. There is no way—'

'I agree with Ned,' said Burbage. 'It is too much. This book you've been reading—'

'Actually, it is Machiavelli.'

'Machiavelli?'

'Stanyhurst was oblique. He took care to make his meaning obscure, and some things he hid in allusions to books such as *The Prince*. I could see he wanted me to decipher his clues and catch his meaning, but for a while I could not understand. Eventually I began to see, and then it came together in a rush.'

His friends sat back to listen, and Shakespeare saw that this was the moment on which his play would stand or fall. If he failed to persuade them now, it was over.

He did not have a long speech in mind, but there was a great deal to say, and once it was clear that he was taking them into choppy waters, no one was inclined to interrupt. He spoke of Florio, of how the two of them had followed Stanyhurst's clues, and how shaken they were when they perceived his meaning. He spoke about fathers and sons, kings and princes, brothers and birthdays. The faces in front of him expressed shock, wonderment and horror all mixed together, as if they were stumbling through a mist. Slowly, the events Shakespeare wanted them to dramatise gained substance, until the monstrous truth stood revealed before them.

He left nothing out. His voice was soft, insistent and persuasive. And as the threads of evidence wound into a thick, stout rope, he could see the astonished resistance of his friends beginning to yield and dissolve.

'My God,' said Alleyn. 'You are beginning to have *me* believing this.'

Burbage coughed. 'Extraordinary. But I still don't like to base a play on such flimsy grounds. We need more proof that this is true.'

'Oh, the truth,' said Shakespeare. 'Who knows what is true? There is no such thing. All we can do is say what we believe.'

There was an embarrassed shuffle of feet.

'Or what we like,' said Burbage.

'Or what we know we like,' said Armin.

'That's clever,' smiled Constance.

Shakespeare had come to take Burbage's support for granted and felt slighted that it was not forthcoming now. However, the last thing he wanted, so close to the end, was an argument, so he did not lock horns. It would do no good to remind them again how often they had changed history to suit the stories they wished to tell. This was different. It struck him that the others were not so aware of posterity as he; they did not feel on their shoulders the judgement of history; they were still busy living their lives.

'Listen,' he said. 'This is our last day, our last hour. Soon I shall take Harvard's script, hide away somewhere and finish this work. I can only fall on your mercy for having been until now as dumb as an ox about this, but I beg of you that we do not quail, or fall short, or censor ourselves. Think how those old sailors must have felt, losing heart that they would ever sight land on the blue horizon ahead. We are so close. Let us not turn back. Let us complete this vision we have dreamed.'

'*We?*'

'Very well. I,' said Shakespeare.

'In truth, *we* want to see this vision finished,' said Armin, glancing at Burbage.

'Who wouldn't?' said Alleyn.

'I agree,' said Constance. 'It is time someone tore the gilt from the memory of King Henry VIII.'

'Others have waited longer,' said Burbage.

'I have a thought,' said Heminge. As always, he had been watchful during the previous exchange, but now, like a skilled pilot, he gave the rudder a nudge. 'Why don't we begin with that moment Will mentioned, where the King has a flash of insight into his own reign? A scene like that will be needed whichever way we go.'

His calm words restored a businesslike atmosphere to the room.

'Yes,' said Armin. 'I love those moments. This is when Macbeth sees how he has been tricked, when Caesar realises too late that his friends are his enemies, when Hamlet understands that he has chattered when he should have acted. What would trigger such a moment here?'

It was a good question. What would melt the King's wrath and grief? Shakespeare closed his eyes and saw it.

'A child. What if the King discovered that he was to be a father again? It would allow him to renew himself, lay down the flaming sword.'

'It would not please the Prince, that is certain,' said Armin.

'But he is not married,' said Constance.

Burbage laughed. 'I hope you are not suggesting, Will, that he really *has* bedded Catherine of Aragon, his son's wife to be. Put *that* in Holinshed, why don't you?'

'Don't encourage him,' said Alleyn.

Shakespeare shrugged. He did not mind being laughed at.

'Whatever the cause,' he said, 'it is important that Henry sees life whole for an instant – he sees how history and destiny conspire against kings, leading them on and cutting them off. We want him to hear the stars laughing at him.'

Once more it was like a choir of voices mingling, separating, echoing and embellishing one another. Shakespeare was again tireless, in his proper element. To watch him at work, Burbage had once said, was like watching a fish swimming – it seemed to require no conscious thought. They took it in turns to snatch up the quill and record what was being said, and though none had Harvard's neat hand, the bones of their work were accurately preserved.

One by one the actors grew fatigued, but Shakespeare continued to rattle off bolts of rhetoric as if selling it by the yard. As the King he delivered resonant epigrams; as the Prince he grunted vicious oaths that chilled the spine. Somehow he permitted the spoiled Prince to steal some indefinable regal quality from his father. The heir's time was coming, and he knew it. Shakespeare gave him lines shaped to make men kneel.

It brought a violent scene to a calm conclusion. Everyone knew that they had taken part in a treasonous slur that could not be repeated outside this room, yet despite their misgivings all felt privileged to be present. Shakespeare often said that his idea of art was simple: to carve out something that did not exist and which hurt no one. It was a pleasing description, though it was not possible to say in this case that no one would be hurt; men had paid for lesser crimes with their blood.

And that, as the saying went, was that.

The end took them by surprise. Shakespeare's shoulders dropped an inch or two as he discarded his royal manner, and it took a long, quiet moment for everyone to realise that their journey was over. The applause, distant and imaginary, might never be heard in a theatre, but they had made a new play.

'Don't move,' said Alleyn. 'We should celebrate. My treat – any requests?'

'Whatever you can find,' said Shakespeare. 'Could someone fetch Harvard? The boy should not miss this.'

Alleyn grinned at his old friend, then left.

'I'll fetch wine,' said Armin.

'Spare no expense,' said Shakespeare. 'Ned is paying!'

A short while later Alleyn returned with armfuls of baskets and cloths.

'Give us a hand,' he said, laying out a spectacular last supper: veal pie and mutton, rabbits from Essex and curd from Kent. The rabbits would be delicious roasted in the fire and dripping with the last of the Moorfields honey. There was spiced ginger wine and ale. Firelight toasted the walls and filled the room with fragrant cherrywood smoke.

There were sweetmeats too – Alleyn evidently wanted them to drown in sugar: jumbal, snow cream, gingerbread and junkets. There were date tarts and pears preserved in aqua vitae. His basket seemed a bottomless reservoir of sickly things.

'Is that Apple Moise?' said Constance. 'It's my absolute favourite.'

'I thought it might be,' said Alleyn. 'I remembered you like apples. I found some of last year's, preserved.'

'Have lots,' said Taylor, carving her out a big bowlful.

'This gingerbread is delicious,' said Heminge. 'Sticky and peppery.'

'What's that orange stuff?' said Harvard. He stared at the spread in amazement.

'It is called marmalade,' said Shakespeare. 'It is made from Spanish oranges, I believe. It is best when it is bitter. Be good with that bread, I should think.'

Armin reappeared with a firkin of ale and a supply of bottles.

'I gather we have you to thank, Ned,' he said. 'That's what I told the inn.'

'Hippocras!' said Alleyn, holding up a bottle. It was the most expensive drink to be had in all London. 'Oh well,' he said. 'Have at thee!'

Anyone passing the Globe that evening would have heard, as the sun sank over Westminster, infectious shouts of laughter booming from the upstairs gallery.

They clasped hands; grabbed shoulders; hugged.

'I don't want to embarrass you,' said Shakespeare, 'but before I lose the power of speech, I have something to say. I was confident that we would finish today, so I brought you all a little something. John?'

Heminge picked up a small casket and lifted out half a dozen identical purses.

'Here's coin for each one,' said Shakespeare, passing them round. 'And my heartfelt thanks, as always. You have surpassed yourselves, all of you. I do not know if we shall ever be like this again, so thank you . . . thank you . . . thank you.'

'It's over to you now, Will,' said Armin. 'Don't let us down.'

'That is hardly conceivable,' said Burbage.

'A ridiculous suggestion,' agreed Alleyn.

'And what's all this about not doing it again?' said Heminge, as excited as any of them. Though alert to all the political difficulties with *Henry VII*, he could not stop himself believing that, with prudent cutting of the more controversial parts, the play would prove bankable. And if it wasn't, there was always *Henry VIII* to fall back on. He knew that they still depended on Shakespeare for their livelihoods – to an extent greater than most of them recognised. It was wonderful to have him back.

'How about *Henry IX*?' said Taylor. 'There's no such person, but after today I see no reason why we should let that stop us.'

'I think we should do another comedy,' said Armin. 'I have just the subject, ready and waiting to go: there are these twins—'

'Oh, not twins again,' said Alleyn.

'Hear me out,' said Armin. 'There are these twins who are separated and live in different countries. And then years later, when they are all grown up, they meet. And they don't know they are twins—'

'Don't tell me.' Alleyn smiled. 'They fall in love.'

'Or kill each other,' said Taylor.

'Or both,' said Constance. 'And one of them is called Romeo—'

'Sounds perfect,' said Burbage. 'But why don't we set a whole play to music? I have always wanted to. With proper minstrels. I came across a great story the other day about a libertine – a licentious aristocrat – who has hundreds of amorous adventures and ends up being dragged down to hell by a statue. Superb.'

'Can I play the statue?' said Taylor. 'I promise to sit quite still.'

'He'd have to be Italian to write a story like that,' said Armin.

'I can't see it catching on,' said Shakespeare. 'Though I did wonder once about setting *Macbeth* to music, or *Othello*. I meant to ask Dowland – but then he went off to Denmark. He may be back by now.'

'I heard an incredible story not long ago,' said Alleyn, 'about an Oriental count who makes himself immortal by sucking the blood of the living – mainly women. He moves through the night like a bat and bites them on the neck. He comes to sleepy England to prey on the daughters of the shires. Only one man can stop him—'

'I've never heard anything so stupid,' said Burbage. 'I *would* say have another drink, but it sounds as though you don't need one.'

And so it went on. They traded jests like duellists, or tennis players, as the sun dipped behind the pinnacles of Westminster.

At one point Shakespeare and Burbage found themselves outside on a flat roof overlooking the river. Lights rocked on the water; waves slapped against hulls.

'Can I ask you something, Richard? Is it a sin to covet honour?'

'How should I know? I am honour's stranger.'

'Seriously.'

'How could it be?'

'Good.'

Burbage leaned on the rail and faced his friend.

'What is troubling you? I know you have work ahead . . .'

Even in the darkness Shakespeare could make out the bulk of the Tower, dark and hunched against the night sky.

'Which of our heroes, would you say, doth please you most?'

'A very Lear-like question. What do you mean?'

'Nothing. But looking back, who is your best man?'

'I know I shouldn't say so, but I *am* rather fond of Richard III. A fiend, of course, but he has been very good to me.'

'I do admire his furious refusal to be cowed. Macbeth is the same: he stays the course, even though he is tied to the stake like a bear.'

'Yes, we did well with those two.'

'I find, as I get older, that it is the Romans I remember best. They seem to grow closer.'

'Oh, I agree with you there. Antony, the old ruffian. Marvellous.'

'I think of Brutus sometimes. A bit like our Henry maybe – a man

297

performing evil from the best motives. Do you recall his death, when he asks that soldier to hold his sword? "Thy life hath had some snatch of honour in it." Antony was sarcastic, but Brutus really *was* an honourable man. His error was to strive for ends, not means. However noble the end, that is a mortal sin. What do we gain if, to prevent killing, we kill?'

'You are very grave tonight, Will. Let me pour you some wine.'

'The other man I love is Barnadine. Remember him?'

'You might have to jog my memory. *Much Ado about Nothing*?'

'That was Benedick. Barnadine is in *Measure for Measure*. A minor fellow, but that is the point. He was one of Kempe's, and he has this one great moment of superb, stupid courage. Do you remember? He is a drunken prisoner whom the authorities sentence to death because they need a head . . . Do you remember?'

'That's right. And he refuses.'

'Exactly. They come for him, but he is a stubborn soul who rejects their authority, and waves them away on the excellent grounds that he is steeped in drink. "I swear I will not die today for any man's persuasion." That is the spirit. He squares his life according to his own lights, refusing to accept a part in another man's play.'

Burbage looked at him with a quizzical face.

'What are you trying to tell me, Will?' His voice was kind.

Shakespeare wanted to divulge to his old friend all the details he had withheld regarding Sir Edward Coke and the long, sharp talons of the Crown. He had never shared the fact – proved by the yellow glass eye left on his table – that the raid on his house was a royal visitation. It was time – well past time – to share this knowledge with Burbage, who had stood with him every inch of the way. Yet he could not do it. Shakespeare trembled to find himself once again on the wrong side of a lie, but to mention it now would trigger a long conversation; the hour was late and he was excessively tired. There would be time for a full reckoning later, he thought. Right now, he needed to devote himself to the Muses. The King's Men's work was done. His own was about to begin.

Happiness is not just fleeting; it is a quality of which we are almost always unaware, and the term we use for a mood that is evident only in retrospect. It implies a suspension of self-consciousness that makes it hard to weigh. As a result, none of the company paused to think that this was a day they would never forget: they were too busy enjoying themselves. The afternoon melted into the evening with careless glee. Even Constance and Harvard, who did not take drink like the men, were caught up in the delirious mood. The sound of their laughter mocked the midnight bell and echoed down the breeze that drifted along the river.

Only one discordant note spoiled the atmosphere. Shakespeare was pointing downriver towards the Tower, and speaking of Sir Walter Raleigh's proud adventures in the New World, when Alleyn coughed.

'You do know, I trust, that old Raleigh never actually set foot in Virginia himself.'

'What?' Shakespeare was taken aback. He had imagined the man wading ashore in giant forests.

'He keeps quiet about it, I am told, but it is the purest truth. He financed those expeditions, but did not lead them.'

'You astound me,' said Shakespeare. He did not wish to disrupt the convivial spirit of the occasion, though, so he forced himself to set this news to one side and rejoin the party.

In their memories, this day would shine out as a bright flare of pleasure made all the more tragic for being so short-lived. Looking over their shoulders, they would see heads thrown back in laughter, feet stamping for joy and arms waving with delight. But they would also see faces illuminated by lightning flashes from the storm that was, though none knew it then, so soon to break upon them.

They had achieved great things together. But they were drunk, and it was easy to forget that great things do not always last.

Shakespeare himself could not sleep that night. He had no way of knowing whether his ageing powers were up to the task to come. And the wine made his heart race.

He was thrilled with the closing scenes and more grateful to his friends than he could say. They had ploughed the soil with supreme skill and invention. But no one could help him now – he was on his own. And though everyone laughed, sometimes dismissively, at the ease with which he could turn out pages of poetry, he knew that it was *not* easy and that the effort would cost him dear. It always did.

Weary with toil, he yet found no repose. He heard every bell. Every now and then he fancied that he slept for a moment or two, but could not be sure. Sometimes he was hot; sometimes he felt the chill. Scenes, words and fragments from the play swirled in his mind like bats in a ruined abbey. He feared that if he took his eye off them they would flit through the haunted night and disappear from view for ever.

Somewhere in the small hours he made a decision. Before he left in the morning, he would seek out Richard and tell him everything. If his friend was disappointed to find that Shakespeare had again been keeping things from him, so be it. The time had come for a full accounting.

It was almost a relief when he heard steps outside and a rap on the door. It must be almost dawn. He pulled a gown over his nightshirt and picked up his candle.

This time there were three rapid knocks.

Andrew?

As soon as he swung open the heavy door and looked into the eyes of the men facing him, he knew who had sent them, what they had come for and why. Their gaze was flat and wary, as if they expected trouble.

They were the King's men, and they had come for him.

'Do I have time to gather my possessions?'

'No,' said the tallest of the men, in an oddly pleasant voice.

He ordered one of his troops to go in, fetch Shakespeare's belongings and bring them down.

'No one needs to know he did not have time to pack,' he said.

Shakespeare flinched. At least Stanyhurst's book was safe; they would not find it here. He knew that these men were not villains. When they caroused, they sang and drank and laughed just as other men did, just as he himself had done the previous afternoon. Life or fate had handed them this assignment, and they did not know what they did. Behind them, however, Shakespeare could see a cruel black hand, hovering over all their heads, twisting the strings that held them up.

For an instant he wondered whether there was some way he could leave a message. Too late. A burly soldier took him by the arm and steered him across the yard. He could have cried out, but there seemed little point. He allowed himself to be escorted into the wings, the shadows, the darkness.

Chapter

15

*N*o one expected to see Shakespeare for at least two weeks. He had left London in search of a tranquil place to find poetry. Only Burbage knew where he had gone and he wasn't telling; he knew how greatly Shakespeare prized his privacy. In the early days the young genius had been able to write through the night, in the back of a barrow, with his left hand if necessary. The words would spill out in an unstoppable torrent; all he had to do, it seemed, was open the sluice gate and let them run on to the page. These days, however, he preferred solitude, even secrecy. Easier said than done. People began to gossip – he was out west, it was said, halfway to Oxford, buried in the country near Uxbridge, perhaps as far as Wycombe. No one knew for sure.

He was a rapid worker who did not spare himself, but even *Henry V*, which had streamed out like wine from a tap, had taken three weeks. And although his friends had cause, this time, to fear a palpable threat, they were content to assume that if violence lay in their stars it would have fallen on them by now. So it wasn't until the middle of May that anyone began to chafe at his absence.

In truth, he was more than missed. Even though they knew he would return in his own good time – he always had – they had once more become helpless dependants. He was not merely the author of their roles; he was somehow, despite his famous incuriosity, the author of their lives as well. And whilst he never troubled to learn about their domestic arrangements or daily predicaments, all of them felt seen through, known. It had taken the King's Men two years to acclimatise themselves to his absence. Now they felt it, all over again, as an acute personal loss.

Nervous messages began to bounce between them. Armin heard that he was in Fulham, with Florio, and actually took the boat there one morning to sidle between the trees, hoping for a glimpse. Heminge called in at the Blackfriars house every day or so, with a mounting sense of unease, yet on each occasion the servants had no idea when Will would be due back. Taylor toured the theatres and trawled up a very unhelpful and contradictory range of informants. Some said that Shakespeare was back in Stratford; others that he was travelling in the Low Countries – a possibility, Heminge had to admit, if he was pursuing Stanyhurst. An actor at the Swan swore that he had seen Shakespeare riding a horse across Blackheath, but he was also said to have taken up a position at court, as ambassador to France. Three people believed he was in Shoreditch; one eager informant had a vague (and misplaced) idea that the playwright was even then taking breakfast upstairs; a couple of others were sorry to have to convey the news that Shakespeare had passed away, God rest his soul.

It was common knowledge that Shakespeare liked to write in neighbourhoods related to the stories he was developing. He had spent a week in Eastcheap during the making of *Henry IV*, and had completed *The Tempest* on an island in the Thames. It was not possible to go to Venice to write *Othello*, or to Elsinore to write *Hamlet* – but in the case of a play like *Henry VII* it was reasonable to think that he might be holed up in Eltham, or Sheen, or Greenwich.

The actors searched but there was no sign of him.

Eventually they rounded on Burbage. With some reluctance – Shakespeare had made him swear he would be left in peace – he took a horse and gambolled out to the house near Guildford where his friend was supposedly working. Loseley, a brand-new manor with bricks, glass windows and all the most modern features, had been built a few years earlier by Sir William More, one of Queen Elizabeth's best friends; the Queen herself had once been a regular visitor.

After Sir William's death in 1600, Shakespeare had remained on easy terms with his son, and the house occupied a place close to his heart, especially its sumptuous, wood-panelled library, where he could write in peace. Its walls were built largely from stones taken from the dissolved Cistercian monastery at Waverley and Shakespeare always said that he could hear, in quiet moments, the remote chanting of monks.

It was also – and Burbage knew the significance of this – the lair of the beast. Henry VIII had built a dozen palaces in Surrey, most of them using materials from abbeys he had destroyed and looted. Shakespeare had said that he felt, in Loseley, as if he were behind enemy lines. He could write as if his life depended on it.

When Burbage returned empty-handed – no one at Loseley had clapped eyes on Shakespeare – their worries gelled into an urgent concern. Alleyn dropped in on Constance to see (he said) whether she had any news. She poured him pressed apple wine and invited him to stay for supper, but she had not heard the smallest word.

No one was any the wiser, and as the days passed, growing longer and warmer as they stole into summer, silence began to hang heavy on the King's Men. When Burbage summoned them to Blackfriars for a meeting that was the exact opposite of convivial, they were dumb. The ghost of their absent leader cast a chill.

'I am truly disturbed,' Burbage said. 'There are places – Nonsuch, Southwark, Spitalfields – we have not explored. We must do so now. He may not thank us for the interruption, but this lack of intelligence troubles me much. I do not like it.'

Taylor pressed. 'Is it true that even in Stratford they don't know where he is?'

'Yes. But how could they? They do not even know he writes plays. They think of him as a gentleman farmer – a man of stature.'

'What?' Armin could not believe his ears.

'It is true. He is better known for his vines than his verse. It is one of the saddest things in this sorry world of ours that our greatest tragedian, the author of all our stories, did not dare go home until he was rich enough to disown his art.'

'I never knew that,' said Alleyn.

'He is not proud of it,' said Burbage.

They could not rest now. Alleyn searched Westminster and the Inns of Court (he was not without friends in high places) but answer came there none. Burbage scoured the bookshops and theatres all over again, but found that no one had seen him for weeks. He kept a wary eye out for anyone who might be taking an interest in his own movements, and though he saw no sign he was distressed to notice so many soldiers on the move. It was almost as if the authorities expected an uprising of some sort: cold eyes scanned the streets by day, and men with torches toured the city at night. London was on edge.

Armin and Taylor investigated the taverns around St Paul's and checked each of the five prisons in Southwark, even going so far as to tour the Marshalsea and the Clink in case Shakespeare had been injured or, God forbid, incarcerated. No one was ever far from gaol in London – Marlowe, Massinger and Dekker had all spent time in gruesome cells – so it was not inconceivable that Shakespeare had fallen foul of the law. But surely he would have found some way to send word to his friends.

Nobody knew anything.

It strained credulity that he could have vanished. He was a well-known man, and it wasn't easy for him to hide. So Burbage sent to Stratford, choosing his words with care. The response was unequivocal. Shakespeare had barely been home since leaving for London back in February. He was expected daily – please be so good as to inform him!

There was no formal procedure for locating a missing person. Although the constables and bailiffs, aldermen and sheriffs all had their networks of confidants, there was no organised way to trace a mislaid friend. And Burbage flinched at the thought of sparking an unnecessary panic. As the days turned to weeks, however, and May tottered towards June, he grew agitated. This was not right. Too much time had passed. If Shakespeare was still at work, he would have found a way to let them know.

What more could they do, though? They embarked on the same fruitless round once more, but this time without any expectation of success. They sought out every person they could think of who might know something – anything. No one was able to help.

One evening there was a knock on his door, and Burbage's heart leaped, but it was only Fletcher. He had good news: he had finished *Henry VIII*. Burbage feigned pleasure, while his heart sank in his breast like a rock. It was not possible – it went against the natural order of things – for Fletcher to write a play more quickly than Shakespeare. For the first time he was forced to concede that something very serious had happened. He sat by the fire until dawn, stirring embers and fearing the worst.

Highwaymen, he thought. The rural byways and drovers' tracks were full of cut-throats, clapper-dudgeons and whipjacks, and Shakespeare loved to ramble – it was one of the ways he rested. Worse, he carried the whiff of wealth about him these days, and walked with a stiff gait, making an appetising target for any rogue or marble-hearted villain in his neighbourhood. Burbage could not avoid imagining his old friend half buried in a wood or hedgerow, valuables ripped from his pockets, a dark crimson gash on his forehead or throat.

Was this, he wondered, how it would end? In silence, in mystery, in . . . nothing? It didn't seem possible that a figure as splendid as Shakespeare could fade, unacknowledged, in this half-hearted manner. Where were the thunderclaps?

Burbage had made a point of keeping John Harvard informed of their progress. One afternoon they were walking together near St Paul's, on their way to enjoy some refreshments at the Greyhound, when the sound of shouting made them pick up their heels and hurry forward. The Guildhall was being assaulted by an angry knot of men in dark clothes with shaved heads. It was an ill-tempered affray.

'Let's go,' said Burbage, taking Harvard's arm.

'But what is it? Who are these men?'

'Puritans. Trying to stop people going to the theatre.'

He did not try to keep the disgust out of his voice. The aldermen had been giving in to Puritan demands for years. Plays were banished from official premises and anyone who gave permission for a performance could be fined a week's wages.

'Listen,' he said.

It was hard to hear exactly what the voices were saying. They warned of *idolatry* and *wantonness* and *licentious acts*. When someone started throwing sticks at the cowering stewards in the doorway, the crowd began to roar. A cry echoed down the hill and there came the tramp of hurrying boots. Soldiers!

'What do they want?' said Harvard. 'I thought Puritans were holy.'

'Some of them are. But these are the most extreme. They want purity: a very dangerous wish. They think the theatre corrupt, damn them. Let's away. Come.'

He did not want Harvard to see that he was afraid. The Puritan tide was rising fast, and one of these days, he knew, it would drown someone. He could not deny that he himself would be a prized scalp in any action against the London stage. He steered Harvard back the way they had come and wandered down to the river.

A few days later the King's Men met at the Greyhound: Burbage, Heminge, Alleyn, Taylor and Armin. No call for the upstairs room this time: secrecy was no longer an issue. They sat at one of the large tables in the gloomy back parlour, behind the big velvet drape that sealed it off from the taproom. The innkeeper brought tankards of ale and plates of bread and sausage, with onions doused in vinegar, but nobody was hungry, not even Joseph.

Their conversation was a dull murmur. With immense reluctance and heavy hearts, they agreed that it was time to notify the parish. What else could they do? He had been gone for six weeks. He was definitely missing. Something unlucky or unspeakable had happened. There was no longer much doubt about that.

A cloud passed across the sun.

A crow flapped lazily overhead.

And then, one day, a bird flew in with a twig in its beak.

Shakespeare had been spotted, and this time there was reason to think it might be a genuine sighting. One of the scene painters at the Globe had followed him across London Bridge, heading south. He was walking, the man said, with a limp.

'I knew it,' said Burbage. 'Damn fool – probably fell off a horse.'

The time for caution had long since passed, so the King's Men fanned out across Shakespeare's known routes and asked people to keep their eyes open. Their centre of operations was the back door of the Globe, and they made public their willingness to hand out coins in return for reliable information.

Reports arrived thick and fast. Shakespeare had been seen eating pie at the Sign of the Pilgrim, the inn where Chaucer had launched his long pilgrimage to Canterbury; he had been spotted stepping into a wherry at Paris Garden, and had bought lemons and brandy in Rotherhithe; he had been glimpsed hurrying past the Blackfriars house, head down; and he had been noticed in the congregation at St Luke's in Aldgate.

His friends waited, bursting with nervous tension. What did it mean?

'I don't know,' said Burbage. 'And I am not sure I want to know.'

The actors peered into the shadows for all the world as if they trod a stage and were waiting for an absent colleague to arrive on cue. They had run out of lines of their own; they could do nothing but hold still, and hope. The story demanded that Shakespeare walk into the lime-light. Had his nerve failed? Had it proved too much, this time?

And just at that moment, quite suddenly and with hardly any fuss, there he was.

They were back at the Greyhound, picking at a beef pie and praying for word, when he slid through the curtain, a fragile shadow of the man they knew: pale as milk and somehow flattened. It was if a bird had flown into the room, in a visitation both vivid and weightless. No one knew how to react.

'They said I would find you here,' he said. He seemed smaller than before: he had lost weight, and the lustre had fled his eyes, his cheeks, his skin.

'Heaven save us,' said Burbage.

'I have been better,' said Shakespeare. 'Perhaps I should sit.'

He stepped forward and stumbled. He hadn't tripped; it merely seemed as if his legs lacked the strength to hold him up.

'Good Lord, Will,' said Burbage. 'What on earth has happened? Are you ill?'

'I wish it were so.'

'Where have you been?' said Alleyn. 'We've been tearing our hair out.'

'Have you?'

'Of course! We've been desperate.'

'I can only apologise. I have been . . . detained.'

Alleyn, like many impatient men, disguised his rush of relief in a cloak of anger. 'Well, thank God you're here. You could have let us know. How's the play?'

'There is no play.'

'What do you mean?'

'Enough questions. Please.'

He did not raise his voice, but it carried a thin strain of anguish that cut through the hubbub like a blade. He sat down.

'A drink would be welcome,' he said. 'Some lemon water, warm, perhaps sweetened with a little honey. I confess I feel a little . . .'

At last they registered that he was in serious difficulty. Heminge fetched the drink. Taylor gathered cushions. Burbage dragged in a stool.

Shakespeare lay with the heavy gratitude of a man who had not slept for days. He looked too tired and weak to move. Only his eyes patrolled the room. They seemed dim and frightened. After a long silence, he sighed.

'I have rehearsed many ways to tell this tale,' he said, 'only to find that I have no varnish to lend it gravity. So I shall, forgive me, be bald. These past weeks I have been held, much against my will, in the Tower—'

'Sweet Mary!' Burbage said. 'I feared as much.'

'I suppose it is a privilege.' Shakespeare gave a weak smile. 'Not all men can say they have seen the innards of the Tower. But I tell you, it is an honour none should covet. You say you have been – what was it? – tearing your hair out? I should not boast, but I found others to perform this painful task. They were not gentle.'

Alleyn blanched. 'Oh Will. I'm sorry. I did not mean—'

'I know. I do not chide you. In truth, I escaped the worst, but they pressed me hard. I saw things . . . such things . . . things that did make me fear to sleep. You have heard of the Pit, I am sure, but no man can describe it. It is a hole in the surface of the earth, a dark burrow stinking of death. They pushed me to the edge, made as if to toss me in. Then they put me in a cave too low to permit standing. I was fitted with irons, weights, hooks. I feared the rack, but they were only playing—'

'How dare they?' said Alleyn. 'On whose authority—?'

'The King's,' said Shakespeare. 'We of all people should know what kings do – you yourself have played enough of them.'

'But this is monstrous. You, William Shakespeare . . .'

'It was no accident. They knew what they were doing.'

'Then—'

'Shall I finish? I will not make a long story of it. The end is that our play is lost. To my shame, I fear I traded it for our liberty. They humbled me. I should have died a martyr, but I have children yet. And still it was an agony worse by far than any punishment they imposed upon my person. Dear friends, I had to watch as brutes set fire to my pages, yes, and little Harvard's too. All is gone, every word. And this is the worst – it was good, my friends. I should not say so, but heavens, it had music in it. We had done such work, and I was capping it with flames as bright as any I ever blew into life. I do swear it might have been our crowning glory. And gentlemen . . . But where is Constance?'

'We will send for her,' said Alleyn. 'Her mother . . . She is on her way. John?'

Heminge gave a swift nod, rested a hand on Shakespeare's shoulder and left.

'We'll do it again,' said Armin. 'You are free now . . .'

'It was not only my life in the barter,' said Shakespeare. 'They said that if they heard so much as a whisper in the shadow of a crevice – and they are trained to hear such things – then all of my companions, that is, all of you, would suffer fates as bad or worse than mine. None of us was safe, nor Constance neither, nor the boy.'

'You did right, Will,' said Burbage. 'You steered the wisest course. But oh, the nerve, to waylay William Shakespeare! This King, I tell you, knows no bounds. He thinks himself a god. But men there are who'll rise against him soon enough—'

'I pray you, pause,' said Shakespeare. 'I know it should console me to hear you speak for my cause. But soft: if you would help me, be at peace – I crave a quiet end. The fault is all my own. You all did counsel me against it – 'twas I who urged us on. 'Tis not unjust that I should suffer for it.'

'I cannot agree,' said Burbage. ' 'Tis most *un*just.'

'Let it rest, old friend. It would cheer me naught to see you hurt. I am punished for my vanity. I did not think they would touch me. I should have known better.'

'Will,' said Alleyn. 'I am sorry, but we have to ask . . .'

'I understand, Ned, and do not take it ill. You are right: they cudgelled me to tell them how much I had shared with you all – oh yes, they knew about our meetings. On this point I showed some mettle. I confessed that I had sketched the outline of the idea, the broad view, nothing more, and promised to enlist you as players when the time came. I added that each of you was quick to warn me of the danger, which is true. I swore you were loyal subjects – the King's Men! They laughed at that.'

'Was it the ending that provoked them?'

'It was the whole play. I am not sure they even read the final scene.'

'Will,' said Armin. 'I don't know what to say.'

'The pain will pass. They could have done worse. But the loss of the play will grow more acute by the hour, I know. It was a noble piece, and now . . . quite lost.'

'I don't know,' said Taylor. 'As Robert says, we can redo it.'

'I'll not countenance it. I lack the stomach, and besides, I pledged all our heads that we shall do no such thing. So no more talk of that. I gave both copies to the fire. Young Harvard's first, and my fair copy after. Both burned well. Animals – how they laughed. Laughed! And our poor play is smoke.'

Alleyn rose to his feet. For a moment he hovered as though preparing to leave, but then something seemed to fix or set in his posture.

'You are right, of course,' he said. 'But Will, though none can know the years to come, we do still fancy ourselves masters of our time. Our play – your play – was magnificent, as fine a thing as I have ever done. I am proud – honoured – to have been part of it. So while I agree that it ends here, I do not believe that history will let it die. A play is like some timid creature of the riverbank. Ours has put its whiskers into the night and been attacked by owls. But they have not killed it. It has been driven underground into burrows and tunnels, into those crevices of time you mentioned. Birds will carry it in their beaks; bees will bear it on their legs. It will survive. Its heart cannot be stopped. Comfort yourself. Greatness finds a way to be heard. I do not believe that *Henry VII* will vanish from this earth.'

Shakespeare was looking at the floor while Alleyn spoke. When he lifted his head his eyes were warm with gratitude.

'I am sorry I ever doubted you, Ned. You are a good man.'

'And a forgetful one,' said Alleyn. 'Burbage gave me this. It is from Fletcher.' He reached down and took a package from the leather bag behind the table. 'It is fierce timing. The gods must be howling. But this is our new play: *Henry VIII.*'

Shakespeare took it without smiling. Alleyn's words reminded him of Raleigh's refrain. What was it he had said? 'The earth spins and nothing goes unpunished.' Maybe he was right. Perhaps the world really would discover their work one day, and wonder at it. In the meantime . . . He glanced at the manuscript in his lap.

'A noble piece, I am sure,' he said.

'I have taken the liberty of reading it,' said Alleyn. 'It wants the hand of a master, but it may pass.'

'I shall dedicate it to you,' said Shakespeare, forcing himself up in his chair with a visible effort. 'If someone could do me the kindness of fetching a pen.'

Armin stepped forward, quill in hand.

Shakespeare glanced at the ceiling, as he often did when lost in thought. People who did not know him sometimes glanced up too, wondering what he looked at, but the King's Men were well acquainted with the mannerism and ignored it.

Shakespeare's fingers gripped the pen and wrote two letters: E.A.

Then he pursed his lips and added: Or Edward the First?

No sooner had he written this than he crossed it out with a bold line.

'I've got it,' he said. '"Alleyn is True." That's better.'

He placed the quill on the arm of his chair.

Burbage looked over his shoulder, and smiled.

'Wait!' Shakespeare took up the pen again and scratched out three letters. 'There,' he said, holding up the page. 'What do you think of that?'

The King's Men leaned in and saw what he had done. The surviving text contained three small syllables: 'All is True.'

'Clever,' said Burbage.

'I am honoured,' said Alleyn.

'See? You will be immortal after all,' said Armin.

'It is never a bad idea to baffle people,' said Shakespeare. 'And I don't want to land Ned in trouble if the play fails.'

'All is True,' said Alleyn, miming a courtly bow. 'Wonderful.'

'Though quite *un*true,' said Armin.

Taylor snorted. 'It is only that "Arm is true" did not work. Or "Bur is true".'

There was a ripple of mirth that owed a good deal to relief. Their adventure was over and it had not ended well. But the globe had not stopped turning, and the dedication – a piece of impish Shakespearian wit that almost made them forget what had gone before – seemed to restore the possibility of optimism in their lives. It wasn't the first time he had taken liberties with dedications. He had once bemused half London by inscribing his own Sonnets to a mysterious figure called W.H. – and tongues had wagged ever since – in an effort to clip a name to the initials. Only Burbage and Shakespeare himself knew that it was a sly joke, a teasing self-dedication addressed to Shakespeare's own extremely private nom de plume: William Hathaway.

'One more thing,' said Alleyn. 'This came for you.'

He held out a letter sealed with purple wax.

Shakespeare tore it open with shaking fingers, read the brief message, and let the paper fall to the ground.

'It is from Stanyhurst. He says he is safe.'

Burbage reached down, picked up the letter and frowned.

'He says that Navarre shall be the wonder of the world, even at this last minute of the hour. "The endeavour of this present breath may buy that honour which shall bate the scythe of time." What means this?'

'*Love's Labour's Lost*.' Shakespeare's face was expressionless. 'He means that our play will be acclaimed by eternity, however great the pain in the here and now. I would that it were so.'

He closed his eyes and bowed his head, as if declaring an end to the scene.

It was almost time to go. Burbage, however, was still frowning.

'Would you excuse us for a moment, Will?' he said. 'Don't move.'

He turned and held out his arms, beckoning the King's Men to follow. Then he began to whisper in earnest. Shakespeare couldn't hear what he was saying, but there was much resolute nodding. Whatever was afoot, the company was of one mind.

A few moments passed. Shakespeare might even have fallen asleep – he wasn't sure. When he opened his eyes Burbage was back, and the others were nowhere to be seen.

'Could you give us another moment?' he said. 'We are almost ready.'

'Ready for what?' Shakespeare pulled the coarse blanket up to his chin and shivered. Although it should have felt good to be safe, but this inn was not home, nor would it ever be. Even his new house in Blackfriars was not home. He was done with London – for good this time. He would go to Stratford as soon as he had the strength. Whilst he longed for sleep, he could not imagine unbending enough to surrender to it. Perhaps he should ask someone to stay with him.

There was a flutter beside him and Constance was falling on his arm in a rustle of lace and a cloud of sweet aromas.

'I can't bear it,' she said. 'Those evil, evil men. I cannot stand it.'

Shakespeare felt his heart lift and expand.

'Constance,' he said, barely loud enough. 'Ah, Constance.'

He could feel moisture on his hand. Her cheeks glistened.

'What have they done to you?' she said. 'And the play: how dare they destroy your work. Those beautiful lines!'

'Ah, beauty,' said Shakespeare. 'Beauty is no defence. There is no flower so fair that it cannot be choked by the meanest weed.'

Alleyn's voice boomed down the stairs. 'Constance! You are just in time! Come!'

She raised her head and looked at Shakespeare. Her face was not far from his, her eyes damp with tears. She looked so very young.

'Go.' He gave a faint jerk of his chin. 'I know not what he wants, but go.'

He listened to the rat-a-tat of her pretty, defiant steps, and for the first time in days his lungs relaxed. Some of the tension leaked out of his body and he felt heavy.

The next thing he knew, he was being lifted by Armin and Taylor, chair and all, and manhandled up the stairs.

'Like a sultan,' he said, dipping his head below the beams.

'Nearly there,' said Taylor.

They parked him in the same upstairs room they had used as a rehearsal space. It was set up as if they were about to work up a new scene.

'Not a word, Will,' said Burbage. 'Not a word.'

He waited while the others lined up behind him. Constance was smiling. She still had a dark stain beneath her eyes, but her faint smile lit up the whole room.

It looked as though Burbage was about to make a speech. Shakespeare couldn't imagine what he might say. At least he had the consolation of knowing, as he scanned the bright faces before him, that none of them had played Judas. The pain he had suffered in prison was mild beside the lancing agony of betrayal.

His heart pounded when he thought of Harvard. The boy must be feeling dreadful. He didn't have the strength to blame him – he was only a boy, and Shakespeare loved boys. What a shame they had to grow into men.

Burbage cleared his throat.

'I pray you, gentles all,' he said, 'permit us to present this day, as best we can remember, *The True and Tragicall Historie of King Henry VII*!'

'No!' Shakespeare tried to struggle to his feet.

'Yes!' said Burbage. 'You have no choice. You are our prisoner now. We are safe. Heminge has sent for Andrew, so we have a man on the door. No one shall disturb us. At least this one time, your final act shall fill a room. And you too have a part to play, for you shall be our audience.'

Shakespeare sat back, defeated, a hand to his cheek. He was white.

Burbage turned and passed before the assembly like a general before a battle.

'This will be the first performance of this play in all the known world, and perhaps – who knows? – it will be the last too. When it is done, none of us shall speak of it again. But here and now, in this room, on this day, in this great and tumultuous city of theatres, where good grapples with evil every afternoon, both on the stage and off, let us fill our roles with ardour. Bend your memories, stiffen your senses. We have a special witness here today, so let us treat him to a special play.'

He turned to face Shakespeare, his voice trembling with the conviction that this was a historic moment, not just for him but in the life of the world. The man before him was the greatest figure the English theatre had known, and they were about to give a one-off performance of his latest, perhaps his final work – it might even have been his greatest, if his tormentors had not destroyed his labour.

Of course it would be a clumsy shadow of the real thing; they could do no more than imagine the rapturous glory of the play Shakespeare himself had written and seen burn. This was the best they could do, and they shivered on the threshold like wet mice.

'Act One,' he began, and the actor in him took the reins. 'Scene One. And let these sober furnishings dissolve, twist and shape into a mighty palace, an edifice of golden stone that reaches to the clouds. For this is Westminster. A wedding party is in progress. Look! The happy faces turned towards the balcony. Band, strike! The King approaches, and with him his beauteous bride. Our Queen, good people, comes arrayed in pink, a perfect sunrise. And yet I fear it rains . . .'

For a moment he saw something flit across Shakespeare's weary jaw, a ghostly, luminous glow that might, just might, have been pleasure.

For the next two hours, Shakespeare did not move. He watched as his friends re-created all those scenes they had rehearsed together, some from memory, some from scratch. He felt dazed, proud and ashamed – at once rescued and lost.

There were times when the action faltered, as members of the troupe swapped roles, filled in for one another and misplaced their entrances, but a few dropped stitches alone could not spoil the texture of the tale they spun before his wondering eyes. Sometimes he smiled, remembering a missing grace note he had applied here or there. Once or twice he winced to hear an infelicity that had not survived his own lyrical revision. But mostly he watched the pageant unfold with an aching heart. Much of it was scatterbrained; dates and faces merged and slid. But there were so many reminders of the time they had spent together. Constance was a study in tender-lipped determination; Burbage played the King with just the right mix of pride and grief; Armin was boundless with his foolery; Alleyn and Taylor were everywhere, sometimes courtiers, sometimes navigators, sometimes printers, sometimes Scots. Through a mist of smiles and tears, he heard every word.

So motionless was this Audience that the players felt, every now and then, that they were performing to a statue – a rare experience for all of them. But the momentum of the play would not let them pause. The story stretched out like a ladder to the sky, and side by side they climbed, eyes raised to the heavens, never looking down as they ascended to regions known to only a chosen few.

If John Harvard had been there, quill racing, the lines that follow are all he would have been able to record. They traced a resounding passage of English history, and held it shimmering before Shakespeare's eyes like the faint suggestion of a phoenix. Alas, no one had summoned the young scribe, so the hasty rhetoric pressed into service as the understudy in this, the final play by William Shakespeare, rose up, frail as a butterfly's wing in the dim back room, glowed for an instant, and died back again like music on the wind.

ACT I

Scene One

Westminster. A wedding party is in progress. Music. Enter King Henry, Queen Elizabeth, Stanley, Dudley, Empson, Morton. King Henry and Queen Elizabeth proceed through applause, Elizabeth in a superb pink dress. Greetings and cheers. It is pouring with rain.

King (with ostentatious ceremony): Good people all, I shower golden thanks
    For gathering on this torrential day
    To celebrate the marriage of the king,
    And this his true and most delightful queen.
    Enjoy this happy deluge at our side
    And celebrate with us the storm of bells,
    From spire to spire, and steeples everywhere
    That hammer out with merry peals the hour
    When we the prideful flowers of this land –
    For so long sundered in a bitter war –
    Have grafted in a single happy stem
    A union of the white rose with the red . . .

Queen (aside): Did ever virgin bride so ache with grief
    To walk the aisle in this too bitter dress?
    'Tis not for love he smothers me in lace,
    Kisses my hand, and strokes my trembling cheek.
    Affairs of state do urge him to the deed,
    As they do bear my body to his bed.

King: But first, some thanks. To you, right noble Stanley,
    A prince among the barons gathered here,
    Whatever you demand of us is yours

Excepting enmity – that you'll never have.
Those words you shouted back at Bosworth Field,
Most bravely, in the frighted din of war –
'I have another son!' – Such was the phrase
You flung in Richard's foul and twisted face
When you did take our part on that grim day,
Furnishing debts we never can repay.

Queen (aside): I hate him, and why not? This is the man
Who killed my uncle with that fateful stroke,
All unprepared, I fear, and quite alone.
The truth will out some day, though lie I must
And with the king, right soon, as his sweet queen.
Oh!

King: Stanley, I name you Royal Chamberlain
Our closest and most trusted counsellor.
Morton, bright Ely, you shall be our lamp
In these dim times. Pray, join us as our lode
And pole. And Oxford, we have need of you.
I here declare: Let every wayside inn
That bore the hated White Boar's name till now
Henceforth take Oxford's colour, and be Blue.
Exeter, Lincoln, Suffolk, come. Let's haste
To Hampton, where we'll have our wedding feast.

Queen (aside): Friends have I still, in Scotland and in France.
Letters I'll send, and my deliverance
Will be as bloody as it shall be swift.
The battle may be lost, my honour drowned,
But war is long, and this one shall not end.

*The King, Queen and councillors move upstage. The wedding feast
is in progress, with jugglers, musicians and platters of food. Enter
Anne, the Queen's sister, and Katherine, her lady-in-waiting.*

Anne: For you, my dearest sister, I choose . . . him!

Katherine: You are too kind, though I have often heard that ugly men
do make the most forceful husbands.

Anne: For me, I'll take a man with salt in his blood. I will to sea, sister. Give me seamen, every time.

Katherine: There, Anne. Look! I choose *him*.

Anne: Which? That flimsy scarecrow, with ears like lobster claws?

Katherine. No! There.

Anne: Katherine, I swear I know not who you mean. Not, surely, that well-buttered oaf, that Friar Tuck. Oh my, he can smile with his mouth open.

Katherine: I know not if he be salty, but assuredly he is well preserved. Anne? Do you yet live? Not that creased gentleman, surely?

Anne: He does look well, I dare say, very well. Not young, but well. Who is he?

Katherine: I'll find out. Play the statue, and move not.

Enter Cabot.

Anne (*advancing*): Good morrow, sir. Perhaps . . . Is't aid you seek?

Cabot: I am looking for the King.

Anne: Why then, you seek unwisely. I am not he, nor hides he among my skirts.

Cabot: What say I look there for myself, my lady?

Anne: Sir! I would not speak to the King with such insolence.

Cabot: Nor would I. I come on other business. In Venice, we ask favours of fathers on wedding days.

Anne: You are from Venice! Wonderful. Is it true what they say? Rivers instead of roads, boats instead of horses?

Cabot: It is true. The lagoon laps the lintels of the houses.

Anne: Such a voice! Oh tell me all, good sir. My heart pines to see such marvels.

Cabot: Mine longs for stranger lands than those. This is the favour I ask the King.

Anne. How can anything be stranger than a city built on the sea?

Cabot: The land across the oceans! That's what beckons me. The terra incognita, out beyond the foaming billows and the icy floes that stud the main.

Anne: You speak good English, sir, too good for me. What do you mean?

Cabot: There are new worlds waiting for us. In Spain and Portugal, ships are rising on their keels, bigger than castles and as swift as eagles. Their ropes and spars are snapping in the wind. Like hawks, they strain to fly. Once slipped, they'll race across the ocean to find unfathomed wonders – ambergris and alabaster, gold and pearls, and unknown peaks to climb. This is what I seek.

Anne: What has this to do with the King?

Cabot: I need money, enough to equip a boat. I'll sail to unconquered lands and claim them in the King's name . . . But I wax too warm in my own interest. What of you, fair lady? If you were seeking royal favours, what would you do?

Anne: I'd have to ask my sister.

Cabot (*disappointed*): A girl's reply. A man attends to business for himself.

Anne: You mistake me. I seek no favours that I cannot have without the asking. The Queen, she is my sister. So be it that my search for the King's ear starts with her.

Cabot: You have the advantage of me.

Anne: Sir, I am too merry. Come, he shall hear your suit. I'll take you to him, and he'll not refuse. But wait awhile, and tell me more of Venice, and the foaming billows, and all else . . .

Exeunt Anne, Katherine and Cabot.

Stanley: We are not safe. I wish that I could give
Your majesty the tidings he deserves,
But he must know that though the Yorkist snake

Beheaded is, and weakened by self-slaughter,
Yet still it lives. In Paris, preening Margaret
Scuttles among our foes, and weaves her webs.
While here the Princes daily grow in strength.

King: Where are they, noble Stanley? Still no news?
They lie not in the Tower, that I know.

Stanley: None, my lord. They've flown without a trace,
Though it is softly noised in sheltered spots
That Richard did himself the boys dispatch
From cruel fear that they his throne might shake.

King: I well believe it, for it is most sure,
As Morton with solemnity will swear,
He did command his brother Clarence killed,
To clear his bloody pathway to the crown.
But those small boys . . . To take such lives as theirs,
What villain would conceive of such a deed?

Stanley: Take all precautions fitting to your state.
Light all the lamps, and bar your royal door.

King: 'Tis not the boys themselves we needs must fear
But those who'll prompt sedition in their name.
Look to it, Stanley, rumours have I heard
Of stirrings in the North against our self.
Dudley and Empson, call our soldiers back
And pledge them further glory. Let us form
A troop of warlike yeomen of our own.
Good sir! I pray thee, let us see your robes.
This brilliant scarlet, with the golden trim,
Shall become our yeomen's uniform,
And let this stomach filled with English beef
Suggest the title of our sacred file.
What else?

Enter Anne and Cabot.

Stanley: Good sir, this may not be the hour

To beg a life, but De la Pole . . .

King (*aware of an audience*):   Release him.
When rain doth into stately puddles fall
The larger body overwhelms the drops.
Know then that England's king wants all the world
To see that e'en his rivals, glad to say,
Are amnestied on this most happy day.

Morton: All?

Stanley: Sir, be not too hasty, sir, I beg.

King: Eat! Feast! No more of this. Be merry now!
Too long on winter evenings we have crouched
In icy darkness, waiting dreadful news
Of sons and fathers, uncles, nephews, friends.
Let this night trumpet in a different world,
Let martial pennants be forever furled.

*Exeunt Stanley and Morton. King Henry whispers with Dudley and
Empson.*

Anne: Rest here. I'll find my cousin. Do not move,
(*aside*) And if I move him not, I'm not in love.

King: Good people, pray forgive another word.
I have no wish this banquet to disrupt
But news has here arrived to shake our thoughts.
There are among us those who love us not.
We would be kind, but must, it seems, be cruel.
There'll be no peace for those who dammed our course.
Instead, I issue here a proclamation.
The date on which I, all against my will,
Humbly took on this grave and heavy crown,
We hereby swear to be the twenty-first
Of August last. So any man still true
To Richard on that date is treason's fool.
He will, and very shortly, know what 'tis
To side against a king. And so, farewell.

Exeunt King Henry, Dudley and Empson.

Cabot: What does this mean?

Anne: I know not, though I fear it brings thin joy. The battle where the King toppled Richard, Bosworth Field, was on the twenty-second. This declaration makes a villain of any man who fought for York. My cousin promised forgiveness, and while I know not what has prompted this change, I fear it bodes ill for your suit. Lodge this with us, and know I shall not rest until I've put our sovereign to the test.

Exeunt Anne and Cabot.

Scene Two

The Queen's bedchamber. Enter Queen Elizabeth. Enter King Henry.

King: I came, my Queen, to bid you pleasant dreams.
    Enjoy your sleep, and know that with the morn
    I must away to draw the rebel sting.

Queen: Away to war on this your marriage night?
    (*aside*) My prayers all are answerèd, and yet
    I cannot let this insult pass unchecked. –
    Will you not stay? Will you not lie with me?

King: With you, perhaps, right soon, but to you? No.
    Never, my faithful Queen. I would not force
    Or try an entrance where I am not urged.
    It is no secret that our wedding vows
    Are bound to panting England's need for peace.
    Ours is a cold transaction, not a dance
    Between two lovers twinned by mounting hopes.
    I know full well that you your husband see
    Not as a gentle friend but as a foe
    To you and your whole family of York.
    I pray that vengeful time may heal the wound;
    I'll not increase the hurt that you must feel.

Queen: I thank the King for his most gentle care.
    I will perform my role while he is gone
    (*aside*) And pray each night that never he'll return.

King: Mine has not been a merry life, my Queen.
    I never knew my father; he was killed
    By Yorkists while I swelled my mother's womb.
    My onion days I spent in Pembrokeshire
    But barely could I walk when our stout fort
    Yielded to siege, and we were all dispersed.
    I have no mem'ry of the day they came –
    The soldiers fell on us like cormorants.
    The story says that just before she died
    My mother lodged me with a stable lad
    Who saved me from the troops, and swift dispatched
    Word to an uncle, who protected me.
    A few months passed in peace until the war
    Crashed over us once more. My uncle fled,
    And I escaped to rocky Brittany.
    There have I lived till now, a banished youth,
    Till fate and fortune brought me to this throne.
    I marvel at it still, and scarce believe
    The man I have to be and must become.

Queen: We all have plaintive stories, good my lord.
    Mine own concerns an uncle and a king
    O'erthrown by wanton treachery and spite.

King: I know we have been bitter enemies,
    But let it end. For my part I do swear
    That never shall a harmful thought from me
    Disturb the smallest ringlet of thy hair.

Queen (*aside*): Right royally he speaks. Is this the man
    Who slew my uncle for his jewell'd crown?

King: There is one other thing I have to say
    Though with a heavy heart, for it is harsh.
    It well becomes you to defend your kin,

But you must know, in honouring his ghost
You do distress another. It is said
That Richard did your uncle Clarence kill
To clear his own rough ladder to the throne.

Queen: I'll not believe it. Oh, I see you clear.
You come to gull me in my misery.
Away to war! Slay other kinsmen! Go!
But do not tell me things that are not so!

King: Enough, I'll leave you, but before we part,
I pray you, hear the marrow of my tale.
We both do know our wedding was arranged
By forces stronger than our humble selves.
But I could not bestow my meek consent
Had I not been beguilèd by your face.
It was thy beauty, fair Elizabeth,
That spurred me on – thy nimble-pinioned grace
That soars upon the breeze above our throne
As eagles do, or haughty peregrines.
And even now, when you my suit disdain,
The colour on your cheek doth drum my heart.
You may not yet believe my love, but I
Do well aspire to conjugated bliss.
I'll give you time, and peace, and hope that we
One day a truly married couple be.

Exit.

Queen: Oh gods, what must I think? Can this be right?
This man that I since infancy have loathed
With all the eager longings of my tribe . . .
Is't possible that he might yet prove good?
Be still, my wedding band. Be patient, ring.
Our husband yet may prove himself a king.

Exit.

Scene Three

The King's court. Enter King Henry with Bergamot his fool, Suffolk, Oxford, Stanley, Morton, Lincoln, ministers and advisers.

King (aside): They see me not, these noble Englishmen.
　They think that I, a Welshman born and bred,
　And exiled in the courts of Brittany,
　Know little of this war-torn realm of theirs,
　Yet I have studied while I've been away.
　Much have I learned, and this I surely know:
　A king must be a panther, or a lion.
　My Queen I've softened, now I must impress
　These great men of the country with my will.
　Look at them chatter, these grey-bearded geese
　Who gabble in the fen-sucked marshy fringe
　Around the island where the swan holds court.
　I will astound them yet. Good morrow, all!
　I trust you know my champion, Bergamot.

Bergamot: 'Tis the company that makes a feast, the wise men say. And
　an empty sack will not stand. So behold, I present an upright man,
　your King!

Suffolk: Your champion hath indeed a merry wit.
　Good morrow to your noble majesty,
　We are your humble servants, gathered here,
　To do your bidding, and our only hope . . .

King: I thank you, gentle sir, but let's be on.
　Much business doth await us, I believe.
　What's first? You, sir, what is it furls your brow
　And weighs upon your honest-hearted soul?

Oxford: Unhappy news, I fear, most royal liege.
　A young pretender has appeared abroad
　In Dublin, so the messengers vouchsafe.
　He claims to be the Earl of Warwick, son
　Of Clarence, murdered uncle to your Queen.

327

Bishops and barons both do flock to him
And raise once more the banner of revolt.

King: I know this news and will away myself
This very night. An army have we raised
To cut this young pretender down to size.
Who's this?

Enter a messenger, one of Oxford's retainers, in full regalia.

Oxford: One of my own, my lord. What tidings, man?

Messenger: There are soldiers, my lord, outside.

Stanley: Summon the Guard!

Enter soldiers escorting Warwick, a ten-year-old boy.

King: Be calm. No matter. Soft, and cool yourselves.
We have already taken regal steps.
See who they bring? Young Warwick, is it not?
Welcome, my boy, and pray excuse our haste.
An Irish army has proclaimed you king.

Warwick: I've never been to Ireland, good my lord,
But if you wish it I will gladly go.

King: I wish you no such thing. Indeed, I must
Insist that you remain with us, our guest
In this, our proud and well-appointed Tower.
You shall be safe here, and your little life
May keep us sound as well.

Exit Warwick with escort.

                              How now, my lord?
This messenger of yours, arrayed in blue
And silver badges, emblems of your house:
Have you not seen our order, lately read
In public on the steps of Westminster?
No baron is to hold a private troop,
And there can be no livery but the King's?

Oxford: I have, my lord, and heartily concur.
    But servants of the house . . .

King: Can soon bear arms.
    I would I could command the law to ease.
    You are my stout right hand, and that is why
    I must not an exception make for you.
    The fine is twenty thousand sovereigns.
    For you, dear friend, and in the name of love
    We'll clip it to a delicate fifteen.

Oxford (*furious*): Your noble wish is ever my command.

King: Good Morton, friend, I beg you, have no fear.
    I will not ask for strawberries today!
    Another favour must I now request,
    Concerning one who wishes us most ill.
    The Lady Woodville, cold Elizabeth
    Cannot, we here avow, remain at large.
    Arrangements have I made in Bermondsey
    To take her into holy orders there.
    Convey her thither with all haste, that we,
    With her enclosed, can breathe and wander free.

Morton: I can but echo Oxford's loyal words.
    It shall be done.

    Exit Morton.

King: There is another task I must perform,
    And 'tis with weighty heart that I declare
    This modest rising in the northern counties
    Is but a ruse to test our royal strength.
    Firm must we be, and to that weighty end,
    Orders have we dispatched to this effect.
    Our noble cousins Lovell, Dacre, Stafford,
    Whom we thought friends, must now prepare to die.
    The scaffold waits; the whetstone grinds the axe.
    Before another dawn has warmed their eyes
    Their souls will fly to heaven, or to hell.

Exeunt all except for Bergamot and the King, who gestures for Oxford to remain behind.

Without ado, let us annul the fine
I lately levied on your noble house.
It was a stratagem, I here confess.
I hoped that when the others heard your fate,
Knowing how close our friendship, they would quail
And look upon our throne with more respect.
How now, good Oxford, let us share a smile.
Thou art our truest friend, but none can say
I have not made my presence felt today!

Bergamot: Necessity needs no counsellors, but truth lies always at the bottom of the well, and a king who is born in a stable is not a horse.

Exeunt King, Oxford and Bergamot. Enter Stanley, Suffolk and Lincoln.

Stanley: This fellow Bergamot is full of salt.

Suffolk: He is proverbial, but methinks he knows
Less than his kipper prattle doth suggest.

Stanley: What think you of this boy we have made king?

Suffolk: I think that he is young.

Lincoln: And Welsh.

Suffolk: And wild.

Stanley: All qualities I hold in high esteem.
What think of you of his manner? Is it meet?
Blunt was he now with Oxford; rough, too rough.
It must be said: he was not born to this.
The crown was not foretold him, and his youth
Was not a preparation for the role.
Unversed is he in statesmanship, and war
And diplomatic arts, and all the show
And glitter that attends a king.

Suffolk: Just so.

330

And this most rough attainder he announced
Will make him rich. He'll confiscate the lands
Of all the nobles on the Yorkist side.
He means to fill the treasury.

Lincoln: 'Tis true.
And look you, sirs, at this unhappy coin
Bearing the King's own likeness, an offence
To all the mortal habits of this land.
See how the face is grim, the eyes a-frown
With heavy thoughts and black imaginings.
I like it not.

Suffolk: 'Tis said he loves to play at games of chance
Like Flux and Plunder, Pillage, Freeze and Plug.
And many other common sports like these.
Whole nights he spends with gamesters on whose cards
He wagers gold enough to ransom kings.
He must amend.

Stanley: So must we look to it.
His claim is small, and on his mother's side,
The bastard daughter of old John of Gaunt.
His grandfather, 'tis true, did wed fair Catherine,
Widow of Henry, Lion of Agincourt.
But these are modest titles. Men will come
With better right by far to England's throne.
When kings are weak, 'tis best to be prepared,
For when they fall, their consorts are not spared.

Exeunt.

Scene Four

The docks. Enter Anne with John Cabot.

Cabot: Wait!

Anne: Are we safe?

331

Cabot: He'll be leagues away by now.

Anne: They follow me everywhere. But here we can loiter. This is your world, so tell me all. What's that, and that, and that and that and that? I would know everything.

Cabot: Then everything is what I shall tell you, my lady. But in return, and first, what of my suit? What says your cousin the King?

Anne: Oh blame me not, but I have failed to advance it. The very morning after the wedding he rode north to fight rebels. He is brave.

Cabot: I am not interested in rebels. I need sails, and bottoms, and men.

Anne: Bottoms?

Cabot: Ships.

Anne: Be patient. We'll beard him when he returns. Meantime, let us not be sad. You said you'd tell me all. How came you here?

Cabot: I am from Venice, as you know, a nautical man. I sailed here on a vessel bearing oil and wine to these cold northern shores.

Anne: In Venice the sun shines always?

Cabot: We have fogs as you do. But they are warmer.

Anne: I wonder you could leave a land of warm fogs.

Cabot: I am barely embarked upon the journey I mean to take. In Spain, Columbus pounds his timbers and prepares to sail. In Portugal, da Gama tars his ropes and stares at maps, calculating unknown tides. The race is to the swift. All seek the same: a route to China and the Indies, but we seek it west, towards the evening sun.

Anne: You hold with those who think our world a globe?

Cabot: 'Tis well attested and a proven fact. Do not you?

Anne: I know not.

Cabot: Imagine! A leaf of parchment floating in the vacancy men call space.

Anne: Space?

Cabot: Have you not heard of Master Galileo, our philosopher, plagued by the Church for having the hardiness of soul to watch the stars in his monoscope?

Anne: Can such a man exist? I never have heard of him. Is he Venetian too?

Cabot: Tuscan. But a great inventor and a mighty soul. He charted the revolutions of the stars, and teaches that it is not the sun that moves across our sky, but the earth.

Anne: You come from a land of seers.

Cabot: Sailors and seers, yes. Giotto, Leonardo, Donatello, artists of such style that you see a hand in bronze and think it lives. I see naught to compare with them here. England is raw.

Anne: We do not mean to be, nor wish it so.

Cabot: And yet I am amazed that you are the King's dear cousin. You do me honour, allowing me as your escort.

Anne: The honour is all mine. We rarely see such handsome adventurers. I fear, sir, you plan to sweep me out to sea.

Cabot: You would not like it.

Anne: I think you do not know what I would like.

Cabot: It is an article of faith for mariners that ladies bring misfortune on a ship. I know better, but I'll not hazard a crew on the chance. When you have seen, as I have, waves tall as forests, drowning the masts . . .

Anne: Oh, take me there!

Cabot: Where?

Anne: To sea. I long to see waves as tall as houses, and your – what were they – the foaming billows?

Cabot: It is not possible.

Anne: Then never shall my cousin hear of your hopes.

Cabot: My lady . . .

Anne: I swear. We may be rough, we English, and lack the skill to make

333

bronze hands soft to the touch, but we are resolute. The King shall
hear naught of you unless you show me deep water.

Cabot: Very well. We are nearly at a place I know.

Anne: They will refuse you nothing.

Cabot (*aside*): I little thought to meet so fine a lady.

Anne (*aside*): So rare a paladin I have not seen
    Such mighty hopes and such audacity.
    I should be such a man, framed to explore
    New worlds that none have ever seen before.

Cabot: Give me your hand, my lady, and we'll sail
    Out to the pool.

Anne: Lead on, kind sir. I'll follow.

    Exeunt.

Scene Five

An open square near the docks. Enter three citizens.

First citizen: There is a sickness so invades the air,
    And so infects the kingdom, some believe
    A pestilential vapour has o'erthrown
    Our native English merriness and strength.
    Some tens of thousands of our citizens
    Have died. The Mayor too has passed away
    And plague-struck are the city's aldermen.
    The King has fled to Guildford, it is noised
    To cleanse himself beside the River Wey.
    See how I sweat and shiver with the chill.
    Malign and icy tremors do assail me quite.
    Much have I heard, and some I do believe
    Of such distempers, that they may—

Second citizen: I know.
    And I have heard of strange events in Kent,
    Of hailstones great as horseshoes that did plunge

And plummet from the steeple-chasing sky.

Third citizen: And wild reports there are that comets fail,
Extinguished in the heavens. Rivers burst
Their green and smiling banks, and flood the fields,
And drown the cattle trapped beneath the trees.
When great men fall, the wheel that crushes them
Will raise up shapes as yet unformed and dim,
And lift them up to realms that scrape the sky.

First citizen: Enough — I am averse to poetry. Now here is a true story
I was told by a baker. People say that the real Richmond was killed
at Bosworth, and that our own beloved King is a royal imposter.

Second citizen: I myself was at Bosworth Field, at the foot of Ambien
Hill, when brave King Richard swooped down from above.

Third citizen: It would be a fine king who swooped from below.

Second citizen: That may be. But I can say that our King is no imposter.
I was there. I saw brave Richmond sword in hand.

First citizen: The baker's point is that the King so loves his bread, all
richly spiced with tender meats, that he eats his fill with wine and
then, by swallowing brimstone and other lotions, voids his stomach,
all for the pleasure of filling it again.

Second citizen: A king who gorges and ungorges. We are most fortunate
subjects.

Third citizen: I have heard this was King Edward's habit too.

First citizen: Some say that at his birth
Three suns were seen to glimmer through the mist
And those same stars were seen at Bosworth Field
When brave Prince Henry cut King Richard down.
And it was cold withal.

Second citizen: So let's away.
Strange sunsets have there been, and heavy dew.
All is not well, when monarchs play the fool.

Exeunt.

Scene Six

The wharves at the port. Enter Tyrell, and King Henry, incognito.

Tyrell: Who's there?

King: A friend.

Tyrell: Uncowl yourself, and come
Into the light of my despondent fire.

King: I shall. Good evening, sir. Fear not, I bring
A token of fair friendship from the King.

The King holds out a bag of gold.

Tyrell (aside): What means he by this gift? What would he have
That his commandment could not have more cheap?
I fear some stealth in this. – Who are you, sir?

King: I called myself a friend, and so I am,
Yet I am no mere royal messenger.
I am the King himself, and here I come,
Unarmed, in expectation of your help.

Tyrell: (*kneels*) Your wishes will be father to my deeds.

King: This is a teeming time. We know how close
You toyed with Richard in the black old days.
And if it pleased us to revenge ourselves
You would by now have tasted royal steel.

Tyrell: I knew him but a little, good my lord.
He had occasion once or twice to ask . . .

King: I know. 'Tis of the Princes I seek news.
They cast a princely shadow on our crown,
And on our royal line. Where are they hid?
I have it on the best of good reports
That you of all men kept the closest guard
On those most trammelled and benighted boys.
Speak, man. I am a patient soul, but peace
Fills me with fear of what it may disguise.

Tyrell: I cannot say. They are not in the Tower?

King: Perhaps I must speak plainly, king to man.
　　'Tis widely thought, and has been written down,
　　That you did kill the pretty Princes. Eh?
　　What think you, sir, of that? Perhaps this gold,
　　A gleaming token of our humble faith
　　Will loosen your tied tongue. What say you, sir?

Tyrell: I would not call myself a cruel man.
　　Deeds have I done that poison sleep and dreams,
　　But harm those Princes? That I never did.
　　Richard commanded me to end their lives –
　　He cared not how. I followed his command.
　　But these too disobedient hands
　　Rebelled against the act. I took the boys
　　And lodged them in a room along the flood.
　　I kept the royal payment for their death.
　　And here I hide, in horror of the wind.

King: Then stand you in the rarest company,
　　For you are two times ransomed by a king.
　　Fear not, I say. Lay off your subterfuge.
　　I only need to know where they reside,
　　That I might make a kingly peace with them.
　　Young they are now, but soon they will be men
　　And claims they have upon this Tudor throne.
　　I would have peaceful talk with them, to end
　　The wars that have this stricken nation torn.

Tyrell: I'll take you there myself. It is not far.
　　You see the windmill, there, across the sand.
　　The row of barges tied against the bank
　　Where otters play at sunrise, and where swans—

The King stands behind him, cuts his throat and takes back the purse.

King: You'll have no need of this, I think, or this.
　　And none shall miss thee, neither. Traitor, die!

'Tis only physic to let tainted blood run free,
The better to relieve the aching heart.
So wherefore do I quake? The sun dims not
To glimpse this minor gash. How many times
My blade has fall'n on bitter enemy heads,
But that's in battle, not in this cold blood.
Oh stars, what have I done? Is this a king?
My brightest hopes for peace and justice sway,
And lean, and shatter in the smiling dust.
When I was but a claimant, I had friends.
Now even my own shadow shrinks in fear.
Like every lord of this accursèd place
I plunge in plots and murthers of my own.
How better can I be than those before
If all I bring is secrecy and blood?
I know not, and am weary, and I fear
The worst is yet to come. There is no peace
For kings in lands where slaughter will not cease.

Exit.

338

ACT II

Scene One

The King's pavilion with the army near Stoke. Enter the King.

King: They think me brave, a dragon warrior
   Who breathes Welsh fire across the battlefield,
   But I would win this fight without a fight,
   And have within the enemy installed
   My acolytes to spread the royal word.
   Sovereigns they have to share with any man
   Who will tomorrow morning cross the line
   And take our part. Those men are not true troops.
   Look at their camps, their fires like tender stars
   A-flicker in the cold, grey Stafford dawn.
   They hold no terrors, these dull worms that glow
   To behold a king. We'll snuff them out entire.
   They fight for shillings, not to save their lives.
   When battle comes, we'll see which army thrives.

*Outside the nobles are gathering. A cockerel sounds. The King sweeps
out into the dawn.*

   Good morrow, gentlemen, I hope you slept
   As easy and as dreamless as did I.
   Know then that on the eve of Bosworth Field
   The black usurper passed a dreadful night
   Of haunting by the shades of those he'd killed.
   Such evils plagued me not.

Stanley: Nor me.

Oxford: Nor me,

339

Though I confess to some unease that tugged
Me from my bed at most ungodly hour.
Your grace, we are outnumberèd.

King: For now.
But soft. 'Tis dawn. The night owl gently glides
Into the mossy, nook-beshotten tree,
And thus swoop I. Your King has set in train
Commotions that may help avert this war.
Give me your shield – I must a sign convey
To enemies who would avoid this day.

He marches forward.

Oxford: My lord! I do beseech you.

Morton: Wait!

Stanley: Hold fast!

The King moves on and calls to the enemy.

King: If any of you brave and eager souls
Possess the stomach to unseat a king
Unloose your arrows now, for here I stand.
But if there are among your number those
Who nurse instead a dream of peace and wealth,
And warm prosperity in this fair land,
Then rise, and join us now. This is no ruse.
Freedom I pledge to all who thus convert
Upon this hour. The rest of you must know
That men who stand enraged against our will
Shall feel the pride and frenzy of our steel.
The choice is yours.

*He waits, watching, as a ragged number of men break ranks and walk
across; bit by bit, and with increasing speed, the opposing army
dissolves. At last the remnant is isolated and alone.*

Bergamot: What can a man expect from a pig, but a grunt? Look at
them flee, those plumed fantasticoes who lead – or mislead – that
inconstant force.

340

Morton: See how their ranks dissolve, like grains of chaff
    Upon a summer breeze. But who comes here?

Enter Simnel.

Simnel: We crave your mercy, for we mean no harm.

King: No harm? An army raised to quell the King
    That means no harm? I like your cheek, you fox,
    And well I see that this was not your play.
    Look on the mighty enemy we faced:
    A boy of tender years, a lamb, a pup.
    Fear not, young man, your head is safe with us.
    The royal kitchen is the place for you.
    Return with us to London: stir our stew.

Stanley: Most gently do you deal with traitors, sire,
    And greatly it becomes you. Yet I doubt
    The kingdom can be safe while such men live.

King: Stanley, my good and noble friend, speaks true.
    Guards! (*pointing at Stanley*) Take this man, and long before this
        night
    Remove that head from these broad shoulders here.
    Knave! That doth seek to flatter and to soothe
    While, canker-like, you grind us from within.
    To foes who show their face I can be kind;
    To friends who veil their thoughts I am of stone.
    Take him. Leave us. Away! Let's to London.

Exeunt all except the King and Bergamot.

Was ever battle won without a blow?
Were ever traitors stunned with such dispatch?
There will be more, I know, while Margaret lives,
But people need to know, their King forgives.
But what think you, my patient Bergamot?

Bergamot: I think that a king has long arms, though his embrace be not
    always fond. And if hesitation be the thief of time, diligence is the
    father of fortune.

341

King: I need no other counsellor. Away.

Exeunt.

Scene Two

London's docks. John Cabot sits on the harbour wall, gazing at ships.

Cabot: Hang me that ever I came to England. But the villain Columbus has captured the ear of Spain and the Italian princes cannot see further than the Mediterranean – a mere lake beside the vast oceans we would cross. And the Germans care only for land. These English are an island people; surely they have nautical dreams. And they do! Look upon this pool – a sea of boats! Cutters, coasters, schooners, barges, barques, carvels, hulks and carracks. How can there not be a hull for me?

Enter Lancelot, a seaman.

Lancelot: Good morrow, Giovanni. The view pleases you?

Cabot: It displeases me much. I would my feet were on a bounding deck, not on this barren stone.

Lancelot: Wait until the first Atlantic storm. Your tune might change. But I have something to show you. Look.

Cabot: A compass? What use is a compass without a ship? See how it points us the way to the west. But where are our masts, our sails?

Lancelot: Be patient. I bring a letter too.

Cabot (opens it): It is from her! Listen! 'My cousin will hear your plea. Come to the Tower tomorrow. He holds his court in the morning, and listens to many such suits. Hurry! Do not delay!' It is from Anne.

Lancelot: Did I not tell you your dark Italian face would win you favours?

Cabot: But when did this arrive? She says tomorrow; that might mean today.

Lancelot: 'Tis early yet. The King will be abed for hours. Come, let us

342

eat. I'll walk with you to Aldgate. I said when I rose that this would be a fine day.

Cabot: Let's pray 'tis so.

Exeunt.
Enter three citizens.

First citizen: They say he won the battle without raising his sword.

Second citizen: He bought the Germans and talked his way to victory.

First citizen: 'Tis a noble skill, to win wars without shedding blood.

Second citizen: They were mercenaries and could be hired. But they say he dealt justly with the pretender, spared his life and set him to work in the royal scullery.

First citizen: I suppose the lad will make a fine spit roaster.

Second citizen: Aye. He can spit on all the roasts. But he can carve a ham as well as any prince in the kingdom.

Third citizen: A rare king it is who has a generous bone in his body. King Richard would have had young Simnel's head.

Second citizen: The new King can be harsh withal. Know you, he has ruled that all mastiffs in the realm be killed. The Portuguese keepers think them a threat to the lions.

First citizen: I would rather he hanged his mastiffs than his subjects.

Third citizen: It may be he is too kind. Kings must be firm, or seem so.

Second citizen: The women at Sheen say the King and Queen dote on one another like fawns. At first the lady was all enraged at how the King had served her uncle, but now they coo like doves, and one said she saw them kissing in the rose garden.

Third citizen: I fear what it betokens, when kings and queens do fall in love.

First citizen: It will not last. The Queen, she is with child. The grooms say they will name him Arthur, if he's a boy, after the great king of the West.

Second citizen: And if a girl, will they call her Guenevere?

Third citizen: Why doom the girl with an adulterous name? I expect they'll call her Margaret. All princes call their daughters Margaret, I know not why.

Second citizen: They have a daughter already. And Margaret *is* her name.

First citizen: I know, but daughters are night, and kings want a rising son. It is for this that the Queen has gone to Winchester, to bear Arthur in the cradle of legends.

Third citizen: What ho. An age of miracles is at hand – quests and dragons, ancient magic and damsels in distress. But still we'll have to haul the water, or sweep the cages. Myths are for the soft-handed. For us the sun is up, and we to work must go.

Exeunt.

Scene Three

A wharf. Enter King Henry alone, in disguise. He watches a man emerge from a house.

King: In olden days, when Mars intended death,
He could assume a shape unlike his own
And range with demons all across the world,
Flying along the wingtips of the wind.
Thus I, a king, array myself in rags
That none may read the throneroom in my face.
I've watched this fellow, and have seen that soon
He'll take his morning walk upon the bank,
Leaving the Princes' breakfast at their door.
It wants a moment to adulterate
The milk with this sweet poison in my purse,
And then I'll wear these shameful threads no more.
This is the place, this is the door. Let's in,
Before our milksop conscience bids us stay.

Come, patient clouds, and swaddle up the sun;
Light must not shine where evil must be done.

Inside the house the two Princes are just waking up.

Edward: What is the hour?

Richard: I know not.

Edward: I heard a noise.

Richard: The wind. The river. Go to sleep.

Edward: I cannot. I had the strangest dream. I fancied we were geese
in a coop, and a fox came among us wearing feathers, and we recognised him not. Again! Did you not hear? There's someone there.
Ralph?

King: Edward? Richard? I am glad to see you well.

Richard: Who are you?

King: A friend. A friend of the King.

Richard (to Edward): I told you, I told you Uncle Richard would find
us. (*To the King*) What news? Have you come to deliver us?

King: Aye, deliverance is what I bring today.
(*aside*) Uncle Richard! They think the old King lives!
But patience must I urge. Pray you, be calm
And wait until a more propitious time.
Here is the breakfast . . . Ralph prepared for you.
Milk, bread and cheese. Enjoy it, eat your fill.
You'll hear from me anon. Till then, farewell.

Exit the King. The Princes fall on their breakfast.

Richard: Did I not tell you? Did I not say? Our uncle promised us that
when he had made the peace hold he would send for us. It is safe
now for you to be king. (*Kneels*) Your most high highness, your
humblest subject greets your most majestic majesty . . .

Edward: Enough. I do remember the Protector's words. He said he
loved us well, and would not rest until he had made the throne

steady. And he patted our heads and said we were dainty fellows . . .

Richard: And I feel much ashamed that we thought he had abandoned us. Steady thrones are not lightly made. It has not been so many months.

Edward: What shall we wear?

Richard: Why clothes, of course. I would not have the new King make his entrance clad only in his skin.

Edward: What think you of this milk? It has a sour taste, of coins, and . . . oh.

Richard: What of it? We shall soon be in the palace, and have cream and cakes.

Edward: It grips. Ugh. My stomach!

Richard: Mine too . . . By heaven!

Edward: Something is wrong . . . Ralph!

Richard: Who was that man? Oh . . . Brother . . . Uncle . . . Mother . . . Help!

They die. Outside, the King waits, still disguised.

King: My conscience has been clear until this day
But now, farewell to sleep and placid dreams.
There is a story that they tell in Brittany
Of one who slew a unicorn, and drowned
In torments of remembrance and self-hate.
So 'tis with me. My conscience will relive
This vicious time in visions that will storm
The battlements of reason, and lay low
The fortresses of all I do esteem.
Dear God, I beg that you avert your gaze.
This grieves thy law, I know, though *you* must know
It was not them I feared, but those who would
Their innocent and royal frames exploit.
Such is the royal choice: a sainted king
Is one who saves his precious soul for thee

And lets his kingdom wither on the bough
Like so much mildewed blossom. I do swear
There could have been no peace for this great realm
Had those boys lived. It was my royal place
Compelled me to deliver them to thee.
England required it; I could not say no.
Enough. I must hold fast or I'll go mad
As Scotland's black usurper, wild Macbeth.
When I do come before the final judge
Let it be noted in my pale defence
That neither lackey nor confederate
Did I ensnare in this most heinous deed.
This scorpion anguish is mine own to bear.

Exit.

Aloft, in her palace, we see the Queen, heavily pregnant.

Queen: What can I do? My anger has grown mild;
I cannot hate the father of my child.

Scene Four

Westminster. The King's court. Enter the King, Oxford, Morton and other dignitaries.

King: We must be brief. I would to Winchester
To tend our Queen.

Morton: God speed your majesty.

King: But first, affairs of state. Thou knowest, all,
That God did bless our enterprise at Stoke.
I thank you. You shall meet the foolish sprout
When you do dine with us, for he is ours.
The boy was harmless. I was merciful.
If we who hold the swords cannot be kind,
Why then should those who shiver in the cold,
Far from the heat of our forgiving flames?

Oxford: Your words will send bright sentinels abroad.
  Happy the land whose monarch sheathes his blade.

King: Well said. And now, what news of those two boys,
  The princely sons of York, whose shades we seek?

Oxford: None, my lord. The search goes on withal.

King: I do confess I think it possible
  That they were slain, perhaps by royal hand.

Oxford: Only your grace's high and royal care
  Allowed you to deny it till this day.
  King Richard strangled their poor fledgling souls
  Like tender larks to salt his regal feast.

King: Where is the thunderbolt to strike
  The man who was the author of this scene?

Oxford: You were yourself the thunder, good my lord
  When you did stoutly brook King Richard's charge,
  Delivering us all from tyrant rule.

Enter Polydore Vergil, William Caxton, and Anne with Cabot.

King: 'Tis so, and to this end I have arranged
  That we be not the last to know the truth.
  Vergil, I bid you welcome to our court.
  Much have I heard of your renownèd skill.
  A grateful king would furnish great reward
  To any man who would accept this brief,
  To write a history of our fair land
  That does not balk to tell such tales as these,
  Blush though we must to own such villainy.
  What say you, sir? I dare say that our lords,
  And even the King himself, would make you one
  With all the secret griefs of these late wars.

Vergil: I would be honoured to perform this task;
  A little time is all I crave, or seek.

King: What news from Italy? How move the stars?

348

Vergil: Sad tidings from the court of Tuscany.
　　Lorenzo, Duke of Medici, is dead.

King: I never knew him save by his repute.
　　He was a friend to music and the arts.
　　Spires he inspired, and domes, and painted walls
　　And gilded doors and ceilings, cloistered courts.
　　How died this Prince, this eagle?

Vergil:　　　　　　　　　　　High on his crag,
　　As great kings should, and it has been much noised
　　That even his great foe, the fiery priest,
　　Consoled and blessed Lorenzo at the last.
　　They say that at the moment of his death
　　Lightning inflamed the tower of the church,
　　A spark divine that flew from heaven to earth
　　To meet the fire that rose into the skies.

Bergamot. Faith, the husk of a prince is rarer than the grain of a
　　common man . . .

King: Enough! We will to Florence send a gift
　　To croak our sorrow at this passing news.
　　Morton, bethink you what would be most fit.
　　Meanwhile, good sir, I thank you for your time.
　　Our nation's history is in your hands,
　　I beg you spill it not, and fare thee well.
　　Morton, my friend, I do require your ear.

　　(*Turns aside.*)

　　If this Italian falters in this task
　　We might a second history arrange:
　　The narrative of cruel Richard's reign,
　　By English hands. Know you a likely man?

Morton: I do, my lord, there's one in my employ.
　　His name is More, and more I cannot say
　　Than that he is right worthy of this task.
　　A youth of tender years, yet great in wit

And more than great, I think, perhaps, in soul.
High things of him I do expect, and this
Shall be his first and most important task.
From me he shall of foul King Richard hear,
How like a bottled spider he devoured
And twisted fate to shape his wicked ends.

King: Right so. We English must take on these roles.
The stories that we tell posterity
Must be the ones we wish our heirs to know.
(*returning*) I find myself in literary mood, and know
That Mr Caxton waits upon our pleasure.
Step forward, sir, what may we do for you
Or you for us, a trade all kings prefer?

Caxton: I bring a book, most great and royal highness,
Warm from the press I recently installed
In this your capital of capitals.

King: I hunger, sir, as always, for the tales
That press themselves on your most willing sheets.
What call you it again? A book, you say?

Caxton: A book, my lord. A very new device
Composed of leaves in paper bound as one
With words from my most humble print machine.

King: The Morte d'Arthur. A French book, so it seems.

Caxton: Originally so, my lord, but now
Translated into perfect English prose
By Thomas Malory, an English knight.

King: I like the title greatly. Dost thou know
That our first-born, whose coming we expect
Within the month, will take the name of Arthur,
If he emerge, as we expect, a boy?
I hope your title presages no ill
We have no taste for works prophetical.

Caxton: I do not think so, sire.

King: No more do I.
We'll let you know our judgement bye and bye.
And now, if that is all, I bid you thanks.
A carriage waits for me. Fortune has smiled,
Ere long we'll have with us a royal child!

Anne: A moment, cousin, please, have you forgot?
You did a promise make to see this man,
This voyager from Italy who comes
In humble hope to honour us abroad.

King: Oh yes. What is your name, my brave young man?

Cabot: Cabot, my lord. I am your humble slave.

King: What would you?

Cabot: Rare and precious sights I seek
In distant seas . . .

King: Excuse me, sir. Make haste.

Cabot: Give me a ship, your highness, and I'll sail
To China by the western route, and pledge
Whatever treasures I unearth for your
And England's glory.

King: Pretty words, Cabot,
But I have not the leisure here today
To ponder such a scheme. Tarry a while.
I would hear more of this another time.

The King holds his hand up, won't hear another word. Exeunt all but the King and Bergamot.

King: You too, good Bergamot. Carve yourself some ease, and eat your fill.

Bergamot: Hunger is the best sauce. But danger lieth always in the path of honour, and the only true history is the one that lies unwritten.

King: I know that you are wise, but know not what you mean. Go.

Exit Bergamot.

See how they answer each of my commands,
Eager to please and anxious to impress.
Like juggling seals in my menagerie.
Thus is it to be king. The whole world smiles,
Laughs at our jests, and hatches plots the while.
And I? I seek the bitter prick of shame
And feel but naught. Awake, good conscience. Rise.
I see a happy kingdom, mild, content,
Busy at last, and greatly thanks to me.
My work was dark, but crueller by far
It must have been, had I let England bear
A crimson age of deep revenge and war.
It had to end. Its ending fell to me.
There it ends. I cannot feign regret,
And yet I am relieved that I was spared
The sight of those young children's bitter fate.
Glad that the slaughter I perforce performed
Allowed me to avoid their final sighs.
They did conceive no malice, nor no harm
And drank their poisoned milk like tender lambs,
Pressing their bashful noses to the teat.
Let me not think on't. So. Who's there? I come!

Exit.

Scene Five

Another part of the palace. Enter Cabot, followed by Anne.

Anne: I pray you, wait.

Cabot: I do nothing else! I will to Norway, a land of real seafarers.

Anne: The King did not say no.

Cabot: He would not listen. I have been much deceived.

Anne: Oh do not say such things. You know they are not true. Have
patience.

Cabot: Patience! I have had the patience of an iceberg. And for what?

Anne: Forgive me, sir, but you have not. You are hot-tempered.

Cabot: Does the King not see that time is all? Tarry a while! While what? While others enter quests that should be ours? Our journeys are governed by tides and seasons, not by ourselves. We cannot choose our time; the time chooses us. Ach, but the King knows nothing of such matters.

Anne: Stop your tongue, sir! Do not speak thus of the King! Think on it. Cares he has more pressing than your own. Not days ago, while you did snoop at ships, he was at battle with a pretender. You shame yourself with this wrath.

Cabot: Forgive me, good my lady. My temper is too Italian, too much in the sun.

Anne: I will forgive you only if you stay. I have money. You may serve me as a tutor, teach me of the tides, the seasons and the stars. I am an eager pupil, you shall see. And if at court I have the influence a sister should, you'll have your ship.

Cabot: I do not deserve such kindness from a queen.

Anne: I am no queen, signor. A year ago I was, like you, a refugee in foreign lands. Believe it, time doth wreak the strangest alterations.

Cabot: It was not time that wrought the change, but thy fair face.

Exeunt Anne and Cabot.
Enter the King, with the Duke of Norfolk.

King: Your offer is most just and generous.
My cousin is of royal pedigree
And that is why the Crown must needs expect
A handsome portion for her wedded hand.
But all the lands of Ely! Were it not
Ungracious in a king, I would refuse.

Norfolk (*through gritted teeth*): Your highness is too noble and too kind.

King: And more I'll do for you. Before I leave
    I'll find the Lady Anne and see that she
    Does not refuse your suit. The Queen herself
    I will inform, and doubt not she'll be pleased.
    Our families shall be together linked,
    Strength'ning England and each other both.

Norfolk: Your hopes shall henceforth also be our own.
    Ripe shall be the fruit that we have sown.

    Exit Norfolk.

King: He thinks by this to polish his own claim
    To this our regal state, but I'll not wait
    To see how he pursues it. Dudley! Here!

    Enter Dudley.

    The Duke of Norfolk is a friend to us
    And now by marriage joined to our desires.
    We would not wish the smallest harm to come
    Within a mile of his dear person. Understand?

Dudley: I do, my lord; you would that he be watched.

King: Thou art the king of plain speech, dearest Dudley.
    Thanks for your royal wisdom and your care.

    Exit Dudley.

    So now I shall the Lady Anne inform
    That she is to be wed. 'Tis passing strange
    The frolics monarchs do perform, that can
    A lady's hand for royal land exchange.

    Exit King Henry. Enter Anne and Cabot.

Anne: Tell me about those dolphins that you saw off Spain.

Cabot: They leaped about our ship like rabbits or birds, at races in the
    foam.

Anne: I yearn to see them.

Cabot: You have such spirit, my lady, I am sure one day you will.

Anne (*aside*): He takes my hand! And though I should remove it, I cannot.

Cabot (*aside*): I can navigate reefs and shoals and murderous banks, but how can I plot a course through rocky feelings such as these?

Enter King Henry.

King: Can it be so? A princess and a sailor?
I should not be surprised, when I myself,
A foundling and a pauper, late in hiding,
Now command the heights. I see it all.
The navigator seeks our royal sail
And he shall have it. Let him depart away
Across the oceans, never to return,
Far from our bride-to-be. My Lady Anne!

Anne: I am surprised to see you, good my lord;
I thought that you had left to travel south.

King: Not yet. Signor Cabot, I come in peace
With news, I hope, that shall your spirit please.
I have conferred with men who know such things
And they speak well of you. A ship you seek,
And so a ship you'll have. To Greenwich, go.
The maritime officials I will warn
To furnish you with England's finest fleet.
And now I must away.

Cabot: Your highness, wait!
Forgive a rough Venetian man who lacks
The proper way to speak to English kings.
Seas shall I cross to China and the East;
Silks I shall bring, and spices rare and fine;
Jewels and gold and snow from towering peaks.
All shall bear England's name.

King: And if you sail
As bravely as you talk, then you'll not fail.

And now, my valiant friend, excuse us, please.
I would my sister's ear detain a while.
Get thee to Greenwich now . . .

Exit Cabot.

Anne: Thou hast done well.
I do believe he will achieve great things.

King: I doubt it not, and pray that he recalls
Your part in all the glory he will gain.

Anne: How is it to be king? To have such power
To make men's dreams come true, and power too
To end them?

King: It goes heavy with my soul.
I find it most perplexing and ill-graced
When all my noble subjects smile and scheme.
'Twas often thus, I know.

Anne: What can I do,
To ease the burden that on you must weigh?

King: There is some news I have concerning you,
But no, it is not fair. I should not ask.
I'll leave you straight.

Anne: Dear coz!

King: Forget I spoke.

Anne: Do you remember, Henry, Richmond, friend,
How once, in Quiberon, we found a hive
And tried to steal some honey from the bees?
How those poor beasts, affrighted from their beds
Flew up in swarms and stung us on the arms,
Perishing freely to defend their hoard?
I do remember, you did say that day
That monarchy required such bravery
From all its people, who must rouse themselves to fight
Whatever foreign arms should break their peace.

King: But people are not bees. No king can ask
    Such sacrifices as those creatures make.
    I should have told him straight. I'll do so now . . .

Anne: Told whom? Said what? A riddle cloaks your words.
    I cannot help if you will not confide
    Whate'er it is that binds your patient tongue.

King: Good cousin Anne, I beg you do not force
    Me into utterance. Thou art a gift,
    And yet I know thou art not mine to give.
    Your kindness would submit to all requests,
    And that is why I must blockade my lips.
    You would say yes, and hate me evermore.

Anne: I may say yes, but hatred, Henry, nay.
    Good cousin, come, why all this mystery?
    We never did have secrets, you and I.

King: You have my battlements entirely breached.
    I'll tell thee all. But pledge me in return
    That you will not let obligation draw
    You to a deed that – though it would secure
    Our crown and underwrite our throne
    More certainly than all the gold in Spain –
    Might not sit well with your devout desire.
    I'll speak it, then. The Duke of Norfolk seeks
    Your royal hand in marriage, thinking by this,
    To bind our warring families as one . . .

Anne: Oh heavens! You do not jest? The Duke of Norfolk . . .

King: But you must not yourself in sorrow drown
    Merely to keep the kingdom free from war.
    The cries of bleeding thousands, limbs all hack'd
    By men they once thought friends or neighbours,
    Banish them from thy thoughts, they are not yours
    To help or heal, but mine alone to bear.

Anne: My lord . . .

King: Your virtues mock my faltering attempt
   To make poor England safe and whole again.
   Much am I shamed that I allowed this duke
   Even to voice his suit. Soon will he learn
   What such temerity shall cost his heirs.
   Farewell, fond Norfolk. Thou art not the first
   To ask too much of kings. Prepare thyself.

Anne: Cousin . . .

King: I know. I feel thy scorn too bitterly.
   Could'st thou forgive a king who for a while
   Thought of his country, and forgot his own?

Anne: Be still, my lord. I am not so surprised.
   We have not spoken in this vein before,
   But I am not so foolish as you think.
   We women know what form our destinies
   Must take, and that our own soft hopes
   Play but a fleeting part in what we do.
   So let us not this Norfolk suit rule out.
   I do not know the Duke, and cannot judge
   How he might fall with me. And knowest thou
   That if our kingdom's peace this may secure
   I will his bride become – if nothing more.

King: You are too good.

Anne: And you, my lord, are late.
   Get thee to Winchester, and bid thy Queen
   Our sweetest wishes at this happy time.

   Exit Anne.

King: Whence comes this fateful power to deceive?
   Is't mine, or dwells it in these regal robes?
   Good Signor Machiavelli, I salute
   Your sage advice. A careful leader must
   Use craft and guile to win his subjects' trust,
   And steer them to a future better far

Than they could find alone. Or so I hope.

Exit.

Scene Six

A courtyard before a tavern. Night. Torches. Enter a Town Crier, bearing a paper. Enter Bacon, a butcher.

Bacon: What have you there, my best and truest fiend?

Crier: A paper, signed by the King himself. See here, his seal?

Bacon: More pup than seal, to my eyes. And what is wrote there?

Crier: I would read it to you, Monsieur Sausage. But I cannot.

Bacon: Why not? Sure it can be no secret, in your hands. You are not known for your discussion. Read on, Macduff.

Crier: Macduff? Think you I come untimely ripped?

Bacon: Why should I wish to untie thee? Read, I pray you, read.

Crier: I cannot.

Bacon: I know you are not blind. You can see a coin at fifty paces.

Crier: I am a hawk for money. And if my name were Egg, we would be a tasty pair.

Bacon: I do not unhand you, sir. How can there be locks on your con-vocation? Is't not your job to speak?

Crier: Aye, though silence is a mark of honesty.

Bacon: And yet you will not read. Honesty ne'er filled a stomach. The paper . . .

Crier: I *cannot* read it.

Bacon: A crier that cannot read? 'Tis like a butcher without a knife. Know'st thou, I was a gentleman once. I kept three servants, and read books every day. (*aside*) But times change faster than a north wind, and now I must play the fool.

Crier: 'Tis possible the servants did not understand you.

Bacon: Four of them condescended me well. One of them, alack, had no earring.

Crier: Poor man, to mishear such a sudden growth in servants.

Bacon: Sometimes I thought that six servants was too many. But there was enough work for all. Our lands were wide.

Crier: Now you have lands?

Bacon: Not now, knave, in the olden times. I built cottages for those servants, hard by the stables. A dozen men waited on me. Here, my hat. Here, my spurs.

Crier: If I tarry, this fellow will house more servants than the Queen.

Bacon: Give it to me. (*Reads*) *The King, to all to whom, etc.* What means this nonsense?

Crier: Read, I pray you, read.

Bacon. Very well. *Greetings: Be it known and made manifest that we have given and granted as by these presents we give and grant, for us and our heirs, to our well beloved John Cabot, citizen of Venice, and to Lewis, Sebastian and Sancio, sons of the said John, and to the heirs and deputies of them, and of any one of them* . . . By God, we have a wordy king.

Crier: Most wordy. Who is this citizen of Venice? A merchant?

Bacon: I once saw a play of that name. It was most dull.

Crier. A play, they say, is as sharp or dull as the ear it falls on.

Bacon: Please! List! . . . *full and free authority, faculty and power to sail to all parts, regions and coasts of the eastern and western sea, under our banners, flags and ensigns, with five ships or vessels of whatsoever burden and quality they may be, and with so many mariners and men as they may wish to take with them in the said ships, at their own proper costs and charges* . . . These lines drift on an empty ocean. I do not think we shall ever survive.

Crier: Arrive.

Bacon: That's what I said.

Crier: Sail on. I think I see land.

Bacon: . . . *to find, discover and investigate whatsoever islands, countries, regions or provinces of heathens and infidels, in whatsoever part of the world placed, which before this time were unknown to all Christians.* At last. A full stop. A manacle.

Crier: You mean, a miracle.

Bacon: I mint, sir, exactly what I sod.

Crier. Is there more? If I list any more, I shall sure capsize.

Bacon: I will tray one mare sintence. A dope breath to fill my lings, and in we drive. *We have also granted to them and to any of them, and to the heirs and deputies of them and of any one of them, and have given licence to set up our aforesaid banners and ensigns in any town, city, castle, island or mainland whatsoever, newly found by them* . . .

Crier: You were slow to leave the harbour, but here is newly found land.

Bacon: Who is this Phoenician, this Cabot? I lake him not.

Crier: You know him not.

Bacon: I lake not what I know not.

Crier: And if ye . . . laketh what ye knoweth, then . . . laketh you all parts of the pig?

Bacon: A straunge quistion. The pig, sir, is of all creatures the most deciduous. Where is my stable lad? Come.

Exit Bacon.

Crier: Was ever man so marvellous a rasher? I know not whether he be better boiled or fried. But to my business. Hear ye! *And that the before-mentioned John and his sons or their heirs and deputies may conquer, occupy and possess whatsoever such towns, castles, cities and islands by them thus discovered that they may be able to conquer, occupy and possess, acquiring for us the dominion, title and jurisdiction of the same; in such a way that of all the fruits, profits, emoluments, commodities, gains and revenues accruing from this voyage, the said John and sons*

361

shall be bound and under obligation . . . For himself, this Cabot will win fame, but such riches as he finds will fall to our shrewd king. How fine, this power to send men for foreign gold. And so the world stands upside down, when all its treasure trickles uphill. Hear ye, hear ye . . .

Exit.

ACT III

Scene One

Flanders. The chamber of Margaret of York. Enter Margaret, with attendants.

Margaret: Leave us! Patched fools! I can the couch arrange!
Be gone, I pray you.

Exeunt attendants.

                   Good. And so to bed,
Though never saw a bed so little rest;
It drinks my tears, but never grants me sleep.
My rebel heart refuses to lie still
While Richmond squats on York's entitlement.
I thought that this boy Simnel would inspire
The noblemen of England to rise up
And peach the tyrant, but I well perceive
That England, like a neutered spaniel, sleeps.
I hear they play at tick-tack in the fields
While nettles crowd the rosy eglantine.
A kitchen scullion! Oh for shame!
The boy is only ten, and well born too.
Who is this king, this lizard, who thus pours
Despite on houses nobler far than his?
Hear now our pledge. Let finer feelings fall
And shrivel at the spurs of our revenge.
This toad hath killed our Richard, and our hopes.
Stafford and Derby, Lincoln, Suffolk, all
Have felt the edge of his self-righteous sword.

Worse, it is said he hath undone the boys
Who carried all the hopes of our great house.
I know not if this horror can be true,
But if it is, then time engulfs all sense.
We cannot let poor England bear the sting
To have so cold a creature on her throne.
Till now we have been gentle, patient, meek,
Obedient to all commands of God.
No more will we be calm. Let no one smile
Until this greedy cuckoo has been mauled.
Our cousin Maximilian, King of Rome,
Hath found a lad most likely to be prince.
We shall persuade this man – and this I swear –
To play the part of Richard's rightful heir.

Scene Two

*The Royal Apartments at the Tower of London. Enter the King,
alone. He is writing.*

King: We have a son. Our future is assured.
   He is named Arthur, and he will be great,
   A mighty ruler, loved and feared by all.
   He is yet young; he counts his age in weeks,
   But every man in Winchester has sworn
   That never was such kingship in a child.
   (*Sets down pen.*) My task it is to sow and feed this land
   With crops so strong and bountiful, that all
   Will think us rulers of another Eden,
   Blessèd above all nations of this world.
   Nor shall my sinews rest till he be girt
   With ships, and gold, and thoughtless fealty
   From all his native peoples, high and low.

Enter Bergamot.

Good morrow, boisterous spirit. What's the news?

Bergamot: It is a wise father that knows his own child, for nothing bites
    deeper than ingratitude.

King: Why, this is well spiced. What ails you?

Bergamot: Nothing, my lord, but early morning beer.

Enter Morton, and other attendants.

Morton: Good morrow, sire. I hope you hear the bells.
    They ring for our new Prince, your first-born son,
    The boldest star in all our firmaments,
    And radiant hope for all our brave tomorrows.
    A thousand blessings peal upon his head—

King: Enough! I mean to hunt today. Be quick.
    I know that there is much to do, but see,
    The sun upon the river sparkles bright
    As topaz. Deer await my bow. What have you?

Morton: Papers, my lord, payments and firm decrees
    From your high throne to England's loyal flock,
    Laws about windows, dogs, and savage sports,
    Hunting grounds, dues from wine and salt and silk.
    And then awaiting your most royal pleasure,
    Ambassadors from Portugal and Spain.
    The one with gifts for your menagerie,
    Which do deserve our thanks . . .

King (*signing papers*):   Our thanks? *Our* thanks?
    If they are *ours*, then you can thank the man
    As well as I. Go to't, I'll see him not.

Morton: But sire, he brings you leopards and gazelles,
    Hawks from the south and eagles from the hills.

King: Then thank him like an eagle, in return.
    Meanwhile, what news from Spain? Let him come in.
    Perchance he has an answer to our hopes.

Enter Spanish Ambassador.

Ambassador: Most earnest greetings, Signor King of England.

Castile does bid thee honour . . .

King: Very well.

Ambassador: And wishes to unite with you in marriage:
　　Your own young Arthur, our fair Catherine.
　　These two, in firm concord, could rule the world.
　　In Aragon and Castile, as you know,
　　The Jews have been expelled, and live no more.
　　With England in our Christian family
　　And all the Atlantic waiting for our fleets
　　None may confound us. So says Ferdinand.

King (*aside*): Poor boy! He is but three weeks out the womb
　　And we do bell his birth with wedding vows.
　　What must we think? We are war's enemies,
　　But love can conquer lands as rich and fat
　　As armies sent at ruinous expense
　　T'expire on foreign soil. Your hand, Monsieur,
　　And tell your king we stand at one with him
　　On all these matters. Let him name the day
　　When his fair child o'er England shall hold sway.

Ambassador: Signor, two mighty nations shall take wing . . .

King: What brings the Lady Catherine to this feast?

Ambassador: Her beauty, royal highness, is most rare . . .

King: But let us not this happy day despoil
　　With vulgar talk of lands, estates and ships.
　　There's time enough for that. So tell me, sir,
　　What news of your explorer, brave Colon?
　　What worlds hath he delivered to your King?

Ambassador: Each day brings news of yet more golden gains.

King: I'm glad. And now you will perforce away.
　　I spy a cloud on my good chancellor's brow
　　That speaks of something ill. Farewell, good friend.

Exit Spanish Ambassador.

What is it, Morton? Why look you so grey?
This marriage disappoints you, I perceive.

Morton: My lord, a new pretender is at large.
    He claims to be Prince Richard, from the Tower.

King: In heaven's name, I say this cannot be!
    Thy words are icicles.

Morton: It may prove false.
    Word we await from Flanders, from the court
    Of Margaret, whence all this treachery flows.
    Our cousin Clifford has imposed himself
    Within our enemies, who think him kind.

King: 'Tis good. We owe our lives to your great care.
    (*aside*) Angels, draw near. There's ample precedent.
    Deeds that do harrow time come back to haunt
    The men on whom the guilt lies dark and hard.
    Like serpents' teeth, these princes do recur.
    I thought 'twas only dreams they could waylay
    But here they sally forth in open day.
    Set down, my heart. Come, breast, expel thy breath . . .

Morton: I see your majesty is much perturbed.

King: A drink, I beg you. We shall want new troops.
    Call Parliament. Sharp taxes we shall need,
    To raise an army to our royal cause.

Morton: I have bethought me on this very case,
    And might a subtle stratagem propose,
    To filter funds from England's finest men.
    Your subjects face a fork. If they be mean,
    Why they must sure have saved enough to share
    With their most faithful and devoted king.
    If opulence defines their daily round,
    If silver plate bejewell'd bears their food,
    Then they can tithe a portion to our throne.

King: Morton, thou art the finest man alive;
   This fork of yours would crack the hardest nut.
   If rich, you pay, if poor, you pay. *Voilà*!
   If God did counsel my archbishop thus
   To advise his lord, he must a Welshman be.

Morton: I do my best to please your majesty.

King: This new pretender's neck is in the noose –
   His head will cap our bridge. Fetch Oxford hence,
   And bid brave Talbot ready now to move
   On any warning. Set our ships to quell
   This impudent rebellion e'er it breaks.
   And send to Scotland, lest King James decide
   To entertain this Yorkist troubadour.
   And since I am a Pandarus today,
   I'll offer him my daughter Margaret's hand.
   True, she is but a girl, and he must wait,
   But she'll be grown ere long, and will be fair,
   And where's the king who'd stoop to raise on high
   The fox who would devour his future bride?

Exeunt.

Scene Three

The formal apartments of Margaret of York, in Flanders. Enter Margaret, with attendants.

Margaret: I think I hear him coming now. Prepare!
   We would upon him stamp a fine impress,
   This chariot of our hopes.

Enter Warbeck.

                              Good morrow, sir.
   Most pleasantly the light falls on the trees
   And glistens o'er this fair and eager land.

Warbeck: Madame, the sun himself doth make a bow

To thy most gracious presence; clouds do form
Like ruffs of lace to please your majesty.

Margaret: A regal speech, and you do look the part.
Think me not rude if I request your age.

Warbeck: I am ten years and seven, good my Queen.

Margaret. Know you the matter why we seek you here?

Warbeck: I do, my lady.

Margaret: Think'st thou to be king?

Warbeck: With all my heart. Papers I bring from Rome.
The Pope himself has pledged to help our cause.
Ships have we brought from Saxony, and our men
Tremble like arrows eager to loose themselves
At England's softened heart.

Margaret: Well spoken, sir.
And know thou then how much we hate this dog,
This Henry Tudor, as he calls himself. A cur,
Who has our prideful family much harmed.
Through you we'll make amends, and, be assured,
Our gratitude will be immense and swift.
Letters I'll send to Scotland. They shall hear
Of this our joint intent. Be keen. Set sail,
And let the Scottish nobles cry, All Hail!

Exit Warbeck.

His father was a boatman, so they say,
And even we can barely fathom how
A boy so humble might be England's king.
Thus fortune sets us all against ourselves,
Beware the tide, most bloody Lancaster,
For when it turns, it sweeps us all to sea.

Exeunt.

Scene Four

The Royal Apartments at Sheen. Enter the King and Queen.

King: I see the Lady Anne has won your ear.

Queen: She's young, my lord, and you should gentle be
    With her affections. Give her yet some time.

King: As ever, thou art wiser than thy years.
    I was too rough, and shall her pardon seek.

Queen: My lord, when first we wed, I thee despised.
    I blamed you for my uncle's horrid end
    And felt that, to be King, you felled a man
    Who might have proved most royal, had he lived.
    But thou *art* good. England has need of thee,
    Be strong for her, if not for thine own sake.

King: I thank thee for thy love and confidence.
    For my part I too know, as you concede,
    Our marriage was in part for outward show.
    I little thought that we might wind as close
    As columbines engathered in one plant,
    With Margaret and Arthur as our flowers.
    I wonder much what men to come will think
    Of love so politic and well arranged.
    Married against our wills, forced to unite
    For high and most profound affairs of state,
    And passing children out to distant courts
    Like pieces in a play of stratagems.

Queen: They'll think perhaps we strove as hard as they
    For happiness, security and peace.

King: But when does striving cease? Is there a time
    When monarchs stand secure upon their throne?
    Each morn brings fresh invasions to our state;
    Each day we have to win the crown anew.

Queen: Ever has it been thus. Since time began,
    A king has had to make his realm a fort

With sturdy walls and pretty turrets proud.
But we are young, and change drifts on the breeze.
If anyone can paint a wintry smile
Upon the face of this sore grievèd land,
It is my valorous and own dear lord.

King: I did a gardener once interrogate,
And this did he confide: that cutting grass
Increaseth growth. The faster flies the blade,
The stronger urge the shoots. So 'tis with me.
Pretenders come to plague us thick and fast.
The more I hack them down, the more they grow,
Like serpents on the foul Medusa's head.

Queen: Perhaps it is Medusa you should slay
More than the snakes she breeds and brings to life.

King: I cannot reach her. She in Flanders rests,
And spits her putrid venom from afar.
Who's there?

Enter Morton.

                Good Morton, you are welcome here.

Morton: You may not think so when you hear my news.
The bold pretender, Richard, Duke of York,
In Ireland has appeared, and raised his flag.

King (*aside*): In what form comes this insolent pretence?
I fear it bears two young and princely brows
In two-faced outrage at their taking off.
But down; I am in view, and must be firm.
What says our cousin Oxford? And brave Talbot?

Morton: Both are westward gone, and both are pledged
To bring the puppet back in iron chains.

King: Why, this is meet, this news. No frowns, my friend,
'Tis better that this quarrel comes to th' point.
Know'st thou, we have in Flanders ears and eyes,
To sow dissent and harvest treachery

Deep in the bosom of our dearest foe.
This battle will be lost before it starts.
'Twas thus I grilled the kitchen boy at Stoke,
And so I'll trim this second vagabond.
When we have plucked this avaricious thorn,
We can parade pretenders far abroad
And advertise them both before the world
As princes brought to judgment for their pride.
No man will send to know, nor ask, nor think
What fate befell those Princes in the Tower,
When we proclaim we have them in our power.
How think you, Morton? 'Tis another fork
With which we may divide the House of York.

Morton: My own poor fork was but a humble pawn
To this most bold and knightly stratagem.

King: Then go. Make all arrangements to disarm
The traitors, and our darkest fears relieve.

Exeunt.

Scene Five

The docks. A crowd gathers to see the ships arrive. Enter citizens, with Bacon and Lancelot.

First citizen: Look where he flies! Cabot! His canvas hissing with Chinese salt.

Second citizen: More likely it is Irish. Who is to say where he has been? Egypt? The Indies? How can we know? Maybe he has sailed in circles, making up stories of cannibals, sulphurous spouts and strange beasts to make his return more glorious.

Bacon: Pish, thou art septic. I do believe he has found new worlds. It is most edible.

Second citizen: Much good may they do us, when this old world furnishes us with neither love nor treasure.

Third citizen: Who needs such furnishings? Thou hast a full belly and a roof to keep the stars from winking at thy sleep. We are not kings . . .

Second citizen: No, though a king wakes with a start, and rubs his teeth as we do . . .

Bacon: I would I were a bitter sailor. I envy these exploders. But I lake not the sea.

Third citizen: Yet fond you are of its creatures. You are wild for oysters.

Bacon: So do I love the wild boar; and yet I am afeared in the florist.

First citizen: The florist? When was a boar ever loose in a florist?

Bacon: It is hime to the boar, you nancompope. It is where he lives, sharpening his tasks against the trays.

First citizen: Quiet. He comes!

Enter Cabot. He is helped on to a platform to address the crowd.

Cabot: Good people, I am from Venice, but today I am your brother. On England's part I have the ocean crossed and found new land. It is the King's land, a valley in the sea, where wolves howl through the forests. The world is smaller now, and men may pass across her waves. I think it will not be long before someone sails west and circumnavigates this globe. Perhaps it will be me – an Englishman!

First citizen: What monsters did you find?

Cabot: Whales as big as ships. White bears and giant eagles. And fish. Seas so thick with life the keel doth nudge the shoal. You can sweep them in with brooms.

The crowd cheers. Lancelot pushes forward. Cabot sees him and leaps down.

Old man! How goes it? Your compass was a marvel. For three days we saw no sky, but still your needle pointed north, and showed us the way.

Lancelot: I am glad to see you, and look forward to your news. What found ye?

Cabot: It has, as yet, no name, and none that we could see did live there. On board we called it New Found Land. Perhaps the King will name it New England.

Lancelot: Here come the King's men now.

Cabot: I'll to him presently. But first I would the Lady Anne waylay. Know'st thou where she is?

Lancelot: She is in Norfolk, it is said. But brave Giovanni, she is not for you. She has married the Duke – against her will. He is not young. Policy twisted her wishes.

Cabot: Then my hopes fall like dead leaves. At sea, in all the Atlantic storms, my thoughts foamed only for her.

Lancelot: Thus is it with kings and queens. Marriage is mere trade with them.

Cabot: I will to the King with all speed. I hope he will permit me to equip a fleet, to raise his glory still higher.

Lancelot: Your hopes, that late were dead, rise like phoenixes. The King might agree to a new venture. He has a son, Arthur. If you suggest a ship named for the Prince . . .

Cabot: My ever faithful Lancelot. If I were a king, I'd knight thee. Come.

Exeunt Cabot and Lancelot.
Enter Town Crier.

Crier: Hear ye, hear ye! Citizens and subjects of the high King, hear this most high and royal proclamation. An execution is announced on Sunday next, the fifteenth of this month, of Arthur Petticlough, for the crime of murder . . .

First citizen: Murder? Who did he kill, this Petticlough?

Crier: One of the King's falcons. For which foul crime he shall be hanged by the neck at the tenth hour . . .

Second citizen: 'Tis indeed foul, to kill fowl – if falcon do be fowl. But this is small news. Have ye not heard? Cabot is returned. He has found new land.

Bacon: He has seen eagles as big as ships. And he has been to Wales.

First citizen: No, he *saw* whales, on his ship.

Bacon. That's what I said. He voyaged all the way to Wales. So is he a Welshman, this Cabot? He sounds not English.

First citizen: He is Italian.

Bacon: A stallion? 'Tis true, he did shout himself half hoarse.

Second citizen: No matter. A brave age is at hand. There are new worlds over the horizon. For me, I would fain follow. If the King gives Cabot another ship, I will aboard.

Bacon: Very good. Necessity is the father of inflation.

Second citizen: What?

Bacon: 'Tis common sense, and most uncommon wise. Does not every man know that importunity seldom calls twace? For myself, Kent would be ocean enough.

First citizen: This man is an empty cellar. There is no meat on his words.

Crier: Am I to understand that this Cabot has discovered land in the King's name?

Bacon: You have it. And if it be not true, I am a whortleberry.

Crier: This is great news. I must about my task. What is it called, this land?

Second citizen: I think he did call it new found.

Crier: Then that is what it shall be. Hear ye! Hear ye! England's greatest sailor, Giovanni Cabot of Ludgate, hath lately returned from his adventures on the Atlantic main, and hath a new country claimed, which shall be New Found Land. Hear ye!

Exit Town Crier.

Bacon: I'll to the inn. I thirst for wine, and as at sea, 'tis first come, first served. Minstrels, play. Where is my best saddle? Heigh and high, will this life never end?

First citizen: What fresh nonsense is this?

Third citizen: How poor a piece of meat is man? His brains fly with the birds. Come!

Second citizen: Sirrah, nothing makes less sense than this man's life. Know ye not, this Bacon was a man of great lands in the time of York, but was stripped of all of his livings by the new king. He has suffered much, and we must pardon him.

Bacon: Faith, I'll do as you bid. Haul me by the nostrils, and I'll not whimper. What would you have me chop? Ah, there's a proper cut.

First citizen: Come. We'll play at being explorers, and sail for new-found supper.

Bacon: Away. No man is a highland. The early beard catches the wart. Why laugh you? You are all knives. Come.

Exeunt.

ACT IV

Scene One

A private room in the Royal Apartments. Enter the King, with Clifford.

King: Make haste and tell me all that you have found
    These recent months in Lady Margaret's halls.
    The Crown will be most grateful for your news.
    What are the blood-stained Woodvilles planning now?

Clifford: His name is Perkin Warbeck, good my lord.
    He claims to be Prince Richard, but 'tis said
    That Margaret herself once gave him milk.
    I wit not if this bastardy be true,
    But she doth dote on him, and softly mew
    As if he were her child.

King: It may be so.
    What of his countenance? Bears he the look of kings?

Clifford: He doth look fair . . . but rather pale, to me.
    Some say that he is handsome . . . but not I.
    He rides right well . . . but not in th' kingly way
    And his commanding eye pleaseth . . . not me.
    In truth he is an actor, good my lord,
    Playing at kingship. Thou art living proof
    That kings need more than velvet, gold and furs.
    They need, among the ermine, streaks of steel.
    This Warbeck is no warrior, that is sure.
    Scotland and France alike refuse him space;
    Ireland has bid him leave, and now they say
    He will in Cornwall raise his traitor's flag.

King: How many has he in his company?

Clifford: Some seven thousand soldiers bear his hopes.
    He will in Bodmin land, and thence to Exeter.

King: Which of our English noblemen
    Desire to claim this tadpole as their king?

Clifford: Fitzwater, Mountfort, D'Aubeney, and Thwaites,
    Cressener, Ratcliff, Astwood, Eaglestone.
    Others there are, but these are Warbeck's friends.

King: My spies inform me that you have been more
    Familiar with this Warbeck than is meet
    A confidant of England needs to be.

Clifford: 'Tis true he thought us excellent good friends.
    We shared a love of food, and wine, and cards
    And horses, music, deer and other sports.
    But never did I swerve from my intent
    To furnish England's crown with tidings true
    Of threats to its most rare security,
    Which now I do deliver to my king.

King: Is this your hand? A friend has shared with us
    This rebel letter from the Netherlands,
    Urging the English people to rise up
    And overthrow the true and rightful king.
    The signature is Clifford's. Is it true?

Clifford: It is my name, but this is not my hand.
    Regard these loops; this is the Flanders style.
    And this is what I feared, your majesty,
    And why I fled across the sea to bring you news.
    My enemies suspected I was not
    What I did seem, and ventured many plots
    To prove me false. I barely 'scaped their swords.

King: Most fortunate.

Clifford: Indeed.

King: Well then, brave Clifford,
Much have you staked upon our holy cause
And your reward will, as I pledged, be rich;
But quit us now, for there is much to do.

Exit Clifford. Enter Morton.

Thou heardst?

Morton: Not every letter, but enough.
It is as we did guess.

King: We must oppose
This prince, this claimant, Richard would-be fourth.
Put our plans in train. Myself I'll scourge
The roots that feed this poisoned Yorkist vine.

Morton: And what of Clifford? We do owe him much.

King: We do, and more than much he shall receive,
Most fulsomely, as true-born monarchs do,
And then, goodnight, we'll never see him more.
Inform him that he never must approach
To forty miles from our most royal house
Or he shall lose his head. It ill befits
A king to be in debt to any man.
He has betrayed his allies, and may us.
And so, to Exeter.

Morton: Before we part,
There is without the embassy from Scotland.

King: We'll see them straight.

Enter the Scottish ambassadors.

                        I bid you welcome, sirs,
And crave your pardon that I am required
Elsewhere. What brings you here?

Ambassador: A humble suit.

King: I'm fully clothed, and have no need of suits.

Ambassador: We are but timid tokens for our king,
    Who, were he here himself, should thee address
    In words more fitting to thy noble blood.
    We do, however, have a gift for thee
    Which Will Dunbar, our bard, shall here recite.

King: God's blood! A poem? Why is it that kings
    Must lend their noble ears to childish rhymes?

Bergamot: If a poem pleaseth not, then certain it is that a fog falls o'er
    the world. But a king who sleeps with dogs shall rise with fleas, and
    more flies are caught with honey than with vinegar.

Ambassador: Your servant too is most poetical.
    He too should reign among the crags and peaks
    That rise in heather clouds in Scotland's sky.

King: I'll hear your lines, but prithee, loose them fast.

Dunbar: London, thou art of all towns a *per se*.
    Sovereign of cities, seemliest in sight,
    Of high renown, great wealth and royalty;
    Of lords, and barons, and many a goodly knight;
    And most delectable lusty ladies bright;
    Of famous prelates in their holy robes;
    Of merchaunts full of substance and of might:
    London, thou art the flower of Cities all.

King: I thank your bardship well and heartily.

Dunbar: There are two further verses, good my lord.

King: Perfection wants no increase, good Dunbar,
    And what this lacks in length it doth make good
    With subtle . . . brevity. I thank thee, sirs.
    And tell your King my daughter may be his,
    When I do see that Warbeck is no friend
    Of Scotland's noble, true and honest heart.
    My Margaret is yet a babe in years,
    But if your King will wait, she shall be his.
    And so I thank you.

Ambassador: Praise your majesty!

Dunbar: I think the King delighteth not in verse.
   But art is long, and will such pains disperse.

   Exeunt.

Scene Two

Caxton's print shop. Enter Caxton, with globe.

Caxton: The world we know is changing every hour.
   Look how this toy, our planet, doth revolve,
   Passing from lustrous day to blackest night,
   With mountains, rivers, cities, deserts, seas,
   Clung fast to this old orb we once thought flat.
   Since Henry plucked the crown at Bosworth Field
   A dozen years have run their fertile course.
   Now England lies, well fed and satisfied,
   In warm and dewlapped pastures of sweet peace.
   And in the calm, life stirs and puts out shoots.
   Our ships attempt new shores, and men explore
   Brave ways to write, and paint, perform and think.
   In Italy, men versed in ink and stone
   Seek God in human shapeliness and grace.
   Columbus and Cabot, with salty hearts
   Find fresh unconquered vistas in the West,
   While brave da Gama dives beneath the Cape,
   Past hungry sharks that leap to feed on seals,
   And pads with tigers in the spice-filled East.
   The Queen spills sons and daughters like ripe fruit
   In some bewitched and melon-spangled wood,
   While Henry makes alliances and deals
   With all the lands that sometime us oppressed.
   Flanders and Burgundy, Denmark, France and Rome
   Afford him pensions to forestall his troops.
   The royal coffers swell, while rebel dogs

Whine in the Tower, growling at the pride
That prompted them to claim the throne as theirs.
A veritable Camelot we've made,
Benignly led, and grown benign ourselves,
No more a land of helmet, spur and blade,
But one where kingfishers sleep safe,
Flashing on rivers in the shade of oaks,
Their mates all furled in gauzy bliss, in nests.
Now men write free, and we do print their words,
In poems, tracts, and cunning sermons too,
And daily news of all the nation's deeds.
As here, for instance, where our history tells
Of Arthur's marriage to fair Catherine
Who sailed from Aragon bedecked in gold
With swan-drawn carriages of tropic pearl
To gild the King's glad heir. But soft . . .

Enter Town Crier.

What news?

Crier: Most solemn tidings, Master Caxton, news to stop your press.
Prepare your eyes to weep fit to drown a fleet. I'll read, and charge
you to print, in the King's name, some thousand copies. Know then
that Arthur, the King's son, is dead, carried off by plague. The
beacon that lit our happiness is dimmed. Tomorrow shall we drape
ourselves in black, and ring out bells, and make such lamentation as
we may.

Caxton: Ill met indeed. I will to work tonight.
How died he? From the pestilence, you said?
And what of his poor widow, that young Queen?
But time enough for that another day.
For now we can do naught but print, and pray.

Exeunt.

Scene Three

Bodmin. The camp of Perkin Warbeck. Enter attendants.

First attendant: The men are ready. All our stores are horsed.

Second attendant: And men do daily flock to swell our ranks.

First attendant: Suffolk awaits at Exeter with supplies.

Second attendant: And spring sends sun to speed our hopeful feet.

First attendant: I pray Prince Richard rises to this quest.
    All England lies before him, as a bank
    Of raspberries before the poacher's knife.

Second attendant: We have been long a-bed. Now we must act.

   Enter Warbeck.

Warbeck: A meet day for a march, my captains say.
    The squirrels are about, and so are we.

First attendant: You only have to say the word, my lord,
    And these fine troops you see before you now
    Will carry you to London, and the throne.

Warbeck: Cornwall delights me. I could rest awhile . . .
    But let's away. What think you: should I lead?

Second attendant: That would be brave, my lord, but first,
    Your highness might a few short words essay,
    T'inflame the hearts of soldiers bold and true.

Warbeck: Indeed. 'Tis fitting. I did so intend.
    Er . . . Men of England, and you Switzers too,
    Let England's summer pasture feel our heels.
    Little doth block our way. The King's a lamb
    Who sure will shrink from wolves as fierce as thee.
    Is this well done?

Third attendant: Most royally, my lord.
    Perhaps a rousing ending for the men?

Warbeck: Should any of us fall, the scribes will say

That we did snort like . . . camels in our time.
There plenty are who can say . . . no such thing,
So on, I pray you, on! Is this the way?

Exit Warbeck, leading his army off. The attendants are aghast.

First attendant: My hairs are all a-tremble on my neck.

Second attendant: And my poor heart, it drums with martial pride.

First attendant: He is not framed for such a reckless stir.
A snorting camel rarely bests a king.
We have not bare begun, and now I fear
We have begun to fail. What thinkest thou?

Second attendant: I too would fain we never had embarked,
But safety lies in victory. Unless . . .

First attendant: 'Tis not too late, I ween, to save ourselves.
The King will favour those who help him now.

Second attendant: 'Tis so. My rebel temper drains away.
Let's leave this doomed invasion while we may.

Exeunt, by another route.

Scene Four

Night. The Royal Apartments. Enter the King, who kneels.

King: The doctors say that Arthur is no more;
I do not, cannot, will not think it so.
Death might have sought some weaker prey to stalk,
Instead of our sweet child. Not fourteen springs
Have passed since we did greet him as our heir.
And he has yet – must I say had? – to bloom.
It is not right. Dear God, art thou a leech,
That conjures with our vows and bleeds them pale?
I have been firm, I know, in England's cause,
When naught but firmness lit the way ahead.
And one sin burns, I know, deep in thy heart,

And in mine own as well. Those princely boys,
It was no fault of theirs they had to die,
But can this be thy high and hot revenge?
If it be so, I'll henceforth none of thee.
I'll be God's gift no more. I'll use my power
To stand athwart thy purposes on earth.
I said I would do good, and I have been
Good as my word. Now I vow much more.
Virtue shall so possess this barren isle
That she shall cry for mercy to the skies,
And thou shalt shut thine ears to human pleas,
Remote in the icy wastes that hide thy will.
So come, you thought-obliterating fires
Stoke my revenge, and scald my black intent
To do such good as will affright the moon.
This is our pledge: England will weep to see
So many Christian virtues thus enforced.
Chaste will we be, and thrifty, and ill fed.
Merriment, kindness, love: I banish thee
From what is henceforth God's own blasted land,
A wilderness of thorns on which sons hang
And, cursing their stern fathers, wilt and die.
Enough. 'Tis sealed. Now listen to our prayer.
Our father, who art not in heaven, harrowed be thy name.
Thy kingdom fail, thy wisdom pale, on earth as it is in heaven.
Give us this day our daily dread. Et cetera. Amen.

Enter the Queen.

Queen: My lord, I have been seeking thee betimes.

King: Thou'dst better seek our son, who is no more.
How can it be? Our boy, our precious child,
No more. There's neither cause nor sense in this.

Queen: There neither is, my lord, nor should there be.
'Tis God's decree. Our part is to endure.

King: I am a king, and would a different part.

For kings have hollow hearts. These robes rebel.
And it is all my doing, dearest Queen;
'Tis for those hapless Princes we are chastised.
They are no more, and now our son is dead.

Queen: Oh do not blame yourself . . .

King: How can I not?
But it is wrong that you, a grieving wife,
Should my confessor be. What must I do?
I thought to rid the nation of its rage
But I am deep in blood enmired, and this
Must be my most lamentable, black reward.

Queen: Sit here, my lord, and rest your head awhile.
Lay down these rods and barbs. The Princes rose.
You acted as a king must act, 'tis true,
Not one ounce more and neither one jot less.
Be calm, my dearest husband, do not lay
The weight of this misfortune on yourself.
Our son was killed by pestilence, not God,
And it is not for us to try his grace.

King (*aside*): See how the world imagines not my crime.
Thou art too fine and noble, good my Queen.
How can'st thou sit so still, and so serene
When heav'n throws down such heavy bolts as this?

Queen: 'Tis inward, all my bitterness, my lord,
Like as the fumarole, swollen with molten fire,
Seems, from afar, as pale and cold as snow.
So 'tis with me. My outward frostiness
Is outward show. But oh, my soul, it seethes
And shakes as water when it 'gins to boil.

King: Much hast thou borne. Thou art too good a queen.

Queen: Too weak, methinks, and lacking nature's art
To bear this deep and diabolic cut.
'Tis best I dwell not on it, for I know

That if I let one drop of my great grief
Rise to the surface, it will swamp me quite.
The only truth is: it cannot be true.
Arthur is gone; he'll never smile no more
Nor lay his head on his poor mother's arm.
I doubt me much that any woman's heart
Could bear so great a loss, and I cannot.
My boy. My prince. Oh . . .

She falls.

King: Dear Lord. Sweet Jesu! Help! Help! Soft. Be still.

Enter attendants.

The Queen's unwell; convey her to her bed,
And, pray you, let your feet ignite the stones
To fetch the surgeons here. Elizabeth!
She answers not! Elizabeth! No sound.
She is not dead. She sleeps. There. Help, I say!

Queen: Be not so troubled. I am peaceful now.
Like as the nervous traveller who, embarked,
Renounces care and bids her soul be still.
Adieu, my dearest spouse and worthy lord!
The faithful love, that both of us did hold
In marriage and in peaceable concord
For many happy years upon this throne
I here restore to thy most loyal breast.
Into thy gentle hands my love I place
To be bestowed on those that yet remain.
Till now thou took'st the father's part alone,
The mother's part I now must thee bequeath.
So go, good husband. Why is it so dark?

*Enter physician. He feels the Queen's pulse and neck, gestures to the
attendants to bear her away.*

King: It cannot be. My son is sacrificed.
And now you stoop to seize my treasured Queen.

Dear God, if she awakes not from this swoon
I'll do . . . I know not what . . . such hellish deeds
As strong men's hearts shall shrivel to believe.

Exit.

Scene Five

*Margaret's court in Flanders. Enter Margaret, Lady Devonshire and
a courtier.*

Courtier: Methinks the man is come. Send him in straight!
We are a-dagger for the news he brings.

Enter Messenger.

Margaret: I will endure no courtesy: what word?

Messenger: The cause is lost. The Claimant is unhorsed,
Dragged naked through the vilest London streets,
And mobbed by all the squalid multitude,
He now awaits his sentence in the Tower.

Margaret: Then dreams, like clay, dissolve into the sea.
There'll be no other claimants. Let's away.

Exit Messenger.

Lady Devonshire: 'Twas all in vain – the oyster bore no pearl.

Margaret: And yet, I think this hand has one more die.
I'll roll it now. My lady Devonshire,
That sometime did prepare our royal bed,
Thou hast two comely sons. Right fair they are
With golden curls and creamy brows.

Lady Devonshire: 'Tis so.

Margaret: To England, go. There, kneel before the King,
Say you'll have none of us, and that you seek
A courtly favour for your noble sons.
Dress them in princely robes. They shall do well.

If, as I do believe, this King has killed
The princes of our blood, then this play might
Unseat his mind, and swift unhinge it quite.

Lady Devonshire: It shall be done, my lady and my Queen.
A dog once burned doth fear the flame, I know.
I'll take my boys, and see what fate unfolds.

Exeunt.

Scene Six

Dawn. The docks. Enter citizens.

First citizen: The sun has passed behind the clouds, and I know not when we shall see bright skies again.

Second citizen: There's plague abroad. The King's own son has been taken, and the Queen heart has snapped like a twig, they say.

First citizen: The fish have fled the Thames, and Kentish apples refuse to blossom.

Second citizen: 'Tis ever thus when princes die. Ships cannot leave the river, their sails flap listless on a glassy flood. Clouds hang heavy o'er the town.

First citizen: I heard they found stones in the eyes of the hyena. Carrion rises to meet the crow. And the hungry leopard pines in his corner. Worse may be to come.

Second citizen: He doth have other sons.

First citizen: But none are named for Arthur, King of the Britons. This was the first-born, the golden fountain from which we all might drink.

Third citizen: I would not be Warbeck. He has not yet been punished.

Second citizen: I saw the Claimant as he marched through London. They lashed him like a dog. The crowd did jeer and pelt him with bad fruit. From upper casements the citizens threw slop. He bore it steadily, but looked afeared.

First citizen: I blame him not. They say his friends abandoned him.

Second citizen: They gave him up like a pig swaddled for slaughter.

First citizen: The King will want his vengeance.

Second citizen: He wanted a confession first. Hast read the proclamation? Look at this. Warbeck is the son of a ferryman in the nether land. His own tongue admits it.

First citizen: Else it had been cut out. Maybe he truly is the Prince.

Second citizen: Say not such things. The King has grown mistrustful, and his spies are everywhere. Were I one, you might pay for such words.

First citizen: We used to long for a firm ruler. Now we have one. The firmness may pinch betimes.

A bell sounds. Enter Bacon.

Second citizen: And here come fresh chops from the slaughterhouse. Good morrow, Signor Back.

Bacon: What is that ringing? If any man here bears the name Beacon, sure he shall hang for it.

First citizen: It tolls from the Tower. I fear me much the Queen is dead.

Bacon: Then sure she is already an angle, in heaven. I love not the King who robbed me of my servants and horses, but she was a nable lody.

Second citizen: The King will thirst for revenge, as you said.

Bacon: The cobbler always wears the worst shoes.

First citizen: What say you?

Second citizen: Yet they live not on any shoestring.

Bacon: This Warbeck was a composter. But look: how are the flighty fallen?

First citizen: Well said, old friend. England can endure all these blows while it still kicks forth nonsense such as this.

Bacon: I endover to give sophistication. And I have not yet broken my fast.

Second citizen: Let's find the man an oyster. He is a fallen star, and light begins to fail him.

First citizen: I know not if there are any to be had. I heard the beds were dry.

Bacon: What, shall we all go oysterless? Then truly night is come at daybreak.

Exeunt.

ACT V

Scene One

The Royal Court. Enter the King, Dudley, Empson, and courtiers.

Dudley: God save your highness.

Empson: Blessings on your crown.

Dudley: And on your noble heart. 'Tis a black time.

Empson: And yet there are some matters we must heed.

Dudley: Though none so dire as your emergencies.

Empson: These trifles should not long detain—

King: Where's Morton?

Dudley: The Cardinal is not himself today.

Empson: A fever, and he charged me to propose—

King: A fever, did you say?

Dudley: I did, my lord.

Empson: He gave me all these papers, majesty.
   Only your royal signature divides
   These simple words from high, historic deeds.

King: Pass me my seal. I'll stamp upon these sheets.

Empson: Perhaps your highness might peruse the list
   Before imprinting your authority.

King: Trouble me not with lists. I will not lean.

Dudley: These are the men, most gracious majesty,

Who proffered friendship to the rank pretence.
Worsley and Mountford, Willoughby and Flint;
Anthony de la Forsa, who did once
Right lovingly defend his king in France;
Savage and Debenham, Cumbermere and Bolt.
There are some ninety here, my gracious lord . . .

King: They all are dead. I do command them so.
They made the false seem true, the true seem false,
And so, goodnight. Put all their heads on stakes.
Warbeck and Warwick, they will this night hang.

Empson: You would not have them tried, my lord?

King: Not I.
They've tried our patience hard and long enough.

Empson: What of this man named here, your majesty?
His name is Bagnall, and his crime, misprision.
Some twenty merchants, it is here alleged,
Supplied provisions to the invading force.
It is not certain that they had a sense
How grim a mouth they fed . . .

King: Remove their tongues.
And have it known throughout this happy land
That any crime committed on this day
Shall seem to us high treason, and shall bear
The highest penalty the Crown can give.

Dudley: Some of these men have fled to sanctuary
In sacred places of great holiness . . .

King: Then tear them out. No sanctuary is safe
From our prodigious justice on this day.
And all who seek a godly hiding place
Shall have a brand upon their thumb embossed.
God did not think to shield my son from harm.
Why should these vultures shelter 'neath his cloak?

Dudley: It shall be as you say, most noble king.

This purge but seemeth cruel . . .

Enter Lady Devonshire, with her two sons.

King (*aside*): Great hell! These devil's pups do freeze all thought.
They've 'scaped their kennels in the nether world
Where I did roughly house them, and come thence,
Dripping with accusations fell and pale,
To stalk our rest. Madam, what do you seek?

Empson: See how he starts, as if an evil ghost
Had come to mock our feast.

Dudley: I know not why,
But in our noble sovereign I smell fear.

The two boys move forward and kneel before the King.

King (*aside*): Bend not your gentle necks, lest I do strike.
Madam, your sons do honour to our house.

Lady Devonshire: Perhaps this news will physic you, my lord.
We three are from the Nether country come,
And dare to hope that we might yet ascend
To some position close to England's heart.

King (*aside*): Fly hence, you feathered fox! If I be goose,
I yet have wings. I'll not be glutted! Vaunt!

Lady Devonshire: What means his majesty?

Dudley: I cannot say.

King (*aside*): Paint me a Theseus, for that I have slain
The bloody Minotaur!

Dudley: Forgive us, pray.
He must have surfeited on some strange fruit.
Do not be vexed. He'll hear your suit anon.

Lady Devonshire(*aside*): It is as we supposed. His conscience
writhes.
I'll back to Flanders ere his will revives.

Exeunt Lady Devonshire and the boys, ushered out by courtiers.

King: Where were we?

Dudley: Branding thumbs and setting fines.

King: Ah yes. And add, that any man of verse
   Inclined to add the white rose to his poesy,
   Shall have his fingers hacked off with a blade.
   Why look'st thou green? Shall we not justice have?

Dudley: It shall be done.

King: And so: to other doings.
   I would debate with both of thee the means
   Whereby our sceptre can impose its weight
   In dues and levies on our citizens.
   My predecessor monarchs, spendthrifts all,
   Have made themselves mere servants of the state
   By wasting all its treasure. England has changed.
   This crown we hold shall threadbare be no more.
   Come Empson, Dudley – what have we devised?

Dudley: We could revive the ancient feudal dues . . .

Empson: And might reap profits in a handsome way
   By introducing fines for all misdeeds
   As, leaving windows open in the night
   And letting cattle stray upon the road.

Dudley: Or failing to observe the quarantine.

Empson: And taking too much water from the well.

Dudley: We could upon a stroke ban certain books
   And fine all those who have a copy scanned.

King: I do approve all these, and more besides.
   I bid you, double all the tolls and tax
   Laden on salt and wine, and cheese and tin.

Dudley: They'll like not that in Cornwall, good my lord,
   Where they already harbour much dismay
   At customs raised for soldiers in the North.

King: Let Cornwall into Irish waters sink.
　　'Tis far from here, and has opposed us thrice.
　　And let us dedicate ourselves to this great task:
　　To make this English throne the richest far
　　In all the certain world. Sell all our lands in France,
　　Save Calais, and inform our noble friends
　　That they have no more need of knightly troops.
　　Instead of keeping soldiers for our use
　　They can one tithe of all their income hand
　　Into our treasury.

Empson: 　　　　　　It shall be done.
　　Your highness may recall a thought we had
　　One time, concerning foreigners.

King: 　　　　　　　　　　I do.
　　We'll double-tax them all. 'Tis only right.
　　And let us also raise the rent on lands
　　We did ourselves perforce appropriate
　　After we slew the hunchback king in war.
　　Is't right that subjects richer grow than me?
　　Are kings obliged to pander for their bread?
　　These men should share a portion of their fat
　　To guarantee the welfare of their liege.

Dudley: What of the Spanish dowry?

King: 　　　　　　　　　　I care not.
　　This prize of Arthur's now belongs to us.
　　Two hundred thousand crowns — 'tis England's now.
　　It is most small of them to seek it back
　　Now Arthur's . . . But no more of this. Away.
　　We shall return to this another day.

Dudley: There is one other task, your majesty.
　　Your daughter Margaret awaits your grace.
　　She is betrothed by you to Edinburgh
　　And must go north.

King: 　　　　　　I will to her anon.

I would I could protect her from this fate,
For I am but a soul-sore, shipwrecked fool,
Who must neglect his most devoted hopes,
And do what England deems the rightful thing.
She is fourteen, my mother's tender age
When she brought me to life. 'Tis very young.

Dudley (aside): Saw you the King? His wits unravelled quite?

Empson: It was those boys dropped brimstone on his soul.

Dudley: I dare not say what this may signify.
When kings are ruled by spleen, honour is dumb.

Exeunt Dudley and Empson.
Enter Bergamot.

King: How now? I prithee, seek not to amuse
Your King today; he is not like to smile.

Bergamot: We are never so thirsty as when the well is dry. And a net catches more than fish. What would you?

King: Solitude.

Bergamot: I leave you with a pair of pretty thoughts. A man who keeps company with wolves will sure howl at the stars. And even on the longest day the sun will set.

King: Whatever you say. Thou art too deep for me. Here's a farthing. Fare thee well.

Exit Bergamot.

I must know less than any man alive
How best to live deprived of those I love.
But this I know full well: in wealth lies power.
No army ever joined that was as strong
As boxes armed with bonds of minted gold.
Henceforth shall money be my only god,
My hollow life I dedicate to gold,
With resolution mighty as an oak.
Yet it is not for me I make this pact.

Opulent pleasures I this day renounce;
No furs shall clad our humble kingly form;
No fatted goose, no Frankish wine I'll taste.
I will a hermit's life pursue, while we
Wax rich and strong as any nation yet.
'Tis strange. Through yonder window I perceive
Fleet larks against the sky, while heaven's coin
Drips radiance on these our treasured stones.
The horses snort and stamp their rapid feet,
And plunge their heads in water cold as frost,
While I this paradise do now despoil
With executions that must rend the skies
With bitter tears and heaven-piercing screams.
And I care less than naught. 'Tis one to me.
I would to Wales, and leave this royal fate
That I did tussle for, and now do hate.

Exit.

Scene Two

The royal gardens. Enter two gamekeepers, pushing a cart piled high with carcasses.

First gamekeeper: The young prince is keen as a cat. He means to leave not a deer alive.

Second gamekeeper: Even the Duke could not check his arrows. The does were like the French chevaliers at Agincourt when the blizzard fell.

First gamekeeper: He did miss one.

Second gamekeeper: And fell to such a fury, he slew four more in pure vengeance.

First gamekeeper: His father is more temperate. His brother was too, bless his eyes. I do fear me what kind of king this Henry will prove, if he learns not to bind his mood. I urged caution, and the look in his eyes . . . I thought he meant to butcher *me*.

Second gamekeeper: He is yet young.

Enter Prince Henry.

Prince Henry: My thanks, good friends. Here's shillings for your
    care,
  And care I urge on thee, if e'er again
  You counsel me that I restrain my bow.
  Your future king will not be cautioned thus.
  The game is his, and he will fly at will,
  Or you *will* feel the fury of his *will*.
  Why look ye now so pale? 'Tis said in jest.
  Where is it writ that princes not amuse?

Exeunt gamekeepers.
Enter Dudley.

  Good afternoon, good sir, I am right glad
  To see you here today. How stands the kingdom?

Dudley: Much as it stood this morning, good my lord,
  When you did take your breakfast with the King.

Prince Henry: Take care, good Dudley, that you do not vex
  A man who one day might your master be,
  And that right soon, if all we hear is true.

Dudley: Be mindful what you speak of, gentle Prince.
  The King has suffered much, but he is strong
  And yet has much to do.

Prince Henry: Long may he thrive!
  But of our sister Catherine what's the news?
  Is't true what men are saying, that in Spain
  They seek her back, and with her wedding gift?
  I would not be unseemly, but perhaps
  I might the lady wed. She is most fresh.

Dudley: Your father is avowed against the match.
  Why do you grieve him so?

Prince Henry: 'Tis I who grieve.

I have a mother and a brother lost.
Why should I lose a wife so richly left
Who glances chestnut Spanish eyes at me?

Dudley: I am your humble servant ever, sir,
But in this wise I urge you to have care.
You will be king: no one shall say thee nay.
It falls to me to counsel some restraint.
The crown is rich and peaceable, and strong.
Study your father's ways. Despise him not,
And know that it is irksome to be king.

Exit Dudley.

Prince Henry: This Dudley lacks all courtesy; I know
That men do hate him for the care he takes
To blight their hopes with taxes, dues and fines.
Restraint! 'Twas much restraint in me to spare
His oily life. 'Tis he who should have care;
This find-fault – I shall make him drink his stale.
When I am king, I'll earn the people's love
By stopping his rude mouth. Till then I'll wait
And let him fill the coffers of the throne
With treasure fit to swell and amplify
Our royal role. In future we'll be bold,
And drape this throne of England with our gold.

Exit.

Scene Three

The King's private apartment. The King sits at his desk.

King: Mine eyes are fading. Soon they will be dust,
Like all my hopes that once were lit with stars.
My people see a king in jewelled robes
But mine's a frozen wilderness of loss,
Confined in all the luxury of state.
I once had seven children wreathed in smiles;

Three now remain, the rest with worms do dwell,
And dead my dearest wife, Elizabeth,
And dead my Morton, my most trusted friend.
Good Stanley's traitorous head I have removed.
The Pope himself's no more, and old Diaz,
Nimble explorer of the southern seas.
All done, all spent, all passed into the night
While I, the King, see less with every dawn.

Enter Dudley and Empson.

Dudley: The King of Scotland doth await reply.
Wilt thou attend thy daughter's wedding feast?
If so, we must some preparations make.

King: It is too far. I'll not away from court.

Empson: Of course your highness never could absent
Himself from London on St Dunstan's Day.

King: I care not for St Dunstan, nor his day.
Speak of th' Exchequer. Bring my monkey here.

Enter Prince Henry, at the outer wall.

Prince Henry: My father does not think it meet or fit
That I attend these sessions of the court.
When I did ask to be admitted here
He sneered at my ambition and did frown,
And doubt him that the tournament could spare
My ever royal presence, bade me leave.
I blushed with rage to be so harsh described.
He loves me not; and sees in me no more
Than tainted ghosts of his more favoured child.
I know he thinks me frivolous and vain
And so I am, and so I shall remain.
I am no Arthur, and I would not be
Despite my father's wish that I be he.
Here is the place. I'll climb this friendly beech
And seek my own plenipotence on high.

Dudley: The annual income to the Crown is now
   One hundred forty-seven thousand pounds

Empson: 'Tis almost thrice the sum that greeted you
   When you in kingship were at first ensconced.

King: 'Tis not enough; there's more that I would do.
   Money is power; power flows from wealth.
   Kings without coin are tigers without claws.

Dudley: The King is wise, and for these royal ends
   We have devised new rakes and sharper scythes
   With which to harvest even riper wheat.
   Windows shall all be taxed, each pane of glass
   On pain of death shall several sovereigns yield.
   The Cornish rebels, *infelicissimi*,
   Still must repent the error of their ways
   That they did cheer the claimant, and the lands
   Of those whose execution we have sworn
   Shall rendered be unto the royal purse.
   The killing of a beast who's great with calf
   Shall earn, in fine, the price of two grown cows.

Empson: We have another scheme, your majesty,
   Concerning stocks where villagers are held.
   Freedom from pain and scorn can now be bought
   In shillings for the King, and to that end
   The sentences in shame have been increased.

Prince Henry (*aloft*): I like these simpletons who do forget
   Whose coffers they are filling with these acts.
   I'll be the richest king in Christendom,
   No prince or pope of Europe shall gainsay
   My sovereignty when I assume the throne,
   As very soon I may; and must; and will.

King: What say the people of these penalties?

Empson: They love them, good my lord, as they love thee.

King: If this be true, then Jack's a gentleman.

Dudley: They love them not, your highness, but their pride
    Is stirred by what their painful duties buy.
    This sailor, this Cabot, they do revere
    For his adventures on the western seas,
    And Caxton, and good Skelton, and the bears.
    They see a kingdom well trimmed for a storm.
    They love thee not, but kingship is not framed
    To be adored, but rather, to be feared.

King: And juggled with by reckless destiny.
    I thank you, sirs, and bid you leave us now.

Exeunt Dudley and Empson. The King opens a chest and lifts out a box.

How now, my priceless babies; come and play.
Dance in the light that flows through this pale glass.
Rubies and sapphires, glitter on this cloth,
Permit a king to feast his fading eyes
On thy imperishable beauties rare.
What's that! Who's there?

Prince Henry (aloft):   What kind of king is this,
    Who treats his gems like pets, to dandle them
    As kittens, mice or foolish hummingbirds,
    And scrabbles in the dirt to do them praise?
    A king must be an eagle, not a vole,
    Worming between dim hedgerows in the dark.
    When I put on the crown I'll bear myself
    As kings were used to in the knightly days,
    And all the world shall marvel at our strength,
    And native pride shall stir in every breast.
    He is my father, yet he stoops too low.
    I would I did not love and hate him so.

King: Who's there? Away! Thou miscreant! Be gone!
    'Twas nought but my poor conscience – and my shame.
    Away, my pretty nothings, back to sleep,
    And know that thou art loved, and by a king,

A king who covets what his subjects hate,
And would most willingly the yoke
Of servitude exchange for this high place.
I had a son well made to be a king,
And now I am a prisoner, condemn'd
To see what I have built to ruin fall.
Is this my final punishment, that I
Should spurn my second son, this lustful boy,
This cuckoo who supplants the royal place
That was for tender Arthur well prepared,
Malign and cruel, reckless, greedy, base.
A braggart and a bully and a cheat?
I know he seeks my treasure: that is sure,
And I cannot deny him: it is his.
I am the King, but I do lack the right
To choose my royal heir. If I do block
My own son's claim, he'd stake it with the sword,
And England would in bloody manner fall
To civil war again. What would that serve?
We kings, we are the playthings of the gods.
They tempt us with the promise of command
And then torment and harry us as slaves.
I hate thee, Lord, for framing *me* to hate
My own dear child, and fear what he will bring.
But I am chained to this.

Exit the King.

Prince Henry: Didst hear?
My father damns his son, his prince, his heir,
Flesh of his flesh, and child of his dear Queen.
I have been true betimes. If war he seeks,
War he shall have. He's old. He's weak. He's tired.
The comet that has lit these winter months
Will soon behind the cold horizon fall.
A meteor is rising. It is I,
And none shall brook me. As for Catherine,

She will a queen yet be, whate'er her mind.
And for this malt-horse, his long day is done.
I would be his successor, not his son.

Exit.

Scene Four

Outside an inn at the docks. Enter the three citizens.

First citizen: The King has not been seen for months. They say he is frail withal.

Second citizen: 'Tis something more than frailty. Sorrow has turned to rage within his breast, like milk that has soured on the stoop. He starts at shadows.

Third citizen: Something pricks his honour. They say that all the things he was wont to like, jugglers and wrestlers, and eaters of live coals, today they please him not.

Second citizen: He hath his luxury still. The women say that in his rooms there is one servant to smooth his sheets, another to fold them, yet another to sprinkle them with rose petals and holy water. The King's law is strict: the sprinkler may not fold.

First citizen: He is a well-ordered man.

Second citizen: I pray that one night before I die, just one, I will lie on sheets.

Third citizen: 'Twere better to tell the truth, where'er thou liest.

First citizen: 'Tis possible the King will languish even unto his death. I pray the succession will hold. The prince seems royal, but he is young.

Second citizen: 'Tis true the King is not well. His eyes are weak, and he has no taste for company that is not gold or silver.

Third citizen: This is the change that came upon him with the death of his son. He never has recovered his spirits since.

First citizen: And then his Queen.

Second citizen: And our Queen too. We all did much lament and grieve her end.

Third citizen: And now the only thing he loves is his box of gems.

Second citizen: When the apartment at Sheen Palace caught fire, the King cared for naught but his jewels. My jewels! My jewels! Such was his only cry. The tapestries and paintings, rugs and plate, and all the royal papers . . . he cared not for these. 'Twas rubies he cried for, rubies most rare, the colour of sunset or of blood.

First citizen: The Crier told me once that the bill for the King's jewels was thirty thousand pounds a year, more than ever we shall see or dream of, should we live to be sixty. And more, he said that no ordinary man could touch them with common fingers – the King has pearls the size of cherries, all wrapped in muslin cloth like babes.

Second citizen: They say he has six million in gold, and never spends a penny.

First citizen: And yet he never sleeps. Some say that late at night, when the city is dark, the lamp in the King's rooms glimmers the while. He doth experiment with alchemy, and seeks, with strange powders, to make gold from iron horseshoes.

Second citizen: 'Tis natural. If a commoner may be a king, why should not gold be conjured from base metal?

First citizen: He ever did like money. And now the country hangs its head as weary as a chained bear, groaning under the weight of the King's taxes.

Second citizen: 'Tis not the King, but his cruel advisers, the Lords Dudley and Empson. They are fiends for tax.

Third citizen: What know you of the King's son, Harry?

Second citizen: He is large. When he is king, oh Lord, there will be sport aplenty.

First citizen: He means to squander his father's store. Meanwhile, the keepers say that the King still loves his menagerie, and keeps a monkey by him all the time.

Third citizen: I saw it once: it had a white face and whiskers. The King kept it in a leather collar on a chain. One day it slipped free and tore up the royal books.

First citizen: He used to like dancing bears, too. In Oxford once, I saw him give the bear ward five shillings, so taken was he with the beast.

First citizen: 'Tis sad, how the cares of kingship weigh upon him.

Second citizen: 'Tis a fine day when we who toil to furnish the King with our pennies shed salt tears for his monkey.

Enter Bacon with Town Crier.

Third citizen: Ah, good morrow, gentle swine.

Bacon: I count no morning fine that does not include meat. What is this great fuffle?

First citizen: Welcome to our Parliament. How like you the King?

Bacon: The King lakes me not. He has dammed all my ponds.

Second citizen: And if he rules us as he has ruled you, we too shall be damned.

Crier: Hear ye! Hear ye! Item: Sir Nicholas Vaux, forfeit, the sum of nine thousand marks, for keeping too many horses . . . Item: Mr Simon Simmes, a haberdasher of Ludgate, forfeit, one hundred marks, for insulting the Queen . . .

Second citizen: On very thin cause. I know this Simmes; he is no ruffian.

Crier: Item: Hawkyns, a draper, one hundred marks, for stealing bread. Item: the Abbot of Furness, five hundred marks, in consideration of which he is to be pardoned . . .

Second citizen: And so it goes with us. We are all in the King's most humble debt, and he must have his portion, though he needs it not.

Bacon: Dost grumble, knave? Wouldst thou not give the King thy testoons? Hie thee to Kent. There is fine land there fit for thieving.

First citizen: I will, and very gladly. Come . . .

Third citizen: I would away from here. I see clouds rearing like horsemen in the sky ahead. There will be squalls ere long.

Enter Cabot, accompanied by three small Indians, clad in skins, with straight, black long hair and carrying brazil-wood bows.

Second citizen: Look who comes here, dressed in rare silks, his sails swollen with royal wind. And what are these creatures at his side?

Cabot: I will to sea, and have much need of men. The King has released prisoners to man my fleet, but I need more. Linger not here in idleness! Sail with me! Together we will make new maps, and walk in undiscovered lands where white bears roll on the ice, and birds do swim like seals, and trees flow with sweet sap. Come, men of England, where are your adventurers now? The ships await. Take axes to the ropes that bind you to this shore and soar like hawks with me, into the blue.

First citizen: Who are these wild boys, Signor?

Cabot: These men are Indians, from the tribes who live in the New Found Land. I brought them here to meet the King. Now I shall take them home.

The crowd presses in for a closer look.

Beware. Their bows may look like toys, but they can knock a squirrel out of his tree. But who is with me? Fail not the tide. Bring astrolabes and nocturnals, almanacs and cross-staffs. We leave tonight. A new world beckons.

Exeunt Cabot and the Indians, followed by a few men.

Second citizen: Very inspiring. But I'll not to sea.

Third citizen: Take this, and this, and keep them for my sake. I will to China with this windy navigator. Farewell. God save this land, and all who sail in her.

Exit third citizen.

Bacon: I too would sail with thee, and raise myself in fortune, but I cannot leave my gardens.

First citizen: The times are disarranged, when some men try for the end of the world, while others pine for gardens that o'ergrow their wits.

Second citizen: The King must wake, or his kingdom will faint beneath him like a horse without water.

First citizen: 'Tis true, our fountain has run dry.

Bacon: I care not for mountains – my heart aches rather for green fields and chalky streams. But I do have most fond care for salami.

First citizen: And also for those other worthy knights: Sir Prise, Sir Vivor, sweet Sir Lyver and mighty Sir Cumference. But look, who comes here?

Enter Anne.

Anne: Excuse me, gentle sir, while I entreat
Your patient ear and gen'rous breast awhile.
I seek the noble seaman, brave Cabot.
He slips the shore tonight, with canvas taut
Against the breeze that flows across the waves.

First citizen: 'Tis true then, what they say, that lords and ladies have poetic souls.

Bacon: Who here addresses me in simple lines?
Who dares to speak in tongues of former times?

Anne: I wish to bid Signor Cabot farewell.
Take pity on a fragile woman's heart,
And guide me to his side, that this sad wretch
Can speed him off with royal blessing sweet.

First citizen: He went that way, my lady, towards the ships whose masts you can see. Look how they rock against the clouds, sheets tense against the wind.

Anne: I thank thee. Thou art kind. Here is a sovereign,
  'Tis yours if you will only lead me there.
  I may have served the kingdom, but my life
  Would happy be were I another's wife.

First citizen: This is the way, my lady. Keep close. There are cutpurses
  enough, but they shall trouble you naught. Else they shall feel my
  vengeance. Come, away.

  Exeunt Anne and first citizen.

Bacon (*aside*): And do not trip, for none shall catch you if you fall. Oh,
  this world's heart is a pound of flesh that wants pepper, and a broken
  one tastes as good as a proud one, or I'm no butcher. And so we men
  are offal, to be weighed in the scales and sold as fodder.

Second citizen: What ails you, friend – are you not hungry?

Bacon: Praise the Lord, I have no children.

  Exeunt.

Scene Five

The King's private room in Richmond Palace. Enter the King.

King: I have instructed them to bring me here
  To Richmond, which doth owe its name to me,
  And I have neither fancy nor desire
  To stir from this sweet river ere I die.
  Yet would I do some good before I part.
  (*writing*) I hereby cancel all recognisance
  Imposed on our authority till now,
  And amnesties I'll grant to those good men
  Unjustly rotting in our royal gaols.
  And God, I know that I have baited thee
  With cruel acts and edicts pitiless,
  But I will raise a chapel in thy name
  At Westminster in honour of my son.
  Who's there?

Enter Prince Henry.

Prince Henry: Good father, how goes it with thee?
I have a rare and dainty sweetmeat made
With nuts, molasses, honey and warm cream.
'Tis very fine. A nectar for the soul.

King: What would you? There is work that I must do.

Prince Henry: I know thou thinkest little of thine heir,
But kingship sought I not, and I, like thee,
Do wish that Arthur had not fallen so.
But if the throne is what my fate decrees,
I needs must study what a king should do,
And where should I for wisdom look
But to my father, now and in this place?

King: Fine words, my son. Someone has taught you well.

Prince Henry: Thou dost but praise thyself, for it is thee.

King: Then know, since you are in this giving mood,
That this I ask: wed not fair Catherine.
I swear – this is no plea, but my command –
She was your brother's bride. It shall not be.
You must to Austria cleave. For England's sake
This child of Aragon myself must take.

Prince Henry (*aside*): Snakes and wormwood! Hell will stoke its
    fires
To see a father swive his son's betrothed!
This shall not stand – I know not how. But, soft . . .
(*to King*) I would say yea to all that you beseech,
But this I cannot swear to. 'Tis too late.
I have already asked her. She is kind
And smiled most warmly on my wedding suit.
She will become my lady . . . and my Queen.

King: Put not your private promptings in the van.
Your wedding is an act of policy.
Bind England to the gentle Hapsburg cause.

Prince Henry: In this I cannot act the royal knave;
　My heart is Catherine's. She shall be my Queen.

King: Then all your father's curses fall upon
　This union, for it cannot come to good!
　Barren you'll be of sons, and your reward
　Shall be a kingdom riven in bitter schism.

Prince Henry: Prithee desist, good father. Thou art tired.
　Take now thy rest, and do not agitate
　Thy noble soul with trivial complaints.

King: 'Tis true. 'Tis true. I'm sorry for my wrath.
　'Tis age and kingship that thus cloud my sight.
　Forgive me, Harry.

Prince Henry:　　　　Perished be the thought
　That ever thou a pardon seek'st from me.
　Take my hand. Revive thy strength awhile.
　And eat this cake, whose sweetness is for thee.
　And so I'll leave thee now. When I return,
　Thou'lt teach me kingship. I have much to learn.
　(*aside*) Be still, my leaping heart, and know thy place.
　I swear that I could crush him for his crown
　But I am not of age. I shall be merciful.
　And still he eats, and so my hopes arise.
　How goes the saying – out of sweetness, strength?

Exit Prince Henry.

King: It seems that I have much mistook my son.
　Kindness and gentleness attend him now
　And he shall need them both, these courtiers firm,
　For England is a deep and treacherous marsh.
　At least he'll start with treasure. Gold is force
　And he'll have both – I pray he use them well.
　This cream is rich indeed. I feel as faint
　And limp as flags on hot and windless days.
　Where is my water? Servants! Where's my cup?

Enter servant with a gift. It is a brand-new invention: a globe. The King spins it feebly.

A drink, I pray you. Even kings do thirst.
Yes, yes. And leave us now. I like this ball.
When I was young I thought the land was flat
And that the world had edges, like a field.
But now it seems we live upon this sphere,
Which men do circle in their wooden ships.
I have too little ventured on these seas.
Look at these rare and oceanic names.
Venezuela – little Venice – there!
And Vera Cruz – the one and only cross.
But Henry is not present on this globe.
Richmond alone, this seat upon the Thames,
Shall bear my title into future years.
I should much more have done. 'Tis now too late.
My eyes grow heavy. I will rest awhile,
And think . . . and dream . . . of Arthur . . . oh, my heart.

Enter Prince Henry.

Prince Henry: This sleep he sleeps is not yet endless sleep.
He will awake. Or will he? What if I
This cushion took and pressed upon his face?
A moment's work is all it would require.
And would it be a crime to lend this hand
To work that Nature sure intends to do?
To kill a child is murder, but to nurse
A dying man to death can be no sin.
But why should I with murder thus be blight?
Too many kings have gained the throne by force,
And paid most foully for their bitter crime.
I'll none of it; the crown will soon be mine
Without my stir. And yet, if he should sleep . . .
(*Sees the King's crown*) How now, you royal bauble, band of
    gold?
Love you your king? Then know that this my head

413

Will soon play pillow to your majesty.
Soft now. It glows, and sits right fair on me.
Angels and choirs . . .

King (sits up abruptly and grasps Henry's arm): I sleep not, and I hear!
I'll have your head for these most treasonous thoughts.

Prince Henry (snatches pillow and presses down on the King's face):
You will not! Father! Down! I'll not be hanged
For something I did not intend to do.
Be bold . . . Be still . . . He struggles yet . . . Oh God!
I did not seek this. It is fortune's slaves
That urge this deed upon us, not ourselves.
Oh heav'n, be still! I cannot spare thee now.
Thou should'st have slept awhile, and been secure.
'Tis done. He sleeps, and never shall awake.
And God, thou seest that innocent am I
Of this foul deed that he did press me to.
I loved him, though he ever me despised,
And his last gift was thus to force my hand.
He lies not as he was. 'Twas thus.
And thus, and so, and thus. And so 'tis done.
I'll take my leave, and well I do believe,
How strange a thing 'twill be to be a king.

A long pause. The King lies still. A servant enters. Prince Henry hides.

Servant: The Prince commanded me not to come into the chamber, that
I should let the King rest in peace, but I fear the King much if he
should lack water. There. I will creep on tiptoe and none shall know
that I was here.

Prince Henry: What dost thou in this place? Did I not bid . . . ?
No matter, I have business with the King.
Your highness! Majesty! (*Shakes him.*) Oh, God in heaven!
Murder! Oh help! Guards! Come! The King is dead!

Enter guards, running, and attendants.

Prince Henry: Fetter this man! I found him in the room

When I did come for conference with the King.
I fear me what foul business he has played.
Escort him to the Tower. Take him hence!

Exeunt guards with the servant (shouting 'No! No!').

I swear I know not now what must be done.
Send for the Earl of Dudley; Empson too.
Inform our ministers and our noblemen
That our dear King is dead. And since I may
Have been too hasty, send for doctors straight.
To them shall fall the heavy task to say
What happened in this room. I never thought
That I would cease to mourn my mother's death,
But I am glad she did not witness this.
He was a king of kings. And so, go to't.

Exeunt all but Prince Henry.

And so this fruit doth fall into my hand.
My father was an honest man, but kings
Want more than honesty: they need wings.
And though King Henry patient was, and just
His reputation rests with me, his son,
And history herself must never see
The blow that fell here, on this heavy day.
I did not wish to win the throne by might
When it was mine in any case, by right,
But I'll not waver now. I'll take this land
And raise it to a glorious new realm.
Princes and popes shall kneel before our will.
Henry the Eighth I am, for good . . . or ill.

Exit.
Enter Polydore Vergil.

Vergil: Nothing can slake our grief when kings do pass.
Sorrow devoureth all: the stars capsize
Upon their orbits bright, and oceans rise
In foaming protest at the mortal blow;

But never did sadder sunrise dawn to see
The mournful fall of one so sure and wise.
Myself am charged to write the history
And so I have. 'Tis here among these leaves,
How cursèd Richard did the Princes fair
Harass to death in his malignant Tower,
And how brave Tudor checked the Yorkist beast
And rid the English garden of those weeds
That choked her scarcer flowers. 'Tis all here.
And thus this Tudor house, planted by might,
Begins its gentle growth towards the sun.
Succession falls on the beloved heir,
Prince Henry, jewel of a great king's eye.
Though heaven weeps hot when such a father dies,
After the night, the son will always rise.

THE END

Chapter
16

*I*n June London took to the streets. The weather was pleasant, the days were long and the theatres were full to the brim. The first performance of *King Henry VIII*, due to be staged at the Globe Theatre at the end of the month, on 29 June 1613, could hardly have come at a better time. The civic mood was as warm as the sunshine, and London heaved in anticipation of a fresh triumph. The great William Shakespeare, acknowledged master of his craft, was back. It was rumoured by some that he had been too weak to finish the scenes, and that John Fletcher had done a good deal of the work. But informed people maintained that the master was as dashing and eloquent as ever, and had tossed the whole thing off in a matter of weeks.

The advance news was mixed: it was said Shakespeare had never done better; but also that his powers had dwindled, that this was the work of an ordinary writer. Almost everyone agreed that Lowin would make a splendid Henry – the King's Men had found their new leading man, by the look of it. One or two well-informed spectators tapped their noses and muttered that, of course, the censor must have diluted many of the best scenes to protect the King's good name. Some went so far as to say that Shakespeare was refusing to have anything whatsoever to do with the preparations, so harshly had it been mauled by the royal pen.

Who knows how rumours start? This one was no more than idle speculation, yet it was close to the truth. Once or twice Shakespeare walked down to the stairs at Queenhithe and looked across the huge, muddy river at the Globe. He was not concerned with Fletcher's lifeless *Henry VIII*, though, because he could not stop imagining his own *Henry VII*. What work they had done! How fine it would have been! He could almost hear the audience gasp at the execution of the Princes, the toppling of Stanley, the death of Arthur and the final, incredible murder of the King.

A searing pain would split his head even to dream of such glories. And as the days passed, so his *Henry VII* seemed ever more transient and ephemeral. It became a ghost. Could a play that no one watched be said to exist? Could so lively a spirit be said *not* to exist? Shakespeare wondered whether the world had been altered in any way by the play's brief, unproclaimed life. The King's Men had come together one last time; they had met and perhaps influenced sweet Constance and dear Harvard; they had kept old truths alive and inspired new ones. But none of this was lasting. He could see it all sliding into the swamp of forgetful history, could imagine marshy mud closing over its final scenes with a slow exhalation of stagnant breath.

As he paced the roads north of the river, refusing to dignify with his presence the momentous opening of this last so-called play, his mind chattered with conflicting thoughts like a flock of birds that sensed a change in the weather. Was it really Harvard's guest who had alerted the authorities? Was Alleyn truly as innocent as he seemed? Was the vagrant who had tried to grab Heminge's leather bag nothing more than a cutpurse? Was Stanyhurst alive? What would Raleigh make of all this? Was Coke smiling?

It was pointless, he knew, to dwell on these matters – one of his rare articles of faith held that life was ruled by chance – but he could not stop himself raking over these and other questions, hoping to hear the pure note of something more solid than speculation.

When he thought of young Harvard, he could not be angry. The boy had done his best to be brave, and had been undone by nothing more than youthful enthusiasm and pride in his work. In any case, it was by no means certain that he was to blame. Any of them could have taken the King's shilling and betrayed the secret.

He smiled. The deepest root of this adventure was the desire to tell the truth, and it looked as though the truth had undone them. It was like some divine, malicious jest. As flies to wanton boys, he sighed, are we to the gods. They kill us for their sport.

Could Burbage have said anything? Impossible.

Armin? Absolutely not.

Heminge? Never in a thousand years. He would stake his life on it.

Who else was there?

Andrew? There was a sort of perfection to the idea, but it was not likely.

Lowin? Taylor? Shakespeare paused. They *were* a possibility – younger than the rest, part of a new generation of lauded child actors with powerful admirers and grand careers ahead of them. Taylor had not shown any sign of unease or double-dealing, but he was a skilled performer. He had played more difficult parts.

Why, though? There was a rapid tumble in Shakespeare's imagination and for a second he glimpsed a pattern – or thought he might have. It was vague, like remote constellations on a bright night. Familiar houses and streets swam and blurred as a vision formed in his inner eye. Taylor and Lowin; Lowin and Taylor. In a flash, like the twitch of a curtain, he seemed to see them with their heads together, whispering in a corner. Treachery would certainly have enhanced their prospects with the royal cause. And they were young. If *Henry VII* seemed too risky for them, then it was a perfect fatted calf for them to present to the authorities. They might easily have been tempted to invest in their own future by staking his feeble, obsolete head.

Shakespeare quailed. He was familiar with these intuitive lunges – cousins of his ability to see shapes in clouds. Events would rhyme and ring; a gong would sound, a light flare; an eagle would cry overhead. Clarity would brighten the sky.

But this time, almost as soon as it had come, the vision flew away. Shakespeare made little effort to detain it and consoled himself with a mere tantalising echo. Having been so wrong about Alleyn, he refused to let himself believe wild notions any more. If he had known what the future held – that Taylor and Lowin would indeed work their way to the centre of the circle and become leaders of the King's Men – he might have dwelled on the theory a little longer, but in truth anyone could have informed on the group. They had not been sufficiently stealthy. Any number of greedy ears could have been pressed to their windows, and if each in turn had just one confidant, each of whom had passed the news to another, then hundreds of people would have heard what they were doing. And it took only one.

Deep down, he lacked the energy to harry such a faint notion into life. For who could say what lay in another person's heart? It was hard enough to know oneself: indeed, Shakespeare tended to believe that no man knew himself, merely the story he liked to tell about himself. And sometimes that story grew stale and had to be refreshed. But he would not, he sighed, seek proof or let himself harbour suspicions against anyone. He knew when he was beaten. He would retire, a wounded stag, to a woodland glade, and be a country gentleman, and offend no one.

He had one significant freedom left: he could refuse to become sour, suspicious and resentful. He had watched his own father submit to these demons, and knew from bitter experience how hollow and ruinous they could be. He would tend to his vines, administer his estate so that his girls did not suffer, and fade from view.

There was one more thing he had to do, however. Late one night, with the candles guttering, he packed various of his books – the Holinshed, the Hall, the Spenser and the Marlowe, the Chaucer, the Malory and a handful of others – into a small sack. They were a bequest, a gift to young John Harvard. He did not want this episode to be a damaging memory; if nothing else, he would have the seed of a library as a souvenir.

Not long after dawn the next day he walked over the bridge to Southwark and tapped on the Harvard family door. John's mother greeted him with surprise and delight, insisted that he drink a beaker of buttermilk with bread and figs, and then, fluttering with apologies, went out to fulfil an appointment at the church.

Harvard could scarcely believe his eyes as he pulled the books from the sack.

'So many,' he exclaimed.

'I suspect you will need more,' said Shakespeare. 'But it is a beginning.'

'King Arthur! *Canterbury Tales!* Boccaccio! It is too much.'

'I am sure you will give them a good home.'

'I am sorry I missed the play. Mr Alleyn came here and told me all about it. He said it was very splendid.'

Shakespeare sighed. Not marble, nor the gilded monuments of princes, shall outlive this rhyme. 'He was right. It *was* splendid, very splendid. I too wish you had seen it.'

Harvard gave a rapid nod.

Shakespeare looked at his open, clear face. An idea stole over him like a finger of smoke: since the play had failed, perhaps Harvard could be the vessel that carried the truth into the future.

'I wonder,' he said, 'did Edward tell you how the play ended?'

'Not exactly. All he said was that it finished with a bang, an explosion that would have shaken the kingdom to its roots. I would dearly love to know what happened.'

Shakespeare hesitated. Should he follow Alleyn's fine example and protect the boy from the mortal peril of possessing too much knowledge? It was possible – to say the least – that this truth might be a curse, a burden on the man who bore it.

No. There had been too many secrets, too much suppression. Harvard had a right to know all there was to know. What he did with it was up to him.

'Do you really want to know? I warn you, it is quite complicated.'

'Please tell me. I'll keep it secret if you want.'

Shakespeare winced.

'Come walk with me awhile. There is much to tell.'

They wandered away from the river, towards open fields, and as they advanced Shakespeare retraced his steps to the beginning of his story, describing his strange encounter with Stanyhurst and his first confused response to the man's book.

'It was a straightforward attack on Henry VIII, I could see that much. It listed all his known vices and many that I did *not* know. But it was clear from the dark happenings surrounding it – Stanyhurst's disguise, his flight, the coded message in the volume itself – that it contained *another* story, one too dangerous to relate in plain words. Stanyhurst wanted me to piece together the story for myself. There were stray lines from Machiavelli, observations on Tudor history, information from witnesses and significant dates, all embroidered together to make a simple, shocking accusation – that Henry VIII murdered his father and stole the throne.'

He glanced at Harvard. The boy was looking straight ahead, concentrating on picking a path through the mud.

'I do not know if it is true, but I am certain that it *might* be. More to the point, in entrusting this notion to me, Stanyhurst was risking his life. The least I could do, I thought, was keep the story alive. That, after all, has been my life's work.'

'How did Machiavelli fit in?'

'There were references to a man called Oliverotto. I had never heard of him, but I visited a friend who enlightened me. Oliverotto appears in Machiavelli's great book, in the chapter "Concerning those who have obtained a Principality by Wickedness".'

Harvard was frowning, as if he did not quite follow.

'I took that to be a signficant clue – a declaration that, so far as Stanyhurst was concerned, Henry VIII had obtained the throne by wicked means. But there was more. In order to steal a kingdom, Oliverotto killed his uncle.'

'Like Hamlet.'

'Precisely. And this uncle was more than an uncle. He was a father to Oliverotto – he adopted the prince and raised him under his own roof. So this was clear-cut parricide. Stanyhurst certainly thought so: in the margin he scribbled a note wondering whether a king has ever been thrown into the Tiber in a leather bag containing a dog, a rooster, a monkey and a snake. This was the Roman punishment for parricide. Stanyhurst was making sure that I saw the connection.'

'I see. Stanyhurst was trying to tell you that Henry VII was murdered by his own son, but thought it safer to tell you in this hidden way.'

It sounded unlikely, put like that.

'You must remember: Stanyhurst was running for his life. If he had been able to see me he could have told me straight out, but he had no time. He had to make sure that no one but I caught his meaning. He had reason to think me a sympathiser.'

'Oh.' Harvard climbed a rough wooden stile made of crossed

planks on logs and waited for Shakespeare to do the same. 'I think I see.'

'Then there was the evidence of the Spanish envoy, Fuensalada, whom Stanyhurst knew in Madrid. This was damning: it seemed that the Spanish were astonished to learn that Henry VIII intended to marry Catherine of Aragon. So far as they knew, he was planning to wed Eleanor of Austria. In fact it was all arranged, and the Habsburgs were delighted with the union. As it turned out, it was the late king, Henry VII *himself*, who was contemplating marriage to Aragon. Imagine!'

Harvard's eyes were wide, but he said nothing.

'It is quite involved, is it not? But reduced to its simplest form, it means that both men wanted to marry the same queen. Wars have begun for less.'

'If this be so,' Harvard said, 'I am surprised it is not better known.'

'That is the point, exactly.'

'I can see why your friend Stanyhurst had to flee.'

'There was one thing more.'

Shakespeare related his struggle with the hidden numbers in Stanyhurst's book, and explained how, in his poor eyes, they gave ballast to the conspiracy.

'The first number turned out to be the date of Henry VII's death. Some say he died the day before, but Stanyhurst thought it was the twenty-second. The second was the date of Henry VIII's coronation. These were sufficient in themselves to solve the riddle, but it was the third date that revealed the full, horrifying face of the deceit. For 28 June 1509 was the eighteenth birthday of Henry VIII – the day he attained the age of majority, the day he could rule without a Protector. It came only days after his coronation – far too close to be an accident.

'Armed with this thought, everything became clear. Henry VII died in April 1509. And Henry VIII was married and crowned half a dozen weeks later, on the brink of his own eighteenth birthday. It is too neat. Henry VIII did not murder his father on a whim.'

'Still, for a son to kill his father . . .'

'Unthinkable? Remember: princes are not like common men.'

'I did read somewhere that Prince Henry's youth was strange.

Unlike his brother Arthur, who was tutored in kingship from infant-hood, Henry was kept away from the public gaze. He was kept hidden, secluded, and given no royal role.'

'There you are. The King loved his first son so deeply that he came to hate his second.'

'I suppose it is possible,' said Harvard, 'that having lost five children, he could not bear to lose a sixth, yet still resented Henry for surviving.'

'That is true,' Shakespeare's voice was soft, 'and very far-sighted of you, John. But it requires us to imagine the lonely Prince Henry nurs-ing his resentment until it became a monster of envy. Where his brother was fêted, he was disparaged. It is ironic that Henry VIII him-self was actually promised to the Church. Had his brother not perished, Henry would have been Archbishop of Canterbury.'

'Perhaps he killed his brother, too.'

If Shakespeare had retained the power to smile, he would have smiled.

'Even *I* would not go quite that far.'

He put a hand on Harvard's arm and indicated that they should turn back.

'This is where we found the end of our play. Oh, we knew it could not be shown to the King in so unroyal a condition, but we made it come alive, by God we did. Burbage was grand – you should have seen him. When the time came to perform the murder we were nervous, but it acquired a flavour none could have predicted, least of all me. We exchanged parts, so the characters slipped and shifted; each was an unlikely mixture of moods; each was both divided and complete.'

'Who wrote it all down?'

'We took turns. You were much missed, of course. But the result, though barely legible, was . . . perfect, in a way. It seemed to me the fruition of something I had worked on for years: not just one king killing another king – that is common meat – but kingship swallowing its own tail. I have never heard of such a thing being presented before. Our murderer was both a father and a son, both king and prince. I am sorry to be telling you all this – you must think me very fond and fool-ish – but the thought of our work being destroyed . . . it is hard to bear.'

'I am sure the others would do it all over again. I too will be glad to help.'

Ahead of them they could see the high roof of the Globe rising above the squalor of Bankside. The clouds were lifting: there was a patch of blue over St Paul's.

'You are a fine young man. I am glad to have had this chance to make your acquaintance. I wonder what you will do in the years to come.'

'My father wishes me to study for the Church.'

'Well.' Shakespeare smiled. 'Fathers are not always wrong. But if I were you, I would not rest in London. Thanks to Cabot, Raleigh and their like, there are many fresh worlds to conquer. Who knows where your compass will take you?'

They parted at the end of the alley where Harvard lived. Shakespeare stood for a moment, watching the boy hurry home, skipping over mudholes in the smelly, straw-filled gutter. His memory skidded, and suddenly he could see his own dear Hamnet, running along the sunlit bank of the Avon River, stumbling over tall, grassy clumps as his weak, unsteady legs fought to keep him upright.

He closed his eyes. For a held breath or two, wreathed in an agony of sorrow, he was even able to forget the anger that had built a nest in his heart.

The wrath refused to leave him, however, and two days later it was a fierce knot. Shakespeare woke with a keen sense that sleep had failed to knit up the ravelled sleeve of care. The loss of his play still cut into him like scalding chains, and he felt both revived and restless. He had marched into this enterprise with a dispirited feeling that he could not hold his head up, even to himself – that he was responsible for false history. Now he felt purified by a martyr's indignant anger, and with a light-headed sense that he was also dreaming. It was exhilarating, in a way.

He fretted away the hours until noon. He could not have said exactly what he was planning, for his thoughts were not organised. One thing was certain: he was *not* going to see the play. *His* Henry had perished in the flames – he had been forced to watch as it brightened the damp stone walls – and he could not bear to be praised for such inferior work as was about to appear at the Globe. Of all the punishments visited upon him, this was the cruellest: he would for ever stand accused of having written this sycophantic waffle, when his own grand master-piece (it was not for him to say, but he could not resist the thought) was mere dust. He would not grace the play with his presence, and people could make of that what they liked.

Why was it, then, he asked himself, that his steps led him across London Bridge and on towards the Globe? What force was dragging him? He could not guess. His clothes were untidy, and no one recog-nised him. He watched the crowd push their way in through warm odours of roasted chestnuts, ale and bread; he heard people gabble and laugh, and felt a gathering fury that was entirely new to him.

The Globe was rarely quiet; the rim of the acting pit buzzed with small workshops. Armourers and haberdashers, chandlers and boot-makers, smiths, porters, plasterers and drapers – the Globe supported a small colony of craftsmen and labourers. Most of them tried to sup-press any noise during a performance, but this only meant that the hectic cries from the river and from the neighbouring markets were free to echo down the alleys. Women hurried by with pies, cakes and baskets of fruit to throw at any actor foolish enough to miss a cue.

Shakespeare could hear music: pipes and drums. It was beginning. The crowd was starting to thin as the last members of the audience set-tled on to their low benches. He imagined Lowin's pampered King arriving on the stage, and suffered a fresh stirring of his new-found rage. He hated kings. It was thanks to his own that he had suffered so much. This popinjay, who gave more treasure to his shallow friends in a single year, it was said, than Elizabeth gave in a lifetime. This blub-bermouth who believed in witches and who had even had a settlement in Virginia named after him, yet showed no respect for English life, English tradition and, most of all, for English theatre.

Shakespeare knew plenty about the vengefulness of kings. He had not needed Raleigh to remind him that James, on a throne so recently occupied by the woman who had executed his mother, might well smirk at the ruin he could bring down on his new kingdom. He felt a surge of the self-righteous, patriotic indignation that had fired him to write about Henry VII in the first place. It was a disgrace that could not long be tolerated. Someone had to oppose this bloated tyranny before it was too late.

Walking round the back, he felt awkward, drowsy and heavy-limbed. It was a hazy afternoon and he was damp with sweat – he should not have come in the first place. He sat on a bale of straw, rested his feet on a bucket and let himself lean back. Something tickled his neck: straw. Thatchers had been working on the roof and had left a few sheaves down here. He imagined he was elsewhere, in a hayrick back in Warwickshire, staring at the sky, seeing the patterns in clouds.

There'd been no rain for a week; the thatch was as dry as tinder. Tinder.

The thought flared through his body.

The loss of his play stung him afresh. It was his own fault, but still, it was too cruel. Every time he thought of himself being held guilty of this lesser drama, pain seared his brain. He could not bear the notion that history would think him the author of the pallid piece about to be paraded on the far side of these walls.

An idea swooped over him, sharp as a swift over water. *Henry VII* had been incinerated. Why should not his son suffer the same fate?

There was justice in it, and poetry, and drama – a heady combination that Shakespeare was powerless to oppose.

He could smell roasted chestnuts.

They were warm.

Fire.

He had tried to oppose a depraved monarchy with a creative act, and they had thrown him into the furnace. Perhaps he too should stoop to baleful flames.

He returned to the hawker's brazier with vacant steps, like a sleep-walker, dropped a coin in the tin and picked out a cup of nuts. When the man's back was turned, he tipped the hot nuggets into his hand, pushed the cup into the brazier and scooped up a glowing coal. When he dropped the nuts on top, he could hear them snap and bubble.

A moment later he was back at his pile of straw. Brassy horns split the air and loud cannons announced the entrance of the players. Inside the theatre he could hear the dreary opening lines of the play.

Shakespeare closed his mind to these distractions. With no attempt at subterfuge he set down his cup on the edge of the cordwood and stood up. No one was watching. He nudged with his toe, let the chestnuts fall and immediately saw a wisp of smoke curling from the thatch.

Arson sounds dramatic, but only a minor effort is required to ignite a blaze. One modest movement – a nudge with a foot, a turn of a wrist – can be enough to bring down a leviathan. Shakespeare felt himself to be a David, unarmed and devout, kneeling before the weak point of this Goliath.

He tipped the cup with his foot and walked away. That was all it took. Such a tiny crime! Nature would take care of the rest.

Within a few seconds he was just one of many unremarkable figures in the throng that criss-crossed the streets of Southwark. And the roaring in his ears came not from the flames but from the verses that swelled in his memory. Fire answers fire . . . fire burn and cauldron bubble . . . I am bound upon a wheel of fire . . . fretted with golden fire . . . I am fire and air . . . Promethean fire . . . gulfs of liquid fire . . . Now all the youth of England are on fire. His own molten rhetoric crackled in his mind as he stepped into a wherry and bade the boatman push off. Had anyone been watching, the only thing they might have found unusual was that he was muttering. 'Our revels now are ended,' he was saying under his breath. 'The cloud-capped towers, yea, even the great Globe itself . . . shall melt, thaw and resolve . . . and leave not a rack behind.'

He had not intended those words as prophetic. Strange, the twists life took.

He was very calm. Something unclotted in his soul, and even his back felt strong. Away to the east he could see the Tower of London, and it pleased him to think of Sir Walter up on his pavement, gazing at the Globe, perhaps with his hands to his temples, aghast at the orange glow that would soon tint the western sky. For one butterfly instant, he felt a warm kinship with the imprisoned man.

What was it Raleigh had said about *Hamlet*? That he liked the crescendo of revenges at the end? Shakespeare reeled under a sudden convergence of feelings and thoughts, memories and notions that blew fierce gusts through his ribcage.

He was always being invited to consider new theories about *Hamlet*. And of course he was glad that the play was rich enough to allow everyone to see in it the reflection of their own cherished prejudices. But though he rarely admitted it, he could never see what the fuss was about. It was simple, wasn't it? In Hamlet he had created a virtuous man forced by unlucky circumstances to perform dark deeds that fought against the sweet grain of his temperament. The ghost was malicious, like all bewitched voices from the grave: it insisted that Hamlet suffer torments for which he was ill suited. Vengeance was a curse, and only at the point of death did the poor, hapless man know peace and happiness. Only then was he free from the hideous tyranny of the revenge plot, liberated from the horrid obligation to do wrong.

That is how Shakespeare felt about his Prince of Denmark, and it was how he felt about himself, in the middle of the Thames. He had been cast as the reluctant hero of a story he had no desire to play, but somehow he had found a way to end it, and now he felt . . . nothing. He had lived too close to the woods to be afeared of owls.

Behind him, flames were licking at the dry walls of the Globe, at the wide cross-beams and delicious tinder. They reached imploringly for the fine drapes as they raced for the roof. The air was full of wild cries, and he could hear a thunderous pounding of feet as the audience shoved its way down the stairs. There was only one entrance, so some ran across the stage; others jumped from balconies. A man beat at his fiery trousers. Another paused to drag a child out of the path of the inferno. If Shakespeare had looked more closely (which he did not) the Globe might have seemed to him like a stricken ship, beached and ablaze, with seamen leaping into the waves.

Something jolted inside Shakespeare. It was as if he had been stung into life. He did not know how, but there had been a curtain drawn across the scene, and now it was raised to reveal an infernal drama he had somehow been able to ignore.

What had he done?

He clutched at his face with his hands and only just suppressed a wounded cry. It had not occurred to him until this instant that he had been destroying not just a theatre, not just a play, not just a falsehood, but real, inhabited lives. In these last few dreamy moments he had been fatally detached, dislocated from his own senses, as abstract as a vaporous wandering spirit. Now, as he watched men hurtling about and stumbling in the path of the flames, he trembled to see the raging heat of his own rash action. What derangement had permitted him to do this thing?

Fortunately, he could not see two of his oldest friends shaking their dazed heads and shouting into the sky, the proud, rich voices that had made them famous hoarse with smoke and ash. Burbage was one of the last to leave. He seemed to hope that by imposing himself he could direct the fire to cease, and bellowed at it with all the power his throaty roar could muster. Heminge, quicker to grasp the implications, paled at the awful scale of the disaster. The Globe was a bonfire – their world was being incinerated. In a few hours, nothing would remain.

Shakespeare bade the oarsman still his blades, and together they bobbed noiselessly on the stream and watched the wild scurrying on the shore. They were close enough to hear shouts, and it seemed to them both, listening to the noisy crowd on the riverbank, that everyone had been brought to safety. Shakespeare peered through the smoke and it did not seem as though anyone was still trapped.

Thank God! The thought that he himself might have been turned into a murderer was too much to bear. What had he been thinking of? It was enough – almost – to make him leap into the reddening flood.

He gestured that it was time to continue and bowed his head as the boat drifted across the water. Away from the conflagration, it was chilling to reflect that first his play, and now the stage on which it should have had its hour, had been consumed in this greedy, devouring fire. In this, his final act, he was erasing his own life from the chronicles. Up in the burning lungs of the Globe was a plain cedarwood box containing the papers, letters, playbills, drafts, pamphlets and commissions he had accumulated in his long and superb theatrical career. For the sake of history, history was going up in smoke.

A hundred yards behind him, his trusted friend John Heminge, coated with sweat as he hauled timbers from the Globe, was already suspecting that this fire could be an extension of the furnace that had devoured *Henry VII*.

This was no accident.

No one had died, but they were not safe.

He had never been so scared.

Lines of men had formed and were ferrying buckets of water from the river, hand to soaking hand. But it was impossible to quench the thirst of the fire – as futile as tossing pebbles at a thunderstorm. The flames paused for a brief sip here and there, then scorched up into the summer afternoon, ravenous as a dragon.

In the days and weeks that followed, London slid into the grip of an intense heatwave. The city, however, was anything but subdued. The Southwark inferno had sharpened the public's appetite for theatre; by pointing up the fragility of things it inspired a minor frenzy of pleasure-seeking. There was dancing on the bridge and late-night carousing kept the constables busy. People even swam in the filthy river to cool off.

There was a good deal of speculation as to the cause of the disaster. Some blamed it on the 'blasted furriners' – the black-cloaked Spaniards and Portuguese who stole about the city like swarthy crows. Others blamed red-faced papists from Ireland or France. More specific gossip hinted that it was a rival theatrical gang, driven to violent lengths to suppress competition. Henslowe, people noticed, was hard at work on the Hope, a new theatre just down the road from the Globe.

Others held that it was a disgruntled actor maddened by the loss of a prized role. Actors, ran the argument, everybody knew they were disreputable fellows.

The truth was: no one had the first idea. So no tongues wagged when, a day or so after the death of the Globe, William Shakespeare stepped on to the footplate of a carriage bound for Oxford and, without so much as a backward glance, ducked into the shadows and vanished from sight. No one came to see him off or even noticed him leave. So no one witnessed the melancholy sight of an extinguished spirit, as he passed out of London for the last time, and into posterity.

It was all over. England's greatest dramatist was going home.

DRAMATIS PERSONAE

(in order of appearance)

William Shakespeare retired to Stratford and vowed never to return to London as long as he lived. He left his business affairs in the capable hands of John Heminge, and the gatehouse at Blackfriars was swiftly let to a good tenant. He devoted most of his time to his estate and was a keen farmer, trading wool and corn in the local markets. His pride and joy was the knot garden at New House, Stratford, which he designed and planted – with a mulberry tree and vines – himself. He entertained guests there (Ben Jonson was a regular) and was rumoured to have worked on a play titled *Cardenio*, which has never, in four centuries, been located.

In 1616 he summoned a lawyer and produced a will that left various tokens to his old friends. The sum of twenty-six shillings was set aside to buy mourning rings for his companions Richard Burbage, John Heminge and Henry Condell (he did not hold Condell's absence against him). At some point in the spring he contracted a fever after some late-night carousing, grew weak and, on 23 April 1616, died. He was buried at Holy Trinity Church, beneath a gravestone on which this verse (sometimes supposed to have been written by himself) was carved:

> Good friend, for Jesus' sake forbear
> To dig the dust enclosèd here.
> Blest be the man that spares these stones
> And cursed be he that moves my bones.

It is said that till his dying day he winced at every mention of Henry VIII.

Sir Walter Raleigh remained in the Tower until 1616, when he was granted his wish to undertake an expedition to the New World in search of gold. He sailed under strict orders not to engage Spanish ships, but off Guyana he could not avoid a fight – in truth, he did not try very hard. His punishment was dreadful: his own son, who had accompanied him on the voyage, was killed in the fray. Raleigh returned home a broken man and was at once executed by an ungrateful King.

Sir Edward Coke was appointed Lord Chief Justice, the most senior legal figure in the land, shortly after the fire at the Globe. Becoming dismayed by King James's haughty attitude towards royal power, he turned into a bold defender of common law, writing numerous judgments that still obtain in English courts. 'Magna Carta,' he famously said, 'will have no sovereign.' This brought him into conflict with the Crown, and in 1616 he was removed from office for his boisterous refusal to kowtow to the King – partly at the behest of the Attorney-General, Sir Francis Bacon. After 1620 he was a resolute spokesman for the Parliamentary cause; in 1628 he was one of the authors of the Petition of Right, an assertion of common liberties that stiffened the sinews of a nation sliding towards civil war. He died a few years before war broke out, in 1634. His wife said: 'We shall never see his like again, praise God.'

Robert Armin was in continual demand for his brilliant performances as Feste, Touchstone, Dogberry and every other fool and clown on the Stuart stage. As ill-health and unhappiness started to get the better of him, he faded from the London scene. He was also a significant playwright – *The History of the Two Maids of More-Clacke*; and *Foole upon Foole*, *A Nest of Ninnies*. 'Better a witty fool than a foolish wit,' he would say, quoting himself. He fell ill and died just two years after the destruction of the Globe, in 1615.

Edward Alleyn remained one of London's most celebrated citizens. As part-owner of several theatres – the Rose, the Paris Garden, the Fortune – as well as the bear and bull rings, he was England's first great entertainment mogul. A good part of his wealth went into the College of God's Gift in the fields of Dulwich, south of London. Centuries later a nearby school – Alleyns – would bear his name, while Dulwich Old Boys are still known as Old Alleynians (some graduates, no doubt, occasionally try a spot of engrossing in the financial markets across the river). In 1623 his wife Joan died and was buried in the chapel at God's Gift. Alleyn, not one to grieve for long, remarried with what some thought unseemly haste. More than a few eyebrows were raised when it turned out that his delightful new bride, Constance, the lovely daughter of the poet and Dean of St Paul's, John Donne, was nearly forty years his junior.

Joseph Taylor did not become a full member of the King's Men until 1619, three years after Shakespeare's death, but he went on to become one of its leading lights, a star of the Jacobean stage and a shareholder in the Blackfriars Theatre. He played major roles not just in Shakespeare plays, but also in works by Jonson, Webster and – especially – by his old friends Beaumont and Fletcher.

John Lowin became a fully paid-up King's Man after the fire at the Globe that interrupted his starring performance in the title role of *Henry VIII*. With Joseph Taylor he formed the vanguard of the new, post-Shakespeare company, and when the old generation passed away (Heminge and Condell died in 1627 and 1630 respectively) it was these two who took over as joint leaders of the Company.

Richard Burbage was, with Alleyn, London's most famous theatrical impresario; but he was also an unwary businessman and amassed no fortune. He adored the stage, so the blaze at the Globe hit him hard; he spent years in a fruitless search for the culprit. No one ever discovered the cause. In the end it was blamed on cannons that had sparked flames on the dry thatched roof. Burbage had misgivings about this theory – he suspected arson – but he was never able to prove it. Along with his brother Cuthbert, he threw his energies into rebuilding the theatre, was a father to eight children in Shoreditch, acted as often as he could, and was vexed by the fact that he was so often mistaken, by passers-by, for his old friend William Shakespeare. When he died in 1619 a waggish comrade contrived a perfect epitaph for him: 'Exit Burbage.'

Richard Stanyhurst surfaced in Brussels, pursuing studies in medicine and chemistry, and revising his unpopular (because bombastic) translation of Virgil. His stealthy trip to London in the summer of 1613 was never made public. He waited (in vain) for news that his work on Henry VIII had not been lost and never dared return to England. When he heard news of Shakespeare's death, it was said he stopped eating. This cannot have been true, for he lived for two more years until his own death in 1618.

John Harvard continued his studies at St Saviour's Grammar School in Southwark, where his father was a governor, and occasionally went to Stratford-upon-Avon to visit his mother's side of the family. He never lost his love of reading and writing, and studied hard at Emmanuel College, Cambridge. In 1625 plague swept through Southwark and killed half his family – his father, two brothers and a sister. A few years later, in 1632, he sailed west in search of religious freedom. He took his books, settled on the Charles River near Boston and became a noted clergyman. When he died childless, his 400-volume library (including books given to him by a grateful William Shakespeare) was donated to a college in Cambridge, Massachusetts. These volumes were the seed from which grew the library and university that bears his name. In 1674 the college burned down, and all but one of his books was destroyed. The surviving title – an exciting narrative called *The Christian Warfare against the Devil World and Flesh* by John Downame – was out on loan at the time.

Constance Donne retreated into domestic life, a course imposed on her by the ill health of her mother. Her father, John Donne, became Dean of St Paul's and one of the most influential figures in London. For a while it looked as though Constance would be true to her word and take no husband, but in 1625 she married a famous old actor: none other than Edward Alleyn, a 'family friend'. The fact that he was so far her senior seemed to present no bar to their happiness although it did, alas, lead to a financial dispute between Alleyn and Constance's father. Donne felt he should be paid £200 a year for allowing the actor to marry Constance; Alleyn expected a dowry of some £500. He did not get his money and his wedded bliss was also short-lived: he died three years later, in 1628, after a chilly business trip to Yorkshire. Constance became an independent-minded widow of distinctly handsome means.

John Heminge stayed on (sometimes with an S at the end of his name, sometimes not) with Henry Condell as a chief executive of the King's Men. After Shakespeare's death the pair of them organised the company's surviving playbooks into a single coherent volume, which was published in 1623 as the First Folio – by universal consent the most spectacular and influential work of literature that has ever been produced. In a rare design flourish, Heminge commissioned an illustration for the frontispiece. The result was a neckless, bulging-eyed portrait of Shakespeare, which, all his friends agreed, looked absolutely nothing like the man.

John Florio remained in Fulham for a dozen years. The second edition of his translation of Montaigne was printed a few months after the fire at the Globe and kept him in demand as a translator and scholar. However, he fell out of favour with the court of King James, which stopped his royal pension and left him destitute. Too old to secure a new income, he died in poverty in 1625, at the grand age of seventy-two. Not long after his death, foolish rumours began to circulate that he had helped Shakespeare write his plays. He denied claims that the wordy scholar Holofernes, in *Love's Labour's Lost*, was to any extent a portrait of him, insisting that Shakespeare loved him too well to deal with him so wantonly. But on his deathbed he did admit to one stinging regret: a proud Italian, he had never once set foot in Italy.